THE SONG OF THE
SKYLARK

C000218072

Liz Shakespeare

THE SONG OF THE SKYLARK

Liz Shakespeare

LETTERBOX BOOKS

First published 2020
by
Letterbox Books
Littleham
Bideford
Devon
EX39 5HW

www.lizshakespeare.co.uk

ISBN 978-0-9516879-6-3

Printed and bound by SRP Ltd, Exeter

ACKNOWLEDGEMENTS

I am very grateful to Alison Harding for her advice and constant support, both for this book and throughout my writing life; to my dear friend Kate Cryan for her proofreading, and to my son Ben for finding the time in his very busy life to design the cover and help with images. I am indebted to Janet Few for showing me the document that originally inspired me to write this book; also to my authors' group and the Buckland Brewer History Group for their support. Thank you also to Ted and Sheila Lott for their hospitality, their insight into the Bible Christian community and for the loan of hard-to-find books.

I would like to thank the Shaw Collection at the Royal Institution Library, Truro for giving me the opportunity to read the diary of Mary O'Bryan Thorne; also the North Devon Record Office and Local Studies Library, and Torrington Museum, for access to documents.

To my brother

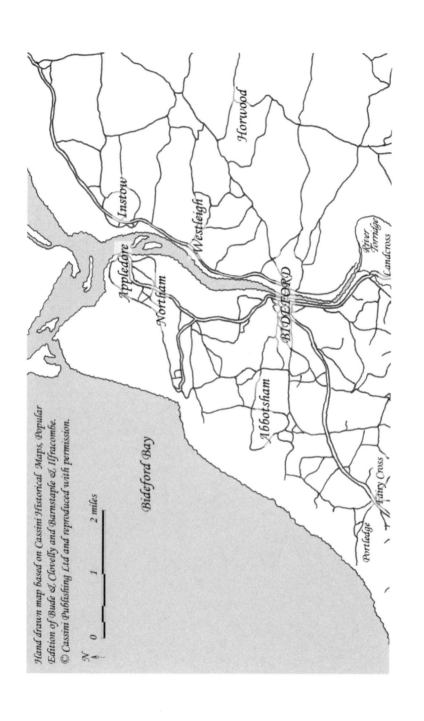

Hand drawn map based on Cassini Historical Maps, Popular
Edition of Bude & Clovelly and Barnstaple & Ilfracombe.
© Cassini Publishing Ltd and reproduced with permission.

N

0   1   2 miles

Bideford Bay

Appledore

Instow

Northam

Westleigh

Horwood

Abbotsham

BIDEFORD

River
Torridge

Landcross

Portledge

Fairy Cross

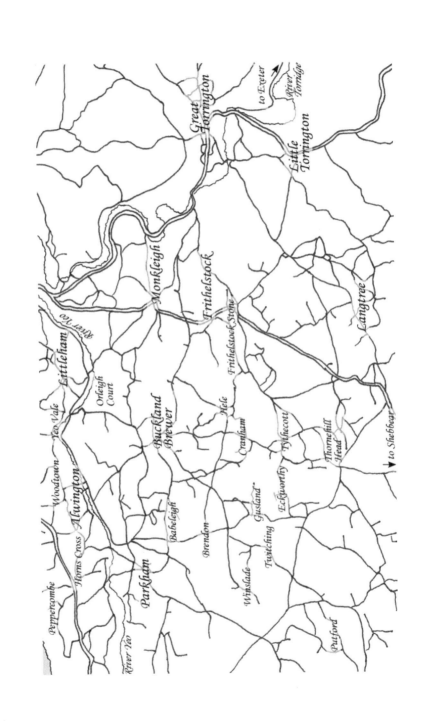

PAROCHIAL SLAVERY.—A number of householders attended at the instance of the overseers of the poor, to take
their " chance " at a " drawing " of parish apprentices.—
There were two boys produced ; and after standing on the
form, like slaves at a market, subject to the gaze and inqui-
sition of the court, one of them was set by as not in a fit
state of health to be bound. For the remaining one, a
drawing took place, and Mr. John Norrington was the unfortunate recipient of the prize.—[It is an utter abomina-
tion and disgrace that such a scandal to a free country should
be tolerated : we believe the barbarous practice is well nigh
confined to Devonshire, which, in this instance, fully makes
out its title to be counted a century behind the rest of the
country in the order of civilization. Why do not the overseers call the parishioners together on the subject? Such
a traffic in human flesh and blood could not survive a full
and free discussion.]—ED.

North Devon Journal, 5th October 1843

Part One

Spring 1842

Chapter One

The street in the poorer part of the town was deserted but for a sleepy tabby cat sitting on the pavement. The early morning showers had passed, but the terraced houses, many unpainted and in need of repair, remained closed against the cool northerly breeze.

The silence was broken by the jingle of harness and sound of trotting hoofs, and the horse appeared from around the bend, drawing behind it a creaking cart carrying the two children. Just as the church clock commenced striking ten, the driver drew to a halt by some iron railings.

Mary knelt up on the straw-strewn floor of the cart. A great stone arch loomed over her, so high she had to tip back her head to see to the top, and beyond the arch stood a tall building with rows of windows frowning down at her. It was bigger than any building she had ever seen, bigger even than the village church that stood next to her cottage home, and she knew that this must be the Bideford Workhouse.

She stared in silence, and her brother Thomas reached for her hand.

'Don't forget us is only going to the Meeting Room.' He gave her a little shake to make her look at him. 'Mary, us isn't going to stay, remember?'

She nodded solemnly. 'Going to the Meeting Room means us don't have to go into that ol' place, don't it?'

'That's right, and I'll be with 'ee, so you'm not to fret.'

The stark walls of the Workhouse drew her gaze again. She knew from the stories she had heard that they contained countless examples of human misery. Somewhere, behind those walls, was the old woman who used to live in the cottage on the corner near Mary's house, somewhere was the orphaned girl with whom she used to play. They had been there for a long time now. In front was a bleak yard, empty but for two women in identical blue-striped gowns and caps who were listlessly sweeping, and Mary could hear the slow scratch, scratch of their brooms. From an open window at the far end of the building came a cloud of steam accompanied by a sour smell, and somewhere a child was wailing, the forlorn cries echoing around the yard.

Mr Fulford climbed down from the cart and tied his horse to the iron railings alongside all the other horses that waited there. 'Come on, my birds, down you come and let's get this business over with.'

He held out his hand to Mary and she took it reluctantly. Mr Fulford had a broad, kind face and the sort of voice that had a smile in it; he had given them each a cutround to eat on the journey, the first she had ever had, and she would far rather stay on the cart with him than enter the Workhouse.

Mr Fulford's footsteps echoed as he passed under the archway to a door on which he knocked loudly. When the door opened, Mary followed him into a crowded room. The next stage of her life was about to begin. She kept close to Thomas, and she watched, and she waited.

When Mary's turn came, she climbed on to the low table in front of the group of men. They stood shoulder to shoulder in their fustian jackets and neckerchiefs, and all of their eyes were on her. She had made the decision not to cry, and she held her head up high. Through a small window high up on the far wall she could see the topmost branches of a tree and some slowly drifting clouds; they must be the same clouds that passed over the cottage home she had left just a few hours ago. The baby would have woken now, and her mother would be nursing it.

The men looked her over and one spoke quietly to his neighbour. She stood tall and proud so that they could see how strong she was and how hard she would be able to work.

She knew what to expect; she had watched while children from other villages were assigned.

'Mary Mitchell, nine years old. Draw your straws, gentlemen, and we'll see who's to win this prize.'

There was some laughter and muttered comments, then the farmers crowded around the magistrate who was in charge, and all she could see were their bowed heads and dark coats.

'Ah, 'tis me!' A stout man, his cheeks flecked with red like apples, held up his straw. 'But I've come to an arrangement. I don't want no more apprentices.' He looked around apologetically at the gathered crowd.

The men stirred restlessly and one or two leaned over to murmur to each other.

'But 'tis your duty as a ratepayer, Mr Heal, you'm aware of that!'

'I know it, but I've nine children of my own at 'ome still, there's no call for me to be taking in more, upsetting my maids and leading the boys astray. So Mr Phillips yer will take her in my place.'

Mary gazed at each man in turn as he spoke. This was different from what had happened before; she was to go with this other man. The farmer who stepped forward was taller than her father and looked well-fed, but he had a stern expression. Mr Fulford indicated that she should climb down from the table so she went to stand next to the tall farmer.

'Hello, maister.' She looked up at him but from where she stood his bushy dark beard obscured his face. He was staring straight ahead and did not return her gaze. Should she hold his hand, like she did her father's?

'Next up, Thomas Mitchell, eleven years old. This young *gentleman* has been apprenticed these two years out at Cranham, but Mr Westaway having sold up and moved to Bradworthy, he's here to be reassigned. Take your straws, gentlemen!'

Thomas was looking down at his feet, and his mouth was a thin, hard line; she wished he would look at her and pull one of his silly faces to make her laugh. Since he had been home they had hardly been parted. While Mam was at work he had helped her with the water-carrying and the fire and even with the washing, which wasn't really boys' work. He was the best brother ever, and he had promised to look after her until they were assigned.

A man was holding up the short straw. 'I'm of a mind with Mr Heal; I've had my fill of apprentices and Mr Phillips has agreed to take this one too. Us talked about it at market a day or two since.'

There was a rumble of laughter. The men were smiling and shaking their heads, but Mr Fulford didn't look pleased. Thomas stepped down from the table and came to stand beside Mary, but when she tried to hold his hand, his fingers were rigid and he did not respond to her grasp. She whispered to him, 'What's happening, Thomas?'

'Us is going to the same farm. Us'll be together.' He gave her a small smile.

Together! Now she didn't mind going to a strange place because Thomas would be with her – he would show her what to do! When she put her arms around him, he gave her a brief hug in return.

Mr Fulford came over to speak to her farmer, her maister, that's who he was now.

'Well then, Mr Phillips, how many apprentices be this that you have now? You'm making quite a collection of 'em, bain't 'ee?'

'Six now. They all sleep in together, I don't make no difference between 'em.'

Mr Phillips stared at the wall as he replied to Mr Fulford. Mary knew that was a rude thing to do.

'Well, see that you take care of 'em, won't 'ee, this little maid especially. They'll be needing some better clothes and some boots, you'll be seeing about that, no doubt? Some warm clothes for the cold mornings?'

'My wife'll take care of that. Good day, Mr Fulford.' As Mr Phillips walked towards the door Thomas grabbed Mary's hand. 'Quick, us must follow.'

Outside, the air was cool and fresh. They hurried after Mr Phillips who was striding towards the line of horses and carts tethered to the railings outside the Workhouse. Thomas helped her to clamber up and when they were sitting in the back of the wagon, Mr Phillips turned around to them before he took up the reins.

'You'll sit there. Try to run off and you'll feel this,' and he flourished his whip at them. Mary pulled a face at Thomas. She'd had no thought of running off.

Bartholomew Fulford stood in the arched entrance of the Workhouse and watched as Mr Phillips drove off with the two children crouched behind in the wagon, poor little mites. All the Mitchell children were brighter than was usual for those of their station; quick to learn, and hard workers. And these two had delightful smiles just like their older sister, though the boy had needed some coaxing and teasing before he would demonstrate it.

The wagon turned the corner and disappeared. Mr Phillips would be driving out Horns Cross way to reach his farm; he rarely went through Buckland Brewer village. Solitary type he was, never had much to say at market. He was not a chapel man and only went to church when he had to, baptisms and burials, and then only for his immediate family. It was hard to know what went on in his head. But then, his father had been a difficult man too.

Bartholomew untied his horse and climbed up on to the cart. He would miss the children's company on the return journey. He had given them a sack to shield them from an early morning shower of rain and when he turned to talk to them, they were peeping out like two little mice, wide-eyed at the unfamiliar landscape. It was the first time the little maid had been on the six-mile journey to Bideford, and likely to be the last until she was twenty-one and her apprenticeship was up.

He clicked his tongue to urge Dobbin to a reluctant trot as they passed the last of the town's cottages and turned off on to the Buckland road. The ringing of the horse's heavy hoofs on the stony lane almost drowned out the languorous song of a blackbird and the murmuring of a few early bumblebees. Where the hedges had been recently laid, Bartholomew could see over into a meadow. The grass was already showing signs of growth here; it was certainly more advanced than at Buckland Brewer. The village was high up and so much colder than the land nearer the river, that it was said even the devil caught cold in Buckland.

The next field was already planted up with potatoes. He stood up in the cart to observe it as Dobbin trotted past. It was neatly done. He had brought his own potatoes in from the thatched pit to prepare for planting but the land was not yet drilled. If the weather continued fair, as it looked certain to do, he could start tomorrow.

On the journey into Bideford he had not paid his usual attention to the work of other farmers, so amused had he been by the chatter of that little maid.

'Mr Fulford!' she had yelled from the back of the cart, as Dobbin clip-clopped along the road.

He had turned to regard her. 'I'm not deaf, chiel.' Mary was kneeling up and twirling a lock of her long brown hair around her finger.

'Mr Fulford! Mam says you can mebbe fix it that I go home along with you so's I can work alongside my sister. She says you'm mebbe not averse to fixing things a bit, even though you'm a preacher over at chapel. I told her you could say sorry to God afterwards if 'twas fretting you. Would 'ee do that? 'Twould suit me to be alongside Catherine.'

'Well, Mary, I don't know that the Lord would look too favourably on me if I'd planned all along to sin,' he'd replied. 'Besides, 'tis only those who'm due to take an apprentice as draws the straws. 'Tisn't my turn, chiel.'

'Land sakes!' He'd looked around again and saw her frown fade as she pursed her lips in thought. Her brother, gazing blankly ahead at the narrow winding lane, did not appear to be listening. Bartholomew could not help wondering whether Thomas had been unhappy in his previous placement, such was his reluctance to be assigned again.

'Well now,' she continued, 'I don't mind too much 'cos I'd like to mind little chiels, that's what I'm used to, see, and you don't have any little chiels, do 'ee Mr Fulford?'

He had agreed that he did not. His children were all grown, he said.

'Might 'ee have some more, do 'ee think? If 'ee do, I'd come and care for 'em! Or be 'ee too old for breedin' now?'

He had not replied to that, but secretly rather wished that he was not too old because he would have liked a little maid like Mary. His only daughter would have been old enough to be a mother now, had she lived.

Before going to the Workhouse for the assignment, he had driven down into the town to collect some laudanum for a villager suffering from toothache and, as he tied up his horse on the Quay, he saw that both children were standing up in the cart, staring.

'What's that?' Mary demanded, pointing.

As he turned to look, he realised what an extraordinary view it was for someone who had seen nothing but village cottages, green fields and rutted tracks. The broad expanse of the River Torridge glistening in the soft morning light reminded him of the words of the Psalm: '*There is a river whose streams make glad the city of God.*'

''Tis water!' said Mary, astonished, before he had time to reply. She would only ever have seen the small rivulets that trickled along lane edges and wound through wooded dells. Thomas, who had seen the river once before, pointed out the tall-masted ships that sailed to Canada, and the fishing boats that brought in the herring. As Bartholomew walked off on his errand, he had turned back for a moment to smile at them as they stared at all the wonders of the busy quayside.

He sighed as Dobbin drew the cart on towards his home village. It was not an easy position, being on the Board of Guardians. He had offered to stand when the New Poor Law was first introduced. He tried to introduce a little kindness and charity to the proceedings, but at meetings he was no match for the likes of Reverend Harding or Major Wren. Just recently he had put before the Board the case of an old

Buckland labourer, crippled with rheumatism and almost blind, whose wages had been cut because he worked at such a slow pace. Out-relief of a shilling or two a week to top up his wages would enable him to stay in his own home and look after his sick wife.

'Nonsense,' roared Major Wren, 'he must move to the Workhouse if he chooses to be dependent.' Bartholomew had then asked that the weekly tea allowance for Workhouse inmates be increased from one to one and a half ounces so that they might have a cup every day.

Reverend Harding laughed; 'Shall we also allow them brandy and port wine?'

Bartholomew was too aware of his inferior social standing to argue with a gentleman.

This business of parish apprentices made him a little uneasy. It was a system that had died out in most parts of the country, but was still embraced with enthusiasm in North Devon because it kept families out of the Workhouse. Most farmers treated their apprentices well. Did he not treat Catherine Mitchell as he would his own child? But not all were so kind and, unlike in towns where eyes and ears were all around, cruelty could go unnoticed on isolated farms. Naturally some children needed to be beaten from time to time to make them behave, but he suspected that some things went on that should never be allowed.

Perhaps he would find some excuse to call at Gusland in a week or two just to see that the Mitchell children were settled. And he must call at their cottage on his way through the village to let their mother know where her children were.

Bartholomew's road wound down into a narrow wooded valley where a stream flowed beneath tangled branches and an old stone bridge, then led to the top of a hill that gave hazy views of the looming bulk of Dartmoor on the far horizon. After another steep descent, Dobbin lowered his head to start the two-mile climb to Buckland Brewer, while Bartholomew mulled over the chores he had to complete that week. Dung must be spread in Barton Meadow – Walter and John could set to and do that tomorrow; he must mend the gate to Broad

Park, then check the sheep and lambs in Higher Meadow. Ninety acres was quite enough – how did Mr Phillips manage Gusland's 250 acres and all those labourers?

As the road levelled and the church tower came into view, he clicked his tongue to urge Dobbin to a trot again. The main street housed a butcher, two bakers, a small general shop and two inns. In addition to these amenities, the number of tradesmen in the village meant that there was little need for anyone to leave Buckland Brewer, and indeed most people did not; similarly new people rarely moved into the village, ensuring that one's neighbours were well-known and could usually be traced back several generations.

Bartholomew's family had always lived in Buckland Brewer. The village stood at the northern end of the parish, the land that stretched for three miles to the south being lonely country with narrow, deeply rutted lanes connecting isolated farmsteads and a couple of small hamlets, but he knew every inch of it. Much of the parish was high and exposed; heavy, unproductive land that was hard to work, often waterlogged and reverting to reed-infested moorland if you turned your back on it. That was where the children were going. He looked back at the meadows of the distant valley through which he had passed. He often asked himself why he did not give up his tenancy to take on more forgiving land, run a dairy herd to stand knee-deep in the lush meadows, but the truth was that the pull of family, community and long association was too strong.

He tied up his horse by the church wall and walked along a drangway that led through a huddle of cottages to the Mitchells' tiny two-roomed dwelling, passing tarred water barrels that caught the drips from the overhanging thatch. Knowing that Mrs Mitchell could be difficult, it was with some trepidation that he knocked at the door and entered. She was sitting on a low stool nursing the most recent baby, another girl whose arrival had necessitated Mary's apprenticeship. A small child, wearing only a ragged shift despite the chill in the gloomy room, toddled towards him and a young girl followed him into the cottage, staggering under the weight of a pail of water.

'Good news, Mrs Mitchell! The children have been assigned and I thought you'd be pleased to hear where they'm to.'

She glared at him. 'Pleased! Pleased that you've taken 'em away to work without wages?'

He sighed. She was going to be awkward. 'Come now, Mrs Mitchell…'

'My Thomas,' she said with great emphasis, 'could earn a shilling a week if he was taken on proper, and Mary was already earning threepence for the little chiel she was tending alongside her sisters! But now me and Mr Mitchell must struggle on with what little us can get, and you know I've been so wored out I haven't been out charring these two weeks!'

He knew it only too well. Mrs Mitchell was a hard worker but the births of the last two of her eight children had taken her right off her feet for several weeks. She was over forty years of age but was still a strongly-built woman; although repeated child-bearing and heavy physical work had taken their toll, there was only a little grey in her hair and her broadly-marked eyebrows were still dark.

He sat on a stool at the scrubbed deal table, moving aside a plate of cold potatoes. 'Now Mrs Mitchell, you know 'tis for the children's own good. They'll be fed and clothed which you'm not able to do, however much you want it. Look at Catherine, how her's blooming because my wife sees to it that her has good food and plenty of it.'

She scowled at him. 'Catherine should get wages to send home to her family alongside the vittles! And because all the farms has got young lads working for nothing, they won't pay wages for the likes of my husband and he has to scratch around for a day's work here and a day's work there! Is it any wonder us can't feed the little ones?'

Bartholomew sighed. Most people accepted their lot in life and thanked him for helping them, but Mrs Mitchell had a way of seeing right into a situation. The older girl leant against her mother and regarded Bartholomew seriously. She was like her mother and sisters, attractive, but strong-featured and determined.

He smiled at her. 'And how old are you now, chiel?'

'Her's seven, so 'twill be another two years before you'm taking her away!' the mother snapped. 'Her'll be caring for these two little ones while I'm working; what else can us do now Mary's gone?'

He remembered his purpose in coming to the house. 'Now, 'tis good news as far as Mary and Thomas are concerned. They'm gone together to the same farm, they'm at Gusland along with Mr Phillips.'

'Gusland? Where be that to?' She was looking at him very directly. He knew she would not like his answer.

''Tis down past Bilsford, two or three miles from here. 'Tis a distance, I know, but you'll find a way to visit from time to time, I'm sure.'

She glared at him. 'Past Bilsford? And where's Bilsford? So they'm not even down the same way as Elizabeth and Edward? 'Tis more than a year since I last saw them, and now my Mary's gone too, and Thomas, both of 'em.'

She was bending low over the child she held, caressing its smooth head. He was embarrassed to see that she was crying a little.

It was true that four of her children were now scattered throughout the parish, and it was only Catherine who was close by on his own farm. As Mrs Mitchell worked as a charwoman six days a week, it was only on a Sunday that she might be able to visit her children, and it was unlikely that their masters would give permission very often. He promised that he would make arrangements to see that the two youngest were settled, and would let her know.

She seemed defeated, and was silent for a moment before replying with unaccustomed humility. 'Thank 'ee. I know you do's your best, Mr Fulford. 'Tis hard, but us must just carry on. What else can us do?'

He touched her shoulder as he rose, not wanting to wait until Mr Mitchell came home for his dinner.

Chapter Two

Mr Phillips had not spoken to them at all since they left the town, and Mary really wanted to know what sort of work she would have to do. Catherine had to do all sorts of things and was very clever at all of them, Mr Fulford had said so, but *she* would not know how to make cream, or what to feed the fowls, or how to oil the maister's boots.

He was sitting very straight in his seat in front of her. His brown hair curled beneath his hat to reach his coat collar, and she could just see some whiskers from his dark beard.

'Mr Phillips!' she shouted. His head turned just a little as if a fly had settled on his cheek, but he did not reply.

Thomas nudged her. 'Ssh,' he whispered. 'Don't say *nothing* unless he tells you to do summat, then you must just say, 'Yes, Maister.''

'But I need to know if he's got any chiels to look after! That's all I can do, Thomas!' She was beginning to feel afraid.

There was silence for a while, apart from the rhythmic clatter of the horse's hoofs and the whirr of the wagon's wheels. Thomas looked anxiously along the road ahead. 'I don't know where us be gwain. Us didn't come this way.'

Mary had never left the village before, so all the roads were unfamiliar. After they left Bideford, the road had been wide enough for them to pass other carts and one on occasion they passed a carriage pulled by two horses like Reverend Colling's, but now the lane was so narrow, a bramble in the hedge scratched Mary's arm and pulled at her hair. Why didn't Thomas know where they were going? He knew everything there was to know; he was always telling her things.

The side of the wagon was bruising her back as it jolted along the rutted lane, so she shifted about to try to get more comfortable. She was hungry. Mr Phillips had not given them any cutrounds, or even a potato.

'Thomas, when will us have dinner?'

He took her hand. 'Soon; he'll give us our dinner soon.'

They passed through a cold, bleak landscape where the wind blew across poor grasslands unimpeded by a few stunted hedgerow trees; after what seemed like a very long time, the wagon turned into a farmyard. By the gate, a pale-eyed dog straining against a chain showed its teeth and barked aggressively until Mr Phillips flicked his whip at it. Half a dozen dark red cows stood aimlessly in the muddy yard with speckled hens strutting and pecking around their feet, and the bellowing of calves could be heard from some outbuildings. Keeping her eye on the dog, Mary clambered down from the wagon after Thomas, and they followed Mr Phillips through a door. They emerged into a large room with a heavily-beamed ceiling from which numerous smoked hams were hanging; a tall dresser holding plates and bowls stood against one wall and a huge, cavernous fireplace hung with pots of different sizes formed another. There was a smell of food, which made Mary's mouth water, and a lot of people eating who all turned to stare at her and Thomas standing just inside the door, but no one said anything. When Mr Phillips took off his coat and sat down at the biggest table, a woman whose face and knuckles were reddened by the heat of the fire hurried up with a plate which she placed in front of him.

He picked up his knife and fork. 'There be two extra for dinner,' he said.

The woman looked anxiously at them and then into a pot hanging over the fire. 'I think I've enough teddies, I hope I have, I didn't know you were bringing anyone home. I'll do my best.'

There were two tables, a big one where Mr Phillips sat and a smaller one tucked in a corner away from the fire, and there were children at both, children of all ages, all of them staring. A girl indicated that Thomas and Mary should stand at the smaller table which had no chairs around it, then fetched plates of potatoes mixed with a little fat bacon and placed one in front of each of the children.

Mary ate quickly. Her father was the only one to eat bacon at home, and then only on a Sunday. When she put down her spoon, she saw that she and Thomas were the first to finish. There were four other boys standing at this table, the youngest about her own age and the oldest almost grown. None of them spoke and when they looked at Thomas or Mary, it was from the corners of their eyes. The plump, round-faced girl who had told them where to stand was eating with them, so was probably a servant, like Catherine was for Mr Fulford. She had smiled kindly at Mary; perhaps she would show her what to do. At the large table two boys and two girls that Mary guessed to be Mr Phillips' children ate in silence, and there was a baby that Mrs Phillips held on her lap and fussed over, but no small children to look after.

The biggest boy, who was tall and rather fat with a silly grin that made Mary want to laugh, shambled over to Mr Phillips and leaned against him.

'Hello, Da, hello!'

He sounded soft, like a girl. Mary giggled, but Thomas dug his elbow in her ribs to make her be quiet.

Mr Phillips pushed him away. 'Sit down, John!' but he reached up to tousle his son's hair affectionately before the boy returned to his seat. John then flung his arms around his younger brother who wriggled away, complaining. Fancy a big boy like that being so mazed!

'Will 'ee find some use for the maid?' Mr Phillips was addressing his wife. What girl did he mean?

Mrs Phillips paused as she collected up the plates. 'Oh! I don't think… I don't need one, not really, Lucy and Rosa is big enough to do all the work along with Sarah. But if you want, if you think I ought to…' As her voice trailed away, she glanced anxiously at Mary. They were talking about her!

'My name's Mary,' she said loudly. She felt all the eyes in the room on her again, but no one responded.

'Her wouldn't be strong enough for the rough work, not really,' said Mrs Phillips, 'and I wouldn't want her upsetting Lucy and Rosa. I don't know what to think really.'

'I don't want to share a bed with the likes of she,' one of the girls said unpleasantly. 'Her'll have to sleep in the barn with the boys.'

14

Mr Phillips pushed his chair back and stood up. 'Well then, if her's not wanted indoors, her can work with the boys. There's plenty of stone-picking and bird-keeping; her'll not be idle.'

Before Mary could take in what was being said, Thomas had pushed his plate away and was glaring at Mr Phillips. 'You can't make her do farm work!' he shouted. 'Maids don't do outdoor work!'

In two strides Mr Phillips was across the room with his arm raised, then his hand shot forward and slapped Thomas around the side of the head sending him sprawling on to Mary's feet, and his voice assaulted her ears.

'Think you can tell me how to run this farm, you young varmint! Didn't they teach you nothing down at Cranham? 'Twill be the whip next time – you'll soon learn who's maister here! Your sister'll work with the boys and her can sleep in the barn with 'em as well!' His huge face and dark beard withdrew and he strode to the door. Thomas was shaking as he struggled to his feet but Mary dared not move to comfort him.

By the time she ventured to look up again, only Mrs Phillips and the servant remained in the kitchen. When Mrs Phillips carried the plates out to a back room, the girl came over and put her hand on Thomas's cheek.

'Be 'ee hurt, boy? It don't do to answer back to the maister, you know that now.'

Thomas looked up with tears in his eyes. 'I knew it before. But her's only nine, he can't make her work outside in all the rain and mud and cold, it idn't right!'

The girl perched on the table. 'Once he decides on a thing, I believe even a chargin' bull would have a job to stop'n. Anyways, if Lucy and Rosa have taken against her, her's better off outside. My mother used to work outside, girls did in them days. What's your name, my lover? And you'm Mary, bain't 'ee?'

They watched as she spread some linen out on the big table and took an iron from the fireplace. Her name, she said, was Sarah Moase and she was fifteen years old. Her mother farmed up the road at Bilsford but money was tight since her father died a few years ago, so Sarah had to earn a wage to send home. She lived in because she had to start so early in the morning.

'You'm not 'pprenticed?' Mary could hear that Thomas was impressed.

'No, Mother didn't have to ask for relief, that's what causes chiels to be apprenticed, to save paying out relief, i'n't it. Us can just about manage but her says if the poor rates go any higher, us'll be paupers too.'

Mary watched admiringly as Sarah leaned on the iron with all her strength, pushing it out over the clean linen as steam hissed and swirled from under it, then folding the cloth in a few quick, easy movements.

'Can't I work in yer along of you? It don't take my fancy working out there with all them girt boys and, and him too, the maister. You'd show me what to do, wouldn't 'ee?'

'Course I would, my lover, but 'tisn't up to me.' When Sarah looked up and smiled, Mary felt she would give anything to stay indoors with her. 'And 'tisn't no good speaking to the missus, her daren't ask nothing of the maister, her won't speak up even when 'tis something her really wants.'

At home, Mary's mother always said exactly what she wanted; a new bucket when the old one was leaking, or another hour in bed when she was tired. Sometimes she said she wanted a new house, new legs and a cupboard full of food. Usually she couldn't have what she wanted, but Mary's father would offer to nail a new bit of wood on to the bucket or light the fire himself to give her another few minutes in bed.

When Mrs Phillips came back carrying the clean crockery on a tray, Mary looked curiously at the woman who was now her mistress. Thin, with pale straggly hair that fell away from the bun at the back of her neck, she walked hesitantly with her head thrust forward, and almost jumped when she saw Mary and Thomas still standing at the table.

Sarah spat on the iron and called over her shoulder as she continued with her work.

'Us must find some clothes for Thomas and Mary, ma'am, and some bedding. You really going to let Mary sleep up in the loft with all them boys?' She winked at Mary.

Mrs Phillips said she thought it best to do what her husband wanted. 'I'll look out some clothes.' She looked at Thomas and Mary doubtfully. 'Her's about the size of Rosa but the boy'll have to have something John's grown out of.'

That evening, after a plentiful supper served as before to the family and the apprentices, Mary followed Thomas and Mrs Phillips up into the linhay. She found herself in a long, low-eaved room where a row of straw-filled palliasses were laid on a wooden floor. As in the upstairs room of her mother's cottage, the thatch was clearly visible between the rafters, and thick dusty cobwebs gathered in the corners; she knew how to use a broom to get those down. Hay was piled at one end ready to throw through an open hatch to the cattle she could hear shuffling below. When she walked to the edge of the hatch and peered down to see the shadowy shapes of the cows, a warm smell of dung and milk wafted up.

Mrs Phillips gestured vaguely to the line of beds. 'Thiccy one's yours, boy, and I thought best to put you in here, maid,' she said, pointing to a corner of the loft where some sacks had been hung from the rafters to create an alcove.

Mary pulled the sacks to one side and saw that they created a small triangular room where a douse mattress was laid. It looked cosy and comfortable. At home she shared a bed of the same size with her two younger sisters.

'Is that just for me?'

'Well, 'tisn't right for a maid to be in with all these boys, not to my mind, but what can a soul do?' Mrs Phillips looked anxiously at the bed then, carefully gathering her skirts in one hand, turned to descend the ladder.

Mary knelt on the bed to examine the space. If she drew back the sacking a little, she could make a spyhole.

'Look, Thomas, I can peep out to talk to you in the night if us can't sleep, and I can give you a poke in the morning if you'm still asleep.'

Thomas was standing with his back to the wall looking towards the ladder that led down to the cattle shed. 'Maybe us'll go to bed afore the others come.' He shifted restlessly from one foot to the other. 'Maybe they'll think us is asleep.'

She tried to bounce on the mattress but it was packed full of chaff and quite rigid. 'No, I want to ask them what work us'll have to do tomorrow. I'll be able to do it, won't I, Thomas? Will 'ee show me what to do?' Her anxiety had passed; she was sure to enjoy working outside once it was explained to her. 'Look, I've got a whole bed to myself!'

'Mary, keep your mouth shut!' He was pulling off his shoes. 'Pretend you'm asleep. Don't come out, whatever happens! Promise!'

She heard footsteps coming up the ladder and looked out to see Thomas scrambling under the blanket. Perhaps he was going to leap out to surprise all the other apprentices.

'Ha, the new baba's asleep!' There was laughter and the shuffling of feet. She thought that the boy who spoke was one of the oldest boys, the one called Lewis Bartlett. She couldn't hear Thomas laughing. What was he doing? She lay flat on the floor and lifted the sacking just a little so that she could peep underneath. The four boys were standing around Thomas's mattress. Lewis had a thin face, pale eyes and an unsmiling mouth. He held a lantern in one hand which swung back and forth, sending circles of light out into the darkening room.

'Geddup baba, time to get up!' The others laughed as Lewis poked Thomas with his shoe. Thomas didn't move. One of the smaller boys stood against the back wall, looking on wide-eyed.

'Where's your sister then, baba? Hidden her away to keep her safe, 'ave 'ee? I wouldn't let my sisters sleep in with us lot.' All four boys glanced over to where the sacking was hung, but they came no closer.

18

'Come on, geddup!' Lewis swung his leg back and kicked Thomas, hard. Mary put her fist in her mouth and bit down to stop herself crying out. She had promised him she would not come out, but if they hurt him again she would, she had to!

Thomas turned to curl over on his side, as if he were asleep.

'He's a hog, thiccy one!' Lewis jeered. 'A lazy hog! Us'll pull'n out from his sty! Come on boys, let's have'n!'

Suddenly Thomas leapt up and crouched on hands and knees next to the mattress. 'Not a hog, a cow, that's what I be!' He made his eyes huge, pursed his lips and let out a long, low 'Mmooo!' which was so exactly like a cow that one of the cattle below called back. The boys stood back in amazement as he crawled along the floor. 'Mmooo! I'm hunnngry!' When Mary saw the desperation in his eyes, she felt a tightness in her chest as a sob rose up inside, and she bit harder on her fist to stop the sound escaping.

Thomas swayed up to Lewis, stuck out his tongue and licked the other boy's hand slowly and deliberately, just as a cow might do. 'I need haaay!'

'Geddoff!' Lewis jumped back, laughing.

'Mmooo! I need haaay!' Thomas crawled over to the pile of hay in the corner and bent forward to take a mouthful. 'Mmmmoo!' His lips worked as he chewed the hay and started to swallow. Mary's throat constricted as she imagined the dry, scratchy hay.

All the boys were laughing incredulously.

'He be mazed!'

'Blimey, he sounds like a real cow – and looks like one too!'

Thomas sat up. 'Me, a cow?' He was grinning and his eyes had a frenzied look as the light from the lantern swung towards him. He kept his back to the wall. 'No, I'm a fowl!' And he started flapping his elbows, squawking and pretending to peck at the floor. At home he had imitated Mr Fulford's hens to amuse Mary. On that occasion they had both ended up rolling on the floor, helpless with laughter.

The oldest boy, James, who was almost a grown-up, had been sitting on his mattress smiling sardonically as if to get fully involved with the proceedings was beneath him, but he was laughing now.

'Go on, boys!' He stood up. 'Who can do a pig! Lewis, can you be a pig?'

Thomas hesitated for a second, then continued with his squawking as he kept his eye on Lewis.

'I can, I can!' The youngest boy got down on to the floor, grunting and snorting. As Thomas crawled towards him demonstrating his best imitation of a pig, Lewis and the other boy joined in until they were all helpless with mirth. Thomas's laughter was the loudest of all.

Mary lay very still as the apprentices gradually recovered, yawned and made for their shared beds, Lewis giving Thomas a good-natured kick as he went. When Thomas lay on his back next to young Joseph Beer, she could see that his eyes were open. As the loft darkened until even the sacking in front of her face disappeared, one boy started to snore; another muttered in his sleep. Mary turned over to escape a prickly straw sticking though the canvas mattress. The bed felt cold and unwelcoming. At home there was the wriggling of her younger sisters, the warmth from their small bodies and, from the other side of the curtain that divided the upstairs room, the comforting murmur of her parents' voices.

Here, there were unfamiliar rustlings in the thatch and a faint creaking from the wooden floor; a cow moving restlessly down below gave a low moan. Then came a different sound, and she turned her head to listen. A swift intake of breath; a sniff. It was Thomas, he was crying; her brave, clever brother was crying! She rolled silently under the sacking while reaching in his direction until she found his hand and they clutched each other tightly. Too afraid to talk, they lay in silence with their eyes open, together in the darkness.

Chapter Three

As the clock struck six, Mr Phillips closed the farmhouse door and stepped out into the darkness. A faint glow above the eastern horizon emphasised the dark silhouettes of the distant hills. It would be some time before the sun appeared, but the cold breeze blowing steadily on to his face pleased him; as he had suspected, it would be dry today and probably for some days to come. The first potatoes could be planted tomorrow.

He strode into the yard where his workers had gathered to await their orders for the day, his children and the apprentices having hurried their breakfasts in order to be out before him. Lucy and Rosa had already set to and were milking on their low stools, a lantern set on the ground illuminating their slight shawled figures as they leaned into the dark red hides of the patient cows.

His five adult labourers had arrived from their cottages at Higher Twitching and North Downs, and stood with caps in hands alongside the young workers. Lewis Bartlett elbowed the new apprentice in the ribs to make him stand up straight; he would help keep the new boy in line. His sister stood close to him.

Mr Phillips was pleased with the previous day's business. He'd got a better price than he expected for the three lambs he had taken to market, and he'd got these two children. The girl was somewhat of a disappointment, but the boy made up for her. Instead of a raw nine-year-old who needed the reality of work whipping into him, this boy had already been out for two years and was ready to set to.

Better still, Mr Phillips now had £20 in his pocket. Farmers who refused to take an apprentice when their time came around were fined £10, so he had hit on the idea of coming to a prior arrangement – he took the child and the £10, and the other farmer avoided an argument with the Guardians. He could not understand those who were so pernickety about having parish apprentices. Twelve years of work one could get from them without paying wages and, unlike others hereabouts, *he* never had any trouble from them, not once they understood what was required of them. The £20 would buy several loads of lime; the lime would grow an even better crop of turnips. Money makes money, that's what he believed.

'What're your names, you two?'

'Thomas Mitchell, Maister, and this yer's Mary.'

The boy's voice was low. He showed none of that brazen attitude today.

'Here, you'm just Mitchell. I don't want to be thinking you'm my son.' His own Thomas, who was six, grinned.

He gave his orders for the day. Littlejohns would tend to the cattle as usual then clear the court of dung, for it would be some weeks before the cows were out to grass. The dung must be carried to Stone Park to be spread at a later date, John Dean and James would help him. They nodded in agreement. David Judd, being past full strength, would take John Phillips, young Joseph Beer and the girl up to Twitching Moor to pick stones.

He addressed the old man. 'Take the ox and cart to move the stones.'

Judd tipped his forelock. 'Ess, Maister. Would 'ee tell John, Maister, that I must drive the ox? He drives 'n too fast and the two of 'em gets so heated, 'tis a job to calm 'em down again.'

Mr Phillips glanced at his eldest son, who was intent on trying to fit a small stick through a knot hole in the barn door, a grimace of concentration distorting his features.

'John!'

'Yes, Da?' His gaze wandered before fixing on his father. Mr Phillips had a fleeting mental picture of his son as he should have been, perhaps already standing here giving the labourers their orders.

'You'll drive the ox today, but at a walking pace. Do you understand?'

'Yes, Da!' He punched the air and began to rock with excitement.

He instructed the remaining workers. John Begalhole to take the larger oxen to plough up at Garden Close with apprentice Jack Lee. Lewis Bartlett was to take the new Mitchell boy up to Five Acres to finish the hedge-laying. William Redacleave would join them when he'd finished tending to the sheep and was to report back on Mitchell's skills, or lack of them. All the hedge-laying must be finished this week before growth started.

Mr Phillips turned to his younger son. 'You'll work along with me today, making spars. You'm getting pretty handy with 'em now. But first us must see to the horse, fetch the hay for 'n now and once you'm set up, I be going to fetch a load of lime.'

Mr Phillips watched as his workers moved out of the yard in their various directions. His daughters remained on their milking stools. They needed no instruction; for them, each day was the same as the one before. Whatever the weather or the season, the cows must be milked, the pigs and poultry must be fed and their houses mucked out. The girls would then help their mother and Sarah Moase with the cooking, the cleaning and the dairy work. Now that they were eleven and eight years old, they could accomplish a lot in a day. He had been able to dismiss the second indoor servant.

John Begalhole led out the second ox and the two beasts bowed their heads submissively as the heavy wooden yoke was settled over their necks. The oxen were cheap to feed and reliable, but they were slow; Mr Phillips would like to replace them with a pair of the big draught horses that were now kept on the largest farms, horses that could plough a field in half the time it took a yoke of oxen. The cost was prohibitive at present but he intended to increase the yield of potatoes this year, perhaps of corn and turnips also. He would soon have enough money.

Mr Phillips had made much progress since his father died. Sometimes he wished the old man was still alive to see the addition to the farmhouse, the renovated buildings and the greatly extended acreage, even though he knew his

23

achievements would have been met with derision. He had been unable to do anything right in his father's eyes.

His oldest son walked heavily over to him, his hands hanging loosely at his sides.

'Pick your feet up, John. What be 'ee, a pig dragging through the muck?'

John stared, his large, pale eyes devoid of expression, then looked down at his boots. He lifted first one foot, then the other, as if seeing them for the first time.

'John! Help Judd get the cart out!' He pointed at the cart shed.

'I gonna drive the ox, Da?'

His irritation rose. 'Yes! Didn't I tell you? Now get the cart out!'

John began to rock with excitement again. 'I forgot, Da! I forgot I gonna drive the ox!'

Mr Phillips' father could not abide being in John's presence. 'That girt slotter-pooch,' he would say of his oldest grandson, 'that half-saved mokus, is that the best you can sire? – you should've drowned 'n at birth.'

Perversely, his father's intolerance had made Mr Phillips more accepting of the boy's shortcomings than he might otherwise have been, but there had been several occasions when he had walked quickly away from his father to vent his anger on others, afraid of what he might otherwise do to the old man.

He had not dared to speak of his interest in taking on Higher Twitching Farm and North Downs, but the week after his father's death, he contacted the landowner, Reverend Moore Stevens, offering to rent the farms on condition that his own buildings were improved. His proposal was accepted because Higher Twitching was not an easy farm to let; the land was heavy and the dwellings were dilapidated, but they were good enough for the extra labourers needed on the larger farm. And the land could be improved; Mr Phillips had heard stories about the changes made on the new model farms. The men he had overheard laughed at the new developments, ''Tis all very well for them gentlemen farmers who have money to throw away, but 'twon't work. You have to work with the land, not against it.'

But they were wrong; they would never progress if they stuck with the old backward ways. Mr Phillips knew he could make the land produce more. He had plans.

As Mary followed the oxcart out on to the lane, she turned to look back at Thomas, just visible in the near-darkness. The ragged, over-sized jacket he had been given reached to his knees, making him look younger than his years. As he closed the field gate after Lewis Bartlett, who had marched ahead into the gloom with a billhook over his shoulder, Thomas paused with his hand on the latch, and their eyes met for a moment. She knew instinctively that the anxiety in his expression was for her as well as for himself, but he waved to her in the funny way he did to amuse their younger sisters, then turned away to follow Lewis.

Reluctantly, she hurried after her three fellow workers. The strange, big boy who was Mr Phillips' son was standing in the oxcart, laughing and cracking the whip while the old man half-ran and half-limped alongside, shouting as he tried to slow the ox down by pulling on its collar. She caught up with the apprentice, Joseph Beer, who trailed along behind the cart, scuffing his boots on the stony lane. He was the one with whom Thomas had shared a mattress. When they all woke in the morning, the others had jeered at Joseph for wetting the bed. She could tell that this happened every day, guessing that Thomas had been told to share with him because the others did not want to.

She looked sideways at him. He was smaller than her with a round, freckled face and brown hair that protruded in matted clumps under his cap. He stared resolutely at the ground as he walked.

'How old be 'ee?'

'Ten.'

He didn't look up, and she regarded him curiously. 'Ten! I'm only nine. Ten's too old for pissing the bed. My sister stopped pissing the bed when her was two.'

Suddenly she was sprawling on the road with Joseph on top of her screaming 'Shurrup, shurrup!'

'Get off!' She was stronger than him and sent him sprawling in turn, but then felt a stinging pain across her back.

'Bloomin' young varmints! How'm I supposed to watch you two and John as well?' Again the old man struck out rather ineffectually with the willow stick as Mary scrambled to her feet and stood shamefaced. Mr Judd hurried after the cart, muttering as he went.

They walked on in silence. She looked over at Joseph once or twice but his face had closed in again as if nothing had happened. Her new boots were beginning to hurt her. Her feet looked as if they belonged to someone else, strange leather-covered protuberances appearing in turn below the heavy serge skirt she had been given. She had never worn boots or shoes before. They were rubbing the tops of her feet where their previous owner had worn deep creases into the leather. How much further would they have to walk?

She knew from a greyness spreading into the sky that daybreak was approaching, but the landscape that was gradually appearing was unfamiliar. Was this the same road that she and Thomas had travelled the day before? There were no houses in sight, only the high hedgebanks either side and, when she looked back, distant fields below the huge sky. There was no sign of Thomas or the other workers.

Would her mother know where she was? She would be downstairs now, making up the fire and wearing her old shawl against the chill morning air; when Mary complained of the cold her mother used to pull her close and wrap the shawl around the two of them for a minute or two, asking, 'That better, maid?' before pushing her away to enable them both to continue with their chores. One of Mary's tasks had been to bring in the sticks. Would Anne have remembered to do it? Maria would be crying for her breakfast as she shuffled down the steep stairs on her bottom, and her father would be grumbling good-naturedly from above. Mary wiped her eyes with the back of her hand, and looked again at Joseph trudging along beside her.

'Where does your mam live?' He didn't answer at once, as if considering whether or not he should speak to her.

'Back there.' He gestured at the empty landscape behind them. 'Tythecott. You can't see it from yer.' He stared at the ground as he walked, sunk deep within himself.

'Does her visit you?'

'Her came once. The maister didn't like it though.'

'Do you go to see her?'

He looked at her incredulously. 'No! Us can't leave the farm!'

As they approached the top of the hill Mary glanced over to her right, then stopped in amazement. In the misty morning light, the dark silhouette of a church tower was just visible on the far horizon, and when she screwed up her eyes she could make out a cluster of low dwellings around it, the only buildings in sight.

'Where's that church?' She had seen other distant church towers from the road to Bideford so she knew there was more than one, but this one looked wonderfully familiar.

'I dunno. Village, I think.'

'Village? What village? Buckland Brewer? That's where I live! Just there by the church!'

Could she see her house? What had seemed just a desperate imagining was now real – her mother was there, within sight! In the increasing light from the rising sun she could now make out a narrow lane winding between the patchwork of field boundaries towards the distant village.

'Hurry up, else Mr Judd'll be coming for you with his stick again,' Joseph called and she ran in the heavy boots to catch up with him without taking her eyes off the distant church tower.

'How do I get to that road?' She pointed to the lane that wound so enticingly towards home. 'I could just run up there without Mr Judd seeing.'

Joseph carried on walking. 'You can't.'Twould take you an hour or more to get there.'

'But I got to!' Her eyes filled with tears of frustration at the thought of her mother being so close, and of being here, in this cold, bleak place with people she hated, 'My mam is there, I got to go!'

Joseph turned on her, his face twisted with anger and his eyes full of tears. 'You can't!' he shouted. 'If you go you'll be brought back and whipped. You can't go home, not ever!'

And he walked off after the cart.

Mary hated Joseph, then. He was wrong; she would find a way to go home.

Their place of work that day was an immense field that ran from the top of a broad ridge. Unlike the small grassy meadows near the village where Mary had sometimes played, this field was made up of heavy clods of bare soil, any grass or wild plants that had attempted to take root having been ripped out by the harrow. In the cold, early morning light the view from the top of the field was devoid of colour; dark earth, dreary sky, as far as the eye could see; even the pockets of distant woodland appeared grey. A sharp breeze sweeping in unimpeded from the east made their eyes water.

Mr Judd closed the gate behind the oxcart. He was a wizened little man with thin grey hair and a little whiskery growth all around the edges of his face which, combined with a protruding lower lip, gave him the look of an old sheep. He seemed not unkind; when he gave Mary a hessian sack and showed her where to stand, she heard him muttering that this was not work for maids. Joseph was positioned a few feet away, then John and Mr Judd himself on her left. They were to work their way down the field, throwing into their sacks any stones greater than a hand's length.

Mary crouched to grab a stone and flung it in the sack. This was easy! The next was larger and had to be wrested from the ground but Mr Judd had given her some rough canvas gloves to wear which prevented the sharp edges from hurting her hands. She took a step forward and picked up two more stones, glancing over at John, who had a look of intense concentration as he placed each stone deliberately in his sack.

She straightened up. 'I done more than you.' How foolish she had been to think that she would be unable to do the work! 'Look!' She laughed and held up a large flat stone. 'That's eight. You've only done six!'

He stopped work and stared at her. 'I done six?'

'Yes, look.' She counted them for him, and he laughed delightedly. 'Now you count 'em,' she told him. He carefully counted the stones in his sack, chuckling all the while, but had to start again each time he added another, and after a while Mr Judd shouted at him.

'Leave off, John! Us haven't got time to *count* the blessed stones.'

'Sorry, Mr Judd.' He stood crestfallen, his large hands hanging loosely at his sides.

Mary continued working. She didn't want to be shouted at, but the gleam of pleasure she had seen in John's eyes made her think of the small boy she used to mind. John might be as strong as a grown man, but he was like a small boy in his ways.

'Nine,' she said quietly as she threw in another stone. 'Ten.' She glanced over at him. He was grinning and starting to copy her, repeating the numbers after her with delight, so she went faster and faster as they vied with each other to collect the most stones, until they were both helpless with laughter. Mr Judd muttered to himself and shook his head when he stood up to stretch his back.

In time, she tired of the game. She had run out of numbers she knew, her legs ached and the sack had grown so heavy, she could scarcely drag it over the rough ground. But she would not need to pick up many more stones before the sack was full. She would be able to tell Thomas that she had worked just as fast as the others! She would be able to see him soon, when they went back to the farmhouse for dinner, and perhaps the next job would be just as easy.

At last, Mr Judd led the ox to where they worked and John hoisted the sacks into the cart, grunting with the weight of them. She sat down to take off the big clumsy boots. There were sore red marks across the top of her feet; she rubbed them tentatively and wiggled her toes, finding that the cold air made them feel a little better. She resolved to walk back to the farm in bare feet.

'Mary, Mary! Count stones again, Mary! Can us count stones again?'

The ground beneath her shook a little as John jumped up and down with excitement. An empty sack had been thrown down next to her. Joseph and Mr Judd had started work again.

'Do us have to fill another one? Haven't us got enough?'

Mr Judd laughed. 'Enough! 'Tisn't about having enough, maid! You'm as green as they come, bain't 'ee! The maister can't sow seed on stones so us has to clear the whole lot.'

He gestured at the land in front of them. They were in the top corner of a huge field. It would take her a considerable time just to walk its length; to clear the whole area of stones was impossible. Mary felt her throat tighten.

'Us can't do all that! I bain't doing all that!' She stared at Mr Judd. It would take weeks - he couldn't make her do it! 'I be gwain home!'

She turned blindly towards the gate. Before she reached it, Mr Judd grabbed her arm.

'No, you bain't!' he shouted. 'Land sakes, why'm I given the new ones? I s'll fetch my stick again 'less you set to, though it won't sting half as bad as the maister's if he gets to hear of this.'

She wrestled herself free from his restraining grip and stood, caught for a moment between her fear of punishment and the overpowering desire to run. She could run through the narrow lanes until she reached the distant village; she could burst in through the cottage door, throw herself into her mother's arms. Taut with anger and frustration, she flung herself down on to the detestable field. She wanted to punch and kick Mr Judd for being the one who kept her here, but even in the midst of her rage, she knew as she stabbed a stone repeatedly into the heavily yielding earth that Mr Phillips was her true target.

Her sobs finally died away. Slowly, she looked up. She was sitting alone, away from the others. Mr Judd had returned to his work and was muttering about chiels and it not being right. Around her there was nothing but bare, brown earth, the grey sky above, and a solitary rook flying heavily across the field, uttering its harsh, monotonous cry.

'I want my mam,' she whispered.

She wiped her nose on the back of her hand. At home, there would be movement and colour – children laughing as they ran in and out of the cottage, the fire crackling and pots rattling, all the family around the table for their morning bread and her mother scolding, her voice rich and warm. All the family, except those that were apprenticed. She was here, in this empty field. Catherine, Edward and Elizabeth were scattered two or three miles from home, far from this place. And Thomas. Where was Thomas? She longed for his sympathetic glance, the touch of his hand.

John appeared beside her. He stroked her arm as one might caress a horse or a dog.

'Come on, Mary,' he said, smiling his open-mouthed smile, the smile of a simpleton. 'Good girl, Mary, us can work together again, can't us?'

Slowly she got up to join him. She had no choice.

Returning from the limekiln at Peppercombe, Mr Phillips stopped his horse in the gateway to observe the workers' progress. Already the land was transformed. When he took it on, it had been suitable only for grazing bullocks; it was too wet for sheep in winter, too poor for dairy. The name of the field said it all, Twitching Moor, moorland a couple of generations back, heavy land that had never been properly cultivated. It had been a week's work for him and his two strongest labourers to dig out the clumps of rushes, then another week to plough it with a team of four oxen. Once the stones had been cleared, it would be manured, limed and sown with turnips. If the season was good, he would have a large crop for winter cattle feed and enough left in the field to be eaten off by sheep, providing further manure. Then there would be a crop of autumn-sown wheat. He sat in the cart with his chin in his hand, picturing the scene the following summer; acres of ripe golden wheat stretching across the hillside where before there had been nothing but waste.

He had talked to the labourers on Mr Pine-Coffin's home farm where they had seen astonishing increases in yields. Mr Phillips could not yet afford clayware field drains, but he would try the new four-course rotation he had heard about. It would be noticed, he knew that. It would be discussed at market, over field gates, at church and at chapel. ''Ave 'ee seen what Mr Thomas Phillips be about?' There would be laughter. He didn't care, not so long as he succeeded.

His horse shifted its weight restlessly. Growling at it to stand still, Mr Phillips turned to observe his brother's farm, Brendon, that lay a short distance above the stream on the far side of the valley. It was a comfortable-looking place, tucked into the hillside and surrounded by some good pastureland and a productive orchard. Since his mother died, the onerous duty of calling there had been lifted; there was no love lost between him and his brother and sister. He had heard that his sister would marry, now that their mother's disapproval no longer prevented her.

His brother would have been observing the work on Twitching Moor. He might be watching now.

'Da!'

John had been working away across the field, so had not seen his father until he rose to haul another sack. Laughing, he ran heavily over the rough ground and crashed into the side of the cart.

'I didden know you'm there, Da! I be comin' up along o' you!'

'No, John, geddown! There's work to do, you'm doing a good job, now get back to it!'

Dejected, his son trailed back to his position. Mr Phillips gazed at the field, estimating the percentage that had been cleared. The children were working steadily, and Judd would ensure that the work was thorough; there was another week's labour for them at least.

The day was interminable. Mary learnt not to look at the huge expanse of field stretching in front of her, because the distance always remained the same. She tried instead to concentrate on the minute details of the field; here was a stone that fitted the curve of her palm; there was one the shape of the axe head with which her father chopped wood. And the field was home to tiny creatures; earthworms writhing in panic when she lifted the stones under which they lived, scuttling black beetles, and long-legged spiders, with bodies no bigger than a grain of corn, that engaged in intricate dances in their efforts to escape. When she saw their distress, her sympathy went out to them, and with careful fingers she helped the beetles over clods of earth and she replaced small pieces of stone on the earthworms' homes. When Joseph deliberately smashed a stone down on an escaping beetle, she shouted and pushed him over in anger.

John did not mind the work. 'Look 'ee this one, Mary!' he exclaimed when he picked up an extra big stone, 'Look!' Sometimes she gave in to his exhortations to count the stones, but soon grew weary of his enthusiasm.

After several hours, Mr Judd and John drove off in the oxcart to unload the stones they had collected. Mary stopped work and sat back on her haunches.

'You can't stop,' Joseph told her. He looked at her bleakly, 'You never know when the maister's coming.'

Temporary relief came at midday when Mr Phillips' daughter, Lucy, arrived with their dinner. Mary stood up and watched as Lucy put a basket down near the hedge, before walking off without a word. The four of them sat with their backs to the hedgebank, too busy eating and drinking to talk. There were thick slices of bread, some cheese, half an onion each and a flagon of small beer to share. Afterwards Mary fell asleep against the hedge until shaken awake by Mr Judd.

When the sun was sinking down towards the western horizon, the final sacks were at last loaded on to the cart. Mary followed the oxen along the lanes with her boots in her hand, almost too tired to place one foot in front of the other, walking with the muddy hem of her heavy skirt slapping against her bare ankles, and her smarting hand tucked into her armpit. When they reached the top of the hill, she looked up just once at the distant church tower. She knew that she could not go there, but on her shoulders she felt the squeeze of her mother's hands, and in her ears she heard the reassurance of her mother's voice, and she started to cry.

As she trailed along behind the other workers, a man on a horse approaching from the opposite direction reined in beside her.

'You all right, maid?' A round, kind face was looking down at her. 'Be 'ee hurt? What's your name, chiel?'

'I'm tired,' she told him, 'and I'm hungry. My name's Mary. I want to go home.' She almost shouted these last words, but the man didn't seem angry with her.

'You'm new, bain't 'ee? A new apprentice to Mr Phillips?'

She nodded.

'Well, chiel, if you'm ever in trouble, if you'm not treated right, I'm over at Lower Twitching,' he pointed, 'it adjoins Mr Phillips' land. You ask for Mr Clement if you needs help, maid.' He nodded and rode on.

She turned to see which way he went, but a bend in the road soon hid him from sight. She would not know how to find him and, besides, Joseph had said she would be whipped if she ever left the farm.

A few minutes later when she came into the yard, walking towards her was Thomas; his familiar height, the shape of his shoulders, and the faraway look in his eyes.

'Thomas…'

He was staggering slightly under the weight of the logs piled in his arms, but his eyes met hers in an instant and held them. She saw that Lewis was behind and Mr Phillips across the yard, and knew that he could not speak to her; but his glance told her that he understood how long her day had been, how uncomfortable the boots that she held in her hand, how the bending had hurt her back and, most of all, how much she missed all the things that were familiar to them both. She breathed in his scent as he passed her.

As they stood at the dinner table, he held her hand under his jacket where no one could see, and squeezed it when her eyelids were drooping and her head falling forward. She saw that his hands were scored with deep red scratches and she could feel the rigid muscles in his thighs, as if he were getting ready to run.

When the meal was over, they were the first to climb the ladder to the loft, and at last he could speak to her.

'Did they hurt you?' There was both fear and anger in his eyes, as if he would like to hit someone.

'No, Thomas.' It had not occurred to her that she might be hurt. 'But 'twas hard. I could do the work, but 'twas too long. I'm tired...' She wiped her eyes with her sleeve. 'Couldn't I share the bed with you, 'tis cold on my own.'

She started to cry again at the thought of lying alone with the rats scrabbling in the thatch.

He pushed her away gently. 'No, 'cos the others be coming. Quick, go and lie down.'

She crawled into her corner and let the sacking drop down to hide her as the sounds of footsteps and voices drew nearer. She heard Lewis's singsong voice;

'Well now, how be 'ee going to amuse us tonight then, Mitchell?'

She heard scuffling, and then laughter, but tiredness overcame her. She remembered nothing more.

Chapter Four

Mrs Mitchell dragged the last of the straw palliasses back up the stairs. Taking advantage of the dry weather, she had beaten them to get rid of the dust and the bugs before airing them out in the yard for a couple of hours, but they were hefty things to carry and she had to sit on the low bedroom windowsill to regain her breath. It was as well to get used to some heavy work again; next week, she would go back to her charring. She did not relish the thought.

It had taken her even longer than usual to recover from this most recent birth. It hadn't been that way when she was young, when Catherine and Edward were born.

A narrow beam of pale afternoon sunlight found its way through the small window behind her to illuminate motes of dust floating lazily in the midst of the bedroom. The spare palliasse was folded against the wall, not being needed now that Thomas and Mary were gone. The room looked empty without it.

She was making a new rag rug from scraps of old clothes sewn on to a flour sack to keep the little ones warm in bed when the cold weather came. Usually there was precious little time for such things because the mending alone kept her busy each evening, but this had been something she could do while regaining her strength. Perhaps she would not have started if she had known Mary would be leaving, because there was bedding to spare now.

She sighed. What was she doing sitting here in the middle of the afternoon like a lady of leisure? She pushed herself up and straightened the wooden boxes that held their few changes of clothes, then drew the curtain between the children's and the marital bed to make the room ready for the evening, before descending the steep, narrow stairs to the ground floor room that served as kitchen, sitting room and washroom combined. Baby Jane was beginning to stir in her wooden crib near the fire, her mouth opening to suck each time one of her hands, waving like tiny starfish, brushed against her cheek. It would not be long before she started to cry. Charity Mitchell gazed down at the perfect little face, the pursed lips just waiting to be kissed. She had not wanted another baby. She still did not want another baby! This was her eighth, and her sixth girl. She would never have chosen to exchange Mary for this scrap, yet that was what had happened because the birth and her subsequent ill health had led to Mary being sent away. Surely, there would be no more babies, not now that she was forty-three years old. She had prayed last year that there would be no more, yet here was Jane. She bent to caress the smooth head with its soft cloud of fine dark hair, the rounded perfection of it.

Charity Mitchell knew from experience what it was to be apprenticed; had she not been sent out when she was twelve, just when she should have been able to earn a few shillings to help her struggling parents? Instead, she had been punished for their poverty by being forced to work for nothing, by being beaten and underfed. She had been determined that her children's lives would be different; she would choose employers for them, good people who would care for them and pay them for an honest day's labour, give them a good character when their work came to an end. But she and her husband Thomas had been unable to find steady employment. They had moved from Northam to Abbotsham, from Littleham to Buckland Brewer, going wherever there seemed a better chance of regular employment but, with few exceptions, all Thomas's work had been as a day labourer. If harvests were poor or the weather wet, he was laid off, and the few shillings she had managed to put aside would have to be spent. When the pennies were gone, she had to turn to the parish for help. That was when the trouble would start. The parish would not help the whole family; they said the oldest children must be sent away to work for their keep. First it was Catherine. When Edward's turn came and she refused to let him go, the family's poor relief was stopped altogether. They tried to survive on turnips that her husband stole from the fields at night and songbirds netted in the hedges until she could stand the children's cries of hunger no longer and, taking Edward by the hand, she walked with him through the village and gave him away. She would never forget that day.

Charity walked to the window and stared blindly through the small panes. Every day she went out charring to increase their income, but when a baby arrived and she was laid low, the money ran out. When Ann was born, Elizabeth was sent away and when Maria arrived, Thomas had to go. If she had not agreed, the whole family would have been sent to the Workhouse and forbidden from seeing each other. Was it any wonder that her husband could not find regular work when the farmers had so many apprentices working for nothing?

Jane's whimpering was developing into a persistent and repetitive wail. Charity scooped her up and, loosening her own clothing, sat down at the table as the baby's frantically searching mouth fixed greedily on to the nipple. She sighed. It was Mary she missed most. They were company for each other; they could converse like two old friends. Mary could be relied on for much of the household work and to look after the younger children. Although strong-willed – she had to be chastised for rudeness occasionally – she was clever at seeing what needed doing, so Mrs Phillips, whoever she was, should count herself lucky to have Mary helping in the house. It was to be hoped that she would treat her well.

Her mind turned to the evening's supper. Last year's potatoes were used up several weeks ago, so it would be bread again, and she had a little dripping, a few onions, there would be some greens, but she must keep enough for herself because last week she had gone without to feed the children and her milk had started to dry up. Please God, her husband would come straight home when he was paid tomorrow; if he went to the inn even for a short while there would not be enough money for the flour they needed. The relieving officer had again allowed them three shillings this week, but it had already gone on flour and there would be no more money until she was paid for her charring.

As Charity sat, her gaze travelled around the room and she enumerated the possessions that enabled her family to survive. The long rough table that stood in the centre between a home-made form and two rickety chairs. Her large, blackened pot in which most family meals were cooked, a cast-iron frying pan and the big, black kettle in the inglenook fireplace. Two old wooden boxes serving as storage, and the plank resting between them that formed a shelf where she kept her tin canisters of flour, salt and a little sugar. Underneath was her copper preserving pan and a large wooden tub which served both as a bath for the children and a container for curing sides of bacon, although the family pig had been sold to pay the rent these last two years, instead of being killed for their own consumption. She longed for a bit of bacon but, still, the tub was there for the future. She had these things; she was not destitute. And she had her two most precious possessions; the yoke which made carrying water so very much easier, and her sewing box, a treasure chest of needles, threads, scraps of cloth and spare buttons. With these, and occasional donations from those who were better off, she could keep the family clothed.

There was much to be thankful for. Her children were all living, and how many women could say that? Once she heard that Thomas and Mary were being well cared for, she would be happy. Mr Fulford would let her know soon; he was a good man.

She cupped the baby's head in her hand and eased her up so that she lay hiccupping gently. Mr Mitchell was working all this week, which was a blessing. He had been hired for a year last Lady Day, but it was only for three days a week and one day's work was in exchange for their cottage, so every week he had to go from farm to farm seeking more work. He was allowed their corn at a cheaper price and the use of a potato ground, which was more than some had. Those who could afford it were leaving Devon and sailing for the New World; some had gone from Buckland Brewer and members of Mr Fulford's family were thinking of it. Letters home spoke of the low costs of food and of land, and of wages five times as high as Devon. What she would give to be able to live there! Men who had been labourers here could become landowners in the New World, but the fares were high.

Charity knew she would never be able to raise enough money to go.

She moved Jane to her left breast and went to the door, cradling the baby in her arms.

She wanted Ann to fetch kindling for the fire. The girl had gone with her younger sister to pick watercress from the damp, sheltered lane edges where it grew early and lush; they should have been back long before this. She walked down the drangway from her cottage and looked up and down the village street. No sign of them. She used to be able to rely on Mary, but Ann was easily distracted from her chores.

Grace Ley was gathering in her washing from the hedge that ran between the cottages. Her linen was always white with barely a darn to be seen, and in her person she was always neat and tidy. She must have at least three dresses. But there, her husband was a thatcher and always in well-paid work. A kinder couple you would not meet; Mrs Ley had several times helped out when she discovered that Charity was unable to feed her husband and children.

'Mrs Ley, have 'ee seen my Ann anywhere abouts? Her's been gone such a time her should have found enough cress to feed the village!'

Grace Ley dropped a folded shirt into her wicker basket. 'No, but my Polly's with her. They'm gone off together hand-in-hand.' She came over to where Charity stood. 'Shall I go and fetch 'em? You'm looking a bit peaky, you know,' she said, putting a hand on Charity's arm. 'Be 'ee sure you'm ready to go back working next week?'

Charity was feeling a little weak. It must have been dragging those palliasses up the stairs. 'Well, I must work, ready or not. Us can't live on fresh air. But how Ann's going to manage while I'm away, I don't know. Her'll have to bring the baby to me to be fed before her's screaming fit to wake the churchyard, and drag Maria along with her too. How her'll do it, I don't know.'

Charity had not meant to confide in Mrs Ley, but her doubts about Ann's ability were weighing heavily on her.

Suppose she should drop the baby? Or let Maria fall in the fire?

Mrs Ley patted her arm. 'Well, I can help out, maid! They can come in along of me and I can set Ann on the right road when the baby is getting hungry. And I'll see that the potatoes go on for dinner and the firings is gathered. The chiel needs a bit of direction, no more than that, and my Polly will be glad to have her alongside.'

As they were speaking, Charity saw the girls walking up the road from the Barton, talking and giggling together. Ann was struggling along with Maria on her hip and a bundle of cress in her hand, but there was barely enough for a few mouthfuls. What had the girl been doing? Charity slapped Ann hard on the bottom as they drew level.

'Where've you been all this time! Don't 'ee know there's more work to do? I'm waiting on firings too but us won't be having much greens with the dinner from the look of that! What do 'ee think you'm feeding, chiel, a rabbit?'

Ann looked shame-faced and Maria started to cry.

'Come here, my lover.' Charity watched with irritation as her younger daughter hid her face against Mrs Ley's shoulder. 'Now Ann and Polly, run back down the lane to see who can pick the most cress and I want you both back by the time the kettle's boiled because Mrs Mitchell's coming in along of me for a dish of tea. Then you'm both going out again for some firings and if you come back with your arms full, there'll be a slice of bread and jam. Quick now, run!'

In Grace Ley's cottage the fire was crackling. Charity, sinking down gratefully on to bright cushions, could not remain cross when surrounded by such comfort and kindness.

'That's a weight off my mind, Mrs Ley, knowing you'll keep an eye on the children while I'm working. I could ask Mary Judd or Susan Clark, I know, but they'm busy enough with their own affairs without taking on my worries.'

Grace Ley had the most compassionate face when she smiled. 'And have you heard aught about your Thomas and Mary? How they'm doing?'

Charity explained that she was waiting to hear from Mr Fulford. 'I haven't the strength to go visiting them even if I did know where to go. I know nothing of the place where they be, that's the worry.'

Mrs Ley cut two slices of bread, spread them with jam and handed one to Charity. 'Could 'ee visit of a Sunday when you've the strength?'

Sundays. There was the bread to bake for the coming week, there was the heaviest washing to do, there was a multitude of smaller jobs which were too difficult or heavy for a young girl. What time did she have for visiting Thomas or Mary or any of her other children scattered about the parish?

Mrs Ley must have seen the expression on her face. 'No; no, I don't suppose you have time. But Mary's a sensible girl, and Thomas has been out before; there's no cause for worry, I'm sure.'

Charity Mitchell took a bite from the slice of fresh bread spread thickly with blackberry jam. 'I hope you'm right, Mrs Ley, but seems to me, if a thing can go wrong, then 'twill.'

The farmyard was colourless in the early evening drizzle. The shippen, barns and sheds, being built from the same grey-brown mud that surrounded them, almost disappeared when Mary looked at them through half-closed eyes, so she could imagine for a few moments that they were not there, that she was somewhere else, until the jostling and complaints of the other workers waiting their turn at the pump brought her back to reality. The rain was finally easing, but the sack she had been given to tie over her shoulders that morning had long since failed to keep her dry and she had spent the better part of the day wet right through to her skin. When she stamped her boots on the cobbles in an attempt to shake off the worst of the dirt, the hem of her skirt, heavy with mud, flapped noisily against her calves.

Lewis pushed Joseph out of the way so he could wash his hands in the bucket, then flicked muddy water into the younger boy's face. Joseph was so dirty already it didn't make a great deal of difference, but he recoiled at the shock and tried to use his wet sleeve to rub the mud from his eyes. Without thinking, Mary knocked Lewis's hand away before he could torment Joseph again.

'Leave him be, you ol' mullygrub!'

He turned on her, his mean, pale eyes narrowing in anger, but at that moment Mr Phillips walked across the yard, his boots and long coat as encrusted with mud as those of his workers.

'Get on with it and inside for your supper,' he barked.

Mary kept her head down until he had gone into the house. She expected Lewis to retaliate then, but Thomas suddenly strutted across the yard, capturing Mr Phillips' loping walk and imitating his voice to make the other boys laugh.

'Thomas, stop!' She glanced nervously towards the kitchen window. If Thomas was seen he was sure to be whipped, but she knew he had done it to distract Lewis's attention from her.

She was still a little frightened of Lewis. He had not hurt her so far, and once had laughed quite kindly at her, saying that she reminded him of his younger sister, but she was careful not to provoke him when there were no adults nearby to intervene.

'Hurry up, John!' Lewis had moved away and John, as usual, was taking far too long at the pump, dipping his hands into the water and lifting them to watch the drips fall back into the bucket. She pushed him aside. 'Come on, mumphead, shake'm dry!'

She sloshed the dirty water out on to the cobbles and refilled the bucket from the pump, pushing down with all her weight on the squeaking handle until the water gushed forth. She was not going to wash her hands in the boys' mess. When she had finished, she stood aside to wait for Thomas. However tired she was, this was her favourite time of the day; the work was done, her belly would soon be full, she and Thomas were together. Throughout the long days there was a tight knot of anxiety deep inside her, but it eased when he was there. Sometimes they managed to whisper together about their days, what had been hard, what had gone well; at other times they didn't have the opportunity, but then their eyes would meet and it was just as if the words had been spoken.

Lucy was calling the hens into their house for the night, her high-pitched *coop-coop-coop* as she tempted them in with grain providing a counterpoint to the deep grunts of the pigs in their sty and the soft lowing of the cattle from the barn. The harmony was broken by the shrill yowling of cats. The big ginger tom that frequently left dead rats on the doorstep had grabbed a small tabby by the scruff of the neck and was forcing her face down into the mud as he mounted her from behind. She kept up an unearthly wail as she struggled ineffectually to escape his straddled legs and restraining jaw.

Mary watched with horrified fascination.

'Yerr, give it to her!' Laughing, Lewis yelled encouragement and Jack Lee sniggered as he imitated the male cat's thrusting movements, an amusement which was quickly copied by big John, but he went one further and held his nether regions as he propelled his hips backwards and forwards, roaring with laughter, while all the while the dreadful wailing continued.

Mary turned away uneasily. She knew what was happening. She had seen other animals mating and knew to associate the act with the rustling and soft moans she used to hear at night from the other side of the curtain that divided her parents' sleeping area from her own. She would like to have chased the big tom away but her instinct told her not to get involved.

After what seemed like an age, the tom cat ceased his assault and the little tabby crept silently away on her belly. The farmyard settled back into the more melodious sounds of animals eating and rain dripping from the thatch. Mary walked quietly to the kitchen door and Thomas moved quickly to accompany her.

They were all allowed to stand in front of the kitchen fire to dry their clothes. They stood as close as they dared to the welcome heat, causing steam to rise from their wet garments, but Mary knew that they would not be allowed to stay long enough to dry completely. At home, when her mother got wet walking back from work, she would go to bed for a couple of hours while her clothes dried in front of the fire, not having any others to change into. Mary had tried taking off her skirt at night in preference to lying in damp clothes, but had been too cold without it. Today, as was usual, while their garments warmed so did the odours of sweat, muck and unwashed clothes increase. Mary moved away from young Joseph Beer, it being obvious that he had not washed in all the time she had been at the farm and probably a lot longer than that, but the truth was, they were all filthy. It was only while standing by the fire that she remembered how dirty she was.

Eventually, when the stench became overpowering, Mrs Phillips shrieked at them.

'Get away, go on, the lot of 'ee, fouling my kitchen with your stink! Get away to your table!' She flapped her apron noisily to clear the air and swept the floor clear of dried mud.

Supper tonight was three thick slices of bread and butter for each person served with a leek and bacon stew. The room was silent but for the scraping of spoons and the sound of chewing, until the meal was finished and Mr Phillips gave his usual order, 'Out, you lot,' with a nod towards the door. Mary was always the first out so that she could settle into bed in the cold barn before the others came up, and Thomas was usually right behind her.

There were many nights when they were all so tired that they went to bed in silence but, if the older boys were sufficiently awake, the tomfoolery could go on for some time. Once, one of them brought in a live rat to hunt down and eventually kill with a pitchfork; sometimes they played jacks with small stones. When it was good-natured, Mary would sit on her bed and join in but too often the entertainment was at the expense of the younger boys. Tonight she went straight to bed behind the sacking before her damp clothes chilled her, and lay on her back watching the vapour rise in the cold air when she breathed out.

The voices and laughter down in the yard grew louder as the boys climbed the ladder.

'That'd be some life, a tom cat! No work to do, just the mollies to hump whenever 'ee want!'

It was Lewis. He made deep grunting noises and the younger boys laughed. James, the oldest, was silent. Mary had noticed that he rarely took part in the mischief, usually looking on with amusement, but sometimes calling a halt to the proceedings when he wanted to sleep.

'Yer, Joseph, you'm small, you can be the molly!'

Mary could hear struggling on the wooden floor, laughter, and Joseph shouting 'Gedoff, Lewis!'

'Leave him be, Lewis, you'm mazed.' It was James's deep voice.

'Where's your sister then, Mitchell? Her's the true molly round yer! Come on Mary, gedout and have a laugh along of we!'

She froze. She hated Lewis; she wanted to scream at him and spit and scratch, but lay rigid in the bed behind the sacks, clenching her fists and feeling her nails dig into her palms. He was stronger than her.

'Come on, Mary, gedout!' Lewis was coming closer but there was a sudden commotion, a scrabbling and shouting;

'You bastard! You leave my sister be!'

She had never heard Thomas's voice so full of hate; then was a cry, it was Thomas, and James's gruff voice.

'Leave off, Lewis, you've hurt'n enough! And leave the maid be. Land sakes, her's nought but a chiel! Now get to bed else I'll call the maister.'

Every nerve in her body on edge, Mary listened to Lewis muttering as he crawled into bed, and other movements that she could not identify. She lay very still. After several minutes, she lifted the sacking just an inch and peered underneath. The room was almost dark but she could just make out Thomas's silhouette curled tightly in his bed. She hoped he would know that she was thinking of him. Her fear had not passed, but it was a comfort to know that Thomas would watch out for her. She pulled her damp skirt close around her legs, and she tried to go to sleep.

Chapter Five

Three weeks later, Bartholomew Fulford was leaning on a gate looking out with pleasure over Long Meadow. His eight red Devon cows, having been let out to graze just two days ago after a long winter in the yard and shippen, were still skittish, jostling each other and frolicking with tails held high, before again lowering their heads to tear greedily at the lush spring grass.

Each year, letting out the cows marked the end of the lean months of winter, the end of the careful eking out of hay and turnips and anxious glances at the sky for signs of warm spring rain. Now that the buds were breaking on the ash trees, he could look forward to the hay harvest, to the emergence of potato foliage through the previously bare soil, then the ripening of wheat and the swelling of turnips, until he could hope that the barns and ricks again held sufficient stores to see them through another winter.

One of the cows – it was Betty – raised her head to bellow loudly, then trotted purposefully across the field before resuming her grazing. The other cows meandered after her. Blossom, Daisy and Fancy, their glossy, dark chestnut hides stretched comfortably over their swelling bellies, would calve in June. He hoped for two heifers, one to increase his milking herd and one to sell, and a bull calf to raise for beef. At the back of his mind was the thought of building up the herd a little so as to have two or three cows to give to his oldest son when he set up on his own.

He moved away from the gate and strolled up the lane. The bright green leaves of wild garlic were pushing through the brown leaf litter at the base of the hedge, and vivid yellow catkins were flowering on the hazel. He stood by the gate to Higher Middle Park and, thrusting his thumbs into the pockets of his Sunday waistcoat, swayed back and forth on his heels as he observed the newly harrowed soil. Today would have been the perfect day for sowing oats, dry and mild; the slight strengthening of the south-westerly breeze on his ruddy cheeks presaged rain for tomorrow. It made his hands restless when he thought of letting the seed trickle between his fingers as he flung his arm in a wide arc, first right and then left, while pacing the field in long easy strides. The soil was in perfect condition; tomorrow's rain would swell and germinate the seed. It was often a struggle not to work on a Sunday, but it was a struggle to which he would never submit. That very morning he had stood in chapel reminding the faithful congregation to keep the Lord's Day. But still, there was no harm in looking at the field and wishing that the day was a different one.

He had been a lay preacher for more years than he could remember. In the early days the meetings had been in a cottage room, until the powerful appeal of John Wesley's message led to larger gatherings than even the most generous cottage could accommodate. A chapel was then built on village land donated by his first wife's parents and it was in this unadorned building with its whitewashed walls and diamond-paned windows that he now spent many of his Sunday hours.

This morning he had spoken from a favourite text. The elderly labourers with bent shoulders, their good-natured wives in black bonnets, the portly ruddy-faced farmers with their rosy-cheeked families, all had nodded sagely at his words, it being a comfortingly familiar message.

Continuing his walk, he paused opposite Spurs, his own farmhouse standing tranquil under its thick layer of thatch. There would be much industry within, his wife and Catherine Mitchell flying around the kitchen so that they might all eat their meal before walking back to the chapel for the afternoon meeting. In the yard in front of the house, however, all was quiet. It always seemed that the animals knew when it was a day of rest; the cockerel's crowing was more subdued on Sunday mornings, the pecking of the hens about the court more leisurely and their cackling reduced to crooning; the white ducks huddled together with their beaks under their wings, and the dog dozed in his kennel, merely thumping his tail a few times to acknowledge his master's presence.

A few dozen paces away on the other side of the lane stood more barns, a mowhay and cottages for his labourers, who generally stayed with their employer into old age. At present, one cottage housed a very old man who had been a loyal workman to the family, but was now so far beyond any useful toil that Bartholomew had asked a widow to live there rent-free in order to care for the old man. The alternative would have been the Workhouse.

In the adjoining cottage was a labourer with his young family. Two small children sitting on the doorstep called out to him.

'Look, Mr Fulford!' The small boy held out a tiny tabby kitten which meowed piteously. Bartholomew leaned on the wall. 'Where did 'ee get that, then? Don't 'ee know 'tis too young to be away from its mother, the poor scraggety thing?'

The children's father emerged to wish him a good morning. They engaged in a satisfying discussion about the possible benefits of killing a pig instead of tilling oats if the next day's weather proved inclement.

'Our stores of bacon be getting low, and 'tis a good job for a wet day, killing a pig and getting it salted down,' Bartholomew told him. 'I'll see that a bit comes your way. Us could sow the oats and mebbe the clover too, Tuesday.'

And addressing the children again, 'Now run and put the kitty back in the barn with its mother, else 'twon't live to catch rats for me when 'tis grown.'

He continued up to the village's main street and stopped to talk to old Mr Squire, who liked to drag a chair outside his front door so that he might see the world go by. The blanket Mr Squire had around his shoulders was his most cherished possession, it being one of a dozen or more that Bartholomew had persuaded the Rector to hand out to the poor the previous winter.

The village was a tidier and quieter place on a Sunday; no clothes spread on the hedges to dry, no children kicking about an inflated pig's bladder, no hammering from the blacksmith's shop or sawing from the carpenter's, but only the 'pink, pink' of a chaffinch calling from the old elm tree, and the mewing of a buzzard soaring overhead. When Bartholomew reached the village green, he perched as usual on the low wall outside Mr John Dennis's blacksmith's shop, because it gave him a good view of the church door. The service would be finishing soon and it gave him a pleasant, if rather guilty, feeling of satisfaction to observe how few people came out of the huge edifice, hardly more than packed the small Methodist chapel.

When the church door at the end of the long cobbled path opened, Reverend Colling was the first to emerge; a tall, imposing figure in his white surplice. Mr and Mrs Speke from Orleigh were next; when pleasantries had been exchanged, they proceeded arm-in-arm towards their waiting carriage, and Mr Joshua Veal with his wife and little daughter, Delicia, appeared.

Today the congregation was even smaller than usual, thirty-nine when last week there had been forty-two. The Reverend Colling lacked the common touch, that was his problem. He was rarely seen out visiting, but spent his days shut in his study with his books, and even the most loyal admitted they could make neither head nor tail of his sermons.

Bartholomew strolled back towards the green, admiring the dark red leaf buds that had appeared on the majestic lime trees lining the church path, and nodding to the people who had paused to converse together. He would not stop to join them. Farmers who stood together companionably at market would affect only a passing acquaintance on the Sabbath if one were church and the other chapel.

As he turned back down the lane towards his house, he heard footsteps hurrying up behind, and a harsh voice.

'Mr Fulford! Mr Fulford!'

He turned to see Mrs Mitchell holding up her skirts as she almost ran towards him with her bonnet strings flying.

'Mr Fulford! You habn't been to see me! I've been waiting and waiting for you!'

When she grabbed his arm, the proximity of the fierce expression on her large face caused him to step back in alarm.

'I've heard nought of my Thomas and my Mary! You promised you'd tell me how they'm doing!'

He had forgotten all about the Mitchell children. There had been so much to do, what with illness in the village and visits from the doctor to arrange. He would have to prevaricate. He patted her hand.

'Oh, they'll be as right as rain, Mrs Mitchell, don't 'ee fret about 'em. They'm together, bain't 'em, they'm company for each other.'

Her grip, even through his Sunday coat, hurt his arm. 'But look what's happened to that poor boy down Mr Seldon's place – beaten so bad he was near enough killed! That's why I has to know! When 'ee saw 'em – were 'em being cared for? Did 'em have enough to eat? My Mary's a good worker but I want to know is Mrs Phillips treating her right? Did 'er look like like 'er was viddy, Mr Fulford, that's what I want to know!'

What could he say? When he hesitated, she drew back, staring at him. 'You habn't been! You promised to go and you habn't! I put trust in you, Mr Fulford!'

The fierceness of her gaze seemed to travel right through him to see all the other things he had omitted to do, unkind thoughts he had harboured and selfish acts he had committed.

'Mrs Mitchell, Thomas and Mary – they'm good, sensible children, good workers. For certain, Mr and Mrs Phillips'll be looking after 'em. I will find out for 'ee though, soon as ever I can find the time I'll ask around for news and let 'ee know, I will.'

He employed his most conciliatory voice and tried to pat her hand again but she flung his arm aside with a force that took him aback. It almost seemed that she might lash out at him.

'For certain! For certain they'm looked after! Just like that poor boy down Mr Seldon's was looked after I suppose, and him whipped 'til his back was red raw! If my Mary or Thomas… Did 'ee find the time to visit that poor boy, Mr Fulford? Did 'ee?'

He knew nothing of the boy being beaten. How could he admit it?

'Mrs Mitchell, I haven't heard of that case as yet, but I will make enquiries.' He knew he sounded lame and her momentary silence was ominous.

'You didn't know?' Her gaze was piercing him again. 'The whole village is talking of it and you didn't know! 'Tis your job to know! Beggar 'ee, Mr Fulford, you'm no better than a workhouse master!'

He took a step back. This was too much.

'Mrs Mitchell, that's not warranted. 'Tisn't my job to go chasing after all the apprentices in the parish – don't 'ee know there's thirty-two of 'em? How could I attend Board meetings if I was to spend all my time with them? And you should watch your tongue. Speaking to your betters like that, you might find next time you ask for relief, it idn't looked on so favourably.'

He turned away in what he hoped was a dignified manner to make his escape, but she screamed after him.

'S'pose it were your chiels out there with no one to look out for 'em! Think on that, Mr Fulford!'

Her words cut through him like knives. He wouldn't give her the satisfaction of a reaction. His back felt as rigid as a poker as he marched down the lane, and it was a relief when a bend in the road obscured him from view. He glanced back to make sure. She had no right to talk to him that way. Had she any idea how many hours he worked each week as Poor Law Guardian, and none of them paid? It was often a struggle to get the farm work done – just the other day had he not been hedge-laying in near-darkness, his fingers numb with cold, when other men were relaxing with their feet up before a roaring fire? And all because he had spent the afternoon sitting around a table in the Board Room at the Workhouse. Did she think of that when she made such accusations against him? But his indignation was tempered by an unsettling feeling of culpability. He had promised her he would make enquiries about the children. Just as important, he had promised himself that he would do so because he had genuine concerns for their welfare, especially the little maid. How had he let it slip his mind?

He heard footsteps behind and turned quickly. It was only Mr Norman with his wife and two daughters returning from church, but nevertheless someone he did not wish to meet at this moment. John Norman was his fellow Guardian; between them they were responsible for the poor of the parish, but they did not always see eye to eye. Mr Norman considered it his duty to spend as little of rate-payers' money as possible. Although on good terms as neighbouring farmers, their relationship as Guardians was uneasy and sometimes antagonistic. Had he heard Mrs Mitchell's comments?

'Bad as a workhouse master then, Mr Fulford! I never thought to hear that of you!' He was chuckling. ''Tisn't hard to upset Mrs Mitchell as we both know, but you seem to have made an uncommonly good job of it this time!'

Bartholomew did not want to get involved in a discussion about Mrs Mitchell, but some of her words came back to him.

'What's this about a boy belonging to Mr Seldon being beaten? I've heard nothing of it.'

Mr Norman walked alongside him. 'The father's up in arms about it, says us has to get the magistrate involved and it do seem that Mr Seldon was rather heavy-handed, though I don't doubt the boy deserved it. Would 'ee look into it?'

Something else to do. But he was determined that he would first obtain news of the Mitchell children. The enquiry would have to be made with care; he had no wish to upset anyone else and Mr Phillips would not take kindly to another man interfering in the running of his farm.

He wished Mr Norman a good day and opened the gate into the yard, lifting his head to savour the smell of roast meat drifting from the kitchen window. As he came through the door into the warm, steamy atmosphere of the kitchen, he was met by the clatter of pans and his wife's exclamation.

'Oh, there you be!' She slid the joint from the cloam oven and carried it carefully to the table where their three sons and two young farm servants were talking and laughing. 'Grace, sit down, do, you've been such a help but you'm getting under my feet now.'

The young girl, one of his three apprentices, scrambled on to the bench that ran along two sides of the table, and Bartholomew took his place in the carver chair to serve the meat. Catherine Mitchell placed dishes of potatoes, cabbage and leeks – the last from the garden – on the table before sitting alongside the others. After he had said grace, he glanced up at her as he carved the joint. She had been with the family since she was nine, the same age as her younger sister down at Gusland. She had her mother's strong, handsome looks; all the Mitchell girls resembled their mother and showed equal determination, but with his wife's careful guidance Catherine had become a conscientious worker.

His sons, Robert, John and Titus, had walked out of the village in a direction different from his own that morning, taking advantage of the Sunday hours of leisure to observe the work of other farmers and engage in pleasurable discussion about the successes and, even more enjoyably, the failures of others. Bartholomew listened as he ate his dinner, but did not join in as much as usual. He kept picturing the two Mitchell children in the cart when he had driven them to Bideford. He could not help feeling some trepidation as to their fate.

He had no right to go to Gusland himself and demand to see them, but if a member of the Mitchell family were to go – that would be different. Mrs Mitchell would tend to be confrontational, but someone who could make a few gentle enquiries would not go amiss.

His wife was beginning to collect up the dinner plates while explaining to Grace where the speckled hen's nest could be found.

Bartholomew interrupted her discourse on the vagaries of hens. 'Do you have particular need of Catherine this afternoon, my lover? I have a task in mind for her. She could be excused chapel for once.' When he explained to Catherine that he would like her to go to Gusland to enquire after her brother and sister, her face lit up. He did not, of course, mention the meeting with Mrs Mitchell.

'You may see Thomas working in the fields as you walk along the lanes 'cos Mr Phillips don't keep the Sabbath, that I know. But if 'ee can't find 'n, you could knock on the door and ask, polite-like, if you can talk to Mary. It may be that Mrs Phillips wouldn't be averse to that.'

He explained in which direction she should leave the village and along which lanes she should walk to have a chance of seeing Thomas on the other side of the hedge. If she left as soon as the dinner things were cleared away, she could be back before dark.

He relaxed in his chair as the womenfolk started to tidy the kitchen, happy to have a good meal inside him and his family around him. He still had to arrange to see the boy down at Seldon's, but all would be well, he was sure of it.

Mary bent to place a potato in the drill, took a careful step forward and reached into her willow basket for another. Her back ached from the constant bending. She paused for a moment to glance across the field to the row of waiting baskets, one for each of the apprentices who were slowly working their way up the field.

She knew it was Sunday because the paid labourers were not at work, and also because that morning she had just caught the sound of church bells drifting on a strengthening breeze from the village. She had stood up and stared past the muted brown and green patchwork of fields to the distant tower on the horizon, small and indistinct in the low cloud that drained the colour from the landscape, and she remembered how loud the bells sounded to those near the church. Her mother would hear them, and her father; Anne might be cradling the baby in her arms, and little Maria squealing and holding her hands over her ears at the noise. Sometimes, when a carriage arrived, Mary used to take the little ones out to watch the lady and gentleman descend and walk through the churchyard. As she stood in the muddy field with the wind whipping her hair across her face, she wondered whether Ann would do that today, whether she would miss her older sister and wonder where she was.

She placed another potato, and another. Her hand still hurt where she had cut it three days ago while working with Joseph and big John. Potatoes from the thatched pit had been piled in the barn so that each one might be cut in two or three pieces ready for planting. The children had to make sure that each piece they cut contained what Mr Phillips called an 'eye', and were slapped if he came in and found one that was 'blind'. She was only slapped once, and was almost enjoying being in the dry barn with the rain dripping outside from the thatched roof, when suddenly the sharp knife slipped in her damp fingers and cut deep into her hand. She had cried, and Mrs Phillips had tied a piece of rag around it, but now the rag kept slipping because it was stiff with dried blood and mud. She had had to ask Thomas to retie it several times. She didn't like seeing the cut because it was still raw, like a piece of dirty meat.

She glanced over at Thomas. His movements mirrored hers; one step forward, bend to place a potato, step, bend, step, bend. You mustn't put the potato too far in front of your boot, or take big steps. Thomas looked like a little old man as he shuffled across the field, bent double in his long jacket.

The field did not feel so big or so empty when Thomas was nearby. They could talk while they worked and when she wasn't sure what to do, she could ask him. But she didn't like Lewis being there.

Sometimes she had bad dreams about Lewis, dreams that she did not like to think about when she woke.

Sometimes she dreamt that she was free to return to her mother, that she was running as fast as she could through the lanes towards the church on the hill, but then she was woken by the ringing of the morning bell and the reality of her servitude returned.

Lewis was spreading dung in the trenches ahead while James followed behind them with the oxen, ploughing in the potatoes they had planted. A flock of gulls wheeled and screeched behind the plough as they dived to fight over worms, their cries mingling with the repetitive song that James chanted to the oxen. The song consisted of just a few notes, and Mary could not make out the words, but if James stopped chanting, the oxen stopped working.

James was the oldest of the apprentices. He only had four more years of his apprenticeship to serve. He rarely spoke except to Mr Phillips about work, and he had a way of staring into the distance while holding his mouth tightly closed as if he were grinding his teeth. He said once that he worked extra hard because he wanted to make sure of getting employment when he left Gusland, so that he could look after his mother. He rarely joined in Lewis's games and that made Mary like him a bit. Sarah liked him too; Mary guessed by the way they exchanged looks at dinner that they were sweet on each other.

'He's yer again!' Thomas's voice was low but she caught his meaning at once and glanced up. Joseph and Jack Lee, working alongside, did the same. Mr Phillips was standing very still at the open gate, watching them with his arms folded across his chest. It was the third time today he had come to check on them or to shout some instructions to James; he did not have far to come because the field was next to the farmhouse.

He was walking towards them. He stopped between her trench and Joseph's. Step, bend, step, bend; she daren't look up. She could smell his strong male scent, and sense his size and strength.

'What sort of planting be that?' The loudness of his voice, when it came, made her jump but he was looking at Joseph's trench, and the relief flooded through her.

'Foot apart, I said!' She glanced back as she worked. He was flourishing a hazel stick with which he measured the distance, then his hand shot out and he struck Joseph around the side of the head, sending him sprawling across the trench. 'Geddup while I watch you do it proper!'

Joseph scrambled to his feet and frantically gathered up the potatoes that had fallen from his basket. He placed a potato, then the next, almost tripping over his feet in his efforts to place them at the correct distance. His face was frozen in an expression of anguish.

Finally Mr Phillips moved away, stepping carefully in the trenches that were still to be planted. He shouted something to Lewis then went back to the gate to watch. Mary had to put a potato right on top of a beetle rather than get the distance wrong, but she placed it gently so that it would be able to escape. They worked on in silence until, at last, glancing up surreptitiously, they saw that Mr Phillips had gone. When Joseph started to hiccup as he tried to control his sobbing, Jack Lee imitated him.

'You gert baby!' Jack's laugh was humourless. He never cried, even when he was hit.

'The maister idn't gonna come out again, I reckon,' Mary told Joseph sympathetically.

He looked up at her. His nose was running thickly. 'You reckon?'

'I reckon.'

After a while, Thomas started to sing. His voice was brave and clear; Mary had never heard him sing like that before.

> *'When I can read my title clear*
> *To mansions in the skies,*
> *I bid farewell to every fear,*
> *And wipe my weeping eyes.*
>
> *Should earth against my soul engage,*
> *And hellish darts be hurled,*
> *Then I can smile at Satan's rage,*
> *And face a frowning world.'*

When he reached the end, he looked at her and at Joseph, a faraway look in his dark eyes as if he wasn't really seeing them, then he started the song again. The tune was slow and steady; he was planting the potatoes in time with it and she soon found herself doing the same.

'Us learnt'n in chapel,' he said, when he reached the end for the third time.

'In chapel? When?' She was missing the song now that it had stopped. 'When did 'ee go to chapel?'

'When I was over Cranham. Sometimes us went to Baptist chapel Sundays and sometimes us had to work. I liked singing. I dunno what it means though.'

'Did 'ee learn reading? Catherine learned reading at Sunday School, and Mr Fulford helped her at home.'

'Didn't learn much,' he said. ''Tis hard, reading. The singing was best.'

'Did all the 'pprentices go?' He had told her very little about Cranham.

'Yes, it was all of us or none of us. I liked it. At Sunday School they couldn't be having none of their nonsense. And it got us away from the maister.'

His face hardened. She waited, but he didn't say anything else, and she saw that he was pushing each potato viciously into the earth.

'Was he bad as Mr Phillips?' she asked tentatively. Joseph was listening too.

'Worse. Probably not worse really, just that I knows now how to avoid a whipping. I was whipped twice at Cranham.' He tried to inject some humour into his voice. 'That's why I be watching out for 'ee. Don't want that to happen to 'ee.'

She watched him, and her eyes filled with tears.

'Mr Phillips gave me a whipping once,' said Joseph unsteadily.

Thomas glanced over at him, then away into the distance. 'And I know never to cry in front of the bigger 'pprentices. Didn't know that at Cranham, not at first. Don't 'ee forget that, Mary, not ever! If Lewis sees 'ee cry just once, he'll torment 'ee even more, I know it.'

He spoke passionately and then, after a moment, shook his head and returned to his work.

She wanted so much to stop and hug him, but they had to keep on planting: step, bend, step, bend. She straightened for a moment to ease her back, and saw again how the field stretched ahead of them in the grey afternoon light.

After a while, Thomas started to sing again and gradually she and Joseph joined in. The words weren't quite right perhaps, but the sound of their voices merging together made her feel happy and sad at the same time, and for a while she forgot that her back hurt.

It was late in the afternoon when she heard a voice, a girl's voice. There was a figure at the far gate, but it wasn't Mr Phillips. It was a girl in a long brown dress, a shawl and a blue bonnet. She was taller than Lucy or Rosa. She was holding her hand above her eyes to shade them from the rays of sunlight finding their way through clouds above the misty horizon, and she was watching them. Mary stood up. Who was it? There was something familiar about the girl's height, her confident stance. A little weak sunlight caught the turn of her cheek, the wisps of dark hair.

And then the girl called out. 'Thomas! *Mary*!'

It was her sister, Catherine! She was coming into the field towards them, running right over the potatoes that James had ploughed in, and Mary dropped her basket and ran, and she threw herself into her sister's arms. Catherine held her close. She was warm; she smelled of bread and soap and other nameless things that overwhelmed Mary with memories of her mother and of home.

'Mary! What be doing here? Look at you! You poor chiel, come now.' She wiped Mary's eyes with a clean piece of rag she took from her pocket. 'What a state you be in! And what've 'ee done to your hand? And Thomas!' She had her arms around Thomas as well now and Mary clung to her brother and her sister, forgetting all about potatoes, and mud, and Lewis, and Mr Phillips.

'Oi, what's going on yer?' James had stopped the oxen and walked a few steps towards them. He shook his dark hair out of his eyes. 'The maister don't like visitors. There'll be trouble if he sees 'ee!'

'Mr Fulford sent me.' Catherine spoke out loudly to James. She wasn't afraid of him at all. 'Though I wasn't supposed to say that, so don't tell 'n. Do 'ee work for this Mr Phillips?' She looked straight at James and he looked down at his boots. He wasn't cross after all.

'If he comes, I s'll have to say I told 'ee to go,' he said. 'Be quick then, us have nearly finished yer.' He returned to the oxen but stood with his hand on the plough, watching the visitor.

Catherine pushed Mary's hair back in a gesture reminiscent of her mother, and wiped her eyes again. 'Don't cry, my flower, don't 'ee cry. Thomas, what be going on yer? What's Mary doing working outdoors?'

Mary clung to Catherine as Thomas told her everything, or nearly everything, while she exclaimed, 'What! In the barn? With the boys?' He didn't tell her that he had been hurt, or say anything about Lewis. Then Catherine asked them questions about the work, and whether they were warm enough, and what they were given to eat.

'Listen, maid.' Catherine held Mary's shoulders and looked straight into her eyes. 'I be going to tell Mr Fulford what be gwain on, and I be going to tell Mam. You know you can't come home, but us can p'rhaps make it better. Now come here and let me bind up that hand.'

Catherine's looks and voice, her smell and her firm caress were all so reminiscent of their mother, that Mary clung to her and could hardly speak for sobbing.

'Is Mam gwain to come? Ask Mam to come! I want to see my Mam!'

'I will, I'll ask her. You know how it is with her, but her'll come if her can, I know it. I'll tell her, chiel.' She looked nervously over her shoulder. 'I must go now, but you be brave, my flower, and Thomas – you see that you look after her. I'll tell Mam what a help you be. And I'll come back one day, I promise.' She gave them both a last hug and Mary watched through her tears as her sister hurried back towards the gate, turning once in the lane to wave. When Mary looked at Thomas she saw that he was struggling to hold back the tears.

'Quick now, back to work before the maister comes.' James's voice was gruff but not unkind. 'Us is nearly finished now. And you,' he pointed to Jack Lee, 'don't 'ee say a word. Leave these two be.'

As Mary started planting the last basket of potatoes, she looked towards the gate again. Catherine had stood there; she really had. The memory of her voice and the warmth of her embrace were still strong. Everything had changed.

Chapter Six

Charity Mitchell clung to the wooden plank seat as the creaking cart bounced around a sharp bend in the narrow, rutted lane. She rarely travelled by cart and was afraid that if she did not keep her wits about her, she would be thrown into the hedge or into Mr Fulford's lap.

It was very good of him to offer to take her. She could not have walked all the way before darkness fell.

She had been walking down the road that morning to do the weekly wash for Mr Fulford's neighbour, when Catherine called out to her. It was with some trepidation that she entered the kitchen, remembering her words with Mr Fulford the previous day, but still feeling justified in her belief that he had let her down. She was surprised, therefore, to be ushered in and offered a seat at the table with Mr and Mrs Fulford and Catherine.

It had come as a shock, the news about Mary. She had feared that her daughter might be harshly treated by Mrs Phillips, but it had never occurred to her that she might be doing outdoor work. And as for sleeping outside with the boys – could you warrant it!

'But there be other maids with her, naturally,' she had said.

'No! There bain't! Just her and the boys!' Catherine had been close to tears. 'And the state of her, Mam, so dirty and wored out, I hardly knew her!'

Mr Fulford had tried to calm Charity.

''Tis wrong,' he had said, 'there's no two ways about it. I know what terrors boys can be and it just idn't right for a young maid to be in with them all the night long. But us'll put it right. Us is going down there this very day, when you'm finished with your work.'

He wasn't going to come to the farm with her, he explained, because he had no right to interfere but he had told her what she should say.

She turned to him now. 'I still bain't clear about it. If the mistress won't find her somewhere better to sleep, then what can I do? I don't know nothing about magistrates.'

'That don't matter,' he reassured her. 'Just say as you'll have to see a magistrate and that'll do the trick, I reckon. If it don't, I'll help 'ee with the next step.'

'But then, the outdoor work! What about that? I want Mary to be taught proper in the house like Catherine be, so's her can go out as a servant when her 'pprenticeship's finished and done with. Her won't find outdoor work! Farmers won't take her on save for harvest and potato-picking!' She was pulling at his arm in her agitation, causing the horse to shy.

He transferred the reins to his right hand. 'I think us must leave that for the time being. I don't hold with maids working outdoors myself, not in all winds and weathers, but 'twasn't that long ago as 'twas commonplace and I don't know that us will get anywhere with the magistrate on that matter. 'Tis only cruelty or starvation he wants to know about, but I think her's in danger of cruelty in with them boys.' He shifted his weight to sit more comfortably on the narrow plank. 'One thing at a time. You'm justified in insisting that her has somewhere better to sleep.'

Charity huddled into her shawl. The sun, obscured by thick clouds, was already sinking towards the horizon and the air was becoming chill.

The long, narrow lane, winding this way and that, seemed endless, nothing but mud and high hedges with occasional glimpses through gateways into desolate ploughed fields, or meadows where a few scrawny sheep with dead brambles tangled in their wool looked up in alarm as the cart passed by. The horse's hoofs squelched rhythmically through the mud as it trotted down into a valley and up a long steep hill on the other side. What a distance it was to the place where her Thomas and Mary lived! She would never be able to visit again.

'See there?' said Mr Fulford. 'The first bluebells! Does the heart good to see their little blue heads, don't it! Sign that the weather'll soon warm up.'

''Twould take more than a few flowers to raise my spirits!' she retorted. 'What of that boy that was whipped down Mr Seldon's, 'ave 'ee seen 'n?'

'Tomorrow,' Mr Fulford sighed, 'I'll see 'n tomorrow.'

Tomorrow could be too late for that poor boy, Charity thought.

Finally the cart drew up at the entrance to a farm lane.

'This is where I must put 'ee down,' Mr Fulford said. 'I shall go in to have a word with Mr Heal here at Buda, and you can walk on to Gusland, it idn't far now, ten minutes at the most. 'Tis better that Mr Phillips don't know I brought 'ee. I'll be waiting here when you'm finished.'

She missed his company as she hurried down the lane. Might she see Thomas and Mary at work here? Although Mr Fulford had told her that she would not pass Gusland fields until almost at the farmhouse, when she heard voices she could not help stopping to peer through the sparse, tangled hedge, but she saw only two older men clearing a ditch.

As instructed, she turned left when the lane met another, and soon saw farm buildings ahead. She paused at the gate to ready herself. She was still wearing the old apron she wore to do the washing – why had she not thought to remove it? She smoothed it down and wiped the worst of the mud from her boots on the grass verge. As she opened the gate she had to sidestep quickly to avoid a dog that leapt out to snarl at her from the end of its chain.

With heart pounding, she knocked at the door. It was answered by a young servant girl, and she found herself in a large farmhouse kitchen which had a less comfortable appearance than the kitchens in which she worked. There were no colourful cushions on the chairs, the copper pans hanging above the fireplace were dull and tarnished, and there was a stale smell as if there were, somewhere, a bowl of cream that had turned or a dead mouse that had gone unnoticed.

A thin, pale-faced woman stood by the fire with a ladle in her hand. She seemed startled by Charity's appearance and stammered out a greeting – or a question, it was impossible to say which.

Mr Fulford had instructed Charity what to say, but it wasn't until later that she realised that she had paid no heed to his advice.

'Where's my Mary and my Thomas? Where be 'em?' Her anxiety turned to anger – how dare this woman mistreat the children! 'If any harm's come to my Mary…'

She marched across the kitchen towards Mrs Phillips, but was pulled back; the girl was clinging to her arm. 'Wait, Mrs Mitchell, 'tis Mrs Mitchell, bain't it? Here, sit down. The children are safe, come, sit here.'

All Charity's concerns poured forth in a jumble of words. 'Safe? My Mary safe when her's sleeping with a roomful of boys! Out in a barn with no one watching over her? The magistrate'll soon change things, you see if he don't!'

It was the girl who tried to calm her; Mrs Phillips looked on in alarm from the fireplace, picking up a baby that had been crawling on the floor and holding it against her chest as if to protect herself. But she was the mistress! Charity was determined that she would prise an answer from her.

'What do 'ee mean by it, serving my maid in such a way? Would 'ee let your own chiels sleep out there? And why haven't 'ee got her working in here along of you, her's the best little worker you'd find!'

What a strange woman Mrs Phillips was, quite unlike Charity's employers who were, without exception, forthright women who knew their own minds. This one stammered and dithered, seeming quite incapable of giving Charity a straight answer.

''Twas Mr Phillips, see; he thought, well, he would have it so, I couldn't…'

In her confusion, she turned away and fussed with the fire.

A young, dark-haired girl with a long apron and rolled-up sleeves, the daughter from the look of her, appeared from the back kitchen and stared at Charity.

''Tis the Mitchells' mother,' Mrs Phillips explained, 'her don't like the maid sleeping outside, and I don't think it's right, not really.' She twisted a lock of her thin, fair hair around her fingers as she looked anxiously at her daughter.

'Well, don't make that 'pprentice sleep along of me and Rosa, Ma; her stinks, us don't want her.'

This was too much; Charity rose to her feet again. 'My Mary's worth ten of you! Her's as kind a maid as you'd ever meet!'

'Wait, Mrs Mitchell, sit down.' It was the servant girl again, a plump, fair-haired girl with kind eyes; she sat facing Charity and took her hands. 'Mary can sleep along of me. I'll take care of her. I sleep here in the house, I'll show you where I be. Her's a good maid and I'll be pleased to help. Her'll be safe with me.'

Charity could have cried, then. She squeezed the girl's hands in gratitude. 'What's your name, chiel?'

Mrs Phillips started worrying about what her husband would say, but the girl, whose name was Sarah, cut her short.

'There idn't nothing for Mr Phillips to be concerned over. I'll explain it to him and I hope as he won't put his foot down over it. He don't pay too much attention to house business as a rule. I'll see that Mary's up in the morning and her'll be out to work same time as usual. 'Tis the best way; he wouldn't want to go up before the magistrate – I'll remind him of that.'

Charity followed Sarah up a winding staircase and along a passageway to a little room with a low door. She looked around. There was a proper bedstead that had a straw mattress covered with sheets and blankets; there was a rag rug on the floorboards and an earthenware bowl and jug on a small washstand, something Charity herself had never possessed.

'I'll see that her keeps herself a bit cleaner than her's been able to 'til now, poor maid,' said Sarah.

Charity peered out from the window at a view of fields stretching as far as the eye could see. Mary would wake in this room. Mary would be able to look out from this window.

She turned to Sarah. 'And Thomas? How be Thomas?'

They sat on the bed together. 'They have to work hard, the two of 'em, really hard,' Sarah explained, 'but they'm well fed. The maister knows they won't work so well if they'm

68

starving, see. He's a hard man, but not cruel for the sake of it
like some I've known. They haven't been whipped, Thomas
nor Mary; but they'll have learned that they will be whipped
if they put a foot wrong. That's something us all knows in this
household.'

She told Charity that the children would soon be in for
their supper so, if she was lucky, she would be able to see
them.

When they went back downstairs, a tall, broad-shouldered
man with a long black beard was coming through the kitchen
door. Charity knew at once that it must be Mr Phillips.

'What be gwain on yer?' He looked at her in an odd
sideways manner, confrontational yet not quite meeting her
eyes.

His wife stammered out an explanation.

'It don't make no difference to me where her sleeps.' He
sat on the nearest chair and started to take off his boots, 'but
us don't have visitors yer.' Again that strange, challenging
look, and his voice grew gruffer, louder. ''Tis time you left.'

Charity took a deep breath. 'Why's my chiel working
outdoors? I don't know of another chiel in the parish that's
working outdoors day in and day out! Her should be in the
kitchen and close to the house, seeing to the hens and calves
and suchlike, I've a good mind to call the magistrate...'

Before she could give vent to all her other grievances, Mr
Phillips took several steps towards her in his stockinged feet
and loomed over her.

'Geddout!' His voice was a roar. 'Geddout of my house!
Think I'll be told how to run my farm by a slommoking old
woman like you!'

She might have shouted back but Sarah took her arm and
guided her swiftly past him. 'Come on, Mrs Mitchell, I'll see
'ee out.'

She felt panic rising inside her. 'But, Thomas and Mary,
I've got to see 'em before I go!'

Sarah, who had somehow pushed her out through the door
before she could protest further, leaned closer and whispered
to her, 'There now, look!'

Trailing up across the yard came a group of weary, dirty children; a small, dishevelled boy, an older hard-faced lad carrying a shovel, then, '*Mary*! *Thomas*!' She slipped and almost fell in the mud as she ran towards them, then her daughter's arms were gripping her tightly, and she drew Thomas in too, feeling his tense, wiry body relax as he allowed himself to be embraced.

They had time for so few words. Afterwards, when she walked back up the lane to meet Mr Fulford, she could scarcely remember what she had said, or what the children had told her. But they were well-fed, they didn't appear sick; that was what she told herself again and again. Then her other thoughts would intrude; they were so dirty, their clothes in a worse state than ever they were at home, they looked so very tired, the poor lambs.

But then again, Mary was going to sleep indoors with that kind, sensible girl; that could not be better. The poor chiel had been so very pleased to hear that. But what about Thomas – was he safe with those much older boys? She realised that she was gesticulating wildly as she walked.

The light was growing very dim when she turned the corner to hear Mr Fulford's horse moving restlessly at the end of the farm track, and relief flooded through her that she was away from that place and back with people she could trust. Mr Fulford greeted her cheerily as he took her hand to help her up on to the cart, and on the way home she told him the whole story.

'Could 'ee talk to 'em for long?' he asked.

'No, just moments, it felt like, then Mr Phillips come to the door and, seeing me still there, shouted that he'd fetch his whip if I didn't leave at once.'

As the air grew colder and the cart swayed slowly back to the village, the contours of the fields dark against the twilight sky and blackbirds clacking their evening warnings from the hedgerows, she felt so very weary she could almost have dropped off to sleep. It had been her first day back at work since the birth of her baby – who would be screaming with hunger by now – and all this to contend with. She had been so very anxious for news of the two children, but now she had seen them, she scarcely knew what to feel.

BIDEFORD.

On the 18th instant a farmer named *Seldon*, of Buckland Brewer, was summoned before the county magistrates on a charge of assaulting and severely beating his apprentice boy, only nine years old, the marks of which were visible for nearly a month. He was fined 12s., and severely reprimanded by the magistrates for his inhumanity, and cautioned that if he should be again brought before them under similar circumstances, the full penalty would be inflicted. It was also noticed by the bench, that an act was about to be passed for the purpose of more minutely inspecting the treatment of parish apprentices by their masters, and requiring them to be brought before the bench every six months, or before a board of guardians whenever required to do so, to see that their education, &c., had been properly attended to.

North Devon Journal, 26th May 1842

Thomas gave Mary a little smile as he moved towards the door with the other apprentices, and then he was gone. The table felt too big to stand at alone. She shifted restlessly, unsure of what she should do next. Mr Phillips had gone into another room with his younger son, the girls were completing their nightly chores outside, and John sat listlessly at the family table. The clock ticked loudly in the corner. Perhaps it would have been better to have gone to the barn as usual with Thomas, but she was jubilant that her mother had made Mr Phillips say that she could sleep indoors.

Sarah stacked the plates and balanced them expertly on her forearm before picking up two jugs in her other hand and turning to Mrs Phillips.

'I'll wash these and tidy up, Missis, then take Mary up to bed.' She winked at Mary. 'Comfortable bed and a bit of peace and quiet for you tonight! Mind you don't snore and stop me from sleeping.' She bustled out of the room, leaving Mary feeling even more alone.

Sarah had always been kind. She would slip Mary or Thomas an apple when no one was looking, and secretly roll her eyes at Mrs Phillips' dithering to make them laugh. She had found Thomas a better pair of stockings when his were full of holes. She was, now Mary thought about it, the only person who ever smiled at them. Sharing a room would be like sharing with a big sister, but she was less keen on being in the house with Mr Phillips, and with the girls who were always unpleasant to her.

Mrs Phillips was collecting up the cutlery and wiping the table with quick, nervous movements. She glanced over in Mary's direction once or twice. Mary shuffled awkwardly, unsure whether she was expected to stand still at the table or to lend a hand. If she showed how useful she could be, perhaps in time she would be allowed to work indoors with Sarah.

'Shall I help, Missis?'

Mrs Phillips looked startled and it was a moment before she answered. 'Er, no. No.' She continued with her work. 'But 'tis good of 'ee to ask,' she added as an afterthought.

Mary looked at the clock. It was tall, housed in a wooden case with its face not far from the ceiling. She had never seen a clock until she came to this place and had been startled when she first heard it strike. Each morning and evening she heard it strike six times, and sometimes seven too, and she had realised that the hands pointed at the same numbers each time. She often studied it after she had finished eating, so she knew now how to read each number, because she just had to count on one more each time. Standing here now with nothing else to do, she practised writing the numbers with her finger on the palm of her hand. She could do it without looking at the clock.

'Come on then, chiel.' At last Sarah poked her head around the door. As Mary passed Mrs Phillips, she paused. 'Goodnight, Missis.' It would have been rude not to say it, but there was no answer.

She had never been beyond the kitchen. They came into a dark hallway where Sarah opened a low door that gave straight on to a steep staircase. She could hear Mr Phillips' voice from another downstairs room, so she hurried after the candle that Sarah held aloft, shying away from the shadows it threw on the rough, whitewashed walls.

'Here you be!' Sarah stood back. The room was clean and neat; a narrow bed, a small-paned window. 'I'll leave the candle here for a minute while I get 'ee some water. I can feel my way down.'

Mary sat on the bed, hoping that no one else would come while Sarah was away. There were more doors off the passage through which they had passed, but all were closed.

Clump, clump, came Sarah's footsteps up the stairs, and she appeared carrying a large jug.

'Now, if you'm sharing a bed with me, chiel, you need to be a bit cleaner than what you are now. That hand too, I'll bandage it proper when it's clean. I've got warm water here and a little piece of soap, see? And a cloth to dry yourself. Take off all your clothes, mind, so's you can have a proper wash, and put your slip back on for bed.'

'Do I have to do that every night?'

Sarah laughed. 'No, chiel! 'Tis just that you'm so very dirty now, baint 'ee! And us don't want the room smelling worse than it do now.'

It was true that there was a strange smell in the room. Mary looked up at a wooden rack on the wall opposite the bed. 'It looks like sheep's wool.'

'That's it, maid, they'm fleeces put there to air for a few months, 'tis dry up here you see. No one else wants them but I'm given no choice. You get used to the smell in time.'

When Sarah had gone, Mary did as she had been told. The air felt cold to her wet skin as she quickly rubbed herself dry. She could see by the wavering light of the candle that the water in the bowl and the cloth on which she dried herself were very dirty; Mam would have been appalled.

Memories of her mother swept over her again as she climbed between the smooth sheets. To suddenly see her standing there in the yard had felt like a dream, and she could not now remember what had been said however hard she tried, but the memory of being held was with her still. Was Thomas remembering that too? Was he missing her, up there in the barn? She would have to find a way of telling him tomorrow about this room.

She had never slept between sheets before. When she ran her hands over them, they felt smooth and soft, except where there were darns. The darns felt like daisies, petals reaching out from a hard centre. She turned over. The bed was warm now and the mattress only a little bit scratchy. The noises in the house were different from those in the barn, slow creaks coming from the roof, a clatter from downstairs, then, once or twice, distant voices and doors opening and closing. She wished Sarah would come.

She hadn't thought to ask her mother about the little ones. Was Anne keeping Maria safe? Once, some clothes drying near the fire had caught alight and the sight of the flames consuming the little skirts and shifts had terrified her – suppose Maria had been tottering near the fireplace wearing those very clothes when a spark flew out? Anne needed to keep a careful watch, but she was often absorbed in her own games, she didn't know all the things Mary knew. And the new baby – Anne had never cared for a new baby before.

When at last Sarah appeared, there were many things Mary wanted to ask, and she sat up in bed.

Sarah was easing off her boots. 'Sixteen hours I've been on me feet! Bain't you sleeping yet, maid?'

'No. But I like this bed! Sarah, how do I know when 'tis time to get up in the morning? And can 'ee ask the Missis if I can work indoors along of you? And, you know the clock downstairs; do the hand take longer to get from eleven to twelve than it do from one to two?'

Sarah laughed. ''Tis too late for all that, maid, 'cept to say in the morning I'll come to wake you. You'll be sleeping when I get up. Come on now, move over and give me some room.'

She lay with her warm back against Mary, her hair smelling of soap and wood smoke, like Catherine when she came to find them in the field. When Mary tentatively put her arm around the older girl, Sarah took her hand and pulled her close.

'There, that's cosy, bain't it? Us'll do just vitty here together. Goodnight now, chiel.'

Mary relaxed into the soft warmth. It was not long before the steady rise and fall of the girl's breathing had lulled her into a dreamless sleep.

Chapter Seven

The weather had fallen into a pattern, each morning dawning bright and chill, the merest wisps of cloud being pushed aside by the sun as it crept up above the distant hills. By mid-morning there was warmth on Mary's face when she looked up at the sky, warmth which lasted until mid-afternoon when the clouds would increase and a few drops of rain would fall, although never enough for Mr Phillips.

There was enough light for them to find their way along the lane although the sun had not yet risen. She and Joseph shared the weight of the basket that held their day's food; breakfast, dinner and supper for all three, but it was the bottles filled with ale and water that made her arms feel they were being dragged from their sockets.

As usual, Thomas realised her arm was aching almost before she knew it herself.

'Yer, I'll take it now.' His smile was gentle; she relinquished the basket gratefully and skipped ahead of them. 'Us've got cake!' she told them, 'Sarah asked Missis if her could put in a slice for each of us. I s'll eat mine with my dinner, I reckon.'

She and Joseph were going to Kitty Park and Thomas would be just over the hedge in Five Acres. She had learnt the names of almost all the fields on the farm now and knew, when they were instructed each morning, whether her workplace would be exposed to a cold wind or in a more sheltered position. There were still many tasks of which she was uncertain but it would be more than a week before she would again have to experience that feeling of dread as Mr Phillips barked out his orders at the early morning gathering, because the three of them were going to be bird-scaring from dawn until dusk until the oat seed had sprouted. It was dull work, but it did not cause her back to ache or her hands to hurt, and Mr Phillips only came to check on them once or twice a day.

'I'm *glad* there's no rain! I doesn't care if the seed dies 's long as us is dry!' She turned defiantly to the two boys, and all three subsided into giggles.

'I doesn't care if the teddies rot in the ground and the oxen all go lame!' Joseph's eyes shone as the laughter burst out of him.

'And I doesn't care if the maister falls on his face in the muck and the dog bites his arse!'

Their voices rang out over the dew-laden fields as they competed with each other to think up ever more outrageous events, knowing that Mr Phillips was safely indoors eating his breakfast.

Earlier, when Sarah gently pushed Mary out of bed, she had crept downstairs to the empty kitchen and held up the candle to illuminate the brass face of the clock as it struck four times. It was strange to be alone in the room, and she sat for a moment on the bench at the family's table, reaching out to touch the smooth, brass candlesticks, before hurrying out to wake Thomas and Joseph. The food basket had been made ready for them the previous evening, so that they could set off straight away and arrive in the fields before the first birds awakened, but a blackbird was already singing from a roadside tree and the first rooks flying in from their night-time roosts when Thomas opened the gate into Kitty Park and put the heavy basket down at the foot of the hedgebank.

'Who's going to eat first?' Mary asked. They had been instructed to eat one at a time so that the remaining two could continue to guard the fields.

Joseph was already looking longingly at the basket.

''Tis best to wait,' Mary warned him, 'tis early yet and 'twill break the day up better if 'ee wait. But you can go first if 'ee want.' The previous day they had finished all the food by mid-afternoon, and the evening had seemed interminable.

Mary picked up her bag of stones and wandered away across the field to take up her position. Although the sun had not yet appeared above the horizon, its emerging light had made visible the now familiar view – the bare, brown earth that ran in harrow-lines from her feet all the way to the hedgebanks that were exuberant with new growth, the distant patchwork of fields, scattered farmhouses and pockets of woodland stretching away to the west, and above it all the huge overarching sky. Yesterday she had, at first, thought her surroundings to be devoid of interest, but gradually she had started to notice the beetles that scurried past her feet and a brave ant that carried away one of Mr Phillips' precious oat seeds; she had heard a cuckoo calling down in the valley and seen that the hedge was alive with buzzing insects, the rustling of small animals, and flowers she could pick and tuck into the waistband of her skirt.

The breeze was cold on her cheeks. She pushed the crown of her hat down firmly, retied her shawl behind her back and pushed her cold toes down into the soft earth. They all had to go barefoot so as to walk lightly over the sown seed, but she knew now that she would not suffer from the cold once the sun was up.

A rook landed twenty yards away. It watched her quizzically with its head and huge grey bill turned sideways, then cawed loudly, 'Grah, grah, grah,' bowing to her with each call. In reply, she gave a little curtsey the way women in the village did when they saw Mr Speke. He too had a loud, braying voice. The rook stared at her, then eyed the ground and started to peck.

'Yay-ay-ay!' When she ran towards it, shouting and clapping her hands, it flew a short distance away to glare at her again. 'Bugger off!' She threw a stone. She had developed a good aim, but only threw stones at the bigger birds, having more sympathy for the smaller, prettier ones. She missed this time and the stone landed at the rook's feet. It jumped in surprise before pecking at the stone to see whether it was edible.

'Yay, ay ay!'

The rook flew to the top of the field where Joseph took up the pursuit.

A flock of starlings arrived next but they were easier to chase away, a shout and a run in their direction was all that was needed for them to take off as one and wheel away with high-pitched whistling calls.

By the time the sun was a perfect circle above the eastern hill, there had been two wood pigeons, a flock of finches and a rabbit, the latter having thumped its back feet in alarm and shot back to its burrow in the hedgebank when she clapped her hands. She allowed a robin to fly repeatedly from its perch among the hawthorn blossom down into the field. She watched it hop, put its head on one side to listen then, in one quick movement almost too fast to see, catch a morsel in its beak. She saw that it only took small insects and worms to feed to its young in the nest but, if it had eaten the oat seed she would have let it, as it was too small for Mr Phillips to see should he appear at the distant gate, and it was obviously hungry. It must be cold too, after sitting in the hedge all night with no blanket.

From where she stood she could see the roof of Gusland farmhouse in the distance. The house was set on the side of a hill which would have obscured any windows on that side so, to watch his apprentices, Mr Phillips had to walk along the lane and look over the gate, but he had a way of appearing suddenly when they least expected him.

A large, white seagull landed close to the far hedge. She had not known what it was the previous day, when Mr Judd was showing her what to do.

'Git on back where you come from, you limmer, you!' he had shouted. The sea, he said, was a great big pond full of water.

'I see'd that in Bideford' she said, 'when I was with Mr Fulford.'

'That bain't the sea, maid, that's only the river. Sea's bigger than that, they say, though I've not seen it myself.'

'How much bigger?' she asked.

'Well, they that go across it in boats, takes them weeks, so folks say, and they don't never come back. The Cole family went, and Mr Darch.'

'What did them go for?'

'Easier times, maid, more money. You can buy your own land there, so folks say. You wouldn't be working for nought if you lived out there, I reckon.'

She had decided that she and Thomas would go across the sea together, one day. Surely Mr Phillips wouldn't find them if they went across the sea?

She ran, waving her arms at the gull, and watched as it wheeled away, pure white against the sky.

Joseph skipped down the field towards her with his long shirt-tails flapping below his short fustian jacket. 'I be goin' to eat my breakfast now; watch my patch will 'ee?' He ran over to the hedge and sat down next to the basket with his back against the bank.

She shouted across to Thomas, invisible on the other side of the hedge, to tell him what was happening. They had recently spent several days labouring together, just the two of them with an ox and cart. At first, Mary had kept well away from the ox's formidable horns, but as the day wore on she realised what a gentle, patient beast it was. She rubbed its forehead where the dark red coat was dense and curly, and talked to it while it blew gently at her hand. It was her favourite now, and it seemed to like her.

She and Thomas had worked their way along the lane that led past the farm for a quarter of a mile in each direction, throwing down straw one day before scraping it up the next and forking it into the ox cart. It seemed futile work to her, but Thomas had explained that every farm wanted more muck to put on the fields to make things grow, the farmers never had enough. Mr Phillips, knowing that a flock of sheep and some cows were being driven to market from a nearby farm, wanted to collect the dung they dropped on the lane. By spreading straw, it could be picked up along with other previous droppings and the rich mud that gathered on the surface. Throwing the straw down was fun, but scraping it up with a shovel made her arms ache terribly. She hadn't minded too much, however, because they could talk freely with no one around to hear.

'Do 'ee remember when us used to play down Barton way?' Thomas had paused in his work, his dark eyes alight with memories of their younger childhood days when, after their chores were done, they had been free to roam. 'Us built a wall of mud and stones in the stream so it flooded right across the road and when Mr Norman came past, he couldn't figure out where the water had come from!'

She remembered it well. 'And us was hiding down in the dell! Ann fell in the water after, sat right down in it and us had to carry her home, dripping.'

Thomas was quiet for a while, and his face clouded over. 'The next week, that was when Maria was born, and Da was out half the night drinking. Then I was 'pprenticed. Mightn't have to have gone if he'd kept off the drink.'

She stared at him. Thomas kicked at the ground. 'You didn't know 'bout that. You were only a little maid, you didn't know aught.' She stood in silence until he continued. 'He don't do it often. But when he do –, 'tis always when there idn't much money, then folks like Mr Fulford don't look so favourably on giving out relief, see.'

'Is that why I was 'pprenticed?' Her voice was a whisper.

He had picked up his shovel. 'I dunno. I weren't there when Jane was born, were I? Maybe not. Probably it was cos Mam couldn't work. Come on, us must finish here soon.'

She thought, now, of her Da; his smile and the way he ruffled her hair.

Thomas's voice floated over the hedge. 'I see'd a fox! Soon chased he off!'

'Well, he idn't come this way!'

She ran to the top of the field. Here, a narrow path, a smeuse, ran up and over the hedgebank where an animal had worn away the vegetation by following its habitual route. Mary clambered up, finding footholds with her bare feet and holding on to woven branches of laid ash at the top to keep her balance until she stood high above the field with the breeze fresh on her face. She had hoped for a view of the church tower so that she could picture her parents in the village; her mother in the cottage or working in some other village house, her father labouring nearby. But there was no view of the church, no distant rooftops, only fields and more fields stretching up a hill that obscured everything beyond. She could have been a world away from everything she had known, as far as if she had crossed the sea.

Thomas had his breakfast next. By the time it was her turn, her stomach was grumbling and her throat dry. The boys had found a comfortable seat against the hedge and she nestled into the alcove they had made. She had carefully calculated the provisions and told the boys how much they could have for each meal; two slices of bread for breakfast and an apple, shrivelled but still sweet, from the loft above the stable. She ate greedily, washing down the dry bread with the bitter-tasting ale and water, then leaned back, lulled by the intermittent burr-burr of a bumblebee as it wandered from flower to flower, and distant shouts from Thomas and Joseph as they chased off marauders. When the buzzing of the bee grew closer, she watched drowsily as it fumbled its way silently into a yellow buttercup near her face, weighing down the stem until both bee and flower almost touched her hand. A wren deep inside the hedge burst into jubilant song. There was some warmth now in the sun; her eyes closed again.

The click of the gate. Had she rested too long? Would he beat her? She leapt up and away from the hedge, poised, ready to defend herself, to explain.

But it was a girl, a woman almost, her clothes more ragged even than Mary's own, stepping back in alarm at Mary's sudden appearance. They stared at each other.

The girl gestured across the field. 'Joseph. I need to speak to 'n.'

Mary saw that she was anxious, and relief that it was not Mr Phillips flooded through her.

'Why? He's busy. Mr Phillips don't like visitors.'

The girl had a sore at the side of her mouth, and had a thin, haunted look. Her red, chapped hands twisted and pulled restlessly at the worn fabric of her skirt. 'I have to. Please.'

'You his sister?'

She nodded, pushing her tangled hair back from her face.

At the top of the field, Joseph had his back to them. When Mary shouted and beckoned to him, he ran down across the field, stopping suddenly when he recognised his sister.

'Is Mam sick? Or be it Da?'

'The little ones are all bad, Joseph, real bad, 'tis the fever, and the baby - Mam's got no milk for 'n, her's not eating see, us 've got no potatoes left, nothing.' The words tumbled out of her as if, having started, she could not stop talking. 'Us can't get the doctor to call but, any case, Mam says he'd only tell us they have to have meat if they'm going to get over it; they've no strength, see, they'm just lying there all day. William can barely lift his head to drink, I have to hold'n, and the baby's scritching all the time.' She pushed her hair out of her eyes again. 'Us have got nothing, Joseph! Can 'ee let us have something? Can 'ee get us some meat?'

His eyes were wide. 'Is Da out of work again?'

'He fell out with Mr Walter.' She glanced nervously over her shoulder. 'I got to get back.'

'Wait.' Joseph went to the basket and took out his share of the food; a cold potato, two hunks of bread, a cube each of bacon and cheese, and an onion. Then he reached into the basket again and took out his slice of cake.

His sister gathered it all into her apron. ''Twill help, Joseph, 'specially the bacon.' She rested her hand on his arm for a moment. 'And I'll come back tomorrow, you'll be here again, won't 'ee?' She turned to go.

'Wait!' Joseph looked distraught. 'Tell Mam... tell my Mam, say, say I hope they'm better soon.' He watched as she disappeared around the corner, then he burst into tears. 'I wish it were my Mam! I wish my Mam had come! What be I gwain to do now? What be I gwain to eat?'

Mary watched as he wiped his nose on his sleeve and walked back up the field, his shoulders hunched in misery. She could think of nothing to say to him.

When she had her dinner, she saw that Thomas had put a portion aside for Joseph. She broke off a piece of her bread and her cheese and quickly ate what was left, but it did not assuage her hunger. She drank some ale and water and started on the cake. It was very good and sweet. When she had finished her portion she looked longingly at the piece she had put aside, and called to Joseph.

She rose again at four the next morning. They were about to leave the yard when there was a sudden shout from the kitchen door and, turning, they saw Mr Phillips tucking his undershirt into his trousers.

'Wait!' Mr Phillips pointed at Joseph. 'Come yer!' None of them dared to move. 'Get 'ere!' His voice rang out over the silent, shadowy yard.

Slowly, Joseph crept towards him, his head down, his arms folded tightly across his chest, until he stopped about six feet from Mr Phillips. There was a moment when the world seemed to stand still. Then Mr Phillips strode forward and tore at Joseph's jacket, and out fell half a loaf and a large piece of bacon.

'Thief! Bain't you fed enough? What are you, a crook like your father! What be gwain to do, sell it?' He had picked Joseph up by his coat collar and was shaking him as he shouted, then he dropped him to the ground and was gone, but before Mary had time to breathe, he was back with his whip in his hand.

She saw Joseph curled on the ground in the dim morning light, and she saw Mr Phillips push him over with his foot, but then she clung to Thomas and hid her face on his shoulder.

The whip hissed in the air, she thought she could feel the air it displaced, then *thunk.* Joseph screamed.

There was a pause. The lash snapped out again. Another cry. Thomas turn his face towards her and she felt the rigidity of every muscle in his body. The whip cracked out again, and again, and now Joseph was gasping and sobbing between his screams. Mary was sure she would be sick.

Then there was just Joseph's sobs, but still she did not dare to look up.

'Get up! Now get out there and do yer work! And if you steal another time, I swear you'll never get up again.'

Joseph was stumbling towards them, his face contorted. Mary hastened towards the gate alongside Thomas, her feet tangling in her skirt in her hurry to get away. She dared not speak or look at Joseph until they had reached the field and closed the gate behind them, and then they gathered together, Thomas keeping watch in case Mr Phillips should come along the lane.

'When did 'ee take it? Didn't 'ee think it'd be missed?' Joseph started crying again, deep sobs that had been suppressed until then, and he hid his face in his sleeve.

'Yer, let me look. Take off your jacket.' Mary tried to ease his clothing away from his back but he cried out in pain. Remembering a remedy her mother used, she quickly gathered some plantain leaves from the base of the hedge and rubbed them between her hands to bruise them.

'This'll help, but you'll have to let me look.'

Joseph cringed as Thomas helped to lift his shirt. There was as yet little light in the sky and Mary leaned forward to look, gasping when she saw the red weals across Joseph's back.

Thomas touched them gently. 'That ain't too bad; 'twill soon heal.'

Mary carefully positioned the bruised plantain on the weals and they tied Joseph's scarf around his middle to keep the leaves in place.

Mary put her hand on his arm and looked at him straight. 'What did Mr Phillips mean 'bout your da being a thief?'

Joseph shuffled miserably. 'He stole a fowl once, and another time some rope to sell. He went to gaol for it, up Exeter. He only do'd it for the little ones, to get some food for 'em.' He looked up at her, desperation in his face. 'William's my bestest brother! He's only this big, and, and the baby, I haven't even seen him, not once, and he's my brother too! He came when the birds were nesting last time.'

'He's a year old then,' said Mary. 'He'll be sitting up now, standing maybe, trying to talk.' She remembered Maria at that age, how funny she was, her bright eyes and infectious laugh.

All day Joseph worked in the bottom half of the field so as to be near the gate, but it was mid-afternoon before his sister arrived. Mary saw him hurry over and, just moments later, saw his sister turn and walk away. Joseph returned to his position in the middle of the field, but for a long time he just stood looking down at the ground, while birds came to feed on the grain with impunity.

The weather continued dry and mild. After a day or two, Mary thought no more about Joseph's troubles, amusing herself by counting the orange and white butterflies that had started to appear in the hedgerows, and trying to imitate their dancing flight as she skipped after the marauding rooks. But then, she noticed the first oat seeds beginning to sprout, and the next day they were told that their work there was finished.

She was eating her dinner with the other apprentices in the kitchen for the first time in more than a week, when Mr Phillips suddenly turned in his chair and looked at them.

'Beer, you haven't yeard, I suppose, that your father's in trouble again.'

Joseph stared at Mr Phillips, his spoon half-way to his mouth.

'Stole a sheep, he did; 'twas found cut up and salted under his bed. He was up before the judge today. He'll be transported this time, I reckon, chained up in a ship bound for Australia. So let that be a lesson to you, boy, that's where thieving gets you.' The room had fallen silent. Mr Phillips took a mouthful of food before turning in his chair again. 'And that's not all...'

Sarah jumped up. 'Please, no, Maister, not that, let me tell 'n that.'

She crouched down next to Joseph and took both his hands in hers. 'Joseph, your brothers and sisters, they'm getting over the fever. They'll live. You'll see 'em again, one day. But the baby, I'm sorry my lover, but he passed away. There now,' she put her arms around him as his face crumpled, 'he's gone to a better place, my lover, a far better place than this'll ever be.'

BIDEFORD.

TOWN-HALL, *May 4th,* 1842.—Before *Charles Carter, Esq., Mayor, Henry R. Glynn, and James Smith Ley, esquires, justices.*

SHEEP-STEALING --*Joseph Beer,* of Buckland Brewer, was charged by *Thomas Holman,* of Allhalland-street, butcher, with stealing a fat sheep on Saturday night last. It appears that Mr. Holman saw his sheep in the field about seven o'clock, and on the next morning found that one had been killed, nothing being left but the skin, head, and feet. Palmer, the police officer, was apprised of the circumstance, who took these remains into his possession. On Tuesday, Palmer, with Gilbert and another constable, proceeded with a warrant of search to Beer's house at Tithercott, where he found 34 lb. of meat salted down in a pan under Beer's bed. On Palmer's comparing the feet and other bones with those found in the house, an exact correspondence was evident; one very singular circumstance is worthy of remark—all the meat had either been cut from the bones or the bones extracted from the flesh, with the exception of those parts that exactly suited to enable Palmer to identify the sheep. Beer is remanded until Friday afternoon, two o'clock, when he will no doubt be committed.

North Devon Journal, 5th May 1842

Chapter Eight

As his carriage swept along the driveway towards its destination, the Reverend Harding leaned from the window to admire the view of Portledge Manor standing proudly above the coastline, its ancient stonework set off on this fine May afternoon by a perfect backdrop of sapphire sea and the emerald cliffs cradling the bay. As they drew nearer he saw that the numerous windows were newly painted and the lawns surrounding the house neatly edged. Withdrawing into the carriage, he addressed his wife, Charlotte, who was sitting very upright, not wanting to arrive with creases to her best silk dress.

'The house is looking in good order; he's made improvements since our last visit. I hear that he is also investing in new methods of farming so must be spending a considerable amount of money, but of course his brother had rather neglected the place.'

The owner of Portledge, Reverend John Pine-Coffin was, like Reverend Harding, a younger son and it was the lot of younger sons to go into the church. Until recently John Pine-Coffin lived a few miles away in Alwington Rectory, but he inherited Portledge when his older unmarried brother died and he now combined the duties of his ministry with running an estate which stretched as far as Harding's own village of Monkleigh five miles away.

'His brother had not the advantage of children to inherit his property,' his wife replied. 'Reverend Pine-Coffin must be delighted that he now has a son to assure the future of the estate. We know how comforting that is, do we not?' She smiled at her husband and held up the small beribboned box containing a present for the new baby boy. 'It is many years since our sons were given such delicate trifles as this.'

'It is, indeed.' He leaned back on the upholstered seat, trying to dismiss the feeling of disquiet he experienced whenever his two sons were mentioned. His wife often told him he should enjoy their successes rather than set ever higher standards for them, but she had limited knowledge of the hazards faced by young men in these difficult times.

Gravel crunched under the wheels of the brougham as it drew to a halt beside the imposing entrance to Portledge Manor and, by the time Reverend Harding had helped his wife from the carriage, a housemaid was curtseying as she held the door open for them. As they passed through the great hall, he paused for a moment to look up at the magnificent minstrels' gallery, then followed his wife into the drawing room where John Pine-Coffin greeted them warmly.

Alongside tea and dainty cakes, the conversation focussed on the matters that must be discussed on such an occasion – musings on whom the new child might resemble, the entertainment to be found in the responses of his two sisters, the enumeration of visitors and the news they brought with them, subjects which John Pine-Coffin appeared to find most entertaining, whereas Reverend Harding was relieved when his wife left to visit the new mother and child upstairs, leaving the way free for subjects of greater import.

He rose and stood with his back to the fireplace to light his pipe.

'The magistrates' court has been as busy as ever; your presence has been missed.' He smiled at the younger man. 'Without your tempering influence our criminals have been shaking in their boots at the prospect of the sentence they might receive.'

John Pine-Coffin laughed. He was young and handsome with a warmth of expression that, Harding knew, would not last. No one combining the roles of Rector, Magistrate and Poor Law Guardian could maintain a generous view of humanity.

'Well, I shall soon be returning to my duties,' he said. 'I like to think that I can feel sympathy for those who transgress – as indeed our Lord did – while keeping to the tenets of the law. So tell me, what recent cases have come before you?'

Reverend Harding puffed at his pipe as he observed the young man, who was awaiting his reply as eagerly as would a puppy.

'You cannot nor should you try to put yourself in their place. It is for us to see them as they are; common criminals who need to be punished in this world so that they might repent before it is too late. A vain hope in many cases, I fear, but if there were not consequences then a multitude of others would follow their sinful ways. Just this week a case of sheep-stealing has been forwarded to the Quarter Session. The thief, a labourer from Tythecott in the parish of Buckland Brewer will be transported and his wife and children have already been sent to the Workhouse, having no means of survival now that the head of the household is gone, so one hopes that their fate will make others realise that crime does not pay.'

The younger man prevaricated. 'An example must be set, of course; however, I cannot help but feel sympathy for some. The man who steals to feed his children, for example – I'm sure I would steal before I saw my children starve!'

The man was all emotion; well-meaning no doubt, but lacking in restraint.

'No, you would not steal, you would work to earn an honest wage. There are too many who use their poverty as an excuse for depredations.' Reverend Harding relit his pipe. 'As far as my recent cases are concerned, there have been the usual thefts of food and clothing of course, that goes without saying. Yesterday I sat with Mr Wren and Mr Tardrew. We had before us a witness who was the most miserable scrap of humanity one could hope to meet; a boy, nine or ten years of age but undersized, who had been whipped by his master a month since. No doubt there was justification for punishment but this was excessive, the wounds on his back were still plain to see despite the passing of time. As one might guess, the boy was a parish apprentice and his master, a farmer named Seldon, came from – where else? – Buckland Brewer. The man was unrepentant, although no doubt the twelve-shilling fine has given him cause to reconsider.'

'Poor child.' John Pine-Coffin ran his hands through his thick brown hair.

'Perhaps. Whipping is an ineffectual way to deal with apprentices because it will cause them to run away, thereby setting them on a pathway of crime. A little kindness would be more effective in restraining them and rendering them obedient. But, as you know, I do not approve of parish apprenticeships. Parents need to realise that they are responsible for their children; they should not expect to have them sent out for others to feed and clothe. I allow few apprenticeships in my parish; better that the whole family is offered the Workhouse. It is surprising how many then find that they have, after all, enough to eat.'

John Pine-Coffin was watching him anxiously. As yet he lacked the certainty of opinion that came with experience, but no doubt he would develop it in time.

'I have in my own parish a handful of apprentices,' he said. 'I believe they are all well-cared for and in most cases treated as members of the family. Certainly when I visit I see no signs of the sort of cruelty you describe.'

Harding slapped his hand on to the mantelshelf. 'But there you are – you visit! Reverend Colling at Buckland Brewer does not visit. Our friend is not a magistrate, he is not on the Board of Guardians and he does not know his parishioners. He shuts himself away in his study – and writes excellent sermons no doubt – but as a result the Methodists and now the Bible Christians, too, win more followers almost by the week, especially amongst the farmers since they know they will be supported in their reluctance to pay their tithes. And how does Reverend Colling suppose he will live then?'

Reverend Harding, realising that he had been striding up and down the room, stopped to relight his pipe. He did not often admit that he feared the threat the Methodists posed to Church incomes almost more than their threat to Church attendance, but one had to live, and his income from renting out the glebelands in Monkleigh and Littleham was a small fraction of that earned by the Portledge estate. He needed the payments from tithes to maintain his household and provide for his sons, but the Methodists were gaining ground in Monkleigh despite his best efforts to keep them down.

He took a few steps across the room and blew smoke up towards the ancestral portraits that were ranged on the wall, male and female members of the Coffin family dressed in antiquated styles but all bearing the fine features and blue eyes of the man who stood before him. He did not wish to discuss his financial affairs with John Pine-Coffin, but fortunately his companion was following a different train of thought.

'Buckland Brewer is a very large parish. It would be difficult indeed for Reverend Colling to visit his parishioners on a regular basis.'

'So he makes no visits at all! Nor gives any encouragement to attend services, as far as I can tell.'

'The Methodist, Mr Bartholomew Fulford, works hard for the Board of Guardians and is a great support to the poor, I believe. He seems a kind and generous man.'

'Kind he may be, but he lacks authority, he is as one with the people. They do not respect him but make absurd demands for relief knowing that he will put the case before the Board, and they plead poverty so that their children may be raised by some unfortunate farmer who neither needs nor wants their labour. My parishioners know that I will help in cases of true necessity, but other than that they must take responsibility for their own families.' He walked over to the window and gazed out at the manicured lawns. 'The truth is, Buckland Brewer is not the only parish that is a problem. There are many areas in Devon that are dark indeed, where people live short, brutal lives with no knowledge of the teachings that could bring them salvation.'

'Come now, surely you exaggerate! My parishioners are good people; they are kind and generous, they are helpful to each other!'

The young rector's idealism was exasperating. 'I do not exaggerate! You are young; you have not seen the depths to which humankind can sink! But what can we do except work tirelessly in our own parishes, and in our magisterial roles to punish wrongdoing.'

John Pine-Coffin had thrown himself down on a sofa with his chin resting on his hand, reminding Reverend Harding of the pose of a classical statue.

'I shall try to converse with Reverend Colling,' he said, 'but he is not the most approachable of men. It is your talk of the children that concerns me most. Do we know how many parish apprentices there are in North Devon? Was there not talk of them being brought to the magistrates' court on a regular basis that they might be questioned about their treatment?'

'There was talk of it, but I think it is unlikely to succeed. Who will make the necessary arrangements for such a plan? What will be done when the master of the apprentice chooses not to give up half a day's work to bring the miserable child to town? No; I fear the practice will continue and the depths of North Devon will remain dark, godless areas for many years to come.'

As Reverend Harding travelled back through the narrow lanes of Fairy Cross and Woodtown, his wife extolling the perfection of the new heir to Portledge, the exquisite dress the child wore and the charm of his mother, he felt satisfied with the afternoon's conversation. There were none in the village with whom he could converse, and it was a pleasure to talk to a younger man whom one could set on the right path; a real pleasure.

The coachman guided the horses carefully over the narrow hump-backed bridge that spanned the River Yeo, where white ducks sat contentedly on the bank next to the mill and speckled hens ran flapping and squawking from the horses' hoofs, and now began the steep climb to Monkleigh. The river marked the boundary of Reverend Harding's parish, but all these lands belonged to John Pine-Coffin, so it was no wonder that he commanded such respect. Tenants have to respect their landlord if they want to retain their tenancy. Besides, John Pine-Coffin always rode a first-rate horse, and everyone likes a man who rides a good horse. He was in an enviable situation; Reverend Harding could not help but feel a twinge of envy.

As they approached Monkleigh, he recognised a man returning from the fields, a hoe at his shoulder. He knocked on the glass with his stick to tell the coachman to stop, and pulled down the window.

'Afternoon, Reverend, 'tis a fine day.' John Rigsby, keeper of the Bell Inn and tenant of a few acres of glebe land, raised his hat.

'It is indeed, and I hope it will be a fine day on Sunday also.'

The man looked puzzled.

'If the weather is fine on Sunday, you might be inclined to take a walk in another direction. It is two weeks now since I saw you in church.'

'Why Sir,' he said, 'my wife has been, regular, but 'tis hard for me to find the time, what with tending the fields and so on.'

'On a Sunday? Tending the fields on a Sunday? On my land? I trust that is not the case, Mr Rigsby. I have heard reports of rowdy behaviour at the inn which I shall most certainly follow up if I find there is not reformation of your general conduct. I will see you on Sunday, Mr Rigsby.'

He pulled up the window and tapped on the glass to instruct the coachman to continue to the Rectory.

One had to keep a close eye on one's parishioners if the Methodists were not to win more souls. A firm example had to be set, whether by a rector or a magistrate.

Chapter Nine

The late June sunshine burned on Mary's back as she wrenched the roots of another handful of poppies from the dry soil. Straightening up to ease her aching muscles, she stroked the scarlet petals that were pushing their way out of the confining green bud, then let the plant fall to the ground. Behind her, a line of wilting flowers ran between the rows of wheat right back to the gate.

That morning, as she stood in the sunny gateway to Little Botown waiting for Mr Judd, she had stared at the soft blue-green sea of wheat intermingled with red poppies, bright blue cornflowers and yellow buttercups, and watched it rippling and whispering in the breeze while swallows skimmed over its surface, catching insects. It was the loveliest thing she had ever seen. She took a deep breath, inhaling the scents of honeysuckle in the hedge and pineapple mayweed growing on the stony ground below her feet; she looked up to find the source of the song that rang out over the field, shading her eyes until she spotted the skylark, a mere dot against the azure sky, its liquid warbling song growing louder as the bird dropped down and down to disappear at last amongst the wavering stalks of wheat.

Her reverie had been broken by the clomping of boots behind her.

'Here you be, maid, you'm better off yer.' Mr Judd had shed his old jacket and rolled up his shirt sleeves, revealing sinewy arms not yet darkened by the sun. ''Tisn't heavy work, better for you than the hayfield.'

She followed him as he limped to the edge of the crop.

'Just pull 'em all out, all the old weeds, but watch that you hold 'em down yer, see, so's the roots come up, else they'll grow back. This charlock yer, 'tis a devil for that.' He dropped a handful of flowers to the ground.

'But,' she stared at him, knowing as she spoke that her response was absurd, 'they'll die, the flowers'll die!'

'Course they will, maid. Us wants wheat, nought else!'

She should have guessed that it would not be enjoyable work, despite the beauty of the field.

Reaching the far hedge, she turned to work her way back down the next row. She could see the gate in the corner of the field now, so would know if Mr Phillips or any of the workers in the adjoining hayfield came to check on her. With a clump of bright yellow buttercups in her hand, she paused to break off two or three of the long-stemmed flowers and wove them together with some delicate corn cockles, some cornflowers which were an even brighter blue than the sky, and a few scarlet poppies. When she had enough she wove the two ends together to make a circlet, gave the flowers a kiss while complimenting them on their beauty, then placed the circlet carefully on her hair, weaving a few strands amongst it to keep it safe from the strengthening breeze. Ahead of her, a thousand flowers awaited their fate but at least she had prevented these from being trampled underfoot.

A metallic scrape-scrape that she knew to be the sharpening of a scythe, followed by voices and laughter, drifted on the breeze from the adjoining field. The high hedgebank blocked her view, but the desire to know what was happening was strong so, finally giving in to temptation, she pushed carefully through the thigh-high wheat and found a foothold on the steep bank, grabbed a low branch and hauled herself up to crouch among the foxgloves just below the top so that she would not be noticed.

She could see all the workers now. Soon after dawn, they had all walked together to Higher Twitching Meadow and there had been a sense of excitement despite Mr Phillips' presence. It was not until they arrived that she had been told she was not strong enough for haymaking, and was to be banished to this field. The maister was working now with his back to her, his body swaying rhythmically as he swung the scythe from side to side, Mr Begalhole worked in unison alongside and two men followed behind raking the cut grass. John, the apprentices, and Mr Judd turned the hay that had been cut two days previously. John, taller and heavier than any of the others, was laughing loudly as he tossed the hay high in the air so that it fell down on top of him, and Mary saw that his pitchfork passed dangerously close to his fellow workers' heads. Thomas had moved away but Joseph appeared to be encouraging the older boy.

'John!' As the voice roared across the field Mary ducked down, but was able to peep through the interwoven branches of the elm to see Mr Phillips striding across and snatching the fork from his son's grasp while the other apprentices backed away.

'What do 'ee think you'm doing? 'Tisn't a game!' He brandished the pitchfork at John. 'Now geddout, go and work with the maids if you can't behave like a man!'

He cuffed John around the ear and John cried out and crouched on the ground with his hands over his head like a small child.

'Go on! Geddout and do the weeding in Botown! I've lost faith in 'ee, John!'

Mary scrambled back down the hedge and started to pull frantically at the weeds. She had become used to the maister passing her in the house or yard – although she was always careful to avoid his gaze – but his anger still frightened her a great deal, and she had learnt that there was no one in the household who did not feel the brunt of it. The mistress was as afraid of him as anyone, something which Mary found extraordinary. When her father was cross, her mother shouted at him and told him not to be so daft, but Sarah had explained that Mr and Mrs Phillips were not like that.

After a few minutes John slouched through the far gate and she saw him sit at the base of the hedge, rocking backwards and forwards with his head in his hands. When she had worked her way down the field, she threw down a handful of weeds and walked over to him. His trouser legs had ridden up above his boots to expose his huge white calves but the face that looked up at her when she called his name bore the expression of an unhappy young child, his lower lip thrust out and his eyes full of tears.

'John, come on, you have to do weeding now!'

'Don't want to!' he wailed. 'Want hay-harvest!'

'You can't, John, 'cos you was bad!'

Despite his being four years older than her, she had learnt to treat him as if he were a much younger brother.

'Come on, help me pick the pretty flowers!'

She held out her hand to him, but had to draw it away quickly when he tried to use it to pull himself up.

'You gotta get up on your own, John, come on, up!'

He followed her over to the crop and stood, uttering deep moans like a sick animal, while she resumed weeding. Surely Mr Phillips would hear him and perhaps blame her for not making him work.

'John, your da will whip you! Be quiet!'

He nodded sadly. 'But Da not make blood come, not for John.'

'Look!' She held up a clump of cornflowers. 'Find some like these, John, blue ones!'

But he had spotted the flowers in her hair. His mood changed suddenly and, smiling, he lunged at her, throwing her right off balance so that she landed heavily on her back with John sprawled on top of her. For a moment, crushed beneath his weight, she could neither breathe nor speak but then he pushed himself up on his elbows and reached up to her hair.

'There's blue ones, Mary, pretty flowers!'

'Get off me, John!' She pushed at his soft, flabby chest and he looked down at her, his huge moon-face just inches from hers and his open, smiling mouth dribbling. She could feel stones and thistles pressing into her back. 'Get off!'

When he rolled off her, she staggered to her feet and tried to pull the crushed wheat back into an upright position, then immediately resumed weeding in case Mr Phillips appeared, but her hands were shaking and she felt as if every part of her was bruised.

John was pulling the flowers one by one from the circlet she had so carefully made. She no longer cared whether he got into trouble. She tore up the weeds as fast as she could, trampling them mercilessly as she moved down the wheat row. When John came to her with a handful of flowers and tried to place them on her head, she snatched them from him and shouted at him to do the weeding.

'Do it now, John! Start there!' She pointed further along the field, well away from where she was working. He took notice this time and walked away with his head down to start work, and every time she looked over at him, he was moving along the rows at a terrific pace, his head bobbing up and down as he bent to pull the weeds. She had noticed before that once he settled to work, he was not easily distracted and it was a relief that there would be less for her to do.

Every day, when she cried because of the repetitive work and her aching muscles, the heat or the incessant rain, she had learned to tell herself that it would soon be over; the potatoes would soon be planted, the turnips would soon be hoed, the oats would start to grow and she would never again have to scare the birds away. It was true that for every field of potatoes they planted, it seemed that another remained to be done; for almost a month they had planted potatoes, but in the end it was finished. And tomorrow, or perhaps the next day, all the flowers would be gone from this field and she would never have to pull them up again. She could put it all behind her.

She paused to rub her back which was still sore from her fall, and she had banged her head too, so she allowed herself to cry a little now that John was out of earshot. Crying was a luxury she could only indulge in occasionally when alone with Sarah, when she was sure to be given comfort. Sarah listened to Mary's fears and told her things that must not be repeated, like the way she and James would meet secretly in the barn after dark, and kiss.

''Tis lovely, Mary!' Sarah told her, with a smile that made her look as if she was in the midst of a wonderful dream, 'but you must never let any of the boys kiss you, do 'ee hear?' Her expression became severe. 'James is a good man, not like the rest of 'em. Don't let 'em near 'ee! If any of 'em try anything you run right off and tell me, or tell James. And pretend to be strong, never let 'em make 'ee cry.'

It was true that Lewis, Jack and Joseph taunted anyone who gave in to tears, although she knew that Joseph cried silently in bed most nights. Her mother would have given her a quick hug had she been here now. It was a very long time since she had seen her mother in the yard; she did not know how long, but it was before the potato planting and the bird-scaring. This made her cry a little more, but by the time her tears had dried she felt better. The larks were up again, two of them ascending as they sang in unison high above the field, and if they were happy, then she could be too. She decided to make up a new game; as she weeded she would count each bee and butterfly she saw and whichever was the first to reach ten would be the winner.

The scythe made a satisfying swish as it felled the long grass, leaving a neat row that stretched back across the field. With every swing of the blade, Mr Phillips assessed the quality of the crop; it was good and rich, although not as well-grown as he would have liked, more rain at the beginning of the month would have been beneficial, but the weather seemed to be set fair now, so it was best not to wait for further growth.

He paused and rested the scythe on the ground, facing to windward. The haymaker must always be watching the weather: the form and drift of the clouds, the clarity or mistiness of the hills on the horizon. The breeze today was due south and sultry but a little strong for his liking; it could bring rapid change, but he did not think that it would.

He took up his scythe again, ignoring the ache in his shoulders. Yesterday he had finished shearing the sheep, a job he carried out singlehanded over the course of two or three days. Some years ago, a labourer had misjudged the depth of a fleece and the shears had cut into the soft underbelly of a valuable sheep. It was not something he would ever forgive and he had undertaken all the shearing himself since that day. The flock was small; it could be done. His brother-in-law, Phillip Fulford, used to offer to help, but he had always turned him down. Other farmers hereabouts travelled with their labourers from farm to farm to shear, gathering at one farm this day, another farm that day, the shearing being followed by food, drink and dancing as if there was no other work to do. That wasn't his way. He wouldn't have all the gossips for miles around coming to his farm.

The fleeces this year were good and would fetch a fair price, but he would store them for the time being. Prices were sure to rise.

When he reached the hedge, he wiped the layer of sweat, grass seeds and insects from his face with the back of his arm, and took the stone from his belt to sharpen the blade with long, slow strokes, before turning to work his way back down the field. The blade sliced cleanly through the grass despite it being dry. It was easier to cut damp grass. Arriving yesterday for the first cut with the sun rising and the dew lying heavy on the rich meadow grass had been a special moment, marking the beginning of the harvest season.

He glanced over at the younger workers on the far side of the field. Their progress was slower now that John had left them. He fed his anger into the swing of the scythe, felling a thick-stemmed dock that had been missed during the weeding. Why could John not be more responsible? Would he always need supervision, would he be a grown man incapable of following simple instructions, less capable than a common labourer?

As his father, he should be employing the whip more often, he should have whipped him this morning. But he could not. Seeing John crouching there on the ground with fear in his face – strange, it was. Unsettling. As if he were John cringing there, looking up at the father he could never please.

The scythe exposed a cup of dried grass deep in the woven thatch above the soil; three mottled blue-grey eggs. Skylark. He kicked them aside and swung the scythe again.

When the Sunday School teacher told him, after just three attendances, that John would never be capable of learning, he withdrew the boy and refused to send any of the younger children when they came of age. His wife could teach them to write their names and to read a few words, but she had soon given up trying to teach John and, for once, Mr Phillips did not impose his will on her. He had held out hope that John could learn to run the farm, even if he didn't take to book learning.

One day he would have to address the problem of his other children's schooling, but he would never send them to the church Sunday School after that woman had been so dismissive of John. He had not attended a place of worship himself for several years, and he would not attend the parish church while Reverend Colling remained the incumbent, a dispute over tithes last year had seen to that. It was a state of affairs that made him feel a little uneasy; he was not as devout as some farmers hereabouts but he had never completed a harvest without uttering a prayer of supplication.

He paused to survey the remaining grass. If the weather had been uncertain, he would have stopped now until he saw what the next day would bring, but he was confident that the weather would hold and, after glancing rather apprehensively up at the sky, he swung the scythe again.

As he worked, he wondered whether his brother was haymaking today. The farm on the far side of Twitching Hill contained good, rich meadows. His brother had bought a draft horse, a strong-looking bay, he had seen it while riding past Brendon, and it had made him more determined to have horses of his own. One of the oxen was almost worn out, so could be put out to graze for a few months to fatten for the butcher. Another would have reached the end of its working life next year but, by then, with the profits from a good harvest, the potato surplus and some fat lambs, he thought he could find his way to buy two horses to replace them. Few farmers hereabouts owned draft horses, most had just one horse for riding and cart work, but they were not forward-looking.

He would need more hay to feed horses. His brother was at an advantage there, with his good meadowland. Mr Phillips held a plan of the farm in his head: where he would grow oats this year, where to follow turnips with wheat. It would be tricky to harvest enough hay but he was sure he could plan it out if he set his mind to it. He could picture the farm evolving and changing through all the years ahead, until it became the best farm in the district, the envy of all around.

Grasshoppers chirped and leapt from under Mary's feet as she moved slowly through the wheat. The sun was beginning to burn her head, reminding her that she had left her hat in the hedge next to Thomas's jacket. Although the wind was growing stronger, it too was hot and brought no comfort.

While straightening up to ease her back, she saw some children come through the gate from the hayfield, a girl a little younger than herself carrying a young child on her hip, and a small boy. They watched her but came no further into the field. She glanced over at them every time she stood up, and when she drew level with the gate she walked over to them, seeing at once from their bare feet and their ragged clothes that they were not farmer's children.

'What do 'ee want?' she asked. All three stared at her but did not reply. 'Where be 'ee from?'

The older girl, almost a head shorter than Mary, with thin straight hair the colour of hay, gestured back across the hayfield. 'Over there.'

Mary had noticed a couple of rundown cottages beyond the field, the only visible dwellings for miles around, their brown cob walls and greying thatch rendering them almost indistinguishable from the landscape in which they stood. The girl put the small child on the ground and it crouched in the dust, pulling at the trampled weeds in the gateway. There was silence but for the singing of skylarks.

Mary tried again. 'What be 'ee called?'

'Maryann.' The girl gestured at the hayfield. 'That be my da and grandad.'

'Who be?'

'There and there.' The girl wiped her nose on the back of her hand.

'Mr Judd's your grandad?' She had pointed out Mr Judd and Mr Dean.

'I dunno. He be grandad.' She pointed again.

Mary looked at her pityingly and resumed her weeding. 'My brother be there with him,' she told the girl, 'that one, with the brown waistcoat, turning hay. That's my Thomas.'

Maryann rubbed her toes in the dirt. 'My brother died. He was going to be 'pprenticed, but then he caught fever.'

'When was that?'

'Back along, when it was cold. And him and him,' she pointed at Mr Redacleave and Mr Begalhole raking hay, 'their chiels died too, same time.'

Maryann told her that the others lived at North Down, 'an old house way over there,' she said, gesturing beyond her own broken-down cottage.

Mary had little to do with the labourers apart from Mr Judd; they were all wiry, hard-eyed men who rarely smiled, and she had not known where any of them lived until today. But Thomas often had to lead the oxen when they were ploughing, she knew that he would rather work with the labourers than with Lewis.

Maryann was becoming a little less shy now, and looked up at Mary confidingly.

'I caught the fever when I was a little maid and Mr Begalhole, all his chiels died then; this many,' she held up four fingers, 'then he had two more and another died.'

'So he's got just one now.'

She looked at her fingers doubtfully. 'Yes.'

Mary wiped the sweat from her forehead; it was almost hotter standing in the sun than it was working. 'Do 'ee want to help with the weeding?'

Maryann told the younger children to stay by the hedge so that she could join Mary in the wheat. It was clear that she had done this work before but she was slow at it, and Mary had to decrease her pace so that they could work side by side. They exchanged glances as they bent over the weeds, and Maryann smiled shyly, showing a toothless gap where her baby teeth had fallen out. It was a long time since another girl had been friendly to Mary. She had learnt to keep well away from Lucy and Rosa Phillips.

Mary held up a large buttercup, its rounded, wide-open petals exposing the bright yellow stamens to the sun. 'Do 'ee like butter?'

Maryann looked at her blankly.

'Do 'ee like butter? Yer, let me see.' She held the buttercup out towards Maryann's chin but she stepped away apprehensively.

'Don't 'ee know that game?' Surely everyone knew it. 'Keep still; there now, you *do* like butter,' Mary declared triumphantly. She held the buttercup beneath her own chin so that Maryann could see the magical, bright yellow glow, but she seemed unimpressed.

'Us don't have butter, home.'

'Well, us don't either, not at home, but 'tis a good game, i'n't it? Us always used to play that in the village.'

She pulled up a clump of poppies and drew some sticky cleavers away from the wheat. 'Shall us make a May dolly from flowers like it was Mayday? Us haven't got a box to put 'n in, but us could make 'n here on the ground where nobody'd see.'

The happy memories came back to her; a crowd of children rushing from house to house carrying the beautiful doll made entirely from flowers and, later, the Club walk, the pretty dresses and the dancing, and everyone smiling.

Maryann looked at her blankly and said nothing.

'Us can make a bed for it from dried grass, hide it in the hedge, and us can come back and tend to it.'

It would be their secret; a thing of beauty concealed among the lush grasses.

Maryann's pinched features drew in and her eyes narrowed. 'It'll wither and die.'

'Well,' Mary felt irritated, 'it'll last the day, the one in the village did. Haven't 'ee been to the village for Mayday? A heap of people come!' Now she thought of it, she had never seen Maryann there, or anywhere else.

'What village?'

'Buckland Brewer! Over there!'

Mary pointed authoritatively, but there was nothing to be seen but fields and more fields stretching into the distance. She was not even sure that she was pointing in the right direction, and had the feeling that Maryann thought she was making it up, that there was no doll, no Mayday, no village. She went back to the weeding, feeling close to tears.

'Mary! John! Dinner's come!'

Mary's mood lifted to see Thomas waving from the gateway, a small figure in baggy shirtsleeves and dilapidated hat.

'Come on, dinner!'

Lucy and Rosa Phillips in their straw bonnets, leaving the hayfield with the empty dinner baskets, eyed Mary and her new companion dispassionately, but made no comment.

Mary sat close to Thomas at the base of the hedge and drank deeply from the bottle of cold tea, then tore off a chunk of bread and ate quickly, alternating mouthfuls of bread with bites of deliciously salty fat bacon. When her immediate hunger was assuaged, she noticed that Maryann was crouching near her grandad, Mr Judd, with the two younger children. She recognised the look in their eyes because she remembered that feeling of hunger, how it built and built and the awfulness of knowing that it would still be there at bedtime and right through the night.

Mr Judd broke off a piece of his own bread, tore it into three small portions and handed it to the children. It was gone at once and Mary, watching, knew that it would not help. Sure enough, the youngest child began to wail loudly and Mr Judd gestured to Maryann to take them home. He watched them trail off across the field; of course he could not give them more, he had to work. Mary looked down at what was left of her own food but knew that if she gave any of it away, she would be weak with hunger by the end of the day.

In a whisper, Mary told Thomas about her new friend and he explained to her about turning hay, and how it made the shoulders ache.

'All across yer, it hurts.' He winced as he showed her. ''Tis as well you don't have to do it.' He regarded her with concern. 'Look, you'm catching the sun, mind it don't make you ill. Yer, you must put your hat on.'

They both fell silent then, and Mary's eyes began to close. She knew that Thomas, too, would be able to relax because there would be no problems from Lewis with Mr Phillips nearby. The maister sat on his own further along the hedge, having forbidden John to sit with him. The sun was warm on her face; a blackbird sang languorously from a nearby tree.

The men were talking of previous harvests; two years ago the hay harvest was light due to lack of rain, this year would be similar, said one. Next year would be good then, said another, it went like that. Did they remember when there were potatoes in Little Botown? When would that have been, four or five years ago? Wish the maister would cut down on the potatoes, said Mr Judd quietly, 'tis fair old work to plant them and again to dig, and our own to till as well. No, remarked another, I reckon he'll have more than ever, next year.

Mary sat up. 'Thomas!'

His eyes opened. 'What's the matter?'

'Thomas, have us finished with planting potatoes?'

'Yes, you know us have, for this year.'

'This year?' There was a cold feeling in the pit of her stomach.

'Us'll have to do it again next year, course us will.'

She stared at him. She hadn't thought about the seasons coming round again, year after year.

'And the stone-picking and the weeding 'mongst the wheat – I s'll have to do that again next year?'

'Course you will, someone will.' He smiled at her affectionately.

She stared out across the field with its soft rows of fragrant cut grass lying pale in the sunshine, and it seemed that all the colours had left the landscape.

'And the year after that?'

'Yes! Farmers have to grow things, else what would folks eat?'

'But when can us go home, Thomas?' She turned to him, appalled. 'When can us go home?'

'Hush,' he glanced over at the other apprentices. 'Not 'til you'm one-and-twenty, Mary. I thought you knew that.' He took her hand. 'I thought you understood.'

She could feel a scream of protest trying to rise up from her heart, a cry that would make even Mr Phillips turn to stare, and she forced it back down. When Thomas pulled her close, she clung to him and hid her face against his lean, hard shoulder, and her silent tears flowed on to his threadbare shirt. She was nine years old. She wanted to go home to her mother. She had not enough fingers to count all those years from nine to one-and-twenty.

The Bible Christians of Shebbear were formed for the purpose of sending Missionaries into dark and destitute parts of the United Kingdom, as Divine Providence might open the way.
A converted ploughboy is more useful in missionary work than a sceptical bishop or a proud ecclesiastic.
The Bible Christians by F.W. Bourne

(The Bible Christian) William Reed's early ministerial labours were devoted to the smallest and most neglected villages in Devonshire and Cornwall, including Littleham, Bradford, Sutcombe, Sheepwash, Langtree and Buckland Brewer. To these he devoted much time and attention, believing that the souls of the neglected people living in those wilderness places were of as much value in the sight of God, as those residing in towns and more favoured localities.
Methodist Worthies by G.J. Stevenson

A busy, hurrisome day, - a large wash, a full school, cheese-making, books to be folded without number.
Spoke at Thornhillhead Chapel this morning. At Putford Bridge in the afternoon, I almost fainted; the numerous congregation made it so warm.
From the diary of Mary O'Bryan Thorne, Bible Christian minister.

Part Two

Autumn 1845

Chapter Ten

Mrs Mary Thorne glanced up at the grandfather clock that ticked resonantly in the corner of the low-beamed farmhouse kitchen. She must leave; a quarter to eight, and she still had to change her clothes. Since arising at four o'clock, she had said the morning prayers, helped the older children to feed the pigs and chickens and milk the cows, she had made breakfast for the family and workers, stood the milk in the dairy ready for the next day's butter-making, and was now helping her only servant, Eliza, to prepare the vegetables for dinner, a job that should have been done before the Sabbath. She quickly counted the peeled potatoes. Including the two farm labourers and two apprentice printers, but minus herself, there would be sixteen for dinner.

'You'd better do another dozen potatoes, Eliza, but I think we've enough carrots and turnips. Then tidy and sweep the kitchen; I'll send Thomazine to dry the dishes.'

She peered under the lid of the pot in which the joint of pork was already roasting; good, she could swing the pot away from the fire a little. Now she must change.

'Susanna, take the two little ones into the parlour so they're not under Eliza's feet; here, have the illustrated Bible to read to them.'

Her seven-year-old daughter pulled a face and sighed. 'But Mother...'

'Susanna! Go, now!'

Ten to eight. She ran up the stairs with her nailed boots ringing on the wooden treads then, overcome with anxiety, came to a sudden standstill on the landing. She pictured herself standing motionless before the congregation, unable to speak, and the eager faces looking up at her. Why, after all these years, did the prospect of speaking in chapel still fill her with fear? She clung to the banister as she whispered a prayer for courage. She had to go. The people expected her.

In her bedroom she quickly unbuttoned her old brown wool dress and let it drop on to the floorboards. Her grey costume had once been of good quality and was still serviceable; perhaps the congregation would not notice the darns. Samuel would never countenance new clothes for her or the children while the printing business was struggling. She used the mirror to button the high collar, put on the close-fitting bonnet and hurried into the next bedroom where her oldest son lay. Taking a deep breath as she approached the bed, she smiled and took his hand.

'I will be going in a few minutes, dear. Is there anything you need?' His prayer book had fallen closed at his side.

'No, thank you, Mother. I shall sleep again, I think.' He managed a smile as she stroked his hair away from his dear, kind face. It had been many months now that he had been lying here; the doctor hinted that the spinal affliction might never be cured. She kissed him and walked slowly from the room, then ran down the stairs.

'Do you know where your father is, James?' Her third oldest son was reading at the kitchen table.

'He has gone to the printing room, I believe, Mother.' He made a rueful face at her and a moment of understanding passed between them. 'Should I tell him you are gone? The horse is ready for you.'

She touched his cheek. 'Thank you for doing that. But I think I must speak to him, I'll call in on my way.' She glanced at the clock again. She *must* go. It would be dark when she returned.

As if James read her mind, he said, 'I will see to the horse on your return. Now go, Mother! I'll make sure that the children are ready for chapel on time.'

James had thoughtfully tethered the horse next to the mounting-block so that she could slide easily on to the saddle.

She rode along the lane to Prospect where the print room and the Bible Christian college run by her brother-in-law were located, dismounted and hurried across the yard. Samuel should not be working on the Sabbath. He would glare at her and tell her that it was not *work* that he was doing, not today, but she knew better. As she entered, he glanced up from the paper he was studying.

'I need to include 'ee on the next circuit plan. Mr Penhale'll be unavailable and Mr Slee'll be absent in February, so I need 'ee to speak at Langtree yer,' he pointed at a date on the complex chart he had drawn up, 'and Putford yer and yer; that's in addition to these two dates here in Shebbear, one at Lake and one at Rowden Chapel.' As he spoke, he pencilled her initials on to the draft plan.

Her heart sank. 'But Samuel, it is too much, I cannot fulfil all those engagements when there is the farm to run and the children to care for – and you so often needing help with the folding of pamphlets.' She felt close to tears. 'And suppose I also have to fill cancellations due to illness, as I do today?'

He looked up at her coldly. 'Be 'ee suggesting that I don't pull my weight? *You* run the farm, you say? Is it you that ploughs, you that scythes? Are you the one that prints the Bible Christian hymnbooks, circuit plans and magazines? And have 'ee not noticed that *my* initials are on the plan, yer, and yer?' He jabbed at the paper with his finger and she shrunk from his anger.

'Of course, dear, I did not mean to suggest... it is just that I am tired, and the thought of more commitments is daunting. I will try to overcome my fears, but I have to leave now. The children will be ready for chapel at nine-thirty, will you accompany them?'

'Of course.' He had returned to his work, and although she listened for a farewell as she walked from the room, none came.

With Samuel's unkind remarks ringing in her ears, she was some distance from Shebbear before she became aware of her surroundings. Samuel's short temper continued to dismay her, even after all these years.

He had been brought up in a much coarser way than she had, so it was not surprising that his manners were not always agreeable to her. She sometimes suspected that his anger was fuelled by envy at her success as a preacher. It was true that the responsibility of the farm and the printing of all the Bible Christian literature put him under a lot of pressure, but she could not help feeling that he should try to be more compassionate. She had learned not to mind too much for herself, but the way he sometimes treated the children upset her a great deal.

Her horse's hoofs rang rhythmically on the rough road. Low cloud obscured any remaining autumn colour in the October landscape, and a fine drizzle blown in by the south-westerly breeze settled on her woollen coat. The straight, treeless road offered little shelter from the light but relentless rain and provided a dull ride at this time of the year; the hedges that were ablaze with wild flowers in summer were now only brightened by an occasional, straggly, red campion. She had been too perturbed when she left home to think of covering her head but now, having lifted her hand to her bonnet and found the fabric quite wet, she pulled her hood from her pocket. If she could prevent the moisture soaking right through, she would at least avoid the embarrassment of standing before the congregation with dripping hair.

Her road ran across the plateau which stretched from Shebbear to Buckland Brewer and from Holsworthy to Hatherleigh, an unforgiving land of lonely farmsteads and scattered hamlets whose inhabitants she knew to be slow of speech and given to suspicions, their lives being linked daily with the forces of nature. There were still some poor, dark, miserable places with little prospect of virtue, hamlets where none worshipped on the Sabbath, where poverty was extreme and unspeakable abominations were said to take place.

She sat a little straighter in the saddle, determined not to let herself be dragged down by such thoughts. There had been encouraging progress in the area since the coming of the Bible Christians; through the efforts of her father, her husband's family and their many supporters, the word of God had been brought to areas where church attendance had been almost non-existent. A hundred yards or so ahead of her stood Rowden, one of many roadside Bible Christian chapels whose congregations had increased rapidly in the last twenty years or so, and she took comfort from the thought that people would gather there to worship at the same time as she was to speak at Thornhillhead. No doubt Mr Whitlock, who would speak at Rowden today, had already left home and was walking the lonely roads towards the little chapel with its welcoming diamond-paned windows and whitewashed walls.

She had always walked in the old days, when she was just a girl, before she was married. On occasion she had walked twenty-five miles in a day and preached in three different places. She had travelled the length and breadth of the land, preaching on village greens in Jersey and the Isle of Wight and on the banks of the Thames in London; she had been jeered at and had eggs thrown at her, but she had also moved some to tears and there had been many converts. What a long time ago it seemed. She would not have the stamina for it now; giving birth to ten children had taken its toll.

Her horse stumbled and began to limp. She drew to a halt, feeling anxiety tightening within her chest. She would have to dismount. She still had several miles to go and would surely be late for her appointment. She slid carefully to the ground and bent to run her hand down the horse's leg. He was a gentle, obliging animal and lifted his foot so that she could cup it in her hand. Her guess was correct; a large stone was wedged in the hollow of the hoof. The only wonder was that it did not happen more often on these rough roads. She felt in the saddlebag for the hoof pick and removed the stone without too much difficulty, then led the horse forward a few paces to check that he was sound. But now she had to remount; it was so much easier for men who could ride astride. She searched for a foothold on the high banks at either side of the road, but they were clothed in brambles, and in any case a ditch stood in her way. Gathering up her skirt she started to walk with the horse following willingly at her shoulder, but she had to go several hundred yards before a field gate came into view.

After coaxing the horse to stand alongside it, she was able to climb carefully up and slide back on to the saddle.

As she drew nearer to Stibb Cross, she saw a family in their Sunday best emerging from a roadside cottage, then a woman reaching the road from a field path, and at the crossroads an elderly couple in a donkey cart and a farmer on horseback. All greeted her, for they were heading to the Bible Christian chapel that stood just beyond the crossroads, and she saw the wonder in their eyes, and heard the whispers after she had passed.

'Be visiting with us today, Ma'am?' asked the farmer.

She smiled at him. 'Not today, my friend, I am bound for Thornhillhead as Mr Slee is unwell. God willing, I shall be with you soon.'

She knew that when she was assigned to preach, she attracted larger congregations than was usual, the numbers swelled by those who chose to come from their usual chapel at a mile or two's distance, and sometimes others who had not previously attended chapel at all but came to see her out of curiosity; she strove, then, for extra power in her voice and inspiration beyond the words she had planned, and it was not infrequent that the newcomers were sufficiently affected to become regular attendees. If she could save just one sinner, then the fear and trepidation she felt at the prospect of speaking was as nothing.

When she had passed the tiny Stibb Cross chapel and the scattering of nearby cottages, her road left the fields behind to lead out on to rough moorland across which the moisture-laden breeze blew unimpeded. It was a bleak place at this time of the year, deserted but for a few sturdy bullocks grazing on the purple moor-grass with their backs to the wind, and she missed the yellow and purple flowers, dancing butterflies and buzzing insects that enlivened the moor in summer. Drawing her hood forward so that it almost obscured her face, she urged the horse to a trot. There was still a mile or more to cover and, as she carried no timepiece, she feared that she might be late, but when at last the chapel and schoolroom came into view it was apparent that the people had not yet begun to arrive. She paused to gaze affectionately at the neat, whitewashed Salem chapel and schoolroom with its far-reaching view over undulating fields towards Buckland Brewer some three miles away. Despite its exposed, windy location, it was one of her favourite chapels because it had been the first to be built in this area. It had a large and loyal congregation, partly due to its possession of a burial ground; this alone persuaded some poor labourers to join the Bible Christians; they struggled to pay the burial fees at the parish church when one of their children died.

As she dismounted she was greeted by an elderly woman hurrying from a nearby cottage.

'Mrs Thorne, welcome! Be 'ee come to speak to us today? Come in, come in now and dry yourself. David'll take your horse. Mr Fry, the steward, asked me to look out for 'ee.'

She followed the woman gratefully into the neat, warm room where her coat and hood were spread near the fire to dry, and she was given a hot drink. By the time she crossed the road to the chapel she felt rested, but paused for a minute or two in the porch to gather her thoughts, and to take several slow, deep breaths.

The congregation was already seated when she entered but many turned to welcome her, and she reached out to take their proffered hands as she walked between the rows of narrow pews to the front of the chapel. She turned to face them, clasping her hands together to stop them shaking as she looked out on the sea of faces.

'Dear friends.' She let her gaze move slowly over the crowd so that they should know she spoke to each one of them: the labourers with faces deeply etched by sun and wind, the tired-eyed women worn out by heavy domestic work and repeated childbearing. 'Dear friends, let us pray for a blessing.'

She had chosen her text from Proverbs, Chapter Three: *'Let not mercy and truth forsake thee; bind them about thy neck; write them upon the tablet of thine heart.'*

'What do we mean by these words, dear friends? What is mercy? Mercy denotes all kindliness, charity, and readiness to do good to others. Let us suppose you walk to the well for two buckets of water. You are weary; perhaps it is washday, or you have been hoeing turnips all day and your shoulders are aching; you long to sit down and it is all you can do to drag yourself to the well.'

Every eye was on her. They knew exactly the feeling she described.

'If an elderly neighbour arrives just as you haul up the second bucket, do you hurry away? Do you leave her to draw up the heavy weight unaided? After all, who will know? Does God take much notice of us poor people, you ask yourself? Surely he made the world for the wise and the rich, else why does he not notice when the harvest is bad, when the fever comes, when there is all sort of pain and trouble? He will not notice if I turn away from my neighbour when help is needed, you tell yourself.'

She paused, and allowed her voice to drop. 'Dear friends, you would be wrong! He sees you, every one! He is here in this very hamlet, watching as you fetch water from the well, guiding you when you stumble behind the plough,' – she saw one young lad nudge his father and look up at him in wonder – 'He knows when you have performed a kind deed and when you have chosen selfishness.' She looked meaningfully at a young woman she knew to have been guilty of a transgression, and saw her eyes widen a little.

'And what does it mean, that you should bind mercy and truth around your neck? Why, if you have something precious, as some might have a locket or a timepiece, you tie it around your neck to ensure that you never lose it! So should you make sure that mercy and truth are always with you, for they are more precious than a golden locket.'

Then, her voice growing louder, she detailed the dire consequences should they turn their back on God.

'"Depart from me," He will say unto you.' Every face gazed at her, wide-eyed. '"Depart from me into the bottomless pit of everlasting fire!"'

She let silence fill the room, then went on to describe how they would be rewarded for choosing kindness, the joys that were in store for them as long as they treated their fellow men with compassion and generosity, providing they were honest and truthful.

'Dear friends, I know what this blessedness is; it is the good news that Jesus came to preach to the poor. Be like him; be kind, be true, be compassionate.'

'Praise be to God!' declared a farmer.

'Amen,' murmured others.

She had moved them. She saw tears in the eyes of women and men alike.

'Now, let us sing, dear friends.'

She sang along with the loud passionate voices, but between the verses took deep relaxing breaths. It was done. She had not stumbled over or forgotten her words. She had found the right tone: a sermon should be aimed at the depths of the heart, not the top of the bonnet.

When the prayer meeting was over she spent half an hour with the people, giving reassurance to those with illness in the family, comforting a recently bereaved woman, and speaking to a small boy who had been restless.

'Now William, you study to be quiet, and be kind and good until I come again.'

He looked up at her and nodded solemnly.

When her horse was led out for her, the people were still gathered in little groups outside the chapel, for this was the day when they had time to catch up on each other's news. Soon, they would drift back to their homes for dinner, but would return for a further meeting in the afternoon while their children attended Sunday School. By then, she would be speaking at Twitching Chapel two miles away. She was being accompanied by Mr Joseph Clement with whose family she would have dinner before the meeting.

The rain grew heavier as they set out on their journey and was soon dripping from her hood and soaking through her coat. Mr Clement walked beside her horse, striding over the water-filled ruts on the muddy lane as they talked. A yeoman farmer who was loyal to the Bible Christian movement, he had helped to build the small chapel at Twitching three years previously. Attendance there had increased; labourers who walked great distances during their working week were more likely to attend chapel if it were not too far away, so the intention had always been to build numerous small chapels rather than larger buildings many miles apart.

As they descended a hill she saw an oxcart ahead in the lane. The ox stood patiently in the rain while two children worked alongside, scraping up dung and mud. Their shovels rang against the stony surface and she saw how weary they looked as they heaved the shovels up to shoulder-height to throw the muck into the cart, how slowly they turned back for another load. When she drew nearer she could see that their clothes were little more than rags, giving them scant protection against the weather, and her heart went out to them.

'What poor, suffering children are these? They should not be thus employed on the Sabbath!'

'They'm apprentices of Mr Phillips at Gusland. I've been concerned for 'm a good many years. They'm not the best treated I believe, but he's not a man that's easy to talk to.'

'Does this Mr Phillips attend church, or chapel?'

'No, his older children were baptised in church but he switched, and a new baby was baptised at Thornhillhead last year. Since then he's been sending the older ones to Thornhillhead Sunday School. He's only attended once or twice himself, just wants free tuition for'm, seems to me.'

The boy and girl were about twelve or thirteen years old and, judging from the similarity of their features, a brother and sister. As she approached, they paused in their work and stared at her wearily. The girl, apparently becoming aware that she was wet through and splattered in mud from head to toe, drew her sleeve across her face to wipe off the worst of the filth.

'This is heavy work for you, dears! What are your names?'

They did not answer at once but gazed at her as if stupefied. The girl wore a chemise that was too tight for her developing figure, and Mrs Thorne wished that she could fasten the torn jacket to preserve her modesty. Poor child; she had no mother to care for her.

'I'm Mary,' the girl replied at last, 'and this yer's my brother, Thomas.'

'So tell me, Thomas and Mary, have you taken Jesus into your hearts? Do you know how he watches over poor children who are tired and sorrowful, whose parents are far from them? Have you heard the good news that he brings?'

They stared at her and did not reply. They had strong, expressive faces and there was sensitivity in their eyes.

'Would you like to go to chapel to learn about Jesus? You would meet kind people who would care for you, you could learn to read. Would you like that?'

'I went, years ago,' said the boy, his face brightening a little. 'The Baptist chapel over Eckworthy. I liked it, but the maister us is with now would never let us go.'

'Thomas, Mary, I can speak to your maister. His children come to chapel, do they not? And, as apprentices, you are entitled to attend a place of worship. You could go to the chapel just over the fields from you at Twitching, but better still for you would be Thornhillhead because there is a school there.' She turned to Mr Clement. 'Perhaps I could call at the farm after this afternoon's meeting. Would you accompany me?'

He scratched his head. 'I'll come, Mrs Thorne, but I don't hold out much hope.'

She looked at each of the children in turn, holding their gaze. 'Thomas, Mary, my dear children, I won't forget you. Do you understand? You are in my heart, just as Jesus holds you in His heart. I will come tonight, I promise.' She felt moved almost to tears by the sight of the two neglected and defenceless children; there was something in their faces that called to her. She gave them one last loving look and rode on.

Mary stared as the lady rode gracefully down the hill, turning once to wave before a bend in the road obscured her from view. Mary lifted her hand to wave back, but it was too late, the lane was empty again, and silent but for the dripping of rain from the elms and the creak of the cart as the ox shifted its weight. It was as if she had imagined it all.

She had been at the farm for three years. The sun rose and fell each day; the seasons came and went. There was no end to it. The days were marked by sunshine, wind, rain or snow and she had learnt to look at the patch of worn grass outside the back door as she left the house each morning for puddles or for frost, so that she should know what sort of day she might have, and to study the sky for signs of a change.

If a day reached its end without fear of a beating, without taunting from Lewis, without rain trickling down her back or frost numbing her fingers, then it was a good day, and if she worked alone with Thomas or was not too weary to share late night laughter with Sarah, it was a day to remember.

But this – nothing like this had ever happened before.

No one had shown concern, or thoughtfulness, or love before.

Mary turned to Thomas. 'Who was she? Will her come, do 'ee think?'

'Her promised her would.' He, too, stared at the empty lane winding between high hedgebanks. 'But, can you see her at the farm? Talking to the maister? I can't. Her's too different, nought like him. Nought like him at all. But her promised.'

They stood in silence for a while.

'Be it true, do 'ee think,' said Mary, 'what her said 'bout Jesus? That he be watching over people like we?'

Thomas shrugged his shoulders, but she could see that he was deep in thought.

Slowly, they set back to work, but Mary kept picturing the lady's gentle expression and remembering the sound of her voice. She had spoken softly but clearly, as if every word was very important, and she had looked at Mary and Thomas intently as she spoke.

'Her did promise, and I don't think her'd tell a lie, Thomas.'

She had sat quite straight on her horse, dressed very plainly in a long, grey coat with a single row of buttons down the front, and a grey bonnet with not an ornament or frill in sight, not even a little piece of ribbon. A Quaker cap, Mary's mother would have called it, and a distant memory came back to her of her mother trying to repair an old bonnet.

'Folks'll think I be a Quaker if I've not so much as a length of ribbon to decorate it! 'Twould be enough to frighten the cows!'

Mary smiled to herself. She had last seen her mother back in the summer. Perhaps twice a year there she would be, suddenly, standing at a gate or calling over the hedge and they would have a few precious minutes together, sometimes half an hour if they were lucky, but they had to be constantly on the lookout for Mr Phillips. Usually Mr Fulford had driven her mother to the farm, having somehow found out where Thomas and Mary were likely to be working. Mary wondered what her mother would have said about the lady.

'I knowed that man that was with her, Thomas – Mr Clement, he spoke to me several times.'

Thomas nodded. 'Me too. He be a kind man, I reckon. And,' he looked up in surprise, 'I mind it now, he called her Mrs Thorne, did 'ee hear that? And they that go to that chapel, folk call them Thorne-ites sometimes.'

'What does that signify, then? Who was she?'

'I don't know. But I reckon her's important.'

'I'll ask Sarah tonight, her'll know.'

'P'raps Lucy and Rosa know, they go there. But they won't have seen her at chapel today 'cos they don't go 'til the afternoon. And us don't want to ask them anyway.'

Would Mr Phillips let them go to the chapel? Since the disastrous harvest last year, he had taken to saying grace before a meal, but it hadn't worked because the harvest was almost as bad this year, and it had been so cold from January through until March that the sheep had to be kept inside. Before long, the hay and turnips had almost run out and all the animals had been in poor condition.

One day in March, when snow had fallen yet again on the deeply frozen ground, Mary was sent to fetch Mr Phillips in for dinner. As she turned the corner in the yard, she saw him standing by the gate to Barn Park gazing up at the leaden sky, and she thought she could hear him muttering. While she hung back beside the linhay, he dropped to his knees in the snow and she realised that he was praying.

His prayers had not improved his mood. They had learned to fear his anger even more than before.

She and Thomas led the ox a little further on and began work on another stretch of the lane. It would take another half an hour or so to fill the cart, after which they could return to the farm to spend the rest of the afternoon with Joseph cutting up turnips for feeding to the cows. They would be in the barn for that work, so their clothes would have a chance to dry a little before the evening.

Seeing Thomas wince as he threw another shovelful of muck on to the cart, Mary stopped and leaned her shovel against the wheel.

'Yer, let me look.' Thomas had several boils on the back of his neck which had been causing him pain for a few weeks. As soon as one cleared up, another appeared. Sarah said it was because he was made to work too hard and was always getting wet. Mary gently pulled down his collar to look.

'I reckon that one's going to burst soon. It'll feel better then.'

Last winter Thomas had been very ill with a cough which had confined him to his bed for several days, but Mr Phillips wouldn't call for the doctor because, Mary thought, the doctor would probably say that Thomas had to sleep in the house to keep warm.

Their shovels scraped on the road again, until Thomas stopped and stared at the ground.

'Mary, I want to go to that chapel. I really want to go.' He looked up at her, his face and hair caked in mud. 'I be so sick of this life! If only us could just walk away from it all – the work, the being ill, most of all, the folks around us; the maister, Lewis. All of 'em 'cept you and James.'

He was close to tears, and Mary could not trust herself to reply without crying.

'When I think of the years us still has to do!' he said. 'But if us could go to chapel, at least 'twould be a thing to look forward to, the singing and that.'

He gave her a pleading look. 'I don't know if us can, but – would 'ee come with me?'

She nodded slowly. 'I want to go too.'

She thought about what the lady had told them, about the kind people there were in the chapel, about learning to read.

But it seemed like a dream. It could never happen.

That evening, they had almost finished eating their potatoes and gravy when there was a tap at the farmhouse door. Mary exchanged a glance with Thomas; callers were rare at any time and unheard-of on a Sunday evening. The knock was followed by the click of the latch, and there she was.

'Please excuse me for disturbing your meal, Mr Phillips, Mrs Phillips.'

Mary saw that as she stepped forward, Mrs Thorne glanced quickly around the room; in that brief moment she managed to make eye contact with Mary and Thomas, and to pick out the owner of the household from the sixteen people present. It was already dark outside but Mary, being nearest to the door, caught sight of a shadowy figure. Mr Clement was staying outside.

'I am Mrs O'Bryan Thorne from Lake in Shebbear. I have been preaching today at Thornhillhead and Twitching.'

Her gaze was so direct, it was as if she could see inside every one of them. The effect of her presence in the kitchen was extraordinary. Everybody stopped eating and stared at her in astonishment, then Mr Phillips rose to his feet, almost knocking over the chair in his confusion.

'Come in, I... will 'ee sit down? John! Give the lady your seat!'

Mary had never seen him so flustered. John slid on to the form with the other children while Mrs Phillips got up to make a cup of tea for Mrs Thorne.

'Thank you, that's very kind.' She smiled at John, who started to rock with excitement until his father growled at him to sit still.

'This is an inconvenient time to call I fear, but it was my only opportunity before I return to Shebbear. I wanted to tell you how pleased I am that your children are attending Sunday School. I have been told that they are making very good progress.' She smiled gently at Lucy, Rosa and Tom. 'And this little one,' she touched Henry's hand, 'I hope he will soon be attending – and John of course! Why do you not come to Sunday School, John?'

John, who had been staring open-mouthed at Mrs Thorne, looked at his father for guidance.

'He's not one for learning, John.'

Mrs Thorne looked at him sympathetically. 'Mr Phillips, all children are welcome at the Sunday School, whatever their ability. John will be able to learn at his own pace; please do allow him to go!'

Mary was surprised to see Mr Phillips flush with embarrassment.

'Ah, but Mr Phillips, does John work on the Sabbath? The Rector, I know, is rather lax on these matters. Have you followed his guidance in the past?'

'Not anymore I don't. Us don't see eye to eye, me and Rector.'

Slowly, Mary finished eating her dinner, listening carefully as the conversation went back and forth. Mrs Thorne must have forgotten about meeting her and Thomas because she had not mentioned it. Mary pulled a face at Thomas, but he was listening intently.

'It is very hard for us farmers,' Mrs Thorne was saying. 'There is always so much work to do that it is tempting to work on the Sabbath and get ahead, although one must of course milk the cows and feed the stock, whatever the day. Life has been so difficult these past two years, has it not, Mr Phillips? The drought last year and the disastrous harvest – was yours bad too?'

Mr Phillips shook his head in despair. 'Us have never known one like it.'

'Then the very cold spring this year when we thought our animals would starve, and the harvest little better. I know my husband and I went down on our knees many times, and I'm sure you did too.'

Mary watched him carefully. She knew that he had knelt in prayer, but he looked down and did not reply.

'However, can we expect God to listen to us,' said Mrs Thorne, in her clear persuasive voice, 'if we do not listen to Him? And the Bible is clear about working on Sundays. Do you recall the words, Mr Phillips?'

She drew herself up in the chair, and her words rang out across the kitchen with such slow emphasis that it might have been God himself who was speaking:

'"*Six days shalt thou labour, and do all thy work.*"'

All eyes were on her, even those of the baby who was sitting on Mrs Phillips' lap.

'"*But the seventh day is the Sabbath of the Lord thy God: in it thou shalt not do any work, thou,*"' she looked straight at Mr Phillips,

'"*nor thy son, nor thy daughter, thy manservant, nor thy maidservant, nor thy cattle, nor thy stranger that is within thy gates.*"'

They all sat in stunned silence. Mr Phillips looked down at his lap.

'Always remember,' her powerful voice continued, 'the great God sees you. When you give the order to work, He can strike you dead in a moment, and in the same moment of time, appoint you in your portion of the lake that burns with fire and with brimstone.'

It was a minute or more before she broke the spell, and her voice was soft.

'I have kept you too long. I am so sorry to have disturbed your meal.' She rose from the chair and adjusted her bonnet. 'So, we will see John at chapel next week? Oh, and these are your apprentices?' She had turned towards the table around which Mary and the others were standing, and her gaze met Mary's. There was love in her glance, and humour too.

'Do they attend church or chapel, Mr Phillips? I expect so, the magistrates are so insistent these days, are they not, that apprentices attend the place of worship that they choose.'

Mr Phillips had risen from his chair. Mary saw that he could not meet Mrs Thorne's eyes, and she held her breath.

'Well, no, they've never asked, see.'

''Well, perhaps they would like to come to Thornhillhead too! How many of you would like to come to chapel, and to Sunday School?' Her eyes were smiling as she waited for the response.

Thomas had scarcely once taken his eyes off Mrs Thorne but the older boys were scowling with embarrassment at being the centre of attention. Mary would not perhaps have dared to answer if Mr Phillips was looking at her, but he was staring at the floor.

'I want to come! My name's Mary.'

'And me!' said Thomas.

'He's Thomas, he's my brother.' She had to stop herself from smiling, especially when she caught the sparkle in Mrs Thorne's eyes.

'I'll come!' shouted Joseph.

'Mr Phillips, will that be acceptable to you? It will keep them out of mischief, and I know what a problem it can be to occupy apprentices on a Sunday. Perhaps the others will come too when Thomas and Mary tell them all about it. I will be at Thornhillhead again next week so I will be sure to speak to all the children; there will be seven, then, from this farm and perhaps even more than that! And, of course, yourself and Mrs Phillips, I do hope you will be able to attend.' She took his hand, 'Mr Phillips, thank you. You will never regret letting God into your heart.'

Then she made her farewells, and she was gone.

Mary sat very still as her gaze travelled from face to face. She was careful to look innocent and unassuming, but inside she was rejoicing. Together they had triumphed over Mr Phillips!

Mrs Phillips was the first to break the silence. 'Well, I ... was that *the* Mrs Thorne?'

'Us have seen her up Sunday School,' said Lucy, 'but only one time, I reckon.'

'Must be her,' put in Sarah as she rose from the table, 'because her said "Mrs O'Bryan Thorne", didn't her? Mother knows about her 'cos her cousin goes to that chapel.' She started stacking the plates. ''Twas that lady's father, Mr O'Bryan, what started the Bible Christians down in Cornwall, then the Thornes took over and her married one of them and they all live down in Shebbear. They've got a school and I don't know what down there. But her's the one folks talk about the most.' She started to carry the plates out to the scullery. 'Her's a good woman, so they reckon.'

Mary watched Mr Phillips, afraid that one of his outbursts of anger would be forthcoming. But he remained silent, and after a minute or two he got up and walked out of the room.

Chapter Eleven

When Mr Phillips had drawn up amongst the other farm carts, wagons and tethered horses outside Bideford pannier market, he jumped down from the cart and grabbed the leather handle of the large wicker hamper. The three fat lambs in the cart jumped away from him, scrabbling wildly at the wooden hurdles that fenced them in.

'Geddown, you buggers! Move yerself, Tom!'

His son took the other handle and between them they carried the heavy pannier into the market. He left his wife to climb down on her own. It was her fault they were late. She had been up half the night preparing her produce for market, then had decided to get up early to kill and pluck a fowl to sell.

She hurried over as he and Tom lowered the pannier to the ground.

'Oh, idn't there a spot undercover?' She looked around anxiously. 'If it should rain, and me with this chill.' She drew her shawl around her and tied it behind her back. 'If you could only give me a day or two's notice of when you'm coming to market...'

He turned on her. 'You didn't have to come! 'Tis you who've caused us to be late so I don't want to hear any more of that!'

Leaving her to unpack, he and Tom passed between the rows of benches where farmers' wives sat with their wares set up on panniers in front of them. Several nodded to him and he saw his sister, Annie, wave from the far side of the market; but he kept walking, noticing nevertheless that several women had chickens alongside the eggs, apples, onions, cream and bunches of parsley they were selling, which meant that his wife would not even get a good price for the fowl. Next time he would put his foot down; she would leave on time or not at all.

It was only a hundred yards to the cattle market but he flicked the whip and drove up Honestone Lane at a fast trot, the clatter of the horse's hoofs echoing from the walls of the tall houses that lined the narrow road. It was imperative that he arrived before the bidding started.

Ever since Mrs Thorne's visit he had been suffering from a deep malaise which kept him awake at night and distracted him during the day. It had caused him to tell Lewis to drive the bullocks out to graze in a field that was planted with turnips, and to set out himself to round up lambs without taking the sheepdog.

He had taken to working on the farm accounts – a job he usually put off for as long as possible – because the necessity of making the numbers add up soothed him, and he felt safer when he was indoors.

It was the sky that made him anxious; the vast, overarching extent of it, its unfathomable distances. There was no escaping it. He had tried. Thinking the woodland canopy would shield him, he had gone to Upper Coppice for kindling although there was already enough stored to last the winter. So preoccupied was he, he forgot that there would be no leaves on the trees at this time of year. He spent hours cutting up turnips in the linhay, just for the reassurance of wooden planking above his head when he looked up. But he had to go outside eventually, and however hard he tried not to cast guilty glances at the sky, he could not help himself; when the fast-moving clouds created alarming images or a sudden shaft of sunlight appeared, he was sure of it: God was watching him.

How long had it been going on? The farm apprentices had worked on Sundays for as long as he could remember, back in his father's time too. Had all those transgressions been observed? Mrs Thorne's words rang through his head once more: '*Thou shalt not do any work, thou, nor thy son, nor thy daughter, thy manservant, nor thy maidservant, nor thy cattle, nor thy stranger that is within thy gates.*'

As if the anxiety about being watched was not enough, another fear had taken hold of him. He had begun to wonder whether his punishment for enforcing Sunday working had already commenced, even before Mrs Thorne's visit. Why else would he have suffered two bad harvests in a row? Why else had he lost his best ewe after a difficult lambing? Why else would the snow have lasted right through until March, only melting when all the roots and hay were gone and the stock close to starvation? As he endured yet another sleepless night, his certainty of the failure of the farm and the inevitability of his family's downfall grew, but when morning came at last he had pulled himself together. The wet summer had ruined many harvests. The snow had not fallen at Gusland alone. Until now he had been too enmeshed in his own misfortune to notice whether he was being singled out for punishment or whether other farmers had suffered to the same extent. Were their sheep fatter than his and their fleeces deeper? Were their bullocks heavier and their calves better grown, their wheat and hay of superior quality? He had to find out.

Mrs Annie Fulford recognised that her brother was in one of his evil tempers. He had deliberately chosen to ignore her when he saw her wave to him from across the market. Although she was busy serving, while she spooned the yellow-crusted cream into the small ceramic pot the customer had handed to her she kept glancing over at her sister-in-law. How poor Eliza kept going, she just didn't know; it was true that her whining and complaining could make you feel like giving her a good shake at times, but heaven knew she had enough to complain about.

As soon as she had taken the money for the cream, she asked her neighbour to keep an eye on her stall and pushed through the crowded thoroughfare. Eliza was still trying to unpack her produce but was getting in a proper muddle because, being late, some of her space had been taken by adjacent stalls.

'Come on now, Eliza, us can do this together. Mrs Grigg,' she winked at the woman on the adjacent stall, 'would 'ee just move your things along the bench a little so Mrs Phillips yer can unpack?'

Quickly she removed the remaining vegetables from the pannier so that the white cloth could be spread over it.

'There now, many hands make light work they say, don't 'em? Now let me sit down aside of 'ee for a minute or two.'

'Thank you, Annie,' said Eliza. She looked tired, and even paler than was usual. 'I be so sorry.'

'Sorry? What's there to be sorry for? Only that brother of mine idn't more helpful to 'ee, that's all there is to be sorry for, I reckon.'

''Tis all my fault that us is late, and I've made him late too. I should have been ready.' She looked close to tears. 'But he only said last night that us could go to market and it took me such a time to gather things up. I should be quicker at it, I know I should.'

'Well, how does he think you'm going to be ready if he only gives 'ee a few hours' notice?'

Annie felt exasperated with her brother, but there was little she could do. He would never agree for the two families to visit one another so she had barely exchanged half a dozen words with him in the last few years, and was only able to speak with Eliza when he allowed her to go to market. She worried about her sister-in-law. Once or twice, when many weeks had passed without seeing her, she insisted that her husband drive her to Gusland to make sure all was well. On the last occasion Eliza, looking worn out after the birth of the latest baby, had been relieved to see her, but as soon as her brother came in, he had made it clear that she was not welcome.

Annie straightened the cloth and tidied the bunches of rather wilted parsley to make them more appealing to customers. Eliza seemed too exhausted to take much interest.

'Now tell me, how be all the family?'

She feared for the children too; her brother's temper knew no bounds.

She had to return to her own stall eventually but did so in a subdued frame of mind, and as she chatted with her regular customers she kept looking over at Eliza, who was sitting staring into space as if in the depths of despondency.

It was her brother who was to blame, she knew that for a fact. Eliza came from a family that was more well-to-do than their own, and as soon as they were married, her brother seemed determined to belittle her. He had been difficult even as a boy; Annie was often terrorised by him, but their father always took her side and would thrash his oldest son when he was cruel to her, so badly on one occasion that she vowed to keep quiet in future.

She had a nagging doubt, which she had only ever shared with her husband, about her brother's parentage. After her mother died, she had discovered that her brother was born before her parents married.

'There you be then,' her husband had said, 'I reckon he's only your half-brother.'

It might explain why he was so different from the rest of the family, and why her father was so hard on him. But she had never shared the thought with anyone, least of all with her brother. After all, what good could it do?

Mr Phillips tied up just inside the entrance to the livestock market before pausing to survey the scene. Most of the pens were occupied already; over to the left were three or four dairy cows, some young stock and a dozen or so fat bullocks, the sheep were in the central pens, the pigs over to the right-hand side, while three restless saddle horses waiting to be auctioned were tethered to a fence at the rear. At each pen two or three farmers in their best clothes and polished boots had gathered to lean on the wooden fences and discuss the merits and failings of each animal. The scene resembled a patchwork, each square pen containing white or dark red animals bordered by the groups of brown fustian-clad farmers; the noise of bellowing, bleating and squealing animals blended with the low rumble of Devonshire voices to form a deafening cacophony.

'Da! Shall us unload the lambs, Da?'

'No.' He walked towards the pens with Tom hurrying after him. 'Us'll see what prices they'm fetching first off.'

Four sheep waited placidly in the first pen. They were full-looking ewes, superior to his, there was no doubt about it. When he pushed his fingers into the fleece of the nearest sheep, he could feel a good layer of fat on its rump. Two years ago, he too would have brought such animals to market but this year's cold spring had given them such a poor start, they had been unable to put on sufficient weight even though he had given them a month longer than usual.

'They'm better than our'n, Da.'

He read the paper label tied to the pen. Mr Withecombe.

'They'm grown on warmer land than our'n. Grass grows sooner and gives'n a start.'

He held the muzzle of the sheep and pulled back its upper lip while it rolled its eyes at him. Mr Withecombe was selling ewes with ill-shaped teeth and hollow backs, neither of which would help them bear strong lambs. Nobody wanted such animals in their flock during the winter.

The sheep in the next pen more closely resembled his own; scrawny animals with little fat on them. These were Mr Heal's, so were grazed on cold, heavy land similar to his own. It was a good sign; he must look at more animals but already he felt relief beginning to flood through him. Perhaps he was not being punished, not yet. Perhaps it was not too late to make amends.

He stared out across the market and his gaze wandered over the intricate pattern of grey rooftops that tumbled down the hill towards the river. He would not look up; he was determined of that. But the church stood amongst the town's houses and he found his eyes travelling up the tower and beyond, to a sky where the clouds were just parting to reveal a glimpse of infinity.

Bartholomew Fulford ran his hand over the bullock's flank, admiring its well-muscled shoulders and dense, dark red, curly coat.

'He'd fatten up bootiful.'

'You'm not thinking of bidding for'n, be 'ee?' Mr Ambrose Galsworthy regarded him quizzically, his small, astute eyes almost obscured by bushy black brows.

''Tis knowing whether there'd be the feed for'n. 'Tisn't worth the risk to my mind.'

'Us have lost confidence, haven't us, with the way the weather's been these last two years.' Mr Galsworthy farmed a hundred acres of well-drained land, but Bartholomew knew that even he was feeling the pinch.

'Oh well, us have managed, haven't us.'

'Ah, us'll live to see another day, I reckon.'

Bartholomew reluctantly turned his back on the bullock in order to listen to the auctioneer whose voice was a persistent drone on one note, until it rose in a sudden exclamation just before the slam of the hammer marked a sale. Sheep were making around sixpence a pound which, although a slight increase on the previous week, was low enough to cause some gloomy expressions. Nevertheless, few had the confidence to take their animals back home to fatten them for another year.

'Takes the swagger out of 'ee, don't it,' he said, 'a winter like that. And wheat's only making seven shilling a bushel despite the shortage.'

'Well, they'm saying ministers are set to interfere with the Corn Laws, bain't 'em, that's what that's about.'

Bartholomew looked at his companion with interest. 'Is that right? That's a turnaround, then. 'Twill not please many, save the poor. Where did 'ee hear that, then?'

'In the newspaper. 'Tis to bring in cheap American corn to feed the Irish since the potato crop failed.'

Bartholomew, who generally only read the local news, decided he really must read the paper more closely.

He nodded to Mr Sanders, the butcher who had bought the last lot of sheep, and was looking around for Mr Fry in order to make arrangements to take a cow to his bull, when Mr Galsworthy gave him a nudge.

'See, Mr Thomas Phillips's here today, 'tisn't often us sees'n.'

Mr Phillips was standing apart from the farmers who crowded around the auctioneer, but was paying close attention to the proceedings. He seemed to lack his usual look of determination and seemed tired and drawn. One of his sons stood with him, a diminutive figure in a large cap, clearly from the same mould as his father. Bartholomew watched with interest. What had brought him here today? It was puzzling to know what was going on at Gusland; he had heard that quantities of lime had been brought in, and when he rode past one day, he had been startled to see that an eight-acre field had been ploughed and planted with potatoes, and another field was being ploughed by two fine draught horses. Most farmers he knew were satisfied if they could feed their stock and their families; few could afford to buy expensive horses, nor were there many who wished to, because they believed that oxen were more reliable. It would appear that Mr Phillips had made money and, seeing as his family clearly could not eat all the potatoes that were being grown, had ambitions to make more. Ambitions were dangerous things, to Bartholomew's mind. He didn't, however, remark on any of this to Mr Galsworthy, whose son had married Mr Phillips' younger sister; in any case none of the farmers discussed each other's business beyond an occasional brief comment and a disapproving shake of the head or a slow nod of approval.

'They say as he's had a visit from Mrs Mary Thorne,' he told Mr Galsworthy. He had heard the news from his cousin, whose wife had had it from Mrs Clements over at Twitching.

'Well, her won't find a convert there too easily, I wouldn't think.'

Both men, not wanting to be seen watching Mr Phillips, leaned on a pig pen and cast only cursory glances in his direction.

'Well, that's not what I heard,' said Bartholomew. He reached out to scratch a large white pig between the ears, whereupon it lifted its snout in appreciation and grunted contentedly. 'They say the whole family's like to go to Salem Chapel, and the apprentices with 'em. Whether that'll please Mrs Mitchell or not, I wouldn't like to say.' He winked at Mr

Galsworthy who, having had Elizabeth Mitchell as his apprentice for the past eight years, was acquainted with Mrs Mitchell.

'Mrs Thorne'd convert the whole world to the Bible Christian way of thinking if her had her way,' remarked Mr Galsworthy, who was a church-goer. 'Folks do seem to be taken with her.'

'Ah, her has a way with her.' Bartholomew did not like to admit that, after once conversing with her, he had almost been tempted to move to the Bible Christians himself.

'Mrs Ley what goes to church regular, when her daughter was poorly her sent a message for Mrs Thorne to say a prayer, as if Reverend Colling's prayers weren't good enough.'

Bartholomew thought Reverend Colling's prayers would scarcely save a mouse, but kept this thought to himself. 'Well, if Mr Phillips do go to Salem, 'twon't hurt those apprentices to get away from the farm for a few hours.'

Mr Phillips waited for two more sheep to be auctioned before he made up his mind.

'Da, shall us unload 'em now? Us'll be too late else!'

'No. They'm staying put.' He turned away and walked towards the cattle pens. There were some good quality bullocks, three-year-olds from the look of them.

'Why, Da?' His son hurried after him.

''Tisn't worth selling 'em for fivepence a pound. Us'll take 'em home again, fatten 'em some more.' The price was an insult, it would be better to feed them for another six months, maybe even nine months so as to benefit from another shearing. The price was bound to rise. Realising that the stock being sold was in scarcely better condition than his own had given him renewed confidence; he was not being punished or singled out, he need not fear for the future. If he made amends by allowing the apprentices to attend chapel on a Sunday, all would be well.

He examined the bullocks carefully, then stood back as other farmers gathered round to watch them being auctioned.

The first, a four-year-old, sold for twelve guineas. It was not a lot. If the young stock was going for low prices… an idea came to him and he edged forward through the crowd, his heart thumping. A three-year-old sold for nine guineas, and then it was the turn of the younger beasts.

'A fine example here, two-year-old ready for butchering now if you'm in a hurry, or can be brought on. What am I bid?' The auctioneer scanned the crowd. 'Come on now, who'll offer me two guineas, two guineas to start 'n off!'

Someone must have lifted an eyebrow or raised a finger because the auctioneer was now asking for three guineas. Mr Phillips edged between two broad-shouldered men and waited, ill at ease in the close contact of the crowd. Four guineas. The auctioneer rattled through his pleas, and Mr Phillips gave a slight nod. The farmer who had offered three was now looking at the floor; he was not a serious bidder.

'Four and half, come on now, who'll give me four and a half?'

Someone must have assented because the appeal was now for five guineas. Mr Phillips felt his breath coming fast and shallow, it would not do to appear too keen, nor yet to leave it too late. He felt the auctioneer's gaze on him and gave a brief nod.

'*At* five guineas, will anyone give me six? *At* five guineas, gentlemen, going for five guineas,' the hammer slammed down, '*Gone* for five guineas to Mr Thomas Phillips.'

Mr Phillips, aware of the raised eyebrows and exchanged glances around him, shifted uncomfortably. It was known that he did not usually buy in store cattle, but what business was it of theirs? There were five more two-year-olds for sale; he bought three at five guineas each and two at six guineas, then pushed his way through the dispersing crowd to arrange payment. Tom, who had been ordered to stand back during the proceedings, hurried excitedly along beside him.

'Shall us get a drover to bring 'em home, Da?'

He nodded his assent; the expenditure was not high and would ensure a safe delivery. When he stood in the queue to pay, he rebuffed the inquisitive remarks from other farmers as he calculated how much weight the bullocks might gain, the manure they would produce, and the probable price when he came to sell. He had done well; he was sure of it.

Chapter Twelve

'Stand still! I'll never get it done else and the Missis'll be shouting for me to help with the dinner soon!'

Sarah had been tugging at Mary's hair with a comb for what felt like hours and was now making a plait at the back. Mary shifted restlessly in her new clothes. Beyond their bedroom window, gentle autumn sunlight fell on the deep lane that wound down between rolling fields to the wooded valley, then up again towards the distant hills.

'Is that the way us'll walk to chapel?'

Sarah glanced up. 'Yes, to start off, but 'tis a long way, 'twill take you best part of an hour, I reckon.'

It was rather daunting to be doing something so different from the usual daily round. Mary twisted round to look at Sarah, who was frowning with concentration as she fastened the plait.

'Come with us, why don't 'ee, please!' Sarah would know exactly where to go and what to say; she wouldn't be shy.

Sarah laughed. 'Me? I'm not going to chapel, all that loud hymn-singing! You can hear them from several fields away when they'm in Twitching Chapel, they'm a bit over-keen, my Mam says. But don't fret, you'll have Thomas and Joseph with 'ee.'

After Mrs Thorne's visit, Mr Phillips had said no more about attending chapel. Mary had almost given up hope when, the previous evening, he had suddenly announced that they were all to go the very next day.

'What, the apprentices as well?' Mrs Phillips said. 'But they'll need clean clothes!'

He had shrugged and pushed aside his empty plate.

Mrs Phillips and Sarah searched drawers and cupboards for serviceable garments, but Lucy's old skirt that was selected for Mary was so tight it was impossible to fasten the buttons, so Sarah found a brown wool skirt that was a better fit and had only a few moth holes. It felt much softer than the serge she wore every day, which was in any case so ingrained with mud it would have been impossible to get it clean.

'Let's have a look at 'ee.' Sarah turned Mary around and stepped back, frowning, to scrutinise her. 'There, that scrap of ribbon I found sets off your hair proper. Now then,' she opened the bedroom door and looked both ways along the passage, 'there's no one about, come and see yourself in Mrs Phillips' mirror; I've done it many a time!'

Mary had never been in the other bedrooms. She tiptoed after Sarah. Mr and Mrs Phillips' room had a big wooden bedstead, heavy wool curtains at the windows, and a musty smell. In the looking-glass on the wall she saw Sarah's face, as cheerful and smiling as ever, and next to her a startled-looking girl with strong dark brows and dark hair. When Mary lifted her hand to her mouth, so did the girl, and when she blinked, the girl did also.

''Tis me!' She was astounded to see how she looked.

'Course it is, maid; oh my, you'm mazed, you be!'

The Sarah in the mirror laughed, and the girl did too; Mary could not take her eyes off her.

''Tis as well you see yourself now you'm all washed and brushed and pretty; you wouldn't have liked to see the way you looked before.'

Mary turned her head to see her hair lying between her shoulders and the plait secured with a green ribbon. The violet and green checked blouse was only a little short in the sleeves; she would be warm enough once she was wearing the thick woollen shawl Mrs Phillips had found for her. She looked straight at the mirror and smiled. The girl who was going to walk to chapel seemed an entirely different person to the one that worked all day in the fields.

The Phillips' family were to travel by cart, so did not need to set off early. When Mary had finished eating, she exchanged apprehensive glances with Thomas and Joseph before summoning the courage to address Mr Phillips.

'Please may us leave now, maister?'

He grunted his assent.

They left the family sitting around the table and walked across the yard and down the farm track in silence, half-expecting to be called back, but once they reached the lane they turned to each other and grinned at the unaccustomed freedom and at the sight of each other's shiny, scrubbed faces.

As their newly-polished nailed boots rang in unison on the stony lane, Mary began to enjoy the walk. Barely a breath of wind disturbed the few russet and yellow leaves remaining on the roadside trees, and there was almost a hint of warmth in the sunlight despite the lateness of the season. A robin sang a sweet autumnal song from the branch of a hawthorn, and a blackbird was so intent on its dinner of berries, it quite ignored their presence until Joseph made an unsuccessful leap at it.

The lane led down into the narrow valley where an old stone bridge crossed the brook, then rose steeply again alongside Gusland's most southerly fields of rough grass and furze where sheep were grazed. They passed the boundary of the farm, and walked on alongside the land farmed by Mr Bartlett. None of them spoke. Mary guessed that she was not the only one to feel a little afraid, so deeply instilled was the knowledge that they must never leave the farm. But they continued to put one foot in front of the other until, when Mary turned to smile at the other two, Thomas laughed out loud.

'Come on, let's run!', and she and Joseph chased after him, trying to outdo each other until Joseph, still the smallest of the three, laughing and out of breath, pleaded with them to stop.

The high hedgebanks either side of them shut out any view of the surrounding countryside, so Mary had no idea where they were, except that they were leaving the servitude of the farm behind, but when they reached a junction with another lane that curved away to the left, Joseph stopped dead.

'I knows that! That goes to Tythecott!'

He had gone quite pale. Mary glanced at Thomas, who pulled a rueful face at her.

'Is your mam there?' she asked tentatively.

'No.' He walked a few steps along the lane, and replied without turning around. 'Her's in Buckland now, charring, so my sister told me.'

Thomas and Mary waited.

'Us used to walk down this way sometimes, me and my Da, when us had been out trapping birds or cutting furze on the moor. Before I was 'pprenticed.'

He stood very still, staring down the lane. Mary knew that Joseph's mother and the younger children had been sent to the Workhouse when his father was transported to Australia, and had remained there for at least a year. The children were now working on farms throughout the parish, and someone else would have moved into the cottage that Joseph had known as home. She felt grateful that her parents were still in the cottage she remembered; she could picture them there, even if she could not visit them.

Eventually Joseph turned to continue up the hill with Thomas and Mary, but she could see that he was still distracted. The lane joined a wider road which, after a short distance, crossed an area of open moorland with an unobstructed view of fields and pockets of woodland stretching south for many miles to meet the huge, overarching sky. Mary strode ahead of the boys, her thoughts leaping forward into the day that was to come: the excitement of visiting a new place, of meeting Mrs Thorne again and perhaps other kind people too, the extraordinary experience of hearing music and singing and perhaps even learning to read if she could manage it. As she walked she lifted her head and gazed up into the sky, trying to locate the skylark which was celebrating its freedom by pouring forth its jubilant song high above. She never thought to look up for it when she was tired and dirty and afraid, but it was always there, always singing.

When she came to a crossroads she waited for Thomas and Joseph to catch up.

'Which way shall us go now?'

Before they had time to consider, she saw a family approaching from the road on their right, the oldest child a girl of about Mary's age.

'Please, which way be it to the chapel?'

'Straight across yer, 'tidn't far now.' The woman smiled at them, so they continued along together. The girl, who had sandy-coloured hair and freckles, told Mary that her name was Thirza. She lived half a mile away in a cottage next to the farm where her father worked.

'I'm 'pprenticed over at Gusland.' Mary looked at the girl challengingly, fearing that she would sneer at her, but Thirza just nodded.

'There! That's your maister coming now!' Thirza's mother declared.

Some way back along the road, Mr Phillips could be seen driving the cart with Mrs Phillips sitting alongside and the children ranged behind on makeshift wooden seats, but before Mary had time to decide whether she should wait for them, Thirza nudged her to indicate that they had arrived at the chapel.

Set in a pleasant, grassy enclosure, it was a low, whitewashed building with arched windows. On the path that led to the entrance porch a group of people had gathered. Several of them immediately stepped forward to greet Mary, Thomas and Joseph as they entered, taking their hands, asking their names and welcoming them to Thornhillhead. Mary felt overwhelmed by so many smiling faces, and the boys looked at the ground while shuffling their feet uncomfortably. The moment soon passed. Thirza took her hand and pulled her away.

'Come on, school'll be starting.'

Mary looked back to see Mr and Mrs Phillips joining the crowd who were beginning to pass through the door into the chapel, then she followed her new friend with Thomas and Joseph trailing along behind.

The air in the schoolroom felt chill and stale, like the rarely-used dining room at the farmhouse, but there were colourful pictures on the walls of a man in a long gown that Mary knew to be Jesus. Many of the children jostling to find a place on the low wooden forms were a good deal smaller than Mary; feeling conspicuous, she hastened to find a seat with Thirza on one side of her and Thomas on the other, while the Phillips children, she noticed, found seats further back. Several children stared curiously at her, but then the teacher said a few indistinct words and they all slid silently off their forms to kneel on the floor, so Mary quickly followed suit. She did not know the prayer that followed, but moved her mouth so that it would appear that she did, afraid that she might be chastised.

The teacher, a stout, clean-shaven man, addressed the six new children.

'Can you read? Do you know your catechism? You will answer "Yes, Mr Reed" or "No, Mr Reed."'

Mary could answer the first question and answered 'No, Mr Reed' to the second as well because she did not understand what it meant. All the new children did likewise, and were then sent to sit at the back of the room, facing the opposite way to the rest. John, who was part of the group, flung his arms around Mary but she managed to wriggle free to sit between Thomas and Joseph. A plump young woman with a round, kind face appeared to be in charge, despite being only two or three years older than Mary. Her name, she said, was Betsy Copp.

Betsy wrote the shape of a letter on a slate. Surreptitiously, Mary used her fingernail to trace the same letter on the palm of her hand. It was an A, Betsy told them. It was the first letter of 'Adam'. She opened a well-worn book at the first page on which was printed a black-and-white picture of a sad-looking man and woman standing next to a tree with some words by the side. John pointed and laughed but was silenced with a frown.

'Listen now,' said Betsy, 'then say the words along of me. *"In Adam's fall we sinned all."* This yer man's Adam, see? Altogether now!'

The next letter, B, made Mary think of the buzzing of insects in summer, but Betsy said it stood for Bible and Book. 'B. *"Thy life to mend this book attend."*'

When they had worked through eight letters they went back to the beginning to repeat all the rhymes again. Mary found that with the help of the pictures she could remember them all and make the shape of the letters in her palm, but she noticed that Joseph was staring angrily at the floor. Betsy carefully counted some sheets of printed paper so that they might have one each.

'This yer's the alphabet for you to take home and learn. Mind you take care of it and don't get it mussed up or torn.'

Mary held her paper carefully. It was divided into squares, each of which held a letter and a picture printed in black. The pictures were different from the ones they had just learnt; here, A was an apple, and she thought B was a cow until Betsy said it was a bull. She folded it carefully in the way they were shown and tucked it under her shawl. It was the first thing she had ever been given to keep.

When they had joined the rest of the class, Mr Reed placed the Bible on a stand and started to read. It was the story of a shepherd boy named David whom God had chosen to be a future king because he had a good heart. There was a battle in which one of David's enemies was a giant called Goliath whom no one dared to fight, but David killed him with a stone from his sling. Mary nudged Thomas; they had all used slings fashioned from twigs and scraps of cloth to chase birds off newly-sown fields. Mr Reed showed them a coloured picture of David holding up Goliath's bloody head by the hair.

'He was a simple shepherd boy, David,' said Mr Reed, 'he wasn't rich and he had no armour when he went to fight, but God had chosen him because He saw into his heart. And *you*,' he gazed fiercely at the children, one by one, '*you* can fight on God's side, fight against evil wherever you meet'n, and defeat'n just as David defeated Goliath.'

Mary glanced sideways and saw that Thomas and Joseph were gazing open-mouthed at the picture.

After a long silence, Mr Reed put the Bible down on his table and told the children they must stand to sing a hymn, while Betsy pointed out the words on a sheet at the front of the class. Mary could not join in but she watched intently. If she could learn to read, perhaps one day *she* would be allowed to stand up at the front of the class, and to help the new children. She slipped her hand into her shawl to make sure that the sheet of paper carrying the alphabet was still safe.

After the hymn, three children, one of them a little boy of only five or six years, stood before the class to recite what Mr Reed called the Catechism; he asked questions to which the children had to reply with a learned response.

'Does the Saviour care for children?' demanded Mr Reed.

'Yes, for he said, "*Suffer the little children to come unto me, and forbid them not*,"' chanted the small boy.

'Was He once a child Himself?'

'Yes, and we read about his infancy in the Gospels of Saint…' The child stopped, looking horror-struck.

'Matthew,' prompted Mr Reed with a frown.

'SaintMatthewandSaintLuke,' the boy blurted out with relief.

One by one, the three children said their pieces. The older the child, the more words there were for them to remember and they had to get them exactly right, but their faces glowed with pride when they managed it. It seemed that they were to recite what they had learnt in the chapel in front of the assembled adults, because Mr Reed alternately praised them and threatened them with humiliation should they falter over their responses.

They all knelt for a final prayer before filing out of the schoolroom's close atmosphere and into bright sunlight and fresh air; the smaller children looked as though they would have liked to run across the grass, but Betsy hushed them and they all walked silently through the chapel door.

They entered a large plain room illuminated by sunlight that found its way through the arched windows to play on the whitewashed walls. Tightly-packed rows of people sat with their backs to the children and a dozen or so more stood behind. There was a subdued shuffling and clearing of throats as the chapel door closed.

'Welcome, children!'

The voice carried the warmth and conviction that Mary remembered so well, and she saw that there in front of them all stood Mrs Thorne.

'There are seats for you here at the front; do come and join us.'

Mrs Thorne waited, patient and smiling, as the children shuffled into the pews. Mary was right at the front, so close she could have reached out to touch her.

'First, let us sing.'

Thirza picked up a hymn book from the shelf in front of them and held it so that Mary could see, and as she scanned the page for the letters she now knew, the singing commenced. She looked up in astonishment. The impassioned and arousing voices filled the little chapel and echoed from the walls. It was like nothing she had heard before, and so loud she would have covered her ears if the sound had not been so enthralling.

> '*Love divine, all loves excelling,*
> *Joy of heav'n to earth come down.*'

She turned her head just a little to find the source of a particularly loud voice close by. Just across the aisle stood a man of middle age who rather resembled her father as she had last seen him, with face weathered and careworn; but this man had light in his eyes as he raised his head to allow his deep baritone voice to reach to the rafters of the chapel and beyond. Beside him, his wife, in a faded straw bonnet, sang in a higher pitch but was almost a match for him in volume, her chest rising as she took a sufficiently deep breath to see her through the next line.

Mary turned back to the hymn book and saw that as Thirza pointed at a second group of words, so the singing recommenced and this time she half-remembered the tune. As she started to hum quietly, she looked up and met Mrs Thorne's smiling gaze. At that moment she felt that going to chapel was the most wonderful thing she had ever experienced.

After the hymn, the three children recited their catechism. When they were warmly praised by Mrs Thorne, and by murmurs of appreciation and the occasional loud 'Amen' from the congregation, Mary resolved that one day she too would stand up there in front of everyone.

After some prayers and another rousing hymn, everyone filed quietly out into the open air and the atmosphere changed; whispered exchanges grew louder, there was laughter, and movement between the groups as people found their friends and relatives.

Mary drew close to Thomas. 'Did 'ee like it?' She saw at once that he shared her delight.

A woman, more shabbily dressed than many but with a kind face, put her hand on Mary's arm.

'You'm Charity Mitchell's maid, bain't 'ee? And be this your brother?'

Mary looked at her in amazement. 'Do 'ee know my Mam?'

The woman gave her a hug. 'Course I do, chiel. I remember when you was a little maid, and I see her most weeks when I visit my daughter in Buckland. 'Tis only just over there, remember!'

She pointed across the fields, their irregular outlines accentuated by darker green hedges and clusters of autumnal trees with, here and there, a huddle of farm buildings; the land dropped away from the high ridge on which the chapel stood before rising again to the horizon, and Mary saw, there against the dove-grey sky, the tiny but unmistakeable shape of Buckland Brewer's church tower. To its right she could just make out a spread of dark thatched roofs, but they were too distant to be identifiable.

'Takes me an hour to walk there,' the woman said, 'but then I live just down there, Tythecott, us has a little shop there.' She pointed down across the valley. 'I'll tell her I've seen 'ee.'

'Tell her... tell her "hello"', Mary said. The word did not begin to express what she was feeling. 'And ask her, are the little ones well? And has the pig been killed yet, or was it sold?'

Thomas was gazing at the woman too. 'Ask her, is my Da in work, and....' He looked lost for words. 'And can 'ee tell us next week what her says?'

It would be almost as good as hearing their mother speak, and the woman assured them that she would.

Throughout the exchange, Joseph had been scuffing his boots against the stone path, his mouth turned resolutely downward. When Mary suggested that the woman might know his mother also, he only shrugged, and did not respond when other well-wishers greeted them, or even when Mrs Thorne came to talk to them.

Eventually the crowd began to disperse. Mr and Mrs Phillips had left as soon as the service ended, so Mary began to feel apprehensive about being punished for returning late to the farm. As they set off, she carefully took the alphabet sheet from under her shawl. There was a picture of a pig, so the letter next to it must be a P, and that one stood for M.

'I s'll learn 'em all in time for next Sunday if I'm able. Sarah can help me. Will 'ee learn 'em too, Thomas?'

'I s'll try. And them tunes is still running through my head. I s'll practise them too.'

He looked happier than she had seen him for a long time. It would be harder for him to learn the alphabet; the other apprentices would tease him, and perhaps snatch the sheet away.

'I idn't gwain to do it,' said Joseph. His hands were thrust into his pockets and he kicked at the road as he walked. 'I don't wanna read. Shan't go to chapel next week.'

Mary glanced over at him, but did not reply. She knew his moods; if she tried to persuade him he was likely to become even more determined not to go to chapel and in his anger was likely to lash out at her. She was not going to allow Joseph or anyone else to spoil her day.

Chapter Thirteen

Mr Phillips shut the gate to Town Close behind him and strode towards the grazing bullocks, his boots hissing through the wet grass. The nearest animal lifted its head to stare at him, snuffling the air noisily before resuming its grazing. He scrutinised each animal in turn. They had lost condition since he bought them in the autumn; even now their ribs were visible under their dark red hides.

The weather had been unseasonably close and damp ever since the middle of May, week after week of overcast skies but no sign of proper rain. The grass had barely grown, and this followed the shortage of winter feed so it was no surprise that the bullocks were still underweight. He had been going to market every other Tuesday so that he could judge the best time to sell them, but there was little demand, even for those in peak condition. If he sold now, he would barely cover his costs, but meanwhile they continued to eat. His only consolation was that they were manuring the ground. This field could have been cut for hay if they were not grazing, though God knows it would have been a poor enough crop. Perhaps the light rain that had come in two days ago would go some little way towards producing some growth.

It had been the first winter that he had the two horses to feed, and he could scarcely believe how much they ate; there had been no hay to spare for the bullocks. By March the stacks were finished. His anger rose once more when he thought of the horses. They might be handsome creatures but they had been unable to plough the heavy ground at Twitching. After watching them struggling in the mud, their massive haunches almost on the ground as they tried to wrench the plough through waterlogged ground, he had bellowed at James to lead them away and bring out the oxen. He had knocked James down when he suggested that it had been a mistake to buy them; when the land was further improved they would come into their own, then he would be able to demonstrate that he knew what he was doing.

He continued to the far gate, slashing at thistles with his stick as he walked, thistles that should have been cut before now. The fortnightly trips to market had cost him time, and the loss of Sunday working was taking its toll. It was seven months ago that he had made the decision to keep the Sabbath; he had had no choice. The only way to replace the lost hours was by taking on extra workers but he had neither the money nor the accommodation for more paid labourers. He had tried to get some more apprentices but the Guardians had turned him down. Why? He would pay for their keep, save the ratepayers the expense! He had been told that fewer children were being sent out these days, but he did not believe it.

He no longer went to chapel every week. He disliked standing and kneeling alongside other people, his shoulders rubbing up against them, so he had taken to walking the farm on a Sunday. That wasn't work, nobody could say that it was. Today was the Sunday School Anniversary. He wanted no part in it because it would go on for hours with chitter-chatter and meddlesome questioning in between times. He had sent his wife, his children and the apprentices; that was quite enough.

The drizzle was now becoming heavier. He could feel the moisture from the wet grass seeping into his boots. They can't have been oiled the previous evening because the whole household had been taken up with preparations for the Anniversary celebrations, but he would ensure that the neglect was pointed out and punished. He paused and looked towards the sky in the south-west; the hills were indistinct, a sure sign that more rain was coming this way but perhaps not a lot. There had never been a summer like it.

He passed into Gratton, latched the gate and stood to admire the clean, levelled surface of the soil stretching away before him. This rain was just what the newly-sown turnip seed needed. He walked alongside the hedge, cast a cursory eye over the dairy cows in The Meadow, and passed on into Stone Park.

The potatoes here had been the first to be planted, the field being sheltered and much warmer at the end of March than the more exposed fields up at Twitching. The lines of fresh green foliage ran up across the field, each row perfectly parallel to its neighbour. The steadily-falling drizzle would be soaking down to the tubers causing them to swell and grow at last. If this was the end of the dry spell, there should be a good early crop which would command a good price at market. At last, something was going well.

The potato foliage alongside the far hedge caught his eye. He stared at it, then strode along the rough grassy verge that ran along the edge of the field. A rabbit thumped its foot and shot into its burrow deep in the hedge at his approach, and a blackbird chattered its alarm call. He bent to examine the potato foliage that had drawn his attention; the edges of the leaves were yellow, the colour spreading along the veins to reach the centre, and some stems had collapsed altogether, causing the leaves to turn brown. He straightened up and cast his eye across the field; the rows were bright green, he could see no other area like this. To make sure, he paced the four sides of the field, searching and appraising until he returned to his starting point. Had the area of damaged foliage increased? Of course not, he had been gone only a few minutes. He knelt on the damp earth and held a stem between his fingers whereupon it buckled, the leaves resting limply on his hand. Could this be the potato disease that was spoken of at market? He stared blankly at the sky to the south, the sultry moisture-laden breeze blowing against his face.

Mary held the hand of a small girl in the line of children. Betsy Copp was straightening the chairs on the wooden platform that Thomas and other boys had helped Mr Reed build in front of the chapel. When Betsy nodded, Mary ushered the children into a row facing the audience, nudging them into position and hushing one girl who was complaining loudly that another child had stepped on her foot.

'Stand straight, now. Keep yer hands still, William!' She spoke in a whisper, acutely aware of the large crowd of people who stood expectantly on the grass behind her. After a final frowned reminder to stand still, she stepped up on to the platform to take her place with the older girls, while the boys formed a row above them.

Now she was facing the audience. She smoothed down her hair which was damp from the light rain blowing in on the breeze, and stood up straight with her hands clasped in front of her in the way they had been taught. There were a lot of people, more than two hundred, so Betsy said. Mary wanted to turn away but had she not just told the little ones to look straight ahead? Shyly, she allowed her eyes to travel across the sea of faces, all of them visible to her because the ground rose away from the chapel, and she listened to the low hum of conversation as people chatted happily to their neighbours. There was Mrs Richards who brought messages from her mother, there was Mrs Brook, the carrier's wife, who had found a white pinafore for Mary to wear on this special occasion, and at the back were Thirza's family, and Mrs Phillips, looking less anxious than usual. Then, through the gate came Sarah and James, hurrying to take their places in the crowd. Sarah had said she would try to come! Mary could not help smiling when their eyes met. She began to relax; these people were her friends.

Mr Reed stepped forward and waited imperiously for the audience to be silent. He welcomed everyone to Salem Chapel at Thornhillhead, and then told them that a very special guest was to speak to them. To Mary's amazement, who should appear but Mrs Thorne. Mary had not seen her standing at the edge of the crowd and was not the only one to gasp with pleasure.

Mrs Thorne stood before the crowd, so close that Mary could see wisps of hair below her bonnet whipped to and fro in the wind.

'Dear Friends, what a pleasure it is to see you all here at Salem Chapel to help us celebrate our Anniversary today!'

It was several months since Mary had last heard her speak in chapel, but she had not forgotten that strong, clear voice which compelled everyone to listen intently, and made Mary feel proud to be part of the Bible Christian family.

When Mrs Thorne had finished her address, she asked everyone to listen attentively so that the children could be heard, then she stepped aside and Mr Reed turned to face the platform. Mary could feel butterflies fluttering nervously in her stomach.

The first hymn was one of Mary's favourites.

> *'Come, let our voices join*
> *In one glad song of praise.'*

She knew the words of this hymn and many others off by heart now, and often sang quietly to herself while she was working on the farm. As she relished the feel of the warm and comfortable words rolling around her mouth, '*Redeemer's love, brightest glories, heavenly truths,*' she could, for a few moments, forget her exhaustion and her cold, muddy hands, she could dream of the glorious life that was to come as long as she followed God's commandments. If she stole or told lies, there was the certainty of burning for ever in a pit of fire, but she could console herself with the thought that she had not sinned and, if she ever did, hell could surely be no worse than Gusland.

When they reached the end of the hymn, it was the turn of a boy behind Mary to give his recitation. She managed to catch Thomas's eye. Standing further along the row, he looked very adult in the jacket he had been lent, and there was a quick spark of humour and recognition in his glance before he concentrated again on looking straight ahead.

When the boy had completed his recitation with only a brief stumbling over the words, Mr Reed again fixed them with his stare to prepare them for the next hymn. Mary's stomach fluttered; it would soon be her turn.

When the hymn came to an end, Mr Reed stood aside and Betsy turned to smile encouragement. Mary lifted her head high and took a deep breath.

There was movement at the far edge of the audience. Some latecomers were hurrying through the gate, a woman ushering children, a man following behind.

"*But you…*"' prompted Betsy in a whisper.

The newcomers found a place to stand at the edge of the crowd. The woman bent down to the children; she pointed towards the platform.

Mary could not move. It was her family; it was her parents and her sisters.

'Mary!' Betsy's whisper was louder this time.

No words would come. She looked at Betsy who nodded frantically at her to begin.

"*But you, Lord, are a shield around me.*"' The words were scarcely audible, and her voice unsteady. She took a deep breath; gradually her voice gained strength.

> "*I lie down and sleep;*
> *I wake again, because the Lord sustains me.*
> *I will not fear though tens of thousands*
> *assail me on every side.*"'

She knew, by the end, that her words could be heard right across the enclosure and out on to the road. The audience applauded. Her legs were shaking. She looked across the upturned faces of the crowd to meet her mother's eyes, and she could not look away. She realised she was crying. As the next hymn commenced she glanced back at Thomas, seeing from his startled expression that he too had seen their parents arrive.

The rest of the performance passed as if in a dream. She stood, and she sang, and she managed to remain on the platform when every nerve in her body was screaming at her to jump down and run to her mother and father. Finally the audience applauded for the last time, Mr Reed announced that tea would soon be served, and the children were given the order to step down from the platform. Mary felt suddenly shy. She held back to wait for Thomas and together they walked through the crowd to where their parents stood.

'Well now!'

Their mother held them both at arm's length for a moment to look into their faces, then drew them close, and Mary was enveloped in the embrace that she had dreamed of so often, the rough woollen shawl against her face and the warm breath in her hair.

'Standing up there so grown-up and important, the both of 'ee! Where did 'ee learn all them words?'

The warmth and humour in Mrs Mitchell's voice was so wonderfully familiar that Mary felt the tension in her body melting away.

'Us learned it in Sunday School! And I can read now, Mam, not all the words but a lot of 'em, and Thomas too, though he's not quite so good at it as me.' She looked apologetically at her brother.

'I don't have no one to help me, I could do it better if I did.'

Mrs Mitchell shook her head in wonder.

Mary's father, though watching admiringly, was standing back a little with his cap in his hand. Mary sensed that having so many people around him was making him ill at ease but she felt too shy to approach him. She had not seen him since she left home four years ago; he seemed a stranger to her.

'You can have tea soon, Da, us can all have tea together and there's cakes too!'

He nodded. 'Say hello to your sisters now, chiel.'

The three girls were waiting shyly, Ann and Maria perfectly recognisable although much taller; and the smallest girl, although unknown to Mary, had a strong family resemblance.

'Do 'ee know your big sister?' she asked them. She longed to embrace them but there was wariness in their eyes which made her hesitate. Jane put her thumb in her mouth and stared at Mary in silence.

'Course us do!' Anne's voice wavered a little as she took a step forward. Mary went to her immediately, pulling Maria and little Jane into her arms as well. Memories flooded back of the time before her apprenticeship when she and her sisters spent their days and nights in intimate proximity, their faces, their limbs and their moods as familiar to her as her own.

'Look, Thomas, Mary, you've Mr Fulford to thank for us being yer! There he is, 'fraid to come in, he is!' Her mother pointed back towards the road.

Mary looked up from where she knelt on the grass and saw, leaning on the iron fence that enclosed the chapel, a stout man with a smiling face that she half-recognised. It seemed a long time since he had taken them to the Workhouse in Bideford.

'He drove us all yer! First time the chiels have been in a cart so 'tis a proper adventure for 'em. Can he have some tea, do 'ee think? He wasn't sure, what with him being Wesleyan and not related or nothing.'

'I reckon he can,' said Thomas, 'I'll ask Mr Reed.'

Mary stood up. 'Us has to get ready for the procession to the Moor where us is going to have tea. Us can all sit together when 'tis ready.' She and Thomas had helped to carry the tables and chairs to Thorne Moor earlier on, and she saw that the other children were now lining up behind the banner that would lead everyone there.

'Come here, maid! 'Tis so good to see 'ee.' As her mother held Mary's face in her hands, Mary winced at the sudden pain.

'What's that? Did I hurt 'ee?'

She saw the concern in her mother's face. ''Tis nothing. I slipped going through a gate and banged myself.' She wriggled from her mother's grasp and hurried off to help the smaller children line up.

Had she told a lie? Certainly she hadn't told the truth, but if her mother knew that Mr Phillips had slapped her, badly bruising her ear and knocking her down, it would spoil her day. God surely wouldn't want that.

She hadn't even done anything wrong. It had happened when she was out weeding with Joseph, Lewis and John. She had known when they were sent out together that the day would not go well and had been careful to keep herself to herself, to continue working in silence whatever they said or did, because she had learned that fighting back just made things worse. It was always Lewis who started it. This time he was making jokes about Mr Phillips taking one of the cows to the bull. As his talk became more and more vulgar, so John and Joseph's laughter grew louder. Mary knew that John did not fully understand all the depravities uttered by Lewis but he understood enough to find it funny, and was encouraged by Joseph's raucous laughter.

Then Lewis changed tack. 'You'm as big as a bull, John! Show us what the bull does, John! Look, there be the cow!' And he pointed to where Mary was bent double over the weeds.

She straightened up as John stumbled towards her with his huge moon face creased with laughter and his hands pulling at the fastening of his breeches, and she knew that at the very least she would be knocked forcefully to the ground by the clumsy weight of him. She did not have time to think but as he bore down on her she kicked out hard and caught him right between the legs. He fell to the ground howling with rage and pain, and it was then that Mr Phillips appeared.

He did not stop to ask what had happened, although she realised later that he must have heard the taunts and the laughter as he approached, and she suddenly found herself lying amongst the barley with a terrific pain and ringing in her ear.

Later, when they walked silently home along the lane in the sultry warmth of evening, John ran to catch up with her and slouched along beside her.

'Mary hurt John.' His lower lip was pushed forward like that of a sulky three-year-old child.

She sighed. He had no understanding of what had happened.

'You was bad, John. You was going to hurt me. You'm not a bull, John, you'm a man. You mustn't do things like that, 'tis rude, do 'ee understand, John?'

'Yes,' he said unhappily. 'I like you, Mary. You'm my friend. Do 'ee like me, Mary?'

She had nodded wearily. It was Lewis she hated, not John. But since then, she had avoided him.

The children lined up. Immediately behind the banner were three musicians with a bass viol, a flute and a clarinet, then came Mrs Thorne, followed by Mr Fry the chapel steward, Mr Morris who often came to the chapel to preach, Mr Reed and Betsy Copp, and then the children in twos starting with the smallest, and all the adults following on behind. The musicians struck up with '*Nearer My God to Thee*' and off they went, marching in time to the music, and singing at the top of their voices. They passed out on to the lane; when they reached the crossroads Mary turned around and saw that the crowd was so large, the last few stragglers were still passing through the gate.

It was only a short distance to the Moor where some of the women from the chapel were waiting, having not liked to leave the tea-things unattended. By the time everyone was seated, the light rain had ceased and the breeze had lost some of its strength, so the white cloths covering the wooden trestle tables did not flap quite so alarmingly, and the slices of buttered bread and wedges of cake piled high on the plates could be uncovered without becoming damp. Mary had offered to fill the cups from one of the heavy pitchers of tea, but had been told that it was the turn of the children to be waited on, so she sat contentedly between her parents while everyone talked and drank and ate until they could eat no more. Her parents told her stories of the village, and she explained the routine of the Sunday School and the people she had met there. She said little about the farm except to talk of Sarah, who was smiling and whispering with James further along the table; but she could hear that Thomas was talking animatedly with his father about which farms in the parish were the best on which to work. It was a subject he liked to discuss with James, who had some knowledge of the surrounding area, having sometimes accompanied Mr Phillips to market and to the lime kiln. During dinner breaks, many of James's conversations with Thomas started with '*When I leave this place...*' James had only a few months of his apprenticeship left to complete, but Thomas had seven years left and Mary eight. She could not comprehend such a length of time and preferred not to think of it, particularly today of all days.

Mr Fulford, who was sitting just across the table from her, was deep in conversation with Mr Stapledon, a farmer who lived less than a mile from Thornhillhead. She understood from their talk that they both had relatives who had gone or were planning to go across the sea to Upper Canada. Before long, Thomas, too, was listening intently.

'My cousin, he's doing very well for himself,' Mr Stapledon was saying. 'He's bought land, a good-sized farm and it's all his own, and the prices he gets for produce and stock, well, you couldn't get near it here, nowhere near at all. 'Tis no wonder so many are going.'

'My cousins say the same,' said Mr Fulford, 'They plan to go in a year or two. But can't be the same, can it now, as being in the place where 'ee was born and all your family around 'ee. 'Twouldn't suit me at all.'

'But then, with so many gone and plenty more thinking on it, you *have* got your family around you in the end, haven't 'ee? And so many of them being Chapel people, they've built Meeting Houses wherever they need them because land is so cheap and there's no one to say you shouldn't, and you haven't got the Church people looking down their noses at 'ee and demanding tithes and I don't know what. I'd think of going, I would really, if I were a bit younger.'

Mr Fulford leaned back on his chair and shook his head ruefully. 'Well, it's not for me, but I do think us'll see more and more going, because I reckon things is going to get harder round here, I can see it coming and things idn't easy now, especially for those who are hard-pressed.'

Mary followed the conversation with interest. It was extraordinary to think of people setting off across the sea on a journey that took many weeks, knowing that they would never come back.

'Can just anyone go?' she asked.

'Well, yes, chiel, anyone that has the wherewithal.' Mr Fulford smiled at her, his eyes twinkling. 'Be 'ee making plans then?'

'No, not really.' She glanced over at Thomas. She could not make plans. She had to stay at Gusland.

When everyone had eaten and drunk their fill, it was time to return to the chapel.

'Us must go now, chiel,' Mary's father told her, 'us have kept Mr Fulford away from his home long enough.'

She looked over to where the children were beginning to line up again, and she felt her eyes fill with tears.

'You'll all come again next year, won't 'ee?' It seemed such a very long time, but she knew she could not have dreamed of even an annual meeting with her family before she started attending chapel.

They said their farewells, then her parents and sisters walked alongside the procession until they reached the crossroads where Mr Fulford waited with his cart. While Mary walked and sang behind the banner with Thomas at her side, she turned several times to see the cart descending the hill in the warm evening light, and her family waving, until they disappeared from view.

The day after the Sunday School Anniversary Mr Phillips went out at dawn, striding past his daughters as they brought the cows into the yard to milk. He felt the dampness in the warm breeze settling on his shirtsleeves, having not felt the need to wear a jacket despite the early hour. He returned first to Kitty Park where the potatoes were planted in mid-April and had recently been hilled up for the final time. He could see that the foliage was dark green and healthy despite the half-light of early morning; he paced right around the field until he was convinced that there were no areas of damage. Returning to the lane, he walked quickly for half a mile until he reached Higher Twitching. Here, the hedges were of no great height, having been planted only when the land was enclosed a few generations back, so he could see the fields of

Twitching Moor, High Botown and Higher Westaway neatly portioned out in green, brown and dun according to the crop that grew there. As usual, it gave him a moment's satisfaction to see cultivation where there had before been only rough grazing and waste, but he had not come here to admire. Over there was twelve acres of potatoes, beyond the wheat field another eight acres, and in Higher Westaway was five acres of potatoes. These fields, being on high, exposed ground, had not been planted until May but the foliage was already reappearing after being hilled up for the first time. All had appeared vigorous yesterday and seemed so again today, but he would not trust first impressions. He walked the circumference of each field in turn, and only when his scrutiny was complete was he able to breathe more easily. Most of his potato grounds were healthy; it was solely Stone Park that was affected. Perhaps this morning the plants there would be recovering. He did not say a prayer exactly but he murmured a few words as he glanced up at the sky, and he began to retrace his steps.

He reached the field, passed through the gate and walked slowly around it. The damage was not extensive, some yellowed leaves here, a drooping stem over there, but it was unmissable; more plants were affected.

It must be the warm, moist air and the lack of rainfall. The weather was unusual, it was bound to affect the crops, but it did not mean that this was the potato disease. He stood there for several minutes, staring blankly at the plants. When there was some proper rainfall they would pick up; they needed rain, that was all.

The first rumbles of thunder came three days later at midday, becoming more frequent until, at three o'clock, the rain began to fall. So heavy was it, within the hour water was running down the fields in rivulets and gathering in large pools in gateways. In the late afternoon he ordered the apprentices off the newly-sown fields and set them to work in the yard; no birds would be feeding in this rain.

The storms and heavy rain continued for four days. On the fifth day he found potato disease in Kitty Park. By the seventh day it had spread to Twitching Moor, High Botown and Higher Westaway.

Chapter Fourteen

'Thomas, what shall I do when 'tis your turn to go?' Mary leaned for a moment on her rake. The thought had been nagging at her ever since they had watched James walking away from the farm that morning, never to return.

Thomas paused in his raking of the stubble field and smiled at her. 'You? You'd manage better without me than I would without you! You've got Sarah to look out for 'ee but who've I got now James is gone, 'cept you?' He pulled a sad face. 'Any case, 'tis years off yet.' He continued with his work.

'Time'll pass though, 'twill come one day.' She could not bear the thought of being at Gusland without Thomas, but when he reached twenty-one she would have to stay on for more than a year.

He had told her of the conversations that had taken place the previous night in the linhay. Having finally completed the last day of his apprenticeship, James had not been inclined to sleep, but had talked at length of his plans. He had secured a living-in position at a farm near Langtree where he would be earning seven shillings a week, and he hoped to be able to save most of his wages so that he and Sarah could marry and set up home together eventually. They might even sail for Canada one day, he said, and leave this place behind.

Mary had seen them that morning from her bedroom window saying their final farewells under the eaves of the barn. Perhaps she should not have stayed to watch, but such tenderness and heartfelt emotion was rarely seen at Gusland; the image of Sarah's uplifted face and the passion in James's gestures as he caressed her hair and ran his hand along the back of her skirt stayed with Mary all day. When Sarah had gone indoors to cry, Thomas and Mary watched from the yard as James strode towards the gate carrying only the clothes on his back, and turned to give them a vigorous wave of his hand before he disappeared around the corner.

His departure had unsettled them all. Quite apart from the desire they all had to leave, he was the one who had provided the voice of reason, calmed their anxieties, suppressed Lewis's more vicious taunts and beatings and had given advice on ways of working to avert Mr Phillips' anger. Thomas pretended to be sanguine about it but Mary knew from comments he had made during the day that he was ill at ease, and Joseph had been very subdued as they worked together in the barley field.

It seemed that James was not to be replaced but it was a puzzle to know how the work could be completed without him. Already they were working longer hours than previously, often being sent out after supper to sweep the yard, stack firewood or pick up apples until it was too dark to see. They expected to work longer hours during harvest, but these extra demands had been made before the harvest commenced and were likely to continue after it was finished.

Today, their supper had been brought out to them so that they could continue clearing the field until it grew dark. Mr Phillips, in a hurry to cut the final field of barley before the weather broke, had moved on with the other workers, leaving Thomas and Mary to clear the ground alone.

'How much more shall us do before us stops to eat?' Mary asked, leaning on her rake again. The sun was low now; she admired the gold and pink streaks it lent to the sky, a welcome distraction from the burning muscles in her arms and the stinging of her calves which were bleeding from the constant pricking of the straw.

'Let's get as far as the hedge and then stop. Us can finish after supper.'

She raked the straw into a swathe, bound it and stacked it next to a stook. 'There, that'll do.'

Leaning back against the hedgebank, she stared up at the vastness of the sky. The land fell away from this field until it reached the narrow valley below Gusland, then rose again to the moors around Thornhillhead Chapel some three miles away, so, when looking up, all she could see was sky. The cloud was increasing, vast stretches of it rising from some hidden place like smoke and, at an inconceivable distance far above, still more cloud glowed softly in the sun's rays. Somewhere amongst it a skylark was singing, but she could not locate it however hard she tried.

She waited until Thomas came to sit next to her by the hedge before unfolding the cloth containing their bread, cheese and apples. A flock of glossy starlings wheeled in to land tentatively in the middle of the field, their brown and purple plumage gleaming against the yellow stubble as they strutted and hopped nervously before deciding they were safe from interference, whereupon they proceeded to probe the disturbed ground for stray grain and insects.

Mary took a bite of apple and picked up the booklet which had been presented to her at Sunday School for good progress in reading. Her most prized possession, it had been wrapped in her shawl and left by the hedge until she had a chance to look at it again. Thomas had been given one too but was less enamoured of it, not least because he could not read it before bed for fear of it being snatched away by Lewis.

She admired the drawing on the cover again and ran her finger under the words.

"*The Child's Magazine.*" She moved her finger to the words at the bottom of the page. "*Printed and sold by S. Thorne, Prospect Place, Shebbear.*"

S. Thorne was Mrs Thorne's husband. Each time she read the words she pictured him as a plump, kindly man surrounded by his children. She turned to page seven which was as far as she had read.

'Shall I read to you, Thomas?'

'Hm-mm.'

He had his eyes closed, but she knew he would not actually go to sleep.

"*God watches over us, he gives us health and strength of body.*" Some of the words were very hard so she had to attempt them several times before she could put the sounds together correctly. "*He provides for the fatherless and the widow.*"

Thomas opened his eyes. 'The Workhouse does that!'

168

'Be quiet and listen! *"And who, whosoever puts his trust in God will be pro, provided with all that is good for him."*'

Thomas opened his eyes again and frowned. ''Tis hard to see how.'

'Well, p'raps us doesn't trust in Him enough yet for it to happen. Listen, this is more interesting.'

She read him a story on a previous page which she had learned already. It was about a bird called an ostrich, '"*tallest and largest of birds, taller than a man on horseback, the head and bill are small, resembling those of a duck, its eye has lashes like that of a man.*" Thomas, shall us see one, do 'ee think, one day? Think of it!'

She leaned back against the hedge, tired with the effort of reading. In her imagination she pictured an ostrich walking along the lane with Mrs Thorne by its side; what a sight that would be!

They were both succumbing to sleep when, hearing voices from the next field, they jumped up guiltily to look over the gate. The field, adjoining the dilapidated Higher Twitching cottages, was rented from Mr Phillips by his labourers for the growing of potatoes. The voices belonged to old Mr Judd and John Dean; with them were Mary Ann and her younger siblings.

'Mary Ann!' Mary waved as the group made their way to the gate. Mary Ann had joined in the work on the barley field the previous day but Mr Phillips had set such a pace that there had not been time to exchange more than a few words. Mary Ann had managed to tell her that she was soon to go off to work on a farm a couple of miles away but, unlike Mary, she was to work in and around the farmhouse and would be paid two shillings a week in addition to living in.

'Come in along of us!' Mary called. 'Me and you can work together!'

The time would pass more quickly in Mary Anne's company, she thought, but as the group approached, they all looked downcast.

'Us may as well start yer,' said Mr Judd, 'Get the worst over first.'

The field, like all the potato fields, was home to black and withered plants with only small areas of green leaves dying back in the way they should. The extent of the damage was not yet known, but they all dreaded the effect the commencement of the potato harvest would have on Mr Phillips' mood.

'Be 'em ready to lift, Mr Judd?' asked Thomas, leaning on the gate.

'Who knows, boy, but us is going to have a look. Us can't hold off no longer, waiting and worriting.'

Mary knew the importance the potato grounds held for the labourers because her father had the same arrangement with a neighbouring farmer. He rented a piece of ground which was ploughed and manured by the farmer, then the rest of the work – sowing, earthing up and digging – was down to him. Some of the potatoes were sold to pay the farmer the two pounds rent while the rest fed the family throughout the winter, spring and early summer. Without the potatoes, they would starve.

John Dean pushed his cap back on his head. He had been harvesting all day and his face was thick with dust.

'The maister's been watching us,' he told Thomas, 'He wouldn't let us dig until us had paid the rent.' He spat into the hedge.

'In my granfer's day,' said Mr Judd, 'Twitching Moors over there was all common land. Us could keep a few sheep there and a pig or two, and try to grow a few teddies in the parts that wasn't too cledgy. But now he's got it all fenced in and it's for nobody but hisself to use. 'Tisn't right, not in my way of thinking.' He gazed out across the potato field. 'But there, us must get on.'

Mr Judd walked amongst the potato plants, studying them carefully, his lower lip thrust out in thought.

'This yer's about the worst of it,' he said, 'so us'll find out the worst and hold out some hope for the rest.'

He pushed his fork into the soil alongside the blackened, withered leaves. As he eased the fork up and the soil fell away, they could see three or four medium-sized potatoes.

They all waited in silence as Mr Judd took one in his hands and brushed off the soil.

'There, look at that. Land sakes!'

The potato was uneven in shape with brown marks on the skin but as Mr Judd pressed his fingers against it, the potato collapsed into a handful of mush and the most fearful smell emanated from it.

'Urgh!' They all took a step back and covered their noses.

'Grandad! Don't do that no more!' shouted Mary Ann's younger brother.

Mr Judd was staring in disbelief at the mushy potato in his hand. 'Never in my born days…'

He shook the mess away, wiped his hand on the grass growing at the base of the hedge then poked at the remaining potatoes with the fork, whereupon the dreadful smell wafted up again.

'They'm not all that way, not all of 'em!' John Dean shouted, as he snatched the fork from his father-in-law and thrust it into the ground a few feet away. But the same thing happened, and he had to hastily bury the plants again.

'Try yer, boy, the leaves yer, they'm not so bad, there's a bit of green in 'em still.'

This time the potatoes he brought up were firmer and able to withstand pressure but their appearance was odd.

'Us can eat them, they'm not stinking. They'll be more like that, see, the leaves over there, they'm not too bad.'

Mr Judd was trying to reassure, but as they stood staring out at the darkening field, they could all see that more than half of the crop was badly affected.

'Us'll dig what us can next week when the leaves is all died back, there'll be more time evenings, now harvest's finished. Us'll store what us can.' He scratched his head.

John Dean did not reply. Mary saw his eyes grow hard and cold, then he threw the fork down and strode angrily back to the house.

'What'll us eat, Grandad?' Mary Ann's voice was thin and tremulous.

Mr Judd was silent for several moments as he stared down at the rotting plants, and his back seemed more bowed than usual. He sighed.

'I dunno, chiel, but us'll manage someways. Us have managed this far.'

He gathered up the few healthy potatoes and they walked slowly back to the cottage together, too downhearted to say goodbye to Thomas and Mary.

Ten days later Mary waited morosely in Stone Park with all the other workers, while a fine drizzle settled on their hair and on their clothes. They had been told the previous evening that they were to gather there right after breakfast to start the potato harvest, but there was no sense of excitement such as often accompanied the hay or corn harvest. Mr Phillips' temper was already bad due to the mediocre crops that had been gathered in, and they all knew that it was likely to get worse. There had been no meal to celebrate harvest home. The labourers always complained that it was a half-hearted affair at the best of times, merely a token dinner in the farmhouse kitchen with none of the drinking, music and dancing that took place on other farms. This year it had not taken place at all, and they felt cheated. There was no doubt that the potato harvest would not improve the maister's mood.

John Begalhole led out the two horses. He harnessed them to the plough which had been made ready along with the baskets and sacks for collecting the potatoes. When he was done, Mr Phillips strode into the field and right up to the group of waiting labourers. Mary felt them all draw back a little.

He scowled at them. 'You all know there's disease in the teddies. These'll do,' he held up a darkened, misshapen potato, 'but them's that's rotten, leave them be to be ploughed back in. But I'll have no sound ones left behind, you're to pick up all the ones you *can* pick up. There'll be little enough.'

Turning on his heel, he took up the reins, spoke to the horses and together they moved slowly on to the field.

Mary took her place on the newly-ploughed ground along with the five adult labourers, four other apprentices and the three Phillips boys – even five-year-old Henry was working today. Usually the sight of the cream-coloured potatoes partly exposed on the dark soil brought back happy memories of the potato harvest on her father's piece of rented ground, when the whole family would go out to collect in the crop that would feed them for the next year, the little ones helping by toddling to the basket with a large potato clutched to their chests, and the latest baby lying on a potato sack nearby. It was a day of merriment when they would laugh at the odd and sometimes rude shapes of some potatoes, compete with each other to be the first to fill the basket, and hazard guesses as to how many sacks would be filled this year. Although the work at Gusland was never fun, and the size of the fields meant that the days were long and of back-breaking intensity, there was usually some satisfaction to be gained from gathering in the harvest.

But not today. After picking up a few rotten potatoes Mary quickly learned which ones to avoid, but the stench remained on her hands and clothes, and wafted up from the others left on the ground. On either side of her she could hear the workers swearing under their breath when they inadvertently picked up a bad potato. When Lewis threw one at Joseph, hitting him on the side of the face so that the stinking mush slid down to his neck, she glared at him.

'You do that again and I s'll stuff one into your mouth and right down your throat.'

The strength of her hatred and the intensity of her resolve must have made an impression on Lewis because, for once, he did not respond.

After ploughing a few lengths of the field, Mr Phillips handed over to Mr Begalhole and walked over the ground that had been cleared. There was tension amongst the workers as he paced in silence. When he went to the sacks that had been filled and tipped one out on the ground, they all watched surreptitiously while their hands continued to seek out sound potatoes to put in the baskets.

'What be'm up to now?' muttered Mr Judd.

Mr Phillips was staring morosely down at the potatoes as he turned them over with his foot, then he walked away and leant on the gate with his back to the field. One after another the workers, still bent double over the ploughed earth, lifted their faces to glance apprehensively at the maister's back.

'You'm all to speed up!' The roar, when it came, made them all jump. Mr Judd stood up painfully and turned to face Mr Phillips.

'Us can scarcely go any faster, maister!'

'You can and you will! This field's to be cleared today and Kitty Park too. If you'm not finished by dark I s'll bring out lanterns 'cos these teddies are going to market tomorrow. And all the other fields to be cleared by the end of the week ready for next Tuesday's market. Now get on with it!'

Mr Judd shook his head. 'Us can't do a proper job, maister, if us is racing along like that! Us'll miss good 'uns or pick up bad 'uns...'

He was not given the chance to finish.

'You'll do it or you'm leaving this farm!'

Mary feared for a moment that he would knock Mr Judd down, but instead he strode off and, snatching the reins from Mr Begalhole, took over the ploughing again.

It seemed that the day would never end. Every half hour or so they were berated for being too slow. Once, Mary was sent sprawling into the mud for missing sound potatoes. She, Mr Judd and Joseph were the main targets of Mr Phillips' anger because it was almost impossible for them to keep up with the stronger workers. The smallest Phillips boy was sent home in the afternoon. The rain intensified, running down Mary's arms and dripping off her nose, and both she and the potatoes were coated in mud. When Mr Phillips was not near, Mr Judd kept up a running commentary under his breath.

'Folks idn't gwain to buy teddies like this; they'm not gwain to know if they'm buying teddies or mud and stones. Dunno what the maister's thinking on.'

They finished clearing Kitty Park just as it became too dark to see. They walked away dejectedly, the labourers to their cottages and the apprentices to the farm, where Mary took her turn at the pump, sluicing off the mud which had crept up her arms and legs and under her clothes.

The next day they had the luxury of straightening occasionally to ease their backs, but they did not otherwise dare to lessen their pace, despite Mr Phillips' absence.

When night fell, Mary returned to the farm with Thomas. They fetched and stacked more firewood before supper, and were the last to enter the kitchen. Mary immediately sensed the tense atmosphere. The family sat around the table in silence, not an unusual occurrence in itself, but today Mrs Phillips sat staring ahead without touching her food and the children were barely eating. Even the older ones glanced fearfully up at their father, who was eating his dinner stolidly as if nothing had happened. Moving quietly, Mary took her plate over to the pot in the fireplace to be filled, but when Sarah turned towards her to take it, she saw that the girl was crying silently. Shocked, Mary placed her hand gently on Sarah's arm but she just shook her head pleadingly.

'Tomorrow us'll take the teddies to Stone Park.' Everyone flinched when Mr Phillips suddenly broke the silence, but it was the apprentices he was addressing, and his voice was even louder and more threatening than usual.

'I habn't sold 'em so they'm going in a pit to store 'til such time as the price is worth taking. You knows what to do, Lewis, so see to it that you do a proper job, and I'll come along to thatch 'n. But you,' he was addressing Mary now. 'You'm going to get the cows in and milk 'em along of Rosa, feed the pigs and fowls too. Then you'm to come out to the fields. Same every day from now on.'

She was stunned. What had brought about this change? Lucy and Rosa always milked the cows together. She raised her eyes carefully to look at the two girls, but they were staring down at their plates. It seemed that no one dared to move or to comment. She met Thomas's gaze and wordlessly they shared their disquiet.

When the meal was over, she went straight up to bed and lay between the cold sheets, her thoughts in turmoil. Usually she slept before Sarah came to bed but tonight she could neither sleep nor read her magazine. She heard the rest of the family come upstairs in silence, then after another long wait with only the sound of the wind and the rain against the window, Sarah opened the door.

Mary sat up. 'What be gwain on? Why be I working with Rosa? I don't know nothing about the cows.' She spoke in a whisper and, quietly, Sarah began to cry again.

'I be leavin'. Tomorrow. He don't want me here no more.'

'Leavin?' She couldn't take it in. 'Why?'

Sarah sat down heavily on the bed. 'I dunno, Mary. Money, I suppose, things idn't going well for him. He thinks Lucy can do my work, that's why you'm having to do her morning chores. What am I going to tell my Mam? What with the poor harvest and all, her needs my wage!' She curled up miserably on the bed.

'But he can't just let you go like that! With no notice!'

'He can. 'Tis Michaelmas tomorrow! He never took no heed of it before, each year I've just carried on the same but he always had the right to let me go. And he says he's going to mark the day by killing a goose for good luck in the future. Good luck for him, maybe.' She sat up and kicked angrily at the leg of the bed. 'I hate him! I'm glad I never have to see his face again, nor the Missis neither!'

Michaelmas; it marked the beginning of dark evenings and the coming of winter. She had not known it to be observed at Gusland, but it had always been an important day at home because it was the day when her father would seek out work for the coming year. If he was successful, it was a day for celebration, but if not, then it was a day of foreboding.

'My work's done now. I'm leaving first thing, don't even have to do the breakfast.' Sarah's voice was shaky, wavering like the candle flame that sent shadows flickering and dancing across the wall. 'I'll tell my Mam then I'll walk from farm to farm 'til I find work. I'll go out of the parish if I have to. Mebbe I'll go to Langtree, try to find James.'

'Do 'ee know the way?'

'No!' She looked stricken. 'And I don't want to make trouble for him in his new job, turning up like that. But I must get word to him someways.'

'But Sarah,' Mary's throat was dry, 'what about me? I'll be all alone! Will I be allowed to sleep up here without 'ee? Will I have to go back out with the boys?' She almost wished that she would, because she did not like the thought of sleeping alone with the Phillips family so close by, and Mr Phillips always so angry, and things getting worse every day.

'Oh, I be going to miss you, maid!' Sarah sat up and put her arms around Mary. 'But you'll be able to sleep here, I'm sure, they don't need the room for no one else.'

Mary cuddled into her and they cried together for a while until Sarah eventually fell asleep, but Mary lay awake and restless for a long time, fearful of what the future might bring.

Chapter Fifteen

When he had passed the last cottage in Monkleigh, Reverend Harding urged his horse to a trot. It was good to be outdoors. The February weather had so far been harsh; first a week of snow, then a week of high winds and driving rain, but today was at last dry and bright even if there was a bitterly cold breeze. His wife had pleaded with him to stay at home because there had been a heavy frost this morning which lingered in the lee of hedges and on frozen mud in gateways, but he had been confined indoors for too long, and his horse needed the exercise as much as he did. Besides, it was important that those in authority were seen to be out and about in these difficult times.

He reached Catsborough Cross and took the turning for Buckland Brewer. The lane descended gradually at first giving him a clear view over the hedgebanks into the surrounding fields. He saw no labourers at work; at this time of year most were employed around the farm buildings, carrying out repairs, winnowing, and tending to the animals that were kept in during the winter. The empty fields sometimes then became the target of those who were under-employed and hungry; he suspected that the instances of prosecution for illegal trapping or the theft of turnips and other winter crops represented only a small part of the problem, many other cases going undetected. He had even heard of cows being surreptitiously milked under cover of darkness, so when he spotted two men skulking behind a hedge at a field's distance he stood up in the stirrups and hailed them.

'Hullo there! Show yourselves immediately!'

When the men moved into view, they proved to be merely labourers clearing a ditch. He gave them a prolonged stare and knew that they would continue to watch him nervously when he trotted on. It did no harm for the lower classes to be aware that they were being observed.

As the lane descended steeply into the cold, narrow valley, the roar of the water wheel at Buckland Mill told him that the mill leat was running, but the little streams that had seeped from the fields and across the deeply-shadowed lane were still frozen; a flock of redwing and fieldfare chattered in the hawthorns, a common sight during a cold spell. His horse stumbled a little in the frozen ruts and he was relieved to eventually climb out of the valley and back into the comparative warmth of the sunshine.

After another mile he reached Buckland Brewer. The village was a tidy enough place and its inhabitants were honest on the whole, but neglect had allowed Methodism to take hold even within the shadow of the church tower, and the remote areas of the parish abounded in criminality. This was particularly concerning now that there was no longer to be a Magistrates' Meeting in the village; his colleagues all agreed that the news made his visit to Reverend Colling immediately necessary.

It was some time since he had called on his fellow rector. He could no longer blame his many duties for this failure. Due to feeling his age these last few years, Reverend Harding had withdrawn from many of his commitments, including the Turnpike Trust and the committee of the Cornwall and Devon Central Railway. He allowed his curate to carry out many of the duties in the parish. But he would never give up the Magistrates' Meetings.

Having turned down Gorwood Road to reach the Vicarage, who should he see but Mr Bartholomew Fulford up a ladder, which only went to prove his point that the village was full of Methodists.

'Good morning, Mr Fulford.' He did not trouble to remove his hat. 'On a day as cold as this, one would be better indoors than up a ladder, I would have thought.'

The man replied with some homily about there being enough work to do whatever the weather. Reverend Harding decided not to mention the matter of the lack of a magistrate in the village. That was a discussion more suited to the

Vicarage than the village street; Bartholomew Fulford's opinions were of no consequence.

'What be his business in Buckland, then?' Henry Chapple, who was assisting Bartholomew, peered over the roof of the field linhay to observe the departing figure of Reverend Harding. 'I dunno who has the biggest arse, him or the hoss.'

Bartholomew chuckled. 'You mind your tongue, Henry, that be no way to speak o' your betters. There now, look, he's turning into Back Lane so I reckon he's yer to call on the Rector. There'll be some as is glad he's not visiting *them*, the sight of him'll strike fear into any that haven't been as good as they should be. Fetch me some more spars, would 'ee?'

From his vantage point he could see over the roofs of the village he loved, and right out across the fields to the distant hills in the south of the parish, all of it so ancient, he could sense the centuries of workers who had been there before. There was little movement, except for Reverend Harding's head bobbing up and down between the high hedgebanks until an old oak obscured him from view.

With one foot on the ladder and one knee against the thatch, Bartholomew settled another roll of straw on to the ridge, pushed in the hazel spars that Henry passed to him and hammered them down with the mallet, the sound ringing out over the village.

'Did 'ee hear about young Mary Beer what was up in the court before him?' Bartholomew bent another hazel spar into shape.

'What Mary Beer is that?'

'Mary Beer whose mother lives over at Rickards. Her father was transported a few years back for stealing a sheep, remember? Younger brother's down at Gusland. Silly maid's followed in her father's footsteps, stole a fowl from Mr Bond; and our Reverend Harding, whose rear end you'm so rude about, sentenced her to three months' hard labour with two weeks in solitary. He's not one to take pity on a poor maid, our Mr Harding. Her had to be punished, 'tis true, but three months was very harsh to my way of thinking.'

He shook his head as he gathered up another roll of straw and tamped down the ends. He had been working on the ridge all morning and was nearly finished.

'Sollitorry? What's that then?'

'All alone. Poor chiel'll be shut in a cell on her own, in the dark I wouldn't be surprised, with neither a sight nor sound of another human, just her meals pushed through a hatch twice a day. Then hard labour to follow, but her knows what that is already, us all does.'

Seeing his cousin, who ran a small grocery shop, picking her way over the frozen mud in the lane below, he leaned against the roof to free a hand to raise in greeting to her.

'Morning, Susan! Or is it past noon now?' He consulted his pocket-watch and nodded. 'Where be 'ee off to then?'

She shaded her eyes against the sun, the better to see him up on the roof. 'Just down to Mrs Norman with some treacle her wanted. My Mam's not so vitty this week, will 'ee look in to see her sometime? Her might need some more of that medicine fetching.'

'I will, tell her I'll be around in a day or so afore I goes into town.'

Henry Chapple ascended the ladder again, this time with more straw. 'So did her get to eat the fowl afore her was caught, that's what I'd want to know? Then leastways her'd have the memory of it when her's all alone.'

'That I don't know,' said Bartholomew, 'but 'twouldn't surprise me to hear that her has more to eat in gaol than her did at home.'

It had been a tough winter, and the spring would be no easier for many if the bad weather continued. The plague had hit all the potato grounds in and around the village to a greater or lesser degree, so both farmers and labourers had been affected. Some farmers, responding to the repeal of the Corn Laws and the consequent drop in the price of corn, had planted more potatoes than usual, so the crop failure had been particularly damaging for them. He heard rumours that some would struggle to pay their rent when Lady Day came, though none would admit to it openly. For himself, he always farmed cautiously, preferring to keep to ways that had proved effective over the generations rather than making big swings to this or that crop. Times were hard, he could not pretend that they were not, but he supposed they would survive.

Hardest hit were the day labourers who depended on their piece of potato ground to feed the family through the winter. When the weather had been favourable they had managed, because when there was enough work they could use their wages to buy flour but, when the weather deteriorated, many labourers had been turned away. Because money was in short supply, even the farms that still had threshing to do used their bound labour rather than employ day labourers. So those families were hungry, that was it in a nutshell, and men would turn to crime rather than see their loved ones starve. One evening last week, just after dusk had fallen, he had come across a man, who lived on the other side of the village, creeping along a hedge in the turnip field with a view to stealing supper for his family. Bartholomew had shouted and seen the man off with threats of a whipping, but he had done so with a heavy heart.

'I went up to see the Rector myself, t'other day,' he told Henry Chapple. 'Told him that if he wants to help those that are hungry hereabouts, he could arrange for his cook to make a big cauldron of soup once or twice a week, tell folks they can come with a pan to fetch 'n, proper thick soup so that folks can feel they've got a meal inside of 'em.'

'And what did 'ee make of that?' Henry leaned on the newly thatched ridge.

'Said he'd think on it. Seemed surprised to hear that there's folks that are hungry, prefers to read of famines in the Bible, seems to me, rather than look about him. Hadn't realised folks are falling ill, they'm so undernourished.'

Every week saw more men and women coming to Bartholomew to apply for parish relief. The Workhouse was full. He had always believed that labouring families should be independent whenever possible but now he could see no alternative to parish relief. The potato plague was not their fault.

'And when I talk to Reverend Harding and others on the Board,' he told Henry, 'they won't see sense. Say people must eat turnips instead of potatoes. So they might, next year, but they'm got to be grown first.'

He was usually an even-tempered man, but the reluctance of the Board to see the seriousness of the problem was making him cross. He had kept his annoyance hidden so far, but it was becoming harder by the day. At least Mr Norman, his fellow Guardian in the village, understood the situation and was now willing to agree an increase in the rates to meet the demand for relief, and Reverend Pine-Coffin could always be relied on for support during meetings. The village community was strong; many of the tradesmen would help out a little when they could, to prevent hungry families having to apply to the relieving officer.

'Anyways,' he told Henry, 'you'm not to worry. I know times is hard but I'll not see your family suffer, you know that.'

'I do, maister, and I thank 'ee for it.'

When they had climbed down their respective ladders, Bartholomew squinted up at the newly-thatched ridge. It would do; the rest of the roof would now last a few more years, keeping the sheep that sheltered in the linhay during the worst of the winter weather dry and warm. He called to his dog that had been crouching in the field trying to outstare the boldest among the flock of sheep, and together they passed over the frozen quagmire in the gateway to reach the lane. Bartholomew hobbled a little, his bad hip playing him up in this cold weather.

'Can 'ee manage the two ladders?' he asked Henry. 'I'll be along dreckly.'

He had seen Charity Mitchell and wanted to talk to her. She walked heavily towards him, her gaze downcast and her hands thrust inside her old woollen shawl in an effort to keep warm. She would be returning home for half an hour before going out charring at the Vicarage.

When he addressed her, her response lacked its usual vigour. He passed the time of the day until two other women had moved on, not wanting his conversation with her to be overheard.

'My wife told me of your message. Her said as you've changed your mind about asking for relief. Mr Mitchell found more work, has he?' He knew that not to be the case.

She looked at him wearily. 'No, Mr Fulford, he habn't. But when I got to thinking on it, I couldn't abide my Ann being taken as apprentice. I'd rather starve meself.'

Ever since Mary and Thomas had been taken from her, Mrs Mitchell had somehow managed not to apply for parish relief, but the hardship of this season exceeded all others.

He placed a sympathetic arm on her shoulder. 'Mrs Mitchell, don't 'ee fret, her won't be sent out. The Board have been told not to apprentice any more children to farms, the magistrates don't like it, it don't marry with the new laws, they say, what have been brought in about children working. So you can apply for relief without fretting about that. Not that I can promise you'll get it, mind, but us can try.'

'New laws? What new laws?' She gave him a fierce look. 'If there's new laws then my children can come home, try to earn a wage!'

He sighed. 'Well, 'tisn't like that exactly, Mrs Mitchell, no one's said as any children should be sent home. Besides, there idn't no work, you know that. They are at least being fed where they be. I know that young Grace's mother wouldn't be pleased if I sent her home for the family to feed and clothe.'

Reluctantly, Mrs Mitchell agreed that the relieving officer should call. 'And what of Thomas and Mary?' she asked, 'have 'ee news of 'em?'

'I did see Mary; last week, 'twas, when I was out that way.'

He didn't tell Mrs Mitchell that, while ice stood in cart ruts, Mary had been crouching in a field exposed to the full force of the biting east wind, drawing, topping and tailing turnips. He knew from experience that it was unpleasant work. Despite her rough leather gloves, her hands would be numb from handling the half-frozen turnips and she would then be at risk of cutting herself on the billhook, an awkward thing to use for a young maid with small hands.

'Her gave me a wave and seemed cheerful enough,' he said.

He stood and watched as Mrs Mitchell made her way slowly up the hill. What a winter it was; he had never known such hard times. What was to be done? Some of his relatives believed they had found the answer. His cousins just up the road at Southwood planned to sell off everything next year, the furniture and the china that had been passed down through the generations, they would leave it all behind and sail for Upper Canada, go off for ever to a place that they had never even seen. The Cole family had gone a few years ago and there were plenty more that talked of it. Perhaps that was the answer, for some if not for him. There wasn't enough work here, that was the crux of it; too many people, too little work. And then disease and poor harvests on top of it all. He sighed and walked back to his farmhouse, too despondent to notice that somewhere, high above the meadow, the first skylark was singing.

No manservant appeared to take Reverend Harding's horse at the Rectory. Reverend Colling was known to keep few servants; since his marriage and the rebuilding of the Vicarage last year, perhaps he could ill afford them.

Eventually, he found Reverend Colling in his book-lined study, his tall frame folded into a chair and his fingers ink-stained. He seemed reluctant to tear himself away from the papers spread over his desk, merely turning around as if the conversation would take only a minute or so.

'Mr Colling, I have matters of great importance to discuss. We need to sit down together so that I may have your full attention.' Surely, if only from politeness, a man could be offered a hot drink after being exposed to the elements on such a cold day?

Reverend Colling apologised then, and called for some coffee to be brought to the library. Reverend Harding dispensed with formalities and came straight to the point.

'You will be aware that the agricultural labourers are experiencing considerable privations at present. It is a very serious situation which, if mismanaged, could lead to lawlessness. It is important that they are reminded of their place in society. We do not want to see riots such as have taken place in Barnstaple.'

There was an unfocussed look about Reverend Colling, as if his interest remained in the study with his books.

'You are aware, I assume, of the circumstances to which I refer?'

'Yes; yes of course, I have had news of it.'

'Hunger provides a powerful impetus to commit crimes; I very much fear that theft is on the increase. You have heard, no doubt, of the burglary at Weare Giffard Rectory?'

'Burglary?' He looked startled. 'No I hadn't.'

'Several items of value were stolen while the ladies of the house were present in another room. One hardly dares think of what could have happened. Two men who were seen loitering in the area are suspected of the crime but they have not yet been apprehended. I have taken to locking the church at night to prevent vagrants seeking shelter therein. The point of the matter is, Mr Colling, that the lower classes need to know that those in positions of authority are observing them, that their actions will be noted and severely punished. There being only one constable in Bideford, it is important that you, I and others like us should make our presence felt.'

Mr Colling was beginning to look flustered. 'That really is not something I could do, Mr Harding! I spend many hours studying, I have my sermons to write and I have to find time to spend with my wife now; I'm sorry, but I really cannot be out riding the lanes in the hope of seeing criminals!'

Reverend Harding sat back in his chair and took a deep breath. He had feared this sort of response.

'It may have come to your attention, Mr Colling, if the news has penetrated the walls of your study, that the regular

Magistrates' Meeting in Buckland Brewer has now ceased to exist. While justice was visible in this village – the magistrates arriving in their carriages and the prisoners marching in their chains for all to see – the common people were reminded of the outcome of criminal actions. But now that the Petty Sessions are to take place only in Torrington or in Bideford, what will the people of this village know of them? Will they not believe that they can steal with impunity? How long will it be, Mr Colling, before your home is the target of a burglary and your wife's safety is put in jeopardy?'

Mr Colling shook his head in bewilderment.

'I have a proposal for you, Mr Colling. If you would agree to serve on the Bench, the people of Buckland Brewer would have a magistrate in their midst, they would remember each time they see your carriage that their actions will have consequences, just as those who see me in Monkleigh remember, and touch their forelocks in recognition of the fact. My fellow magistrates all agree that your appointment would be most valuable.'

Reverend Colling uncrossed his legs and sat forward in his chair. 'Mr Harding, I know you are comfortable in your role as magistrate.' He ran his hands through his hair. 'I would not be! It wouldn't suit me at all. Surely there are other ways of dealing with the problem. If the people are hungry, perhaps we can give them food so they do not see the necessity of theft. My wife would like to help in some way in the parish; we had thought of asking the cook to make some soup once or twice a week. Such a role would suit us better. The people could come to the back door so need not inconvenience us a great deal.'

For the sake of politeness, Reverend Harding tried to hide his irritation.

'Handouts will merely make them dependent, as does poor relief! The poor of Swimbridge are being supplied with half-price rice, peas and fish by Mr John Nott which is at least preferable in that it has to be paid for.'

Mr Colling had the temerity to laugh. 'Good heavens, we are not fishmongers! I'm sorry, if I can help the poor in some small way then I will, but I'm afraid the role you suggest does not appeal to me.'

Reverend Harding felt disappointed as well as annoyed as he rode back through the village. Buckland Brewer would benefit from the presence of a magistrate, just as Monkleigh and Littleham profited from his own presence. He was always on hand; complaints could be made to him of undesirable or criminal behaviour and he could issue a warrant straightaway. A firm hand was needed in these troubled times.

> The Bideford Board of Guardians have made several complaints to you respecting the distress occasioned by the failure of the potatoes, and last week they sent up to you the case of a man with six children, earning 7s. weekly, whose main dependence was on his potato crop, the whole of which had failed. The Tiverton Union made similar complaints, and on the 30th of December they sent to you two cases of labouring men, one having a wife and four children, earning 7s, a week, and cider worth 1s.; the other a wife and five children, earning 6s. weekly, neither of whom had a single potato left, and were consequently wholly unable to support their families. The guardians added that these were " only two of innumerable other similar cases."

From the report to the Poor Law Commissioners *'On the Failure of Potatoes and its Effect on Labourers'* quoted in *The Morning Post* 19th September 1846.

Chapter Sixteen

The day was dry and so warm that, as the sun beat down on Mr Phillips' back, he could feel perspiration running down his neck. The potato plants he was weeding were undersized; one would think this was the beginning of June rather than July to look at them.

He stood up to observe the labourers working alongside him, their bent backs forming a ragged line across the field. It was Beer who was falling behind; he shouted at him and watched as the boy redoubled his efforts. A movement up by the gate caught his eye: the girl coming from her duties in the dairy, scuttling along by the hedge with her head down.

'JOHN! Git on with it!'

His oldest son had stood up, grinning and simpering, when the girl appeared beside him to start her weeding. Progress would be a little quicker with one more but, when this field was finished, there was Little Botown to do and the hay harvest to finish between times. He glanced up at the sun and, bending again to the task in hand, redoubled his efforts. He and John Dean were using hoes, but the weeds closest to the plants still had to be pulled by hand. He had hoped to buy a horse hoe before now like the one Reverend Pine-Coffin had at Portledge, but the cost was prohibitive.

He needed more labour. However hard they all worked, there were not enough hours in the day. Last year's potato crop had been a disaster; he had earned nothing from it. The potatoes he had stored, hoping prices would rise, had rotted in the pit, too far gone even to feed to the pigs. Many farmers had tilled turnips instead of potatoes this year, but he had made the decision to continue as before because with less competition, potato prices would rise. If the plague did not return.

He gritted his teeth. Please God, it would not return.

Did he not ensure that no one worked on the Sabbath? He kept to that promise, despite all the work there was to be done and despite the farm looking so unkempt, the gates sagging on their hinges, the ditches full of standing water even after weeks of dry weather. And they went to chapel every week, the children and his wife, and didn't they say grace before every meal? He had kept his side of the bargain. The clouds drifted, and he glared up at the sky.

From here he could see across the valley to Brendon, his brother's compact parcel of land, much of it meadow. His brother grew only enough potatoes for his own consumption, some wheat and oats, and a few turnips to feed the cattle in winter. He went every week to the Bible Christian chapel at Twitching. He produced fine lambs and good quality hay.

Mr Phillips could make out three workers gathering hay in the meadow next to the farmhouse, and knew that one of them was his brother. From time to time, when the breeze fell, laughter drifted over the valley. It irked him to know that just as he could observe his brother's farm, so could his brother observe Gusland. He would have noticed the ambitious plans, and he would have seen the failures.

His brother had experienced no setbacks. He had no family to feed, no sons to inherit the lease. He could walk away from it when the time came, free of it all.

It was several years since they had spoken to each other.

At dawn, Mary and Rosa walked across Town Close in silence. To their right were the dark silhouettes of the grazing bullocks, the sound of their teeth tearing at the grass just audible. In the shadowy half-light, a hare leapt almost from under Mary's feet and loped away. She watched it, opening her eyes wide as it grew more indistinct and finally disappeared into the darkness. She was so tired, she felt that if she let her eyes close she would sleep immediately, perhaps complete all her work without waking. The long meadow grass brushed against her bare ankles, the dew that lay heavy on every blade running down into her boots. Before long, her feet squelched with every step.

They reached the gate to the meadow. Rosa stood in silence; she had not spoken a single word since they met in the kitchen. She surely could not be as tired as Mary since she had no evening chores to do once supper was cleared away, and could go to bed straightaway. Mary looked at her, then opened the gate and started to call the cows herself.

'Co, co, co, co, co-hobe! Co, co, co, co, co-hobe!'

Her voice echoed down in the valley. For a while, nothing happened but then, one by one, the dark red cows started to appear out of the gloom at a slow but purposeful walk, their udders swinging beneath them. As they passed through the gate, Mary placed her hand on each by way of a greeting. There were only five. She turned to Rosa.

'You gwain to fetch 'er?'

Bella nearly always had to be fetched. She would be found grazing at the bottom of the field and would only move after being given a hard slap on the rump, after which she would trot happily after the others. Mary felt herself swaying with hunger and tiredness. She could not do it today.

Rosa was looking at the ground, her dark hair almost obscuring her face as she shook her head.

''Tis your turn,' Mary told her. 'I did 'n yesterday.'

They often had this argument. Even in the summer there was deep mud in the gateway created by the frequent passage of hoofs through the spring that rose a few yards further up the field, so whoever waded through was likely to get a bootful of mud.

Rosa looked up and stared challengingly at Mary. 'Well, I bain't doing it.'

Mary stared back, narrowing her eyes. She would like to have pushed Rosa over into the mud; one day she would do it.

'Don't then, leave her be.' She turned and followed the cows back towards the farm.

She was determined not to look back, but she listened for Rosa's footsteps above the sound of her own, swishing through the long grass. Only when she reached the gate into the yard did she allow herself to turn around. The faint glow from the eastern sky showed her that the field lay empty; Rosa must have gone to fetch the cow.

Mary had come to like milking. Despite the discomfort of crouching in the deep mud of the yard, there was pleasure to be gained from resting her cheek against the warm flank of a cow, the soft rubbery feeling of the teat in her fingers and the satisfying hiss of the milk spurting into the bucket. She always milked the same three cows; they had become her friends. She liked their smell that was milk and grass and muck all at the same time, and she liked the way they turned their heads to huff and puff at her, blowing warm breath into her hair from their wet noses. When her hunger got the better of her and no one was watching, she could bend forward to squirt some milk right into her mouth. The cows did not mind.

When Rosa came through the yard gate behind Bella, Mary kept her cheek against the cow's flank but watched through her lowered lashes as Rosa stomped through the mud to fetch her stool and bucket from the outhouse. It seemed there was to be no immediate retaliation.

By the time she carried the full buckets into the dairy, she was so weak from hunger that she staggered and almost fell on the step. When Thomas gently touched her hand as they went to fill their mugs from the cauldron of burnt crust tea in the fireplace, she felt her eyes fill with tears. She longed to lean against him and feel his arms around her, but the silent watchfulness of so many eyes in the room prevented her. She knew that such a display of affection would be greeted with jeering insults, either now or at some later time.

Breakfast was just one slice of bread. The amount of food they were given had decreased steadily ever since the failure of the potato harvest. The family had more – there was a loaf on their table from which Mr Phillips cut freely – but even they had less than had been customary. If the pantry and the dairy had not been locked at night and a close eye kept on the hams that hung from the ceiling, Mary would have risked taking some food because she was sure it would not really be stealing, but only taking what was hers by right. Jesus would not want her to starve.

But today, when he was given his bread, Thomas continued to hold out his plate to Mrs Phillips.

'Please, can I have another slice?'

The apprentices stared at him. They had complained to each other about the diminishing quantity of food, but not even Lewis had ever dared to ask for more. Thomas's eyes seemed to burn in his face as he held his gaze steady. Mary noticed for the first time how thin and drawn he looked.

'What? What be sayin'?' Mrs Phillips looked confused. She glanced nervously towards her husband who was giving Tom his instructions for the day.

'I'm hungry. Us is all hungry. Us needs more to eat, 'tisn't enough.'

His voice was quiet, but hard and determined. He pushed his plate towards Mrs Phillips again, and she backed away.

'No, there idn't no more, Mr Phillips, he said...'

'What's that?' Mr Phillips looked up with a scowl on his face. Mary held her breath, pleading silently for Thomas to look down, to pretend he had not spoken, but he looked straight at Mr Phillips and in the same cold, calm voice said,

'Maister, us needs more to eat, us is all hungry.'

She could see that he knew what was coming, but he did not back away as the other apprentices did when Mr Phillips strode towards them. When the shouting and the blows were over, Thomas got back on his feet and ate his slice of bread, but he held himself as upright as an iron bar and his eyes burned with anger. Mary struggled to force down the dry bread she was eating when she saw the swelling that was appearing on the side of his face.

When the men and boys had gone out to work, she carried the heavy bucket of slops across the yard to the pigs. Closing the sty door behind her, she looked furtively up at the house, but there was no one at the kitchen window. While the three pigs grunted and butted impatiently at her thighs with their long snouts, she rested the bucket on the trough out of their reach and dipped her finger into the mush. It kept the pigs alive so must have some goodness in it. It smelt like dishwater and felt like earth in her mouth when she crammed a handful into her mouth, trying not to gag. She quickly poured the rest into the trough, watching as the pigs snorted and wagged their tiny tails as they gobbled it down. Perhaps she could find a way to give some to Thomas. The pigs, the fowls, the cattle and the sheep, they were all cared for, fed, given clean bedding. They were cherished. She and Thomas were not.

She replaced the bucket in the outhouse and went to the barn to fetch straw for the pigs. It was cool and dim inside. The air was very still. A shaft of hazy sunlight found its way through an opening below the vaulted thatched roof. She stood for a moment to watch the dust motes that danced in its beam, then kicked up more dust from the earth floor to watch it rise and twirl. No one could see her in the barn; no one except the white owl that sat motionless on a rough oak beam far above, its wide, dark eyes observing her closely.

She was gathering a large armful of straw when she heard footsteps.

'Mary!'

John, with a beaming smile, stumbled towards her with arms outstretched.

She had become increasingly nervous of John. His affection for her was undiminished, but there was something about the way he now looked at her that made her feel uncomfortable. He was eighteen years old, as tall and broad as an ox, but she could still make him do what she wanted by talking to him sternly, as if he were a small boy.

'John! Stop where you be!'

She saw him hesitate for a second, but then he kept coming.

'Mary! I didn't know you was here!'

When he flung his arms around her she was thrown right off balance, falling into the straw with him on top of her, and although the straw cushioned her landing, the force of the fall with John's weight on top of her knocked her breath away. She felt a sharp pain in her chest and could neither breathe nor speak; she was sure she would die. Only as she began to take her first ragged breath did she again become aware of John. As he moaned her name, his hand was stroking her neck, and then moved down to her breast.

'John, get off me, get off!' Her voice came out as a croak and carried no strength. She tried to squirm from under him but she could not even free her hands or move her face away from the huge head and slobbering mouth that hovered just above her own.

'Mary, you'm so soft, you'm soft like a kitty,' and he squeezed her breast so hard she cried out in pain.

'Get off me!' She was sobbing now and wriggling frantically in an effort to escape, but he was so very heavy she could not even free an arm or a leg. She felt she would be crushed to death. He started to moan, a deep sound like a cow in pain, and to rub himself against her. Suddenly he knelt up between her legs, a surprised grin on his face as he clutched at the front of his trousers.

'John's big! John's big like a bull!'

In a second she was on her feet and out of the door. She heard John wailing her name as she stumbled across the yard and ran into the kitchen crying, 'Help me, help me!'

She could barely get the words out, but she managed to say that John had hurt her, that he had been rude, but afterwards she could not remember what else she had said, because what came next shocked her so much.

Mrs Phillips, Lucy and Rosa had turned around when she burst in. They stood staring at her, their mouths open in surprise. Then it came.

'You been leading him on!' Mrs Phillips' face was twisted with dislike. 'John wouldn't do that! Look at you! Fancy going out workin' like that when there be boys around! Straighten your clothes and don't 'ee ever make up such tales about my boy again!'

Rosa and Lucy were smirking now.

Mary was aghast. 'I didn't! He came in when I was fetching straw…'

'Be quiet! And where be the eggs? Fetch 'em right now or I be telling Mr Phillips what you'm up to with John!'

'I didn't do nothing! It were him!'

'Get out!' Mrs Phillips picked up a pan and came towards her as if she would hit her with it, and Mary ran for the door.

She stood outside, her breath coming in deep, ragged sobs. Mr Phillips had gone to fetch three sheep in from the field for shearing, and was now on the far side of the yard, shouting at John. For a moment she thought that he knew what had happened, but then she caught a few words and realised that John was only being scolded for not making the shears ready. She knew it would be no good to tell the maister.

She ran up the steps and past the garden plot to the hen house where, pulling the low, wooden door closed behind her, she crouched on the dusty straw in the half-light and cried until no more tears would come.

Gradually, she grew more aware of her surroundings. The grey speckled hens crooned gently as they peered at her from their perches, holding their heads on one side, as if puzzled by her presence.

'You wouldn't hurt me, would 'ee. You'm better than folks, any day.'

She drew a deep breath as her sobs threatened to return. She was aching and bruised all over, but much as she feared John, she knew he had not meant to hurt her. He had not fully understood what he was doing. It was Mrs Phillips she hated at that moment; she *knew* that John was to blame. Mary had noticed how embarrassed she was by John, especially when Mr Phillips was angry with him and blamed her for his son's behaviour. She could not impose her will on him the way his father did, and as Mary used to be able to do; instead she managed John by bribing him with scraps of food as if he were a dog. She was almost certainly afraid of him.

Mary leaned back against the wooden wall of the henhouse.

'What be I gwain to do?' she whispered.

John was sure to try again to do *that* to her. She could not bring herself to use the words she knew – they were to do with animals, they had nothing to do with her and her body; but nevertheless her imagination kept conjuring up images that appalled her. How could she stop John? However hard she tried to keep away from him, there were times when he could follow her into a barn or a field when no one else was around. Even into her room at night. If she screamed, would anyone come? The horror of it almost overwhelmed her.

She got up suddenly. How long had she been here? She would be in trouble. Quickly she pulled up the hatch for the hens and, as they tentatively made their way out, flapping and squawking as they emerged into daylight, she gathered the eggs from the straw-filled nesting boxes, placed them in her apron and hurried back to the house.

She paused for a moment outside the door to calm herself, then walked past Lucy in the kitchen and into the dairy. Mrs Phillips was pouring milk into a bowl to let it stand for cream.

'What I said, 'tis true. I don't tell lies.' She spoke quietly, trying to keep her voice steady. 'Please, help me, I don't want it to happen again. Would 'ee tell John…'

'You saying I habn't raised him proper?' Mrs Phillips' startled grey eyes turned on her. 'What do 'ee think Mr Phillips'd say if he knew what you'm telling on? He'd blame me for not watching out, that's what he'd do! Now get out with 'ee, get out to the fields and don't you be telling no more lies, not about John nor about me neither!'

Mary tried to tell Thomas as they walked back to the farm together that evening. She could not find the right words for what had happened, but he soon guessed what she was trying to say, and the relief at having someone believe her made her cry again.

'I'll tell'n, I'll tell John if he do's it again…' He was very angry. 'Sometimes he do listen to what I say. But Mary, us must tell other people, us must tell the magistrate! They'm supposed to fix things that are wrong. Folks tell them when a 'pprentice has been beaten bad, and this is bad too. And us bain't getting enough to eat, nowhere near enough! '

She had not thought of telling a magistrate. 'But how can us tell'n? Where can us find'n?'

He did not know. How could they tell anyone when they could not leave the farm?

However, she decided to talk to Betsy at chapel on Sunday. Surely she would know what to do.

The opportunity arose when they came out of Sunday School and were waiting to join in with the chapel meeting. They were a little early so she and Betsy allowed the younger children to run about on the grass in the sunshine.

'Betsy, I be in some trouble. 'Tis John Phillips, you know, as used to come to Sunday School.'

Betsy looked at her in alarm. 'Mary, what 'ave 'ee done!'

'Nothing! I habn't done nothing!' She hadn't expected this response from Betsy. 'He tried to, to touch me…'

Betsy, in her high-necked dress and scraped-back hair, suddenly looked very stern. 'Mary, you got to keep yourself pure! 'Tis a sin, what you'm telling me, and you know what happens to sinners, they burn forever in a pit of fire! You got to keep away from the boys and you got to trust in God, ask him to keep you from temptation. He'll help you!' She smiled encouragingly, and put her arm around Mary. 'You'm a good girl, ask God to keep you on the right path.'

It was not what she had hoped to hear, but perhaps Betsy was right, she should ask God to help her. She would still like to see a magistrate, even though she was not sure where that would lead, but Betsy was not impressed with the idea.

''Tisn't a magistrate you need. Put your trust in God and He will help you.'

Over the next few days, Mary said carefully-worded prayers every morning and every evening, she never smiled at John or said anything that might encourage him, and she never went into any outbuildings without first making sure he was nowhere nearby. At night she tied up the latch to her door with a length of straw rope that Thomas found for her in the linhay.

She neither spoke to nor looked at Mrs Phillips if she could help it.

Mr Phillips watched the cows grazing. Old Fancy was restless, she was approaching the other cows; there was no doubt about it, she was bulling. He cursed silently. He was on his way to turn hay and had not the time for this, but he had no choice, if he left it a day later there might be no calf next year. The service fee for Mr Furse's bull was expensive but produced good calves, so the money must be found from somewhere. He strode on until he came to the meadow where John Dean and old Mr Judd had made a start on the hay.

'I'm taking Old Fancy to Babeleigh for the bull, carry on yer 'til I'm back.'

'Look, maister.' Mr Judd lifted a forkful of hay. ''Tis mouldery, sure nuff. Us can turn 'n but with this ol' drizzle 'tisn't good dryeth.'

He had guessed it. He had held high hopes of a good crop from this field, but in the days since the hay was cut a warm dampness had pervaded the air.

'If 'tisn't turned 'twill compact down and rot.' He looked up at the sky; more cloud was coming in from the south-west. What else could go wrong?

He turned on his heel. Returning to the yard, he fetched a rope halter from the linhay, then put his head around the kitchen door.

'I'm to Babeleigh to the bull. Tuesday I'll to market, you'm to take cream and butter, cheese too, whatever 'ee has that'll sell. The money you say you need for flour must come from that.' Any cash he had, he was keeping for servicing the cows.

'But,' the woman was as timid as a mouse, 'us haven't enough, I think, not enough for market, not really.'

The way she stammered and quivered made him grit his teeth.

'Then some'll have to go without, won't 'em!' He slammed the door.

It was a two-mile walk to Babeleigh Barton and there was no hurrying Old Fancy; she trotted beside him well enough on the level but made heavy weather of climbing up out of the valley towards Brendon. The steep, sunken lane passed between high mossy banks, the fields on either side being on a level with his head, but he had no wish to look into his brother's fields running along on his left. He cursed under his breath, therefore, when he heard the swishing of footsteps up in the field, and kept his gaze on the rutted surface of the lane. Perhaps it was one of his brother's labourers.

'Mornin', Thomas.'

He would recognise that voice anywhere. He continued to walk. 'Mornin'.'

'Come now, Thomas, there idn't no harm in passing time of day. Where be 'ee gwain then?'

'Babeleigh.' He stopped, but kept his gaze on the road. His brother stood six foot above him on the bank, his boots just perceptible at the edge of Mr Phillips' field of vision. He had no intention of looking up to his brother.

'Ah, a fine bull there, 'tis. And the family, they'm all well?' The boots came forward a step.

'Ay, they be.' He wanted very much to get on his way and pulled the cow away from the bank where she had started to tear at the grass.

'Thomas, us is seein' hard times, all of us. If ever you want some extra hands, 'twould be no hardship for me to send over a couple of my men for a day or two.'

He nodded, and walked on with Old Fancy at his side. What had Richard observed that made him think that help was needed? He would never be beholden to his brother. Never.

For the last quarter of a mile of his walk, he passed alongside Babeleigh land. There was some rough grazing similar to his at Higher Twitching, but the bullocks grazing there were doing well on it. He thought of all the work he had put into improving his land, and the poor returns it had delivered – but all due to factors outside his control, the weather, the potato disease. This season would surely be better; he would then see the true benefit of his work. The fields nearer to Babeleigh were in good heart; a field of turnips and two meadows that had already had hay taken and safely stacked before the damp weather came.

He led the cow past the ancient but well-kept farmhouse to find Mr George Furse spinning ropes in the barn, and the purpose of the visit was soon established. Together they leaned on the gate to the paddock where the fine, heavily-muscled red Devon bull circled around Old Fancy. This was the part Mr Phillips disliked, not observing the cattle, but the necessity of responding to the inevitable questions while the two men waited for the mating to take place. Old Fancy was already standing still to let the bull sniff at her, so he hoped that it would not take too long.

'You've another cow to bring when her's ready, I b'lieve?' Mr Furse's relaxed, affable manner made Mr Phillips more uncomfortable than if his neighboour had been hostile. ''Twill make further links between our farms. You know I have a young maid here now, the chiel of one of your labourers? Mary Ann, John Dean's chiel. Her's a good maid, her didn't know aught when her came, but the missis is pleased with her now. Hard worker her is. And I've got young William Beer, younger brother of – what's his name? Joseph, i'n't it? The boy whose father was transported. And the sister sent to gaol. Bad business, that. But there, us has to help out when us can, doesn't us? A shilling here or there can make a world of difference to a family when they'm hungry.'

Mr Phillips grunted in reply, but did not comment. Did Mr Furse know that Joseph Beer was apprenticed without wages? Was he implying that John Dean was paid less then he should be?

The bull made a first attempt at mounting Old Fancy. She moved out of his way, but allowed him to sniff at her again as she grazed.

What was Mr Furse saying now?

''Tis a wonder how they do live, some of 'em. And the repeal of the Corn Laws habn't helped the way 'twas supposed to; prices is low for they that wants to sell, but high for they that wants to buy, seems to me. And now that the teddies look set to fail again, well, there's more hard times ahead for some, seems to me.'

'What's that?' He must have heard incorrectly.

'Well, 'tis back, i'n't it, teddy disease.'

He must have seen Mr Phillips' expression.

'Hadn't you heard? 'Tis over Bulkworthy way, bad as ever for all that it's early, and up in Thornhillhead too. Moving this way with the wind, I reckon. This damp old breeze don't help, that's my opinion. You haven't seen none then?'

Mr Phillips heard no more. As Mr Furse chattered on and the bull did his work, all he could think of was getting home. He had to check the potato fields. They were thriving; he had checked them only two days ago, and they were thriving then.

Mary was working in the turnip field with Thomas and Joseph. They were to return to the house for their dinner, the field being at no great distance, so when their stomachs told them that the time must surely be right, they set off along the lane.

'Look over there!' whispered Thomas.

Two fields away, she could see Mr Phillips walking amongst the potatoes with his head down, as if he were searching for something. They had seen him returning with Old Fancy about half an hour previously and had expected him to shout out some instruction or exhortation to work harder, but he had kept on walking as if they were not there.

'P'raps 'e's lost the cow 'mongst the teddies,' Joseph said, and they all laughed, walking together in a close huddle as they exchanged witticisms.

'Lost 'is senses, more like,' put in Mary, and they watched the solitary figure pacing between the rows of potatoes until Mr Phillips reached the far hedge, whereupon they quickly turned around and hurried towards the farmhouse, trying to stifle their giggles.

Mary had a quick wash at the pump and took her place at the table for the meagre portion of bread and half an onion.

'Where be Mr Phillips? I don't know whether us should start...' Mrs Phillips looked anxiously out of the kitchen window. When Joseph told her what they had seen, Tom, who was becoming more inclined to take his father's place when the occasion warranted it, made the decision that they should all eat, in order to return to work as soon as possible.

Later, Mary lived through the subsequent events over and over again, trying to make sense out of them. It all happened so quickly, yet changed the course of her life forever.

The meal over, Rosa and Lucy started clearing away the dishes while the apprentices put their boots back on for work. Mrs Phillips came out of the dairy carrying her big earthenware bowl of milk to put near the fire until the cream formed a crust. The kettle had been left on the stone hearth, and she called to Mary to move it. It all happened at once; as Mrs Phillips tripped on the hearth, the bowl flew out of her hands and smashed on the flagstone floor, the milk soaking them both and spreading in a large pool on the ground.

The door opened.

'What the devil's gwain on yer?' Mr Phillips' thunderous voice made them all jump, and when his wife saw his face, she started to back away.

'It slipped, 'twas an accident...'

He strode across the kitchen and grabbed her roughly by the arm as she pressed back against the wall.

'You think I'm made of money, woman?'

'No, no, I...' Mary and the other apprentices watched in dismay as she shrank away from him, her eyes rolling in fear.

'You should be helpin', not making things worse! Do 'ee think us can afford a new bowl?'

And it was then that Mrs Phillips screamed out, 'It weren't me, I didn't do it!' And her terrified eyes fixed on Mary. ''Twas her!'

In a second he had turned and, grabbing Mary's shoulder, shook her like a dog shakes a rat, so that she felt her teeth rattling in her head. It was several moments before she could shriek, 'I didn't! I didn't do it!'

'What! You'm lying as well!' His huge face was so close to her own that she felt his beard against her mouth. 'You a Thorne-ite and you'm lyin'! Well, I've had enough of it!'

He threw her to the ground and as she scrabbled to get away from him, there was a familiar hissing sound and she felt the whiplash across her back. Probably she screamed then; when she tried to remember afterwards what had happened, it seemed to her that someone was screaming. The pain was intense; two, three times it came as if her back were on fire, but then suddenly it stopped, and all was shouting and confusion.

She dragged herself under the table in an effort to protect herself from further lashes, and it was only when they did not come that she turned, shielding her face. Mr Phillips raised the whip and brought it down hard, but not on her, and she saw that he had Thomas twisted under his arm. As the whip came down again and again, he fought to hold Thomas who was struggling and kicking with all his strength, but then Thomas stopped fighting and the shouts changed to screams, and then cries. Eventually the whip was thrown aside and her brother was discarded on the floor in a heap.

'Now GEDDOUT! Geddout and get back to work!' A vicious kick accompanied the words.

What had she done then? She must have helped Thomas, and perhaps Joseph did too. Her brother was conscious but could barely stand; but she knew that they did get out of the kitchen, and quickly too, perhaps half-carrying him until they were in the lane and out of sight of the farmhouse. She remembered that they were shaking and sobbing, all three of them, and could hardly get their breath.

Gradually, Thomas recovered enough to get up. 'He'll come out. Us has to get to the field.'

He was very unsteady on his feet. Mary held tight to his arm and he leaned heavily on her, but their limbs shook so much they veered from one side of the lane to the other, and when they reached the field they fell against the hedge, exhausted.

'I'll keep a look out,' said Joseph, 'I can see up the lane from here.'

Mary knelt up. 'Let me see your back.'

Thomas turned around gingerly. 'He was so angry he didn't think to rip off my shirt. That'll have saved me a bit. It's here on my side where he kicked me that's the worst.'

Lines of blood were seeping through the shirt and he cried out when she carefully lifted the cloth away from the wounds.

She gasped when she saw the raised, bleeding wheals across his back.

'Us mustn't let the cloth stick to it as it dries. I'll get some leaves. But Thomas, *why* did he whip you? You hadn't done nothing.'

He turned to her then, crying. 'I fought 'im to stop you gettin' hurt, of course.'

They had to work that afternoon because they were afraid of what would happen if Mr Phillips found them sitting by the hedge, but he never did come near them. Over and over the events played in Mary's mind, and every time she thought of the moment when Mrs Phillips turned on her, her breath caught in her throat. Every movement she made hurt her lacerated back and her bruised arms, but she knew it was nothing compared to what Thomas was feeling. She could find no words for what had happened, and Thomas, too, was silent, but she heard him gasp with pain as he worked.

Later in the afternoon, when Joseph was working further up the field, Thomas moved close to Mary and spoke in a low whisper.

'Mary, us has got to go.'

'Go? Go where?'

'Leave Gusland. I've thought of it afore, but now I know that us has to do it.'

She felt numb. 'But, us can't!'

'Yes, us can. He could kill us, next time,' his voice shook a little. 'I reckon he really could, if he don't starve us first. I've thought on it, and I've got a plan.' He looked around to make sure no one was near.

'But where can us go? Can us go home?' She started to cry when she thought of her mother, and of the feeling of safety inside the close walls of her cottage home. She could still remember it, although it was so long ago.

Thomas's eyes were filling with tears too, but he shook his head. 'That'd be the first place the maister'd look for us. And

Da'd be in trouble for taking us in.' He pulled abstractedly at the weeds. 'No, us has got to get right away.'

Mary pictured the enormity of the world beyond the farm, all of it unknown. 'Can us go to the chapel, ask folks there to help?'

'Anyone who helps us'd be in trouble, James told me 'bout that.'

His face was drawn and anxious; he looked much older than his sixteen years, almost like an old man, Mary thought.

'Us'll get right away from this place, away where no folk know us. And us'll be together, Mary, always.' He was crying openly now.

'When?' she sobbed, 'when shall us go?'

Despite his tears, his gaze was determined. 'Us'll go tonight.'

'I think apprenticeship a good thing: a labourer gets rid of his children, and the children are better off, if in a good place. I was in a good place, but I was lucky. I know many places where I should not like a child to be sent to: the children in such places have no clothes to wear; they are beat and half-starved. There are many such places; but, generally speaking, places are good.'

A Devon Labourer, *Report into the Employment of Women and Children in Agriculture, 1843.*

RAN AWAY, on the Morning of the 13th instant, from his Master, Mr. CHARLES DUNN, of Ash Farm, in the Parish of Braunton, WILLIAM LOVERING, his Parish Apprentice. The said Apprentice is 18 years of age, about 5ft. 4in. high, light hair, rather sore eyes, ruddy complexion, stout made, rather awkward in his walk, wore away a fustian jacket and trowsers, and carried other things with him. Whoever harbours or employs the said Apprentice after this notice, will be dealt with according to law.
Dated Ash, October 16th, 1848.

APPRENTICE EI
RUN AWAY, from his mas PEARD, of *Pippacott*, in the on Sunday the 21st instant, JAMES PUNCHASE, his Parish Apprentice.
The said Apprentice was 19 years of age, light complexion, blue eyes, rather dark hair; and wore away a blue frock coat, green waist... fustian trousers, and blue stockings.
Whoever har notice will be notice that h which the sa Pippacott N
London

RAN AWAY from his Master, Mr. THOMAS HEADON, on Tuesday the 1st instant, JOHN LEE, his Parish Apprentice, 16 years of age, about five feet three inches high, with light hair, light complexion, and rather small hazel eyes. He wore away a fustian jacket, fustain trowsers, and cloth cap.
Whoever harbours the said Apprentice after this public notice will be dealt with accordig to law.
THOMAS HEADON.
Dated Parkham, Devon, Feb. 1st, 1848.

RAN AWAY from his Master, Mr. ... LERWILL, of Verwill Farm, in the parish of *Combmartin*, on the 4th instant, HENRY REED, his parish apprentice.
The said apprentice is 19 years of age, short in stature, has a peculiar shaking of the head and rolling of the eyes, wore away a smock frock and a pair of half-boots.
His said master will which he may contract ploys the said apprentic prosecuted.
Combmartin, July 9

RAN AWAY,
FROM his Master, Mr. EDWARD FURSE, at *South Pillavin*, in the parish of *Bishopsnympton*, on Monday the 13th instant, WILLIAM BOWDEN, his Parish Apprentice ; aged 13, round favoured, light complexion, and light hair, rather short of his age, wore away a smock frock, fustian trousers, and had lost part of the brim of his hat.—Whoever harbours the said Apprentice after this public notice will be prosecuted ; and the said Master will not be answerable for any debts the said Apprentice may contract.
South Pillavin, Bishopsnympton, 29th January, 1840.

Part Three

1847

Chapter Seventeen

Mary sat on the bed in the dark, listening. The door at the bottom of the stairs opened, and the stairs creaked. Her heart was pounding. The footsteps came along the passage; it was Mrs Phillips, walking slowly, her feet dragging a little. Suppose she should come in? Mary had not tied up the latch, she would be seen sitting here on the bed fully clothed, she would be found out; but the footsteps passed on, and a door closed.

It was not long before there were heavier footsteps on the stairs; her heart was beating so loud he would surely hear it, but again a door opened, and closed. Now she had to wait. She had to wait until the clock struck ten, and perhaps longer. The grandfather clock was in the kitchen below her room so she nearly always heard it strike; the sound came through the floorboards as a deep clang quite unlike the musical chiming one heard in the kitchen. Suppose she did not hear it tonight? And how would she know whether Mr and Mrs Phillips were still awake?

Her thoughts went out to Thomas lying in the barn. He had to pretend to be asleep until the time was right; he had to climb down the ladder carrying his boots, without any of the apprentices waking. Suppose his wounds should make him cry out?

She had asked him whether they should take Joseph with them, but Thomas had been adamant that it would be harder with three. She felt sorry that Joseph would wake in the morning to find them gone, that he and the other apprentices might be whipped for not raising the alarm. But, she and

Thomas might be caught before they even left the yard. She clasped her hands over her mouth to stop them shaking.

Carefully, she rose from the bed and went to the open window. A half-moon only partly obscured by cloud gave enough light for her to make out the shadowy silhouettes of the barn and the linhays around the cobbled yard, the dung heap, the dark lines of the five-barred gate and the meadow beyond. The pigs were shuffling and snorting, a gentle sound as if they were conversing together; there was a deep thud as a horse stamped its hoof in the stable.

She stood and waited. She could not tell how long she stood there.

Then, the sound of the clock. She counted ten chimes, almost missing the last because her heart had again started thudding. Now she must wait again. Thomas would not know what time it was; he had to wait until he was sure all the apprentices were asleep. She stared out, trying not to blink lest she miss a movement below in the gloom of the yard.

At last it came; a shadowy figure moving in front of the barn, edging around the yard, and disappearing around the side of the stable.

He was out, and now she must leave the safety of her room.

She tied her shawl over her clothes and, holding the latch in both hands, gently eased it up. She opened the door, and looked out on to the passageway. Slowly, so slowly, she stepped out. She inched the latch back into place. She could hear snoring, John, perhaps Mr Phillips too. Was it Mr Phillips or was he lying awake, listening?

It was pitch-dark in the passage but she knew her way. Carefully she placed one foot in front of the other until her outstretched hands felt the end of the wall, telling her that the stairs were ahead. There was a sudden creak of bed springs from one of the rooms; she froze, tried to calm her breath that was coming too fast, did not move for what felt like minutes. Then her bare feet edged forward and down the first step. Now the second. The wood was cold beneath her feet. Now she had to reach right down to miss the creaking third step;

she touched the wall on each side to keep her balance; there. Now the fifth, and the sixth. She reached forward, moving her hand gently until she found the door, and then the latch, and inched it upwards. She was through.

The door to the kitchen was open, the room dimly lit by the embers glowing in the fireplace. She trod swiftly and silently across the floor; she knew every shadow, every silhouette – but she had seen something different on the table and knew immediately what it was. It had happened before, Mr Phillips taking a loaf of bread from the locked pantry to assuage his hunger before bed, then forgetting to replace it. Here was breakfast, and dinner too; it was theirs by right. Putting the loaf inside her shawl, she moved back to the front door, slipped on her boots and laced them. The latch here was heavy; she tried to still her shaking hands before lifting it, pulling the door open just enough to squeeze through, not so much that it reached the place that made it squeak. And she was out.

The cool breeze on her cheek felt like freedom. Placing each foot carefully in turn she stepped slowly along the side of the barn, keeping close to the rough cob wall, not daring to look back at the house for fear of seeing a face at the window. She reached the stable and a soft, throaty whicker from one of the horses made her freeze for a moment. The horse moved restlessly inside, stamped its hoof, while she waited for it to settle, her heart thudding. Then she crept around the corner of the stable and Thomas's shadowy figure came towards her as she fell into the warmth of his arms.

'Quick, this way now,' his voice was just audible in her ear, ''cos of the dog.'

A sudden movement made them both turn but it was only the white owl floating down, as silent as a ghost, from the little window below the eaves of the barn. It raised its wings to land neatly on the post beside the dung heap, settled its feathers and turned its heart-shaped face as if to watch over them.

Thomas carefully opened the gate to the meadow and then they were walking quickly between the swathes of cut hay in the shadow of the hedgebank. Mary glanced back to see the moonlit fields, the black trees, and a dark shape that was the back wall of the farmhouse, but she knew that there were no windows at the back from which they could be seen.

They climbed the gate at the far side of the meadow and started up the lane.

'Us must walk fast,' Thomas whispered, 'at first anyway. Get as far as us can.'

Their feet were invisible in the darkness, but the moon faintly illuminating Thomas's face made it look feverish, and she saw that he although he had set a fast pace, he was moving with difficulty as if propelled by willpower alone.

'Us have gotta keep listening, and looking back.' The whites of his eyes were shining. 'Gotta know always where the next gateway is, case us has to get off the road.'

They passed beside Kitty Park and then Twitching Moors, every undulation of the fields familiar to them, yet strangely eerie. Small creatures rustled and squeaked in the hedges; a rabbit, invisible in the shadowy lane, thumped its foot at their approach before scurrying over the bank and into a field; a tawny owl called breathlessly from the trees in the valley and was echoed by another up on the hill.

And then they passed the boundary of the farm and went on into a region they did not know. When they had crossed the stream and were halfway up the hill, they paused to regain their breath. Looking back, they saw the lane along which they had passed, empty and silver in the moonlight.

'He could still catch us if he rode the horse,' said Thomas.

Mary spoke quietly. 'They won't know I'm gone, not 'til morning. But if Lewis or Jack wakes and finds you'm not there, would they tell, do 'ee think?'

'I dunno.' Thomas was silent for several moments. 'But I don't reckon any of 'em will wake. Us is all that tired.'

They walked on.

'Thomas,' she whispered, almost afraid to ask, 'where be us gwain? Be us gwain to find the magistrate?'

'I've thought on it, I've been thinking on it for months, even afore John – did what he did. Us has got to get as far

211

away as possible, where the maister'll never find us. I reckon the magistrate'd just send us back to him.' He turned to her, his eyes wide with apprehension. 'I want to see if us can get to Canada.'

'Canada!'

'The ships sail from Bideford. If us offers to work in return for our passage, work on the ship and after us gets to Canada, too, to pay back what us owes, then p'raps they'd let us sail. There's folks out there that would help us, Mary, Bible Christians that come from these parts. And if they don't let us on the ship then us'll keep walking, get faraway from yer and then start asking about for work.'

Mary didn't know what to say.

'What about Ma and Da?' Her voice sounded very small in the night air.

'I know.' He reached out and touched her hand. 'But maybe if us does well in Canada us can send for 'em.'

As they hurried on, she tried to take in the idea of fleeing to Canada. She had always dreamed of leaving the farm in order to return home, but they could not go home now; and she was only fourteen, so if she waited until her time at the farm was over she would have to wait another seven years. Thomas was right, they would not survive that long. Besides, they had escaped the farm! Other people went to Canada, so why shouldn't they? And suddenly she felt exultant.

'Thomas, us have done it! Us have got away!'

And he turned to her and grinned. 'I reckon us have.'

As the night wore on, so Thomas's pace grew slower; every step was a struggle for him. He barely replied to Mary's remarks. She felt very tired and her back hurt, so she knew that after the whipping he had received he must feel much worse than she did.

After walking downhill for some distance they reached a broad straight road where bats skimmed the tops of the hedges and fluttered beneath the trees where water flowed.

'Which way now?' Mary asked.

Thomas hesitated. 'Straight across and up that lane, I reckon. This must be the turnpike to Bideford but I think us must make for the coast first. First places he'll look for us will be Buckland Brewer and Bideford, maybe Torrington too.'

She saw him flinch at the thought of Mr Phillips, then he pulled himself together and smiled at her. 'Fancy going to the sea, do 'ee?'

They were both thirsty so they went down to the stream, finding their way by sound and touch alone because the moonlight did not reach the valley floor, then they followed the lane that wound steeply up the hill. When they had climbed for a while, Thomas started to stagger as he walked, and Mary decided that he must rest. He did not protest, so she led him through a field gate where they sat against a hedge looking back into the dark valley through which they had passed. Thomas closed his eyes.

Mary took the loaf from her shawl and tore off a piece for each of them, thanking God for the good fortune that had brought it to her.

'This must surely have been part of God's plan for us. Yer, Thomas, you must eat.'

He ate the bread without opening his eyes, then fell asleep.

Mary sat very upright; if she went to sleep, they might not wake until dawn. She was beginning to be afraid that Thomas might not be able to walk as far as the sea tonight, but she guessed there was nothing but farmland between here and the coast, and it was not safe to be near farms during the day. All the farmers for miles around knew each other and, even though he kept himself to himself, Mr Phillips would soon get to hear that they had been seen.

When she guessed that Thomas had slept for about half an hour she started trying to wake him. He muttered in his sleep and tried to push her away, but she persisted until finally he opened his eyes, looking at her as if he barely knew who she was.

'Come on, Thomas! Us have got to walk again; get up, come on, you have to!'

When she pulled him to his feet, he stood there for a few moments, swaying so much she feared he would fall, but eventually she pushed him through the gate and together they continued up the hill.

By the time they reached a large thatched inn, he was more awake.

'I reckon this could be Parkham. I think that's what James said.'

'Did 'ee plan this all that time ago, before James left?' She could hardly believe that he could have had such things going on in his head without telling her.

'Not exactly, but us used to talk. He was gwain to leave, one time.'

Thomas told Mary about one of the conversations they had.

'I had it all planned out,' James told him. 'I'd wait 'til I was working alone and the maister was out for the day, then I'd go. Walk far enough so as no one'd know me.'

'So why didn't 'ee do it?' Thomas asked.

James had paused in his weeding and, sitting back on his haunches, stared at the sun low on the western horizon.

'You have to reckon it up. Will the next place be worse? Will I be caught? I reckon I was afraid, if the truth be told. Then, in the end, I thought, well, 'tis two years now afore I'm free. I thought I could wait two years, having done ten. And there's Sarah to keep me here now.'

He had smiled as he told Thomas that.

'He said 'twas best to head for the coast,' Thomas remembered. 'Us talked it all over. But I don't think I believed us would ever do it, but then I never thought things would get so bad.'

They paused again at a fork in the road.

'Us needs to keep the moon on the left, but that's no help yer.'

'There's a church up there, let's go that way.' The sight of the church tower silhouetted against the almost black sky reminded Mary of Buckland Brewer. If only they were there now and could go to their parents' house, even if only for a few minutes.

Next to the church some cottages were clustered around a small village green. Wood smoke hung in the air. Mary could picture the small cottage room where the fire was banked up for the night, the table where the family would sit in the morning. She and Thomas moved quietly past, but a dog heard them and barked, once, twice, before settling again. A cat slipped easily under a cottage gate and padded silently towards them to rub its head against their legs, until they hurried on.

At another fork in the road Thomas pulled a long stick from the hedge and set it at the junction to see which way it would fall.

'There, that's the way us shall go.'

After a while the clouds increased, bringing light, misty rain and obscuring the moon altogether; it was then so dark that it was only the bulk of the hedgebanks that guided them on their way.

Thomas's pace was slowing again. Mary glanced at him anxiously from time to time. When she saw his head dropping forward as he walked, she took his arm.

'Come on, I know you'm tired, Thomas, but us have got to get there. I'll help you.'

Before long she was having to support him as he staggered.

'I'm sorry, Mary.' His voice was slightly slurred. 'So tired. And my back is hurting so bad.' It was the first time he had admitted it.

She was frightened. She did not know where they were, and it seemed they would never reach the sea, but Thomas could not continue any further. She had to be the strong one now.

'Come on, us'll rest again.'

And she helped him through a gateway into a hay-field where he lay down on the damp ground and slept immediately.

This time Mary slept too, lulled by the sweet smell of hay. When she awoke it was with a cry – Mr Phillips with the body of a bull was coming towards her with a whip and she was scrabbling to escape; but then he was gone, and there was just the hayfield with Thomas asleep beside her. She jumped up – how much time had passed? She could see now that the hay had been cocked; she had not noticed that before. But then she realised that there was a faint glow in the sky, a barely perceptible lessening of darkness that told her dawn was approaching.

'Thomas, wake up!'

Rosa would be getting up now, she would expect to walk with Mary to fetch in the cows.

'Thomas, 'tis morning, come on, us'll be missed!'

She pictured Rosa going into the bedroom and finding it empty, waking her parents to tell them that Mary had gone.

'Thomas!' She shook him quite roughly and he cried out in pain. 'Oh Thomas, I be so sorry but you have to wake up!'

At last he opened his eyes.

'Thomas, us has got to go on, us can't stay here; look, 'tis a hayfield, they'll be coming to ted it!'

He was so stiff and sore she had to help him up and guide him out of the gate.

As the sky lightened so Mary's anxiety increased. Farmworkers would soon be about in the lanes and the fields; there was nowhere she and Thomas could hide.

'Thomas,' she spoke in a whisper, 'how far be it now to the sea? Can us get there, or should us go somewhere else?' She had no idea where that somewhere might be, or indeed what they would find when they reached the sea.

It was an effort for him to talk and walk at the same time. 'It can't be far now. But Mary, mind, I've not been there.'

She said nothing, and felt close to despair. There was no choice, they could never go back.

When the lane widened, they saw farm buildings ahead, and smoke rising from a chimney. Thomas hesitated but she urged him on.

'Us can't go back, so us must go on.'

They walked steadily with their heads down, not daring to look towards the gate that led into the yard. A black-and-white sheepdog came over to them giving short, sharp barks and wagging its tail, its presence telling them that someone must be around. Holding Thomas's arm to guide him, Mary kept walking until they were around the corner and the farm was out of sight. She did not think they had been seen.

Before long they reached a cluster of cottages at a crossroads with another turnpike road. An inn stood on the corner opposite them.

'The Castle Inn,' Mary read from the sign. 'Which way now?'

Thomas was looking down at the road as if he no longer cared or had the strength to hold up his head. She felt a wave of panic. When a carriage drawn by two trotting horses went by, its lanterns still lit despite the gradual passing of the night, Mary felt too discouraged to attempt to hide, but in any case its occupants did not trouble to observe two weary children.

Should she and Thomas follow the carriage travelling on the turnpike road? Or cross over to the lane that would lead on and down? There were no distant hills in that direction to obscure her view of the sky, which was gradually lightening from darkest blue to a silvery grey. Lower down, the sky seemed to retain its deep colour. She stared at it; she had never seen such a thing before, not in all the times she had been out at dawn. There was a horizontal line across the sky, silvery grey above, dark blue below. Could the dark blue be water?

'Thomas, look!'

'Hmm?' He barely lifted his head.

'Look! There! Is that... can that be the sea?'

He looked up and blinked, then gave her a tired smile. 'I reckon that be it.'

Elated, they crossed the turnpike road. A skylark started from the earth and rose up singing, ascending higher still and higher until it was a mere speck far above, yet still its song filled the air, and at that moment Mary shared its joy and its freedom: she was no longer on the farm, she did not have to live in fear of being beaten or molested, and the sea was ahead, just a short walk away.

The skylark's liquid notes must have summoned the sun because, just then, it crept above the eastern horizon, and colour began to emerge from the high hedgebanks; purple foxgloves, yellow buttercups, the delicate white cow parsley, and then every shade of green appeared where before there had been darkness.

They followed the lane down into a steep, wooded valley through which a stream babbled far below their path, its music almost drowned out by the birdsong that echoed all around now that the sun had started to find its way through the woodland canopy. A silent cottage stood alongside the path, its chimney not yet smoking, and further houses were visible through the trees on the other side of the steep drop to the stream. There were two or three small fields, one of newly-cut hay, but there was nothing that resembled a farm as Mary knew it, and the sea was again visible ahead.

Thomas tripped several times on the stony track, crying out in pain as the sudden jolt wrenched his injured back. Mary did her best to support him, but her own exhaustion was increasing with every step; she was not sure how much longer she could continue. They had to find somewhere safe to sleep.

At the foot of the valley, their path met the stream before it rushed through the trees to disappear over the edge of a rock face.

'Here, Thomas, us must drink. I don't know whether us'll be able to get to the edge of the sea to drink.' She could not yet imagine how the sea would meet the land, or whether they would be in danger of falling in.

She scrambled down the mossy bank, showing Thomas where to hold on to tree roots so that he would not fall, and they drank thirstily before climbing back up to the lane. Which way should they go now? The track turned to the left, but there were signs of habitation that way and the track appeared well-used, so she did not think they would be safe to remain on it for much longer. To their right a sheep path led off through a meadow with woodland alongside.

'Come on, Thomas, us'll go this way.'

He followed her as meekly as a small child, and they had not gone far when a wide view opened suddenly before them. The sea was immense; a glorious expanse of blue that went on for ever, its surface sparkling in the early morning sun. The air was filled with the squealing of gulls and the rhythmic swash of gentle waves running up on to the pebbled beach, before retreating with a churring sound as the pebbles were drawn back with the water. The green cliff on which Thomas and Mary stood continued on around the bay, gentle slopes clothed in yellow gorse, sometimes dropping through a wooded valley before falling in a sheer drop of dark red rock to the beach. Within their sight there were no farmhouses or barns, no cattle, no cornfields or fields of potatoes.

'Thomas, us have done it!' She put her arms carefully around him. 'And you were right, the sea's the best place to be.' She would never have believed it could be so big.

'Us would never have got yer if it weren't for you.' He gave her a sheepish smile. 'I've been no good to you. And now I really got to sleep.'

'Me too. Us'll find somewhere close by.'

The track wound up between yellow flowering gorse bushes and then down through a low, windswept copse as it followed the undulations of the cliff. Mary gathered plantain leaves to soothe Thomas's back while she looked out for somewhere to sleep.

They came to a place where the cliff fell away to a grassy ledge before dropping again to the beach.

Mary stopped. 'This may do. Wait yer.'

A small path made by the regular passage of an animal led down to the ledge, then on at an oblique angle to the beach. Mary followed it carefully. The ledge, about fifteen feet deep and a similar distance wide, was clothed in a thick mat of wiry grass. She sat down. It was damp from the light rain that had only recently ceased to fall, but it was soft and comfortable. Once sitting there she would not be seen from the beach, nor could she see Thomas standing above.

'Come down yer; this'll do!'

She reached up to take his hand as he made his way gingerly down, then they knelt together to eat the remaining bread. It was more than they would have had for breakfast at Gusland.

Mary leaned back against the ledge wall. They were safe; no one knew where they were and they could be seen neither from the sea nor from the land above. Mr Phillips could not find them. Her relief, coupled with her exhaustion and the horrific memories of the previous day threatened to overcome her, and she started to cry.

'Hey, come on.' She had thought that Thomas would be too tired to notice her tears, but he put his arms around her and pulled her towards him. 'Us is safe now.' He wiped away her tears with the tips of his fingers. 'He won't find us yer; I promise. Now give me some of those leaves, I know your back needs easing too.'

They pressed the bruised leaves against each other's injured backs, then lay down carefully to keep them in place. Mary's last thought was that she had never in her life been so tired, and then the soothing sound of the waves and the comfort of Thomas's hand holding hers lulled her into a deep sleep.

Chapter Eighteen

It was a fine morning, sunny with a soft breeze, just the thing for drying clothes. Charity Mitchell bent low over the washtub and scrubbed hard at her husband's trousers. They were full of dust from hay-harvesting, despite being beaten outside before washing. She would just have time to get this basketful out to dry before going to do the rough at the Rectory; being a Saturday she started later, so could do some chores first.

'Maria!'

Charity left the washing for a moment and opened the door. The village was sparkling as the sun lifted last night's raindrops from the roofs and hedges. Where *was* the girl?

'Maria, where be 'ee with that water?'

Here they came, Maria and Jane carrying the bucket between them, and slopping the water over their bare feet because Maria was taller. Being thoughtless, she did not lower the bucket to her sister's level.

''Tis in yer I need the water not all down the path, maid!'

Charity wrung out the trousers and added them to the pile of scrubbed clothes.

'Now, one more bucket of water'll give me enough for boiling the puddings as well.'

The two girls skipped off to the well again. They were good maids; a great help to her. And now that Mr Mitchell was busy with the hay harvest there was a little more money coming in, so what with that and the sums that Edward and Catherine sent home each month, things were a little easier. When Catherine finished her apprenticeship last year, Mr Fulford had helped her secure a good position. Next year Elizabeth would finish; that would leave only Thomas and Mary without wages.

She poured the bucket of clean water over the clothes. She certainly did not want another year like the last one. The failure of the potato harvest had hit them very badly; she did not know how they had avoided the Workhouse. And now it was said that signs of the disease had been seen again. Her husband had checked their piece of ground last night in the near-dark after harvesting.

She had barely started wringing out the clothes when there came a loud hammering at the door. No one ever knocked. She had not even time to drop the washing before the door was thrown open.

'Where be 'em?'

The voice was loud and hard. The man stepped right into the room.

'I said, where be 'em?'

'Who? Where be who?' She was confused; who was he? He was familiar…

'Those bastards.'

She cried out as he grabbed her arm, brought his dark, bearded face close to hers. 'Where've 'ee hidden 'em?'

It was Mr Phillips. It was Thomas and Mary.

'What's be gwain on?' she cried.

With an expression of disgust he pushed her aside and took the stairs two at a time. Within seconds he had returned.

Her hands were shaking. 'Where be my children? What have 'ee done to 'em?'

He thrust aside a chair that was blocking his way and it fell with a clatter on to the floor.

'They've runned off. If I find you've helped 'em,' he grabbed her arm again, 'you'm gwain to be locked up, I'll see to that!'

He strode down the path, heedless of Maria and Jane returning with the bucket, and then Jane was crying in the dirt and much of the water was spilled.

It did not take long for Charity to leave, despite her agitation. Maria would wring out the washing as best she could, she would hang it out while standing on a chair.

'Then put the puddings on to steam but don't 'ee scald yerself. And go to Mrs Ley if there be any trouble.'

Jane was crying quietly on the floor, Maria wide-eyed and tearful. 'But where be 'em, Mam? Where be Mary and Thomas?'

'I've told 'ee, I don't know. I be gwain to Mr Fulford afore I go to work.'

She hurried down the path and out into the main street, her thoughts in turmoil. Almost running down the middle of the road she found herself looking left and right; were they hiding down that alley, behind that tree? Long since accustomed to being separated from her children, she nevertheless thought of them often, picturing them working in the fields or eating a good dinner in a warm kitchen. Why had they left?

She turned the corner and stopped suddenly. Mr Phillips was mounting his horse outside Mr Fulford's house. He did not trouble to rein in the horse, which was rolling its eyes nervously, as he passed her at a fast trot.

'I'll find 'em! By end of the day I'll have 'em back!'

Charity watched him go, and she feared for her children.

When Mary awoke, the sun had already travelled towards the west. Thomas was still deeply asleep, curled on his side with his arm supporting his head, but he looked less pale and drawn than he had that morning. She knelt up, her muscles stiff from having slept for so long. The grand sweep of the coastline and the endless sea took her breath away. The waves were catching the light from the sun as they rolled in towards the beach and, further out, a small boat made its way along the coast. She could just make out two people, one rowing and the other dangling his hand in the water. In the distance a sailing ship inching its way across the bay appeared no bigger than her hand.

She reached up under her blouse and felt the hard, sore weals on her back. She had been too tired for the pain to keep her awake. How strange that it was already evening; she struggled to remember how long it was since they had run away. They had left on Friday night, so it must now be Saturday evening. When would Rosa have realised that they had gone? Mary had made the bed look as if it had been slept in so that Rosa would go to the meadow expecting to find Mary bringing in the cows. But it would not have been long before Mr Phillips found out that Thomas had gone too. She shivered when she imagined his reaction.

She shuffled forward on the ledge for a better look at the beach. To her right there was an area with a smooth tawny surface where a party of black-and-white birds strutted and probed with their long bills. She was very thirsty. She saw that she could easily climb down on to the beach and would only have to cross over a short distance of pebbles before she reached the water, and if Thomas woke he would be able to see her.

Despite having put on her boots, the pebbles were very difficult to walk on; she had to hold out her arms to keep her balance. She was glad to reach the level area which she saw to be sand, just like Mr Phillips sometimes carried home to put on the fields. She ran to the water's edge and crouched down until a wave ran in, then cupped a handful of water to her mouth.

'Ergh!' She spat it out forcefully. It was salty! She tried some more from further up the beach but it was just as bad. She would have to find water elsewhere.

Wandering along the beach, she enjoyed the feeling of the breeze in her hair and drawing the fresh, clean air deep into her lungs. From here she could see the full sweep of the cliffs from a distant, hazy point to her right, around to the ledge where Thomas slept and beyond to a cliff that sloped gently into the sea, but further on there were yet more cliffs that were so far away she was sure it would take a week of walking to reach them.

She might not be able to drink the seawater, but she could wash in it. She pulled off her boots and tiptoed tentatively into the cold, clean water, the sand soft and yielding under her feet, then she hitched up her skirt and rinsed the dried mud and dust from her legs.

Returning to the ledge, she saw Thomas had rolled on to his back and was snoring quietly. It would be a shame to wake him; she would hurry to the stream for a drink.

Shortly before she reached the stream, as the path led her down into a dip and around a corner, suddenly there was a woman in front of her. She had her back to Mary and was picking peas in a small garden that had been cleared from the dense bracken and brambles surrounding it. She looked quite elderly; her grey hair was arranged in a knot on the back of her head. As Mary stood, uncertain whether to go back, the woman turned and saw her.

'Hello, chiel, what be doing?' She had a kind, weather-worn face and wore a blue apron over her threadbare dress. 'You'm lost, I reckon! Haven't seen 'ee afore.'

'I just be gwain to get a drink from the stream.' Mary did not move. Perhaps she should run back, the woman would not catch her.

'Well, why don't 'ee come along with me and have a dish o' milk? Us has some fresh from Mrs Hortop's cow each morning and it's not finished yet. Yer, you can carry the basket for me.'

There seemed no harm in it, and the mention of milk made Mary realise that she was hungry, as well as thirsty. Taking the basket of peas, she walked with the woman back to the track that she and Thomas had descended early that morning; then they crossed a bridge and passed along the top of the low cliff, where a large house backed by wooded hills came into view.

Mary hesitated. 'What's that place?'

'That? That's the Castle of course, where Mr and Mrs Wood live. You *are* a stranger, bain't 'ee! They'm a lady and gentleman as keeps theirselves to theirselves, us don't see a lot of 'em. Now, just a bit further down this yer path and us'll come to our cottage. Mr Prance, my husband, he be out fishing with our son Joseph so 'twill only be me at home.'

Mrs Prance told Mary that she had ten children, but all except Joseph were living away, the girls in service and the boys fishing or gone to sea.

'Us have lived yer at Peppercombe all our lives, near enough, and all that time in this yer cottage.'

'Is that where us be, Peppercombe?' The question was out before Mary had time to think. Mrs Prance was bound to ask more questions now.

'There, didn't I say you'm lost? Course it's Peppercombe, chiel. Now, yer us be.'

They had descended a path almost to the beach and there, perched on the edge of the low cliff was a thatched cottage with roses around the door and a few hens pecking in the tiny front garden. A pile of nets and strangely-shaped baskets were heaped nearby.

'They'm Mr Prance's lobster pots,' Mrs Prance laughed in response to Mary's question. 'I can tell you don't know aught about fishing, maid!'

In the kitchen, a welcoming fire flickered in the deep fireplace.

'Come on in, chiel, and sit yourself down.' Mrs Prance went into a dimly-lit pantry to fetch the milk while Mary looked around. A brightly-coloured rag rug lay on the floor in front of a small dresser which carried a display of blue and white china; gleaming copper pots hung above the fireplace, and a posy of buttercups, forget-me-nots and red campions stood on the scrubbed deal table. A window looked out on to the sea where Mr Prance and his son were visible in the distance, their little white boat gleaming in the light of the lowering sun. It was very different from the kitchen at Gusland; nothing cruel could ever take place in this room.

As Mary drank her milk, Mrs Prance asked her the inevitable questions about who she was and where she had come from. Her expression was one of concern; her face carried no lines of malice or displeasure.

Mary hesitated. 'Do 'ee know the farmers hereabouts?' she asked.

'Farmers? Well, us knows Mrs Hortrop of course and others nearby but us don't mix with them, I wouldn't say. They looks to the land and us looks to the sea and neither one of us understands the other.'

So Mary told her story. She was determined not to cry, but when Mrs Prance exclaimed with dismay and sympathy, it was difficult to hold back the tears that had been suppressed.

'That maister! He idn't fit to have care of children.'

Mrs Prance warned Mary to avoid the valley during the day because there was a frequent passage of farmers' carts coming to load up with lime. It was burnt in the limekiln just a short distance from the cottage; they leaned out of the window so Mary could see it, still smoking, above the beach.

'Even though 'tis the Sabbath tomorrow,' Mrs Prance said, 'there'll be folks about keeping an eye on the kiln so 'twould be as well to keep away.'

Mary suddenly remembered then that she had heard of Peppercombe before: Mr Phillips used to say that he was going there to fetch lime. She jumped up.

'Us must go; us must leave now.' He might arrive here in the valley at any moment.

'No, maid, no.'

Mrs Prouse took her hand, drew her back to the chair.

'No farmers come here weekends. Any case, I know the place you've told of, where your brother be. You'm safe there; no one'll see 'ee there.'

It was clear that she meant what she said, and Mary felt reassured.

As far as finding a magistrate was concerned, Mrs Prance was dubious whether this would be helpful.

'They'm the ones that lock folks up, not help 'em, or so I'd have thought.' She was also uncertain of their chances of getting to Canada, but said she would ask her husband.

'Now you must go, and go quick, chiel, or your brother will be worried sick. But oh, that mistress of yourn, how any woman can be so cruel I just don't know.'

She gave Mary a loaf of bread cut in half and filled with cold, cooked mackerel, some raspberries and an earthenware bottle of water so that they need not visit the stream during the next day. Mary almost ran back along the cliff path, full of gratitude and longing to tell Thomas of her adventure.

He was just waking when she returned. He was confused at first and could scarcely believe he had slept for so long, then very anxious when Mary told him about Mrs Prance.

'You should never have told her! Suppose word gets out that us is here!'

'Her won't tell nobody,' Mary reassured him, 'you'll know that when you meets her tomorrow. Her's the kindest woman I ever met, even kinder than the folks at chapel.'

By the time they had eaten half of the food they had been given, he felt better. When Mary told him everything she had learned from Mrs Prance, they decided to stay where they were the next day, visit the Prances' cottage again in the evening as had been arranged, then perhaps set off for Bideford the day after that.

Having slept so long, they stayed awake until late, talking over all the events that led to their escape, wondering how everyone on the farm had responded to their absence, and planning their future. As it grew dark, the moonlight tracked a path on the water, silvering the waves as they washed up on the beach with a measured music that soothed Mary's fears. When they lay back to watch the stars appearing, the sky seemed even more immense than the ocean.

Mary passed a restless night. Despite the reassurances she had given Thomas, she was a little anxious that Mrs Prance would tell someone of their meeting and that word would get around, not from any malicious intent but purely through her concern for them. She worried about missing chapel, the next day being Sunday, and wondered whether all her friends would be told what had happened, and whether she would be considered a sinner. And she was cold despite her shawl, and lying close to Thomas. The temperature seemed to drop still further towards dawn, but when the sun came up she slept deeply for several hours.

The next day they walked along the clifftop path where butterflies danced over pink and yellow flowers, and climbed down to the beach to jump in and out of the waves. Their part of the beach was hidden from the Prances' cottage and the limekiln by a jutting cliff, so they did not have to fear being seen by strangers, especially on a Sunday. They vied with each other to go in as deep as they dared and screamed with delight when an unexpected wave soaked their clothes. While Thomas wandered further along the beach, Mary stood at the edge of the tide where the sun warmed the water as it ran in over her bare feet. Staring at the distant ships sailing out across the bay, she wondered about the people who travelled on them.

They had come to realise that the height of the sea varied according to the time of day, enabling them to walk on the sand that was so much easier than balancing on the pebbles. When the tide came in they returned to their ledge to read Mary's Bible Christian magazine which she had carried hidden inside her clothing, and they sang hymns so loudly they drowned out the cries of the gulls.

When evening was approaching they set off for the cottage, stopping at the stream on the way to wash their hands and faces. It seemed to Mary a complete delight to have spent a day without working and now to be visiting sympathetic people, but she could see that Thomas was anxious.

'The maister won't come yer,' she told him, 'not on a Sunday.'

'No, it ain't that. I've thought on it and he won't be yer at all this week, too busy with harvest. Same for all the farmers, I reckon.'

'What, then?'

He stopped on the narrow path and gazed out at the sea. It was a moment or two before he replied.

'The folks us is seeing, us knows nothing of them. Us don't know that us can trust them.'

She knew she only had to say the word, and he would have returned to their ledge.

'Come on,' she said, 'you'll know when you meet 'em.' And she walked on.

Mr Prance was a tall, broad-chested man with dark, curly hair and deep-set eyes; when he greeted them rather gruffly, Thomas drew back.

'Come on in now, my birds,' Mrs Prance called from within and before long they were seated at the table. She gave them bread and a stew made with lobster.

Mary tasted it. 'I never ate fish 'til yesterday; us mostly had bacon or cheese on the farm, or just bread lately.'

'Never ate fish!' Mr Prance slapped his knee and roared with laughter. 'Maid, you've not lived!'

Things were easier after that.

'I been talking to Mr Prance,' said Mrs Prance, 'of this notion of yourn to go to Canada, haven't I?' She looked at her husband.

'That you have.' He stroked his beard thoughtfully. 'I've known of folks who've taken a passage. 'Tisn't something that's done on a whim, takes planning and costs money. Have you two got money?'

They shook their heads.

'That's what I reckoned.'

'But us'll work for our passage,' said Thomas defensively, 'and work when us gets there too, to pay back what us owes.'

Mr Prance folded his arms against his chest. 'But the two of you hadn't ever seen the sea 'til yesterday! There's a heap of folks that would like to take a passage; fishermen, sailors, folks that know about boats, they'd be the ones to get the work if 'twas there for the taking.'

Mary put down her spoon. She had begun to get used to the idea of going to Canada. When she spoke her voice was very quiet.

'What can us do, then?'

Mrs Prance looked at her kindly. 'Now don't fret, chiel, and listen to what Mr Prance has to say.'

He told them that Mr Richard Heard, who owned three ships, might be prepared to help them by lending them the money for a passage, provided they worked off the debt when they arrived in Canada.

'I believe I've heard tell of such a thing,' he said, 'so you could pay him a visit in the High Street and put your case before him.'

They could also call on Reverend Pine-Coffin, a magistrate who lived nearby and owned most of the land thereabouts.

'As I understand it,' said Mr Prance, leaning back in his chair and hooking his thumbs under his waistcoat, 'you've done wrong by walking away from your apprenticeship, but then your maister's done wrong by the way he's treated you, so it may be that the Reverend will know the right thing to do. He's a fair man and I've not known him to be cruel. One year when times was hard, he returned a tenth of the rent to his tenants to make life a little easier for 'em.'

Thomas was in favour of visiting Reverend Pine-Coffin, even though his name made them both laugh. 'Us can find out if he can help, but whatever he says, us isn't going back to Gusland.'

Thomas thought that they should stay in Peppercombe for another couple of days because it would not do to arrive in Bideford on Tuesday; it being market day many farmers would be in the town, perhaps even Mr Phillips.

'Now, that's sensible,' said Mrs Prance. She told them that her cousin who lived in Bideford would help them. 'Her'll give 'ee a morsel to eat when her knows I've sent 'ee.'

It was beginning to grow dim outside. Mrs Prance lit a candle and its light shone out, pushing away the shadows that had begun to gather in the corners of the room.

She patted Mary on the hand while saying that they must come to collect some food the next day and, having questioned Mary closely about the likelihood of comfort when sleeping out on a ledge above the sea, also insisted that they take a blanket.

Together they wandered out of the cottage to watch as the sun sank down towards the horizon. Mr Prance pointed out Lundy, an island that lay some miles out to sea, and made them laugh by suggesting that Mr Phillips would never find them if they went there. Then they walked up the track where he showed them the yard where culm for the kiln was stored, and the warehouse where farmers bought lime. It was a desolate place in the fading light; Mary was glad to leave it.

For the next two days, knowing that farmers might be coming into the valley, Mary made sure that they did not leave their ledge very often. The time passed slowly; she and Thomas slept frequently, they read a little and they talked a lot, looking back over their time at Gusland, able to wonder at the privations they had endured now that it was over.

Late on Tuesday afternoon, when they were sure that there would be no more farmers' carts, they went to the cottage by the sea to say goodbye. Mr Prance was sitting outside on a stool mending his nets; his manner was brusque when he wished them well but Mary could see by the warmth in his eyes that he was sincere.

Mrs Prance came out, wiping her hands on her apron.

'Now, you take care of yourselves, midears.' After a moment's hesitation, she took Mary in her arms. As they clung to each other, Mary tried not to cry but could tell by the way Mrs Prance repeatedly patted her on the back that she was similarly affected.

After a final wave of farewell, Mary and Thomas walked along the cliff path, past their ledge and on, into unfamiliar territory. It was some time before they spoke. Mary paused to look back at the cliffs that had become so familiar, the waves washing up on the pebble beach below and the folds in the landscape where Peppercombe Valley was hidden, just as the cover of a book conceals the story within. Thomas strode on with his head down, and she hurried after him.

They had not gone far when the path turned inland next to a large manmade pond, just the way Mr Prance had said it would. He had told them that it led to Portledge, the home of Reverend Pine-Coffin, and beyond that to the Bideford road, should they still need to go there.

After walking through a small wood, they saw a huge house before them. The scale of it astounded Mary; it was bigger than a church – bigger than ten churches! How many people lived there? There must be space enough for several hundred.

The track led them to a large stableyard some distance from the house. It was nothing like the farmyard at Gusland; here, everything was immaculately clean as if someone came along with a broom the moment a horse lifted its tail. As they stood close to the wall they could see polished brass and leather harnesses through an open door and a glimpse of gleaming paintwork in the carriage house. Somewhere, a horse whinnied gently.

'Which way shall us go?' Thomas whispered.

'Us could try that way.' Mary pointed across the yard. There were further buildings in that direction beyond which the roof of the main house was visible. They walked tentatively out into the yard but were barely halfway across when a man shouted from behind them.

'Oy! Where do 'ee think you'm gwain?'

Thomas jumped and would perhaps have run off if Mary had not grabbed his arm. She turned to face the man in knee-high boots and a long apron who had emerged from the stables with a leather halter in his hand.

'Us is looking for Maister Pine-Coffin.'

'Be 'ee now?' His tone was more amused than angry. 'And what would 'ee be wantin' with the maister then?'

'Us needs to talk to 'n,' said Thomas, who still looked ready to run. 'Us needs to talk to a magistrate.'

'Do 'ee now? Be 'ee in trouble?' He walked closer and Thomas flinched, but Mary was sure the man meant well.

'Not in trouble, but us needs to ask'n what us should do,' she told him.

'Well, he idn't at home, won't be back for a week or more. Do you two want a morsel to eat afore 'ee go, 'cos I can't have 'ee hanging about yer. Go up that path there and you'll come to the kitchen door. Ann'll give 'ee summat to eat, the Reverend will always have it so.'

Half an hour later, they were walking quickly along the back drive to the main road. They had been allowed to sit on the kitchen steps while they each ate two slices of bread and ham with a cup of milk, but it had been made clear to them that they were then to leave the estate immediately. Although Mary felt secretly relieved that they did not have to explain their predicament to Reverend Pine-Coffin, they now had to face the next stage of their journey.

'I don't think us should walk on the turnpike road in daylight when there's folk about,' said Thomas. 'If us can find somewhere to sleep for a few hours, us can walk to Bideford afore it gets light. 'Tis only a couple of hours away I reckon.'

The strangeness of the landscape and the daunting thought of the trials ahead of them made Mary wish desperately that they could turn off this road and walk to Buckland Brewer. What a welcome they would receive when they arrived at her parents' cottage! For a fleeting moment she thought even the familiarity of Gusland would be preferable to this uncertainty, but then she remembered the sight of John coming towards her, the look of hatred on Mrs Phillips' face and the sound of the whiplash, and she thrust the thought aside.

After walking for a short distance along the turnpike road, they came to a small copse. They pushed through the undergrowth, their clothes catching on brambles as they ducked under branches, until they came to a little glade, secluded from the road and from the fields on either side, where they were able to make themselves reasonably comfortable on a bed of bracken. They lay in silence for a while, but Mary felt far from sleep.

'Thomas, what will happen to us, do 'ee think? Will us get to Canada?' It was hard to voice the next thought, and her voice came in a whisper. 'Or will us get sent back to Gusland?'

He reached for her hand. 'Us idn't ever going back to Gusland, I promise.'

He always spoke that way; their time was over, they would never return. Mary said nothing, but secretly she was afraid that Thomas might be wrong.

EMIGRATION

To Quebec, Montreal, Upper and Lower Canada, Prince Edward Island, &c.

 THE following well-known first class Ships will sail from Bideford and Bristol, on or about the 2nd day of April next, (weather permitting,) taking Goods and Passengers.

The Barque 'DEVONIA,' 950 Tons Burthen, will sail from Bristol for Quebec and Montreal direct.

The Barque 'SECRET,' 600 Tons Burthen, will sail from Bideford for Quebec and Montreal direct.

The Barque 'CIVILITY,' 450 Tons Burthen, will sail from Bideford for Prince Edward Island and Nova Scotia.

All of the above vessels are well known as very substantial and fast sailing Ships, carry experienced Commanders, are very roomy in the twixt decks, and can afford accommodation (in each Vessel) for about Ten Cabin Passengers. A more desirable opportunity for individuals and families about to emigrate cannot be offered, as only a limited number of passengers will be taken in each Vessel, which will very much increase the comfort of the passengers

Every accommodation possible will be given to the passengers, and no expense spared to make them comfortable during the voyage.

For particulars, apply to Mr. R. HEARD, Merchant, Bideford.

Each of the above Vessels will return direct to Bideford.

R. HEARD ... this opportunity ... for his ...

North Devon Journal 29th March 1849

Chapter Nineteen

'So remember His words, dear friends, and take Him into your hearts.'

A chorus of 'Amen's echoed around the chapel. Mary Thorne shifted her weight uncomfortably while smiling out at the people gathered before her. She did not feel she had spoken well but the Lord had assisted her, enabling her to keep going despite the horrible aching in her legs and back. She knew that this was a trial she must accept. This pregnancy was even more difficult than the last but, as it was her eleventh, it was inevitable that she would suffer.

'And now let us sing hymn number two hundred and twenty-three.'

She would have to stand during the singing, and then greet the children as they came in from the schoolroom, but perhaps she could then quietly ask Mr Fry if he would hear them say their catechism so that she could sit down. Meanwhile the words of the hymn would distract her from her discomfort:

> *'Weary of wandering from my God*
> *And now made willing to return,*
> *I hear, and bow me to the rod.'*

When at last she was seated she was able to listen properly to the children, something that always gave her pleasure. It was several months since she had been to Thornhillhead so she was able to see some very agreeable progress. Little William, who had been so distractible and fidgety, stood beautifully while he listened to the other children – or at least pretended to listen because he knew she was watching him – then gave his responses without hesitation. It was disappointing not to see Mary Mitchell; she was one of the most dedicated in the group but was not present today, nor was her brother Thomas. It was to be hoped that they had not been kept on the farm to work.

Mrs Thorne spoke a few last words before walking through the congregation to the door. She was uncomfortably aware of eyes sliding towards her as she passed; the less observant in the congregation who had not previously noticed her condition most certainly knew now. It was foolish, but she was a little embarrassed.

When the greetings and enquiries after health were completed she walked slowly towards the gate where a couple of horses waited patiently. Her husband had driven her to Thornhillhead before going on to speak at Frithelstock; but she was now to ride with Mr and Mrs Clement who had invited her to dinner, and after she had spoken at Twitching Chapel in the afternoon, Mr Phillips of Brendon would kindly drive her all the way home.

'Come, Mrs Thorne, take my arm now.'

Mr Clement helped her into the cart and she sat next to Mrs Grace Clement, who had thoughtfully placed a cushion on the hard wooden seat. She could relax a little now; she was in good company and the day was partly over. They spoke of those who had been present and she remarked on how impressed she had been with the children's progress.

''Tis a pity,' said Mr Clement, 'about the two Mitchell children. 'Ave 'ee been told what's come to pass? They've runned off from Gusland, a day or two ago it happened and not a sign of 'em to be seen despite Mr Phillips being out searching for 'em most of the day yesterday, as I understand it.'

'Run off?' She was startled; they were good children who worked hard at school. Mary in particular had made excellent progress. 'I would not have imagined they would do such a thing.'

'That's just what I said meself,' said Mrs Clement, 'and seems to me that they wouldn't have gone unless there was something to run from. Not that I'm excusing them, Mrs Thorne, but I've always thought Gusland a hard place for anyone to work, if you take my meaning.'

'Where are they, I wonder?'

She tried to imagine where such children would go. To a town, surely, because only there would they have some hope of hiding, perhaps finding work and lodging; but it was also likely that they would fall into bad company in a town. She remembered her anguish when James had run away after being beaten by his father; it had been almost a week before he was found.

'Mr Richard Phillips, who is to drive me home, is the brother of the farmer at Gusland, is he not? Does he have any insight into the matter, do you suppose?'

'I don't reckon he does, Missis,' said Mr Clement, pulling a sad face. 'They don't talk, the two brothers, haven't done for years, but you could ask 'n.'

After a good dinner in sympathetic company, and after speaking to the small but attentive congregation at Twitching Chapel, she did ask him as they drove home. While the old grey horse pulling the cart was making its way along the sunlit lanes, and the smell of freshly-mown grass was making her drowsy, she remembered the two children who had run away.

''Tis a bad business, Mrs Thorne.'

Mr Richard Phillips was a quietly-spoken man who had never married, but seemed content with his lot in life. Everyone at chapel spoke highly of him. He was at ease on this summer's evening as he swayed along with the movements of the cart on the uneven surface of the old lane.

'I don't want to say nothing 'gainst my brother, but 'twouldn't surprise me to learn that they'd reason enough to run off. But of course if they'm caught, or perhaps I should say *when* they'm caught, there'll be worse in store for 'em, I reckon.'

The scent of cut grass had been replaced by perfume drawn from honeysuckle by the warmth of the evening sun. Mrs Thorne tried to focus on the beauty of the flowers that intertwined with dog roses and climbed up the stems of foxgloves in the hedges but, try as she might, what appeared before her were images of cruelty and wretchedness.

'Mr Phillips.' She stared straight ahead as she spoke. 'If you have news of Thomas and Mary, or if you think there is anything I can do that would be of help, please would you send word to me?'

It seemed little enough, but at least she would know that she had tried.

The moon rose soon after Thomas and Mary started out on the turnpike road, but its light was scarcely needed, so wide and straight was the way that led them towards Bideford. They walked fast, energised by the sleep that had eventually come to them and encouraged by the apparent safety of the empty road and the silent fields on either side. Once, when they heard a horse and cart coming up behind them, they would have run to hide behind a hedge if a suitable gate had presented itself; but when the cart caught up with them they saw by the light of its lantern that its driver was slumped asleep in his seat with his hat pulled over his eyes, while the horse trotted on quite independently towards its destination.

They paced on in silence as the road took them past shadowy pockets of woodland from which owls called, and dark fields where a sheep coughed or a distant fox barked. Only occasionally did they see the dim shape of a silent cottage at a crossroads or at a short distance down a track.

The road had been gradually descending for half a mile or more when they came to the first houses. The sky was beginning to lighten a little, allowing them to see that these rows of dwellings were humble cottages, no different from those in Buckland Brewer.

'I thought all the houses in town would be grand ones,' Mary whispered. It was strange to think of all the lives being lived in such a small area, when at Gusland the nearest neighbour was half a mile away.

They had only gone a short distance further when she suddenly stopped, and gasped.

'Look!'

Behind some iron railings, there was a high stone arch, and beyond the arch loomed a grim edifice with row upon row of windows.

She reached for Thomas's hand. ''Tis the Workhouse.'

They stood together, staring at the building that had marked the turning point in their lives.

'Suppose,' said Mary slowly, 'us had been kept in there. P'raps you wouldn't have got whipped, p'raps…'

'No.' Thomas pulled her away. 'Don't think that way. Why would us want to be in that ol' place! Us would still be in there and us wouldn't be together. And us wouldn't be gwain to Canada!'

He grinned at her but there was nervousness in his expression, and she knew that he was trying to be brave for her sake. They took one last look at the forbidding building, and hurried on.

The road wound down between rows of houses until, suddenly, as they emerged on to a broad thoroughfare, there before them was the river at high tide, as it had been when Mary first saw it all those years ago.

'Do 'ee remember when us came down yer in Mr Fulford's cart?' she asked Thomas. 'I didn't know what 'twas, then.'

The river looked smaller than she remembered it, but of course now she had seen the sea, and everything was small by comparison.

From where they were standing, close against the wall of a large stone building, she could see the many graceful arches of the old bridge and a jumble of warehouses, sheds and yards on the opposite bank of the river. But on this side along the length of the Quay were clustered vessels of all sizes; a tall-masted clipper, elegant schooners, red-sailed cutters and twin-masted brigs alongside more modest barges and fishing smacks moored three or four deep. Their masts and complex rigging stretched high above the Quay, some even higher than the three- and four-storey buildings that stood alongside, and a gentle creaking and slapping of water as the boats moved on the tide was carried to Thomas and Mary on the breeze.

Unlike the farm, which had been a small, contained realm they were told they could never leave, this town spoke of other worlds. For every boat there on the Quay, Bideford was just a temporary resting place; within days or weeks all would sail away to undreamed-of places taking many people with them, and others would arrive in their place. Even the wind came fresh from the sea, and they drew it deep into their lungs as they stood there.

Although it was barely light, Mary could make out a few figures beginning to emerge; a man appearing from a side street and walking to a fishing boat, another emerging on the deck of one of the ships.

She moved back against the wall.

'When us goes there,' she said, 'us has got to look as if us has a right to be there, not skulk about like rats in a granary.'

'Well, us *has* got a right to be there. But 'tis too early yet, I reckon. Folks will notice us less when there's a crowd.'

They walked alongside the river in the opposite direction until they left the houses and wharves behind. They found a secluded grassy place where they could rest and watch the broad river gliding past them towards the arches of the long bridge.

'I be very hungry.' Mary turned to lie on her stomach. It seemed a long time since they had eaten on the kitchen steps at Portledge Manor.

'Me too.'

'Thomas, us needs money.' They could ask Mrs Prance's cousin for help, but could not expect to be fed more than once or twice. 'Even if us can get a passage to Canada, the ship might not sail for days, or maybe weeks. Us needs money so us can eat, and that means finding work. And when it rains where shall us sleep?'

She rolled over to look at him. He was staring at the river.

'Us can't wait weeks. Us have got to get out of yer soon as us can, 'tisn't safe yer.'

Mary's hunger presented a more pressing need. 'If I'm offered work, I s'll take it, safe or not.'

Thomas looked very tired. There were smudges of dirt on his face and his clothes were torn and grubby. She sat up to look at her own garments.

''Tis a pity us couldn't carry our chapel clothes, no folks are going to give us work while us looks like this. And in any case, there be no stone-picking or harvesting here.'

She suggested that they each take a turn to keep watch while the other crouched on the steep bank to wash. While Thomas turned his back, Mary pulled off her blouse and chemise to wash herself thoroughly and rub the worst of the dirty marks from her clothes. The river water was cold on her skin. It had twigs and leaves floating in it, but otherwise was clean enough. She spread her blouse on the grass to dry while she combed her hair with her fingers. She felt ready now to go in search of Mrs Prance's cousin.

'Come, let's go now and see 'bout some food.'

Thomas was aiming small stones at a log floating in the river and did not reply.

'Thomas!'

'No, us must ask 'bout a ship to Canada first. S'pose a ship was sailing this afternoon?'

He sounded despondent so, reluctantly, Mary agreed. 'All right then, but us must leave now.'

She walked off, and he trailed after her.

The Quay had been transformed during the couple of hours they had been away. Horses and carts lined each side of the road, children ran between the groups of people gathered beside the boats, and the air rang with the shouting and hammering of men at work, the clatter of horses' hoofs and the cries of gulls wheeling over the fishing boats. Surely, no one would notice them amidst the hubbub.

As they passed by the low bay windows of an old inn, a woman standing in the doorway called out to them.

'Would 'ee like some breakfast, my lovers? There's several folk in here eating some good bacon with hot tea, plenty of space for more'

Mary shook her head. 'Us haven't any money.'

'Well, my lover, you looks to me like you need some vittles.' She had a kind face. ''Ave 'ee eaten today? Well then, wait right there.'

She disappeared into the inn but was back in a moment with two bread rolls and some water. 'There you be, and when you come into some money you can come back and have a proper meal!'

They thanked her, and Mary asked if she knew of anyone needing work done.

'Not me, my lover, I do's it all meself!'

As they continued, Thomas suddenly grabbed Mary's arm. To reach the quayside, they had to pass a group of men talking and laughing next to some tethered horses and wagons.

'Do 'ee recognise anyone?' he whispered.

She studied the faces apprehensively. She almost wished she could see someone they knew from chapel, but none of the faces were familiar.

Now that they were close to the boats they realised that every one was different. They admired the heavy oak hulls, the painted figureheads, and tipped back their heads to see to the tops of the masts, trying to imagine how they would look when in full sail like the distant ships they had seen out at sea; and they wondered at the purpose of the multitude of ropes that ships seemed to need.

Eventually Thomas plucked up enough courage to address one of the men unloading timber.

'Can you tell us which ships sail for Canada?'

The man barely looked up from his work. 'The *Devonia*, that barque down the end there.'

Hurrying past other moorings, they saw hastily drawn-up carts being unloaded by workers who then carried the large wooden trunks, sacks and canvas bags on to a ship, while a group of people gathered alongside shouted instructions and warnings to take care.

'Look!' Mary pointed to the side of the ship. 'That's the *Devonia*.'

It was difficult at first to know what was going on but as they watched, it became apparent that families were bringing their belongings to be loaded on to the ship; when their cart had been emptied, each family strolled off, smiling and laughing, into the town.

Mary addressed one of the homely-looking women who was watching to ensure her family's belongings were carefully handled.

'Be 'ee gwain to Canada?'

'Yes, maid, tomorrow! 'Tis a long time us have waited for this day!' And she shouted at a man to take care of her trunk. 'That has all my best china, that does!'

'Tomorrow! Thomas, us has to be quick!' It was now a matter of urgency; perhaps they could sail the very next day!

Thomas went boldly up to one of the working men. 'Please, us wants to take a passage to Canada.'

The man hoisted a sack on to his back. 'Go to see Mr Heard in the High Street then, boy. But you won't be going this year, not from Bideford.'

'This year? Why not?'

'This sailing's full, the next on the *Civility* too, then there'll be no more 'til next year.' He paused before walking up the gang plank. 'Us can't sail later in the year, risk of ice coming back, see. All these folk have been planning for months, boy!'

And he disappeared into the hold.

Mary sat with Thomas on the quayside, looking back at the *Devonia* and the smiling passengers. Neither of them spoke. Mary had come to believe that they really would be able to go to Canada, to leave everything behind and start a new life.

Thomas's expression was bleak. She hardly dared speak to him.

'Well,' he said eventually, 'there's other places besides Canada. All these ships is going someplace. I be gwain to ask around, see where us can get a passage to. Us has got to go today, or tomorrow at least. You wait yer.'

'Ask about work too!'

It was half an hour or more before he returned. He told her that ships going to South Wales to fetch limestone and coal might be able to take a few passengers.

'Wales idn't as far as Canada, they said. The man us needs to ask idn't around now, but us could wait.'

There were Bible Christians in Canada, but Mary had not heard of anyone going to Wales. Thomas seemed tense and anxious, but she felt she had to ask him.

'What work would us do there? Who would us ask?'

A man whom Mary had noticed standing nearby while Thomas was away, sauntered over to them.

'You'm looking for work then, be 'ee?'

'Yes.' Mary looked up. 'Do 'ee know of any? Us can work hard.'

'I knows of some for maids. Indoor work, nothing too hard.'

Mary stood up; she had begun to wonder what work she could do on the Quay as she knew nothing of ships, but indoor work would be welcome. She could surely manage cleaning or kitchen work.

The man looked her up and down. 'You could earn good money, maid, enough to feed the two of 'ee. Who is he then, this boy, your lover?'

'He's my brother.' She didn't like the way the man looked at her.

'Where is this work?' Thomas asked. 'Indoors where?'

The man said it was just a short distance away, in one of the back streets beyond the Quay.

'Leave your brother here and I'll show 'ee.'

The man wore a grubby embroidered waistcoat under his jacket and his hat was perched jauntily on the side of his head. He smiled at her, but the smile did not reach his eyes and his gaze kept moving up and down her body.

'No, her's not going.' It was a relief when Thomas spoke out; she had begun to be afraid that he would want her to go with the man.

'Come on, Mary.' They walked quickly away together, and did not stop even when the man shouted something after them. She had a vague notion of what the work might have entailed, and was appalled, but Thomas did not speak of it and she could not find the words to do so.

Retracing their footsteps they came to the bottom of a broad street near the inn where they had been given bread.

'I reckon this is High Street, where Mr Heard has his shop,' said Thomas. 'There's no point us going there now.'

'Well, us can walk up that way.'

She wanted to leave the Quay, and could see that the High Street had colourful window displays. Carriages and carts were stopping for their passengers to enter the shops, while other people carrying baskets gathered on the pavements to talk. She was aware that Thomas was trailing behind; probably he did not want to go into such a busy street but the shops were enticing, and as it was not market day there would not be any farmers in town.

The first window carried big, coloured signs advertising tea and sugar, the next a display of fruit and vegetables amongst which Mary recognised oranges, having seen the Phillips' children eating them with juice dripping down their chins when they had each been given one at Christmas. She walked on towards a display of different fabrics, blues, greens and a deep purple such as could be used for making dresses, indeed there was a drawing alongside the fabric of two women wearing wide skirts that must have had numerous petticoats underneath.

Mary was distracted by the sudden loud ringing of a handbell. On the opposite side of the road, a man in a black hat held the bell still before starting to shout in an extraordinarily loud voice.

'Oyez! Oyez! Oyez!'

Alarmed, she looked around for Thomas and finding that he had retreated into a doorway, she hurried to join him.

'Who's that man?'

He pulled her off the street. 'I don't know. Let's listen.'

Most people were walking on regardless, but the man seemed unperturbed.

'Missing from this town!' His voice really was extremely loud, and each word was slowly and carefully enunciated. 'A black and white dog of medium size and gentle disposition.

Whosoever finds it will please return it to Mr Cann of Mill Street. God save the Queen!'

He walked a little further up the street before ringing his bell again.

'Oyez! Oyez! Oyez! Missing, having run from the farm where they were apprenticed, a brother and sister aged sixteen years and fourteen years, of dark complexion and medium height. Whosoever sees them will please report to the constable of this town. God save the Queen!'

The words rung in Mary's ears. She could not take in their implication. She could not move. The man had continued up the street and was announcing the departure of a coach to Barnstaple.

'Thomas?'

She looked up at him. The colour had drained from his face; he was staring unseeingly across the street.

'Thomas? Did he mean us?'

His eyes flicked down to hers. 'Us have got to get out of town. Now.' He grabbed her hand; his was shaking. 'But us mustn't run. You hear? Walk slowly. Now.'

They walked down the High Street to the Quay. Mary kept her eyes on the ground, terrified that she would be recognised if she met anyone's gaze. Thomas hesitated for a moment before turning right. Would they go back to the spot by the river? No, they were crossing the road, walking on, turning on to the bridge.

Thomas leaned towards her and spoke in a whisper. 'Other way goes to Torrington. Us have got to get right away.'

He moved stiffly, a little ahead of Mary. Her legs felt awkward, as if she had just learned to walk for the first time. A carriage passed them, then a wagon. They both flinched when a man pushed past them, but he hurried on. Their boots rang in unison on the bridge that stretched far in front of them, and the thought came to Mary that if they could not run forward or back, the way was over the parapet into the river below. Walk slowly, she told herself, while her heart pounded and below them the river flowed on heedlessly.

'OY!'

The sound of running footsteps behind them.

Thomas looked back. 'Run, Mary!' and he took off at a run, but immediately Mary was overtaken by a man in a black coat and top hat who, in a few strides, caught Thomas and wrestled him to the ground. For a fleeting second she saw his terrified eyes seeking out hers.

'Mary, run!' His voice was a scream and then he disappeared as the man, who was carrying a stout stick, knelt on him.

She started to run back the way they had come but after just a few paces, she froze. Where could she go? There was nowhere she could go without Thomas. Her legs felt so weak that she staggered, then suddenly she was grabbed from behind and her arms were wrenched behind her back.

'You're Mary Mitchell.' A man's rough voice. It was not a question, but she replied, the word coming out as a sob.

She was pushed along the bridge. Thomas was now on his feet, fighting for his freedom, but his energy was wasted; the man who held his arms was twice Thomas's size.

'Now walk! Walk, both of you!' The man behind Mary pushed her hard with his knee; she would have fallen if he had not been holding her arms so tightly.

As they were marched onward across the bridge, a crowd gathered around and walked alongside them; men and women alike jeering, laughing in Mary's face and shouting questions at the two men.

'Be they thieves?'

'Shame! Poor chiel.'

'They them runaways? This yer's a pretty one!'

She had never in her life felt so frightened. Her legs could not hold her; she was almost carried along by the man behind her. Thomas was still struggling and the man in the black coat wrenched his arms even further back until they must surely be broken; she cried out to him in anguish, but her voice was lost amidst the clamour of the crowd.

She could feel the man's breath on her hair, and then heard his voice in her ear as he shouted to the crowd to stand back. They were no longer on the bridge but outside a tall building.

Between the warehouses that stood opposite, she glimpsed the white houses of the town on the far bank of the river and the graceful ships on which she and Thomas should have been making their escape. The sunlight gleamed on the soaring beauty of their masts and the delicate filigree of their rigging, but then she lost sight of them as she was hustled through a doorway into a gloomy passage. Crying again to Thomas, she saw him turn and she recognised the desperation in his face. Then he was gone, and she was being pushed into a small, dark room. As she sank to the floor, she heard the key turn in the lock.

Chapter Twenty

She did not know how long she sat there alone; perhaps it was an hour, perhaps more. The events of the day replayed over and over in her head, and her heart would not be still.

After a time, she rose from the brick floor and stood motionless while her gaze travelled over four bare walls and a heavy door. The walls were thick and the low ceiling arched. Above the door and on the opposite wall were small barred windows less than a foot square; she was not tall enough to see out, and very little light could enter. There was a bed of hard wooden planks with one blanket thrown upon it, and a bucket with a lid.

She neither knew what this place was, nor why she was there.

'Thomas?' She whispered his name, and it hung in the stale air.

There were sounds from outside the room; a distant banging, and a muffled voice that she could hear if she held her breath.

Perhaps Mr Phillips had been sent for. He might arrive soon.

She would think of other things. If she and Thomas were still at Peppercombe they would see the sky stretching to infinity and the waves rolling in towards the beach; they would hear the cries of the gulls and they would walk along the flower-lined clifftop path.

How dark it was in this room; dark, cold and devoid of colour.

When Mr Phillips came, she would pray. She would close her eyes and say the prayers she knew, quietly, so that he could not hear. The whipping would end. It would be bad, but not so bad that she and Thomas could not work afterwards; Mr Phillips needed them to bring in the harvest. It would end and she would be back in a place that she knew, with Thomas. She hugged her knees as she sat on the hard wooden bed.

Suddenly there were footsteps; the key grated in the lock. Mary jumped up and stood with her back against the wall.

'Some tea for 'ee, maid.'

It was a middle-aged woman in a grey dress. She stared at Mary.

'Why, you'm nought but a chiel!'

She shut the door behind her.

'My husband said he'd brought in a maid but didn't say how young you be. What age are you, chiel?'

'Fourteen,' Mary whispered.

'Well, now.' The woman observed her closely. 'You don't look like a troublemaker to me. If you come and drink your tea by the fire in the kitchen, will 'ee be quiet? The doors is all locked so 'tis no use thinking you'm getting out.'

Mary followed her along a narrow passage and through a door into a warm kitchen.

'Now, sit down there and you'm not to move. Do 'ee want a slice of bread? You may as well have it now as later.'

The woman busied herself in the kitchen. Mary was thirsty but when she tried to swallow the hot tea, her throat seemed to close up.

'Please, where be my brother?'

The woman slapped a slice of bread on to a platter.

'Why, in the lock-up, of course. Proper struggle they had getting 'im in there so ' *e* won't be let out in a hurry. I s'pose it was 'im that got *you* into trouble, was it? You shouldn't have listened to 'n, maid, then you'd still be back where you comed from, instead of a heap of trouble ahead.'

The woman started to roll out pastry.

Mary sat very still. Thomas had not got her into trouble.

'Please, where be the lock-up?'

The woman put down her rolling-pin.

'The lock-up? This be the lock-up, of course, Bideford Gaol! Land sakes, chiel, what did 'ee think it was? And your brother's in a cell, same as you will be again before long.'

Gaol? She was aghast. Why was she in gaol?

She started to cry. 'Please can I see Thomas? Let me see my brother, please.'

At that moment the door opened and a man in a black coat entered. As soon as he spoke, Mary knew that he was the man who had brought her here. She shrank away, but he paid her little heed, instead engaging the woman in conversation about some goings-on in the town. Mary was still trying to take in the information that she was in gaol, when she realised the woman was talking about her.

'Her's no idea where her be, poor maid. Now that you'm here, you'd better bring the boy in as well and tell 'em what's what.'

Before Mary could take in what was happening, there was Thomas standing in the doorway looking dazed, his shirt torn and the side of his face bruised. When Mary jumped up and clung to him, she could feel that he was starting to cry too, despite his effort to keep himself under control.

They sat very close together on stools by the fire. The man told them that his name was Mr Gilbert, he was a constable and the keeper at the gaol. His wife was the matron. Thomas started to ask the man questions. His voice was very low. Mary knew that, despite his apparent calm, he was deeply upset.

When would Mr Phillips come? he asked. Mr Gilbert replied that Mr Phillips might come, or he might not. If he came it would be to identify Thomas and Mary, but since they had freely admitted who they were, this would scarcely be necessary. No, he said, taking another mouthful of tea, it would be a magistrate who would come, either the next day or the one after, to decide whether they should appear in court.

'In court? Why?' Mary cried. They had stolen nothing, hurt no one.

Mr Gilbert threw back his head and laughed. 'You'm apprentices! You've runned away! Course you'll go to court, maid, and to prison too I don't doubt.'

His wife nodded, her lips pursed as if regretting that such a thing was true.

But it could not be true. She, Mary Mitchell, could not go to prison.

Thomas's voice was barely audible. 'Us was badly treated at Gusland. Mary was whipped, and me too, you can see the marks on our backs still. That's why us ran off. If us tells the magistrate, will he let us go?'

Mr Gilbert knocked back the last of his tea, wiped his whiskers on the back of his hand and stood up.

'You can tell 'n, boy, but the law's the law. You shouldn't have runned off and that's the end of it. Now the both of you's gwain back in the cells 'cos I don't know that I trust 'ee not to make trouble here with Mrs Gilbert on her own.'

The rest of the day passed with interminable slowness. Mary sat on the hard bed, the thoughts of what might be to come returning to her constantly, despite her efforts to think of happier times. When she suddenly remembered her Bible Christian magazine she jumped up. Its stories would take her away from this place. Where was it? In desperation she searched under her clothes and shook out her shawl. It was such a precious reminder of her time in chapel; where could it be? She looked under the bed, she lifted the bucket and she paced up and down the room. There were no more places to search. Then she remembered the struggle on the bridge, her shawl almost pulled from her back.

She curled up on the bed, but there was no comfort in the wooden boards.

Mr Phillips leaned on the gate, watching the bullocks grazing in Barn Park. The old oak on the western boundary of the field threw a long shadow across the field; it was time to return for his tea, but he stood a few minutes more. The bullocks had fattened up well after such a slow start. They might make a good price in the autumn, but he would not hold out too much hope. Expect too much, you'd only be disappointed.

It had been a blow, finding disease in the potatoes again. He still couldn't take it in. What with that and losing a whole day's work over the two apprentices…. There were times when he felt he had had enough; enough of constant striving, enough of trying to wrestle produce from unforgiving land. There were times when he thought to let Twitching Moors revert to grazing; he could grow enough potatoes for the house, give up on the rest. Raise a few more bullocks on it. But too much toil, too much sweat and anxiety, had gone into trying to improve that land.

If he could have found those brats himself, brought them back to the farm, by God they would have learnt their lesson.

He pulled a hazel switch from the hedge, snapped it in half, and half again.

But for now the magistrate was to deal with them; he would keep out of it. He wasn't going to go to court to be asked a lot of prying questions. They were the ones on trial.

They deserved the beating they got, he wasn't going to answer questions about it. Suppose he were fined for it?

He threw the hazel switch aside.

He couldn't afford a fine. There wasn't the money now for buying lime, none for buying in hay if this year's crop didn't last the winter, none for extra hands during harvest.

Thanks to those bastards, he'd be harvesting with two hands short! Last year he had James as well as the two of them. It was going to be hard; there were no more apprentices to be had and he had never welcomed outsiders at harvest. But when those two were back, he'd see to it that they worked twice, three times as hard.

The rhythmic tearing of grass as the bullocks grazed was drowned out by the clanging of the dinner bell. The sound was uneven; that would be John, he would be standing in the porch, swinging the bell high above his head, then stopping to examine some detail on the handle that had attracted his attention.

Mr Phillips did not immediately return for his tea. He gazed out across the field.

If he were to let Twitching Moors revert to grazing, there'd be less need for labour.

There would be those who would laugh at him, they would say that he had always been set to fail. Just let them say it to his face; they'd never say it a second time. What did he care what others thought?

Yet, he had hoped for so much from that land. He had hoped, one day, to make his sons proud when they looked back on his achievements.

The shadows were lengthening; he turned and walked slowly back towards the house.

Bartholomew Fulford helped Mrs Mitchell down from the cart. Now that they had reached the gaol, she had at last fallen silent. He savoured the few moments of peace and quiet, knowing that there would be none on the return journey. He could understand her distress, of course; the worrying news of the children's disappearance and then the shock of their arrest had been the talk of the village, and indeed had been in his thoughts a good deal over the last few days. He would now find out what the true situation was, but he rather feared that the outcome would not be a good one.

He hammered on the door. Mrs Mitchell, who was wearing her Sunday clothes in an attempt to convince the gaoler that the children came from a respectable family, held her hand in front of her mouth, but he could still hear her murmured supplications for the Lord to save her poor children. She groaned when Mrs Gilbert unbolted the door, and he kept his hand on her arm to restrain her while he made their introductions, before following Mrs Gilbert through a narrow passage into the kitchen.

'Wait here 'til I'll fetch 'em.'

They heard more bolts being drawn, and Mrs Gilbert declaring 'Visitors to see 'ee!'

Bartholomew stood aside when Mary, looking pale and bewildered, appeared in the doorway, then mother and daughter fell into each other's arms, and a moment later were joined by Thomas. It was affecting to see the strength of emotion between them; he had to turn away for a moment when he imagined how he would feel if they were his children.

Through her tears, Mrs Mitchell was asking one question after another without waiting for answers, while hugging each of her children in turn.

He stepped forward. 'Come now, shall us sit down, if Mrs Gilbert don't mind, and us'll see what's what.'

'Has the magistrate been to see 'ee yet?' he asked. There was a chance that it might be decided no crime had been committed, but Bartholomew did not feel optimistic.

'The magistrate!' exclaimed Mrs Mitchell, 'They shouldn't have to see the magistrate!'

'Mam, listen, us has to tell Mr Fulford what happened,' said Thomas. He was an intelligent-looking lad, but appeared tired and anxious. 'Yes, he came yer and said us have got to appear at the next petty sessions in Torrington.' His eyes were searching, as if desperate for some positive news from Bartholomew. 'Be that the court? What'll become of us?'

'Well now,' Bartholomew leaned back in the chair. 'Tell me first, who was the magistrate as came to see 'ee?'

''Twas, I think his name was Mr Harding.'

'That's right, 'twas Reverend Harding,' put in Mrs Gilbert as she poured some tea, 'and 'twill be him sitting at the petty sessions.'

Bartholomew did not often curse but he did now, albeit under his breath. This was bad luck indeed; other magistrates might have sentenced the children to a week or two weeks in Bideford Gaol, most of which they would have served by the time the case came to court, but of all the magistrates Reverend Harding was the toughest. He would show no leniency.

'I see.' He scratched his head. 'Yes, boy, petty sessions, they be the court and 'tis there that 'twill be decided what's to become of 'ee both.'

Mary was staring at him wide-eyed. His heart went out to her; such a girl should not have to go through all this.

''Tis likely, I'm sorry to say, that you'll stay in prison for a few weeks, but then 'twill all be over and you'll be out. You must be brave, keep thinking of that time.'

'And then what?' Thomas had jumped up and was almost shouting. 'Then us has to go back to Gusland? Us isn't going! Us isn't never going back there!'

So, now the truth was coming out. 'Now then, boy, sit down and tell us why you'm so set on not going back.'

The tale that they told was worse than he had expected. Mrs Gilbert must have been used to hearing all sorts of stories in this room because she carried on with her ironing regardless, but it was a hard thing for Mrs Mitchell to hear. And when he asked Thomas to lift his shirt to show them his injuries, Bartholomew was shocked into silence for a few moments, and poor Mrs Mitchell was quite overcome. It was clear that it had not been a fair punishment, for the skin had been badly broken. The boy must have been given at least twenty lashes and his side was badly bruised where he said he had been kicked while on the ground. In addition, if Thomas and Mary's story were true, and certainly Bartholomew was inclined to believe it, there had been no call for any chastisement at all.

It would also appear that Mary's honour had been in danger of being compromised. It was difficult to make out that part of the story at first because both children found it hard to find the words for what they were trying to tell him, but he soon got the gist of it, helped along by Mrs Mitchell who used more graphic terms in her questioning.

How could Mr Phillips have served them so badly? Bartholomew was angry. He determined there and then to do whatever he could to help.

'Did 'ee tell Reverend Harding any of this?' he asked.

'I tried,' said Thomas, 'but he wouldn't listen. He said as it was us who were to be tried, not the maister.'

'There idn't nothing much I can do to alter what happens in court,' he told them, 'but I will do all I can to see that you don't go back to Gusland. I don't know as yet how it's to be done, but I s'll do my best to find out. You have my promise on that.'

There was not much time. If by any chance Thomas and Mary were acquitted, he knew that they would be sent straight back to the farm.

Each day, Mary was taken from her cell to exercise in a dreary passage about fifteen paces in length. Mr and Mrs Gilbert were not unkind; they allowed her and Thomas to walk together and, although they could only march up and down as they talked, even this was a relief after the close confinement of the cell. Having been accustomed to open air from dawn until dusk, Mary hated being shut in without even a view from a window, unable to gauge either the time of day or the weather. In the exercise passage she could look up to see a small area of sky; sometimes there was a passing seagull, and once she felt rain. There was nothing else to see except the chimney of an adjacent building, and nothing to hear except occasional muffled banging from a nearby workplace.

'Thomas,' she said one day as they walked up and down, 'be us criminals? Will folks think that of us? I couldn't bear it if chapel folk turned away from us when us goes back.' She felt a sinking in the pit of her stomach. 'If us ever goes back.'

'Mary, us have done nothing wrong!' His eyes burned with anger and frustration. 'Folks ought to see that – the magistrate ought to see it! – and if they don't, then they're the ones that're wrong, not us!''

He started to pace up and down the passage but had to stop when he knocked his shin on the corner of the wall. He stood beside her, rubbing his leg.

'P'raps I should never have said us would run away.' He stared down at the ground. 'P'raps us should have put up with it. Then you wouldn't be in this place.'

'No.' She leaned against him. 'Think on it, us couldn't stay there. Perhaps in time things'll be better for us.' But it was hard to be optimistic when she did not know what the future held.

The next day Mrs Gilbert came to tell them that they had another visitor. Mary jumped up. Would it be her mother again? Or Mr Fulford? But when she and Thomas came into the kitchen, there, sitting by the fire, was Mrs Thorne. Mary stopped dead. Of all people, Mrs Thorne was the one that Mary was most anxious of meeting. When she came to Thornhillhead, her presence always made that Sunday particularly memorable. Invariably she would find time to make some special remark to Mary; a word of praise for her reading, a comment on how well she cared for the younger children, or an observation on her growing understanding of the Scriptures; and always the remark would be accompanied by that long, loving gaze that seemed to see right inside Mary, and approve of what she saw.

To think of disappointing her was unbearable.

'Dear children, come in. Come and sit by me.'

Mrs Thorne, wearing her usual grey coat, was sitting very upright with her hands folded in her lap. She was a commanding presence in Mrs Gilbert's untidy kitchen and Mary faltered, not knowing whether to go forward or run back.

'Missis, what be 'ee doing here?'

'Come,' Mrs Thorne smiled and held out her hand. 'I have been looking for an opportunity to visit you, so when Mr Thorne told me he had business in Bideford, I immediately asked to accompany him. You have both been much in my thoughts.'

Mary, feeling tearful and unsteady, sat on a stool next to Thomas.

'But you shouldn't come to this place, this is just for bad people.'

'Mary,' Mrs Thorne reached out to take her hand, 'you are not bad, you are one of God's own children.'

'We haven't been wicked, Mrs Thorne, I don't think us has, but then why is us in gaol? Will God forgive us? Will you forgive us?' Once she started to talk, the tears flowed freely. She could not stop however hard she tried.

'Hush now.' Mrs Thorne held both of Mary's hands. 'Hush. I have heard a little of your story from Mr Fulford, and from your master's brother too. I know you have suffered and I fear there is more suffering to come, but please believe me when I tell you both that I do not think less of you for what has happened. Perhaps you should have tried a little harder to withstand the suffering, for we do not know what God has in mind for us, but you have been sorely tried. Perhaps the action you took was unwise and perhaps it was hasty, but it was entirely understandable. It was certainly not wicked.'

Mary looked up into the clear grey eyes; her own were swimming with tears. 'You don't think us is wicked then? Us won't be cast into the burning pit?'

'No, Mary, I don't think you are wicked, but you must ask for God's forgiveness and ask Him to guide you through what lies ahead. Come, let us pray together.'

And they knelt there on the cold, brick floor and prayed while Mrs Gilbert continued to wash her dishes in a wooden bowl on the table with no attempt to be quiet.

Afterwards, Mrs Thorne told them that Mr Fulford was working to ensure that they would not have to return to Gusland, and that she would do whatever she could to help.

'You may have noticed,' she said, 'that I am to be confined before long.'

Mary nodded, blushing a little. She had seen to her surprise when Mrs Thorne got up from the floor that she was pregnant.

'Nevertheless I shall be able to write letters. But you must realise that the outcome is by no means certain, and you must pray for forbearance.'

They talked for a little longer, Mrs Thorne asking them whether they were given sufficient food – hearing which, Mrs Gilbert sighed in an exaggerated fashion and muttered to herself – and whether they were warm enough.

'Now,' she said, 'I have brought something for you.' From her bag she took two books. 'I have the Bible Christian magazine that Mr Thorne has just printed, and I have a small Bible for you.'

Mary gasped. 'I lost my magazine! But I knew it almost by heart and now, to have another, and a Bible...' She could not find words to express her pleasure. How many hours would now be occupied! Thomas took over from her confusion and thanked Mrs Thorne for them both.

'I'm sorry that I did not have a Bible for each of you because I know you will not always be together in the days ahead, but perhaps it can be arranged for it to be passed from one to the other. And see here, I have marked some passages that I think will be helpful to you.'

When she had gone, Mary found time to whisper to Thomas as they returned to their cells.

'I think her visit is a good sign, Thomas. Perhaps when us sees the magistrate he will let us go free. Us can hope and pray that it'll be so.'

Chapter Twenty-One

The day came for Thomas and Mary to attend the petty sessions. Constable Palmer, whom Mary recognised as the man who had arrested Thomas, took them outside and ordered them to climb into a waiting cart. Mary was almost dazzled by the view over the river with its graceful ships, so bright was it after the gloom of the cell.

When they were seated on the rough wooden bench behind the driver, Constable Palmer climbed up after them. He stooped down to some iron chains which were fixed to the floor.

'No, please, us don't need those!' Thomas cried.

'What are they?' Mary had thought the chains might be to stop sheep or pigs escaping from the cart. She gasped when Constable Palmer clamped one of the irons around Thomas's leg and turned the key.

'Don't think I fancy chasing you across the bridge again, boy.'

And then, Mary felt the cold iron around her own leg.

She would never forget that journey through the town. People soon noticed their predicament. Before long a crowd was walking alongside the cart as it crossed the bridge, some laughing, others offering sympathy, but whatever the response Mary could not meet their eyes. With the iron chain dragging painfully on her leg, never before had she felt so ashamed. She gripped her Bible in her hands and she kept her eyes straight ahead, staring blindly out at the eastern bank of the river, the shipyards, the warehouses and the green hills above, as the cart carried them away. At the end of the bridge the size of the crowd increased, as workmen on the Quay and loiterers outside the inns hurried over to join in the fun.

'What did 'ee do then, maid? What did 'ee steal?'

'Jump down, can't 'ee!'

The sea of grinning faces moved along with them as the driver urged the horse to a trot. People clung to the back of the cart; a man with a dirt-streaked face and wild eyes tried to grab Mary's leg.

'Come 'ome with me, my lover, us can go thievin' together!'

Thomas gripped her hand as they sat bolt upright, flinching at each cruel remark. When some boys started to throw stones, one of which hit Mary on the arm, she could bear no more.

'You'm liars! Us idn't thieves! Leave us be!'

Her shriek was so compelling that the boys, grinning uncomfortably, dropped their stones. The driver turned around and used his whip to drive the crowd away, then urged the horse on at a faster pace until they had left the town behind.

It was a long time before the shock of their humiliation abated. While the horse trotted on along the turnpike road, empty now but for the occasional jingling pony and cart or dusty, trudging traveller, Mary gazed miserably at the fields and woods laid out in the summer sunshine. The river, which was greatly reduced in breadth as they travelled farther from the town, wound through meadows where cattle grazed knee-deep in buttercups, then past a village where children played on the green. She would only ever be an observer of such things; she was to be locked away again, that seemed certain now, and when she was released she would return to Gusland where the ground was stony and the wind was cold. She gazed hopelessly down at her feet and the ugly chain that tethered her to the cart.

Thomas could always sense her mood. 'Read me one of they verses that Mrs Thorne picked out.'

She found one of the places in the Bible marked with a slip of paper.

'*We are troubled on every side, yet not distressed; we are perplexed but not in despair; persecuted but not forsaken; cast down, but not destroyed.*'

She could not read the passage with any conviction. Although it had helped her in the cell, it brought little comfort now.

'Thomas, I don't know what all the words mean but I think I *be* in despair.'

'Then us'll sing. That'll make 'ee feel better.'

When he launched into a hymn that was one of their favourites at chapel, the driver looked back in surprise. Thomas continued unabashed, and his clear tenor voice rang out over the countryside. It was not long before Mary joined in.

> *'Good Thou art, and good Thou dost,*
> *Thy mercies reach to all,*
> *Chiefly those who on Thee trust,*
> *And for Thy mercy call.'*

She felt a little better by the time they reached the end.

'Now, listen,' said Thomas. He turned to her, his face still freckled from exposure to the sun despite his time in confinement, and his brown eyes burning with emotion. 'When us gets to Torrington and goes into the court, us is going to hold our heads high. Us have done nothing wrong, remember that.'

She nodded, too deeply affected to speak.

'And whatever happens today, Mary, even if us has to go back to Gusland, us have got each other, always.'

> *John Symons*, parish apprentice of *Mr. William Shute*, of Atherington, yeoman, was committed to the house of correction at Exeter, for 6 weeks, for absconding from the service of his master on the 25th day of December last. The complainant stated that Symons had also been guilty of divers misconduct and ill behaviour prior to his absconding.

North Devon Journal 16th January 1840

SOUTHMOLTON.

At the Southmolton Petty Sessions on Monday last—present, the Right Honourable Earl Fortescue, John Budd, Esq., the Rev. W. H. Karslake, and the Rev. J. P. Benson; *Ann Burgess*, aged 14, a parish apprentice of Mr. Crocombe, yeoman, of Northmolton, was committed for 14 days to the county house of correction, for absconding from her apprenticeship.

North Devon Journal 24th July 1845

Bartholomew Fulford dismounted from his horse when he reached the open gate. The workers in the field had their backs to him; it was hard at first to identify any of the men in their broad-brimmed hats or the women with the scarves about their heads to protect them from the strength of the sun. But then he recognised the height and confident movements of the lead reaper.

His own wheat had been reaped and stooked that morning. He should now be weeding turnips along with his labourers, but this visit to Gusland could be put off no longer.

He had wondered how Mr Phillips was managing the harvest. It was no time to lose two workers, and he never asked for help from neighbouring farms, nor gave it; but Bartholomew could see now that he had called on his workers' families as well as his own children. There were four reapers in the first field and another four in the field beyond, each followed by a woman gathering the corn and a man or boy binding. It was, of course, just the way Bartholomew had worked that very morning, albeit on a larger scale; it took him a minute or two, standing there with the bees buzzing in the hedgerow and the skylarks singing overhead, to realise why this seemed so very different. Here, there was no laughter, no calling out to friends across the field, no singing. They worked in silence.

He would have to attract Mr Phillips' attention. He rehearsed again the words he had planned, his lips moving silently.

He felt uncomfortable about the whole business. He had many roles; husband, father, farmer, Guardian of the Poor, Methodist minister, but his aim in all the roles was the same: be kind, offer sympathy, give practical help. To challenge and to criticise did not come naturally to him at all.

He lifted the reins over his horse's head and looped them around the gate. Someone had alerted Mr Phillips to his arrival; he was staring across the field, then putting down his scythe. Bartholomew took a deep breath and walked through the stubble to meet him, the brittle straw crunching and grasshoppers leaping with every step he took.

'Beautiful day for it!'

Mr Phillips eyed him suspiciously. They stopped a couple of yards from each other and Bartholomew tried to smile reassuringly.

'It looks a fair crop despite the dry weather.'

Mr Phillips gave an abrupt nod.

'The rain'll hold off a bit longer, I reckon. You should be well enough there.'

Mr Phillips stared past him but still did not reply. Bartholomew tried not to be distracted by the seeds and insects thrown up by the reaping and caught in the other man's black beard.

He wiped the sweat from his forehead. 'I won't beat about the bush. I'm come about Thomas and Mary Mitchell.'

A brief, hard stare, then Mr Phillips looked away.

'The Board of Guardians has discussed the matter.' Bartholomew did not say that he had instigated the discussion, refusing to let the matter drop until it was resolved to his satisfaction. 'They referred to the eleventh clause of the 1844 Act concerning the treatment of parish apprentices.'

Mr Phillips continued to stare at a point somewhere behind Bartholomew, and his mouth tightened.

'They feel that your duties as their master haven't been carried out in a satisfactory way. So they feel the best course of action would be for you to agree to discharge both apprentices.'

There, it was said.

'Discharge 'em! Why should I discharge 'em? They'm needed yer!' He was glaring at Bartholomew. ''Tis costly enough getting harvest done with two hands short, I'm not going on through the autumn and winter like that!'

Bartholomew longed to take the easier course by backing down, but he reminded himself of the fear in the children's eyes, the marks on the boy's back. He had kept that in mind throughout his fight with the Guardians. There had been opposition initially, but one or two had supported him from the outset, Reverend Pine-Coffin in particular. He took a deep breath.

'What they said, the Guardians, they said as you could sign the discharge papers – I have 'em here with me – and the discharge'll go through at the next petty sessions. However, if you won't sign, given the seriousness of the children's injuries, you'd be liable to a summary conviction, and a fine too, I don't doubt.'

'I'm not signing no discharge!' Mr Phillips' face darkened as he took a step forward. 'They belong to me!'

Bartholomew stood his ground, and a wave of rare anger swept over him.

'They don't belong to you, they belong to God! They'm God's own children! You've served them cruelly and if you don't sign this paper here and now, I'll see to it meself that *you* appear before the magistrates the way those poor chiels have to. The fine could be sizeable. Now, will you sign or won't you?'

Only when he finished did Bartholomew realise that he had been shouting.

Beyond, in the field, the labourers looked on in shocked silence. Bartholomew's heart was beating fast, but he did not shift his gaze from the other man's face. Mr Phillips stared past him, his mouth set in hatred. And so they stood in silence for what felt like many minutes, while the skylarks sang overhead.

It was Mr Phillips who finally broke the spell.

'They'm a waste of my time, those two! Always have been. I'll be glad to see the back of 'em. Now give me that paper; us haven't got time for idling yer.'

He signed the paper in the place Bartholomew showed him, then threw it back at him.

'Now get off my land!'

And he strode back to his work.

It was with intense relief that Bartholomew rode away from Gusland. It was done. He could return to his farm, continue with his work with a clear conscience. Now that this was over, even the thought of weeding filled him with pleasure. He could enjoy the long, peaceful ride back to the village, the rise and fall of the hills and valleys, the patterns of green pasture, golden harvest fields and pockets of woodland with farms and cottages folded among them.

The Mitchell children's court case was that very afternoon; Mrs Mitchell was going to attend. If they were lucky, they might only be sentenced to another couple of weeks in Bideford Gaol, and would then be able to return home. The good news would soon be disseminated around the village.

'What'll happen to those Mitchell children?' was the question he had been asked countless times. There would be those who would offer practical help now, once the news was out, once it was known that Thomas and Mary were not going to return to Gusland.

Charity Mitchell paused in Torrington Square. Which way had Mr Ley said she should go?

'Mind now, my lover!' A woman selling posies of flowers pushed past her on the narrow pavement and Charity moved back against the wall of an inn. Her anxiety rose; she was not used to towns.

Everyone in the village had been very kind. People stopped her on the street to say how sorry they were to hear about what had happened and Mrs Fry had come especially to tell her that Thomas and Mary were very well-thought-of in chapel, and that she was not to worry. However, when Mr Phillips' sister, Annie Fulford, arrived on the doorstep, Charity had been ready to fly at her. Annie had quickly calmed her, saying that she did not know quite what had happened but she was very sorry for it, and would do her best to put things right.

It had been a relief when Mr Ley, hearing that she wanted to go to Torrington, told her that he had business in the town and offered her a lift there and back. Thomas and Mary were sure to be released today. She wanted to be there to take them home. She had brought a cloth bag containing some bread and cheese for them to eat on the way home because they would surely be hungry.

She would have to ask someone the location of the Plough Inn; that was where the magistrates met, just as they used to meet at the Coach and Horses in Buckland Brewer. She had never been in an inn before, and she had certainly never been to a Magistrates' Meeting, but she could not sit at home, not knowing what was happening to her children.

When a large wagon drawn by two heavy horses stopped next to her to unload, she hurried out of the way, past a dog basking on a doorstep and some boys playing marbles. The town was busy with cottage people and carriage people, all of whom seemed to know where they were going. The front doors of the imposing buildings on the Square opened right on to the pavement; the one outside which she now hesitated had a brass plaque next to its door, but others had entrances through which women passed with baskets on their arms; that one, she saw, was a grocer, over there was a baker and next door was an inn, but how would she know if it were the Plough? Apprehensively, she made her way to the other side of the Square, dodging a farmer's cart carrying two noisily bleating sheep.

Several people passed her before she summoned enough courage to address a woman carrying a small child on her hip.

'Missis, can 'ee tell me where's the Plough Inn?'

'The Plough? There look, right opposite! Busy today 'cos 'tis the Magistrates' Meeting.'

Charity saw that three men were at that moment passing through the door of the impressive building just across the road.

'Do 'ee know, can I go in?' Mr Ley had said she would be permitted to enter, but now that the moment had come, she felt doubtful.

'I reckon so, look, follow them men!'

Charity hurried across the road, caught the door before it shut in her face, and followed the men into a room which carried a smell of ale and roast meat. A wooden counter spanned the width of the room, and men sat here and there at tables. She hesitated; women clearly were not allowed in here, but the three men she had followed were passing through another door, so she hastened after them.

She found herself at the back of a large oak-panelled room. Rows of seats faced the front where a long polished table and two high-backed chairs stood in waiting. The three men had found seats, so she slipped into an empty chair near the back.

About half of the seats were occupied, mostly by men, but there were half a dozen women who she guessed had accompanied their husbands. She looked around nervously. She could only see the backs of heads, but the hats seemed to belong to ordinary working people and the whispered voices nearest her did not sound like carriage people's way of talking. Another man and woman entered behind her and sat down without paying her any heed. Perhaps she would not be told to leave after all. She held the bag of bread and cheese carefully on her lap.

Suddenly a door at the front of the room opened. Three gentlemen entered. One sat on the left and the other two sat at the polished table where they shuffled through some papers and spoke quietly, while pointing at things that were written down. They must be the magistrates, she thought.

'First case please.' The stern-looking man who spoke wore a collar like Reverend Colling.

A man with a shambling walk was led in and made to stand behind a high desk. He kept his eyes on the floor and was told to speak up when he mumbled in response to his name.

The magistrate consulted the papers. 'You were inebriated on Bideford Quay on July 28th. What have you to say about it?'

The fierceness of his expression was lost on the man, who continued to look at the floor as he muttered a reply.

'I cannot hear you, man!' The powerful voice made Charity jump. 'Do you have anything to say for yourself?'

'No, Maister.' His voice was barely audible.

The two magistrates exchanged a few quiet words.

'You are fined five shillings plus Court costs of six shillings. I do not expect to see you in this Court again, do you understand?' He had the most fearsome stare. 'Next case please.'

The man raised his head when he heard what his fine was to be; it would probably be equivalent to a week and a half's wages. Charity shifted uncomfortably on her seat. She had realised that she had seen the stern magistrate, Reverend Harding, once or twice in Buckland Brewer. She had heard that he was a man to be feared.

Next, a man from Hatherleigh charged with begging on the streets of Torrington was ordered to leave the town immediately and was threatened with imprisonment should he ever return; then came a man charged with assault. Each time a new case was called, Charity's heart was in her mouth. When would Thomas and Mary appear? And suppose they were fined? They had no money. She had twopence in her pocket, but that was supposed to be for buying bootlaces for her husband and a packet of needles.

The door opened again and a well-dressed man was brought to stand behind the desk. This case was more complicated. It was claimed that the man had left his wife and children chargeable to the parish, while he lived with another woman in comparative comfort. The man boldly claimed that he had believed his wife to be dead, but the three witnesses gave evidence that suggested that this was not true. Reverend Harding sentenced the man to three months' hard labour. He would have to return to his wife when he left prison, and Charity could imagine what a miserable life they would have together.

A terrified-looking woman was led in next. Before the questioning even started, she pleaded with the magistrates not to send her to prison.

'Please, Sir, I've three little chiels, please don't let 'em go to the Workhouse, Sir.' Her mouth was rigid with distress and her knuckles white as she clung to the front of the desk. Charity watched, appalled.

Reverend Harding, ignoring her pleas, consulted his papers.

'You are charged with stealing potatoes valued at eightpence from a field. I understand that you plead guilty.' He fixed her in his fierce gaze.

'Sir, I'm so very sorry, but they'm so hungry, the little uns, I just couldn't abide their crying no more…'

Her sobs filled the room. The onlookers sat in shocked silence.

The magistrates consulted in whispers.

'You are fined eighteen pence with six shillings costs, plus you must repay the value of the potatoes which I understand have been eaten. Next case please.'

There was a collective release of breath as she was led from the room. How could the woman possibly pay the fine if she had no money for food?

A pause. The constable held the door open. When Thomas and Mary appeared Charity stood up – perhaps she called out – she could not help herself; then Reverend Harding's stentorian voice filled her ears. Reprimanded, she sat. She would be silent; she would not be made to leave. She knew her place.

They both looked so young; her heart went out to them. They were doing their best to be brave, Thomas with a defiant look, Mary holding her head up, but with lips quivering. They had seen her, they knew she was here, and as they stood together behind the desk Mary turned to meet her mother's eyes before facing the judges.

'My name be Mary Mitchell.' First Mary, then Thomas spoke out loud and true, and it was perhaps only Charity who detected the slight tremor in each voice.

Reverend Harding laid out the charge; they had absconded on Saturday 10th July from Gusland Farm; they were apprenticed to Mr Thomas Phillips. Surrounded by the polished surfaces of the courtroom, the children looked poor and dishevelled; Thomas's hair was in his eyes and his faded shirt was ripped; Mary's boots were missing a lace and her blouse needed darning. Charity wished she had her needle and thread.

The constable was speaking. 'No, Sir, Mr Phillips was of the opinion that his presence was unnecessary seeing how the prisoners are pleading guilty. And he didn't care for them to be returned to the farm until after their punishment, Sir.'

'I would have preferred him to be present, Constable.' Reverend Harding fixed the children in his glare. 'I understand you plead guilty.'

'No, Maister, us idn't guilty,' Thomas's voice was surprisingly loud and strong, 'us was driven to run off, Maister, us was whipped real bad.'

'Were you now?' There was sarcasm in the magistrate's voice. 'And what had you done to deserve this whipping? Your master is not here, so you must answer in his place. Was it larceny? Insubordination?'

Thomas hesitated, looking confused.

'Us didn't do nothing, Maister.' Mary spoke out for the whole room to hear, her eyes burning with indignation. 'The missis said I broke a dish but I never; her said it just to save her own skin. Us didn't do nothing wrong; us allus worked hard even when us didn't have enough vittles.'

Reverend Harding cleared his throat in an exaggerated fashion and folded his hands deliberately on the table. 'We are not here to discover whether you worked hard, whether you had enough "vittles" as you term it, nor yet to decide whether or not you broke a dish. We are here to discover whether or not you absconded. Mary Mitchell; did you run away from Gusland Farm?'

'Yes, Maister, but...'

'That is enough!' His voice would have silenced the most courageous of rebels.

'Thomas Mitchell; did you run away from Gusland Farm?'

A long pause. 'Yes, Maister.'

Charity sat on the edge of her seat, her fist in her mouth. The magistrate *had* to listen to her children. If only he could be made to see those dreadful wounds that were seared into her memory, he surely could not then find them guilty.

He was talking to the other magistrate; he rose to his feet.

'Thomas Mitchell; Mary Mitchell; I find you guilty as charged. You are each sentenced to a month's hard labour in the House of Correction at Exeter Borough Prison. Court dismissed.'

And he swept from the room.

Charity cried out, she leapt up and thrust her way between the chairs. The constable and another man were pushing Thomas and Mary towards the door, someone tried to block her way but she saw Mary struggling, she heard her anguished cry.

'Mam! Mam!'

Then they were gone and the door was closed; it would not open however much she shook it.

A woman consoled her. A man said that it was not a fair judgement; you could see that they were good children. And someone helped her out, back to the street, where the sun was shining and people were going about their business as if nothing had happened.

She stood on the pavement. She did not know how long she stood there while people pushed past her, and carts passed close by her feet. And then she saw him through the glass of his carriage window: Reverend Harding, sitting back comfortably, a look of satisfaction on his face.

'Liar!'

Her scream ripped through the peaceful afternoon.

'Liar!'

She leapt off the pavement and she chased after the carriage; she lashed out at it with the only weapon she had, the bag of bread intended for her children.

'Liar! Liar! Liar!'

The cloth bag could not dent the polished steel of the carriage. Her screams could not penetrate the closely fitting windows. The horse trotted on and she was left standing in the street, out of breath and sobbing as if her heart would break.

Summary Conviction of Thomas and Mary Mitchell.

Original document, Torrington Museum.

Chapter Twenty-Two

The locked room echoed with noises that came from Mary knew not where; distant metallic clangs, a muffled cry that was neither a shout nor a scream. She sat on the bench where she had been told to wait, her nails digging into its underside. It seemed an age that she had been sitting here, alone in the room that contained nothing but a table and a locked cupboard.

The journey here had been interminable. It must have been mid-afternoon when they left Torrington, she and Thomas and a well-dressed man sitting in a row with their backs to the driver. The turnpike road cut through woodland and moorland, ran alongside meadows and through narrow valleys. Mary was grateful that the villages were few and far between because she dreaded her chains being noticed, but as the afternoon stretched into evening the road grew busier; they were hardly out of one village before they reached the next. If one person noticed their predicament, it was not long before a noisy, curious crowd was running alongside the cart, only falling away when the last houses of the village were left behind.

Thomas, looking out at the labourers working in the fields, leaned over to whisper to Mary. 'Us is being taken a good way from Buckland. Maybe us can find work yer when us comes out, or on far side of Exeter. Maybe us can save for a passage to Canada.'

Mary nodded, but her mind was filled with thoughts of her mother, and fears of what this day would bring. She could not consider the future, and was afraid of Thomas being overheard by the man who sat in despondent silence alongside them.

By the time the sun had slipped towards the horizon and the air had grown cool, the road grew even busier; grand houses stood back from the road amongst gardens and, in the distance, there was a huge church with houses all around.

'Do 'ee think this be Exeter?' Mary whispered.

Thomas nodded. It was a minute or more before he spoke, his voice a little unsteady.

'I don't reckon us'll be together in – the place where us be gwain. In a month's time, when you'm let out, wait for me, please. Don't go without me.'

She nodded, unable to speak.

Shortly afterwards, the cart drew up next to a high stone wall with steps leading up to a heavy door. It all happened very quickly then; Thomas was taken away, and she was sitting alone in this room, remembering his last anguished glance.

Footsteps approached; the key turned in the lock. Mary sat tense and still. The same woman who had told her to wait here came in and looked through some papers at the table. She wore a dark grey cotton dress which looked uncomfortably tight around her ample waist and must have had many starched petticoats underneath to make it stand out so. The dark ringlets that hung next to her cheeks made her face look even plumper than it was. She was not pretty.

'My name is Mrs Gully. You will call me Ma'am.' She did not look at Mary.

'Yes, Ma'am.'

'Now you are…' She paused, looking at the papers.

'I be Mary Mitchell, Ma'am.'

The woman stabbed her finger on the paper. 'No, you are number 351 while you are here. Repeat it; you need to remember it.' She looked at Mary dispassionately.

'351, Ma'am.' She felt a coldness in the pit of her stomach.

'It says here that you are fourteen years of age. Are you certain of that?'

'Yes, Ma'am.'

'That is a pity; if you were only thirteen you would be with the children which would be easier for you. Now follow me; you have to bathe.'

They passed through into another room where a younger woman was sorting through a pile of clothes. She glanced up at Mary without interest.

'Remove your clothes and take a bath.'

A tin bath full of greyish water stood in the corner.

'Is there any warmth left in it?' Mrs Gully tested it with her finger. 'Better add a jug of hot water.'

Mary fumbled to undo her buttons with shaking fingers while stooping to hide her nakedness; but the two women, talking about the clothes they were examining, showed no interest in her. The tepid water made her shiver despite the jugful that had been added; she washed quickly with the bar of strong-smelling soap she had been given.

Mrs Gully glanced over. 'Your hair as well, we don't want any more lice in here.'

When Mary had dried herself, a pile of clothes was pushed towards her.

'Just put the shift on while the doctor examines you,' Mrs Gully told her.

The long coarse shift reached to the floor. She had only just pulled it on when a man in a black coat came into the room. Mary backed away when he marched up to her, but he merely grabbed her arm to pull her towards him.

'Stand on the scales.' He pushed her towards a small wooden platform. 'Six and half stone, and height,' he placed a stick next to her, 'five foot one. Dark hair, brown eyes.' Mrs Gully was writing while the doctor peered into Mary's ears and mouth, lifted her arms and placed an instrument on her chest. 'Calluses to the hands and feet, a birthmark on the left collarbone, recent scarring to the back. Is this one for hard labour?'

'Yes, Doctor,' replied Mrs Gully, 'is she fit for it?'

'She'll do. Have you eaten today?'

When Mary realised that the doctor was addressing her, she could not think how to answer. Had she eaten? It had been such a long, confusing day that it took her a few moments to remember. 'I had breakfast, maister.' Would Thomas be given something to eat? He must be hungry too.

'Give her some food before she goes to the cell, Mrs Gully.' And he left the room.

The soup she was given was greasy and the bread dry; it was a struggle to eat it with Mrs Gully waiting impatiently beside her, but she finally forced down the last mouthful and followed Mrs Gully down a brick-floored corridor while the lantern-light cast grotesque shadows on the cold walls. Mary's heavy grey skirt, being longer than she was used to, seemed to tangle around her boots and the high collar of the brown pinafore chafed her throat.

Mrs Gully held up the lantern as she unlocked a door. The light shone on to the walls of a small cell. There were two low beds, one of which had blankets folded upon it. The other carried a huddled human shape.

'There's your bed,' indicated Mrs Gully. 'Undress immediately and lie down, it is late. There will be enough light from the window.' The heavy oak door clanged in its metal frame. Mary heard the key turn in the lock.

She stood motionless in the cell. There was a very small barred window opposite the door through which cold night air and a pale light found its way. Mary could no longer see the shape on the bed, nor could she hear breathing, but she was sure that whoever lay there was awake. She moved carefully to her own bed and started to undress, finding the buttons that ran all down the front of the pinafore by touch alone and prising them out of the buttonholes in the stiff fabric. Finally she was able to lie down and pull the coarse sheet and the blankets over herself. She lay very still, every sense alert, and tried to breathe silently.

Bartholomew lowered himself carefully into his favourite chair. An afternoon of weeding turnips, with all that bending, did his hip no good at all.

'All finished now, the weeding,' he told his wife.

It had been a good day; that business at Gusland had gone better than he expected, the turnips were growing well and, from the look of the sky, the weather would be staying fine. After tea he would finish the straw ropes.

But no sooner had his wife put his plate in front of him, than news came to alter his mood.

'You had a visitor,' she said, sitting down next to him. 'Such a hammering at the door, there was! I wondered whoever it could be, and why'm didn't just come on in instead of making that ol' racket!'

'So who was it?' He took a mouthful of ham.

'Charity Mitchell. In a fine ol' state, she was. Seems Thomas and Mary have been sent off to Exeter. A month with hard labour, poor chiels.'

Bartholomew was stunned. He had been so taken up with work, he had almost forgotten that the Magistrates' Meeting was that afternoon. He had expected they might have to stay in Bideford Gaol for another week or two, but not this. He put down his knife and fork.

His wife had made Mrs Mitchell a cup of tea, but it was some time before she began to calm down. Even when told that Thomas and Mary would not be returning to Gusland, she was not appeased.

'I got quite cross with her,' his wife told him. 'Her says 'tis your fault for sending 'em to Gusland in the first place. When I think how hard you works for this village and not a word of thanks do you get! I've said it before; you should give up being Guardian. 'Tis too much, what with the farm an' all.'

The news stayed with him all the while he sat on his stool in the barn, twisting straw. A month's hard labour; Mrs Mitchell was right, none of this would have happened if he had not had the children apprenticed. But he had only been doing his duty, it had always been the way for poor children to be sent out to work on farms; it had happened all his life and in his father's time too. The children were generally better fed and clothed than they would have been at home, and the family were able to avoid the Workhouse. But times were changing. In the last year or two, it had been increasingly rare to send children out. He would not now be happy to do so.

He could have made more enquiries. If he had known what was going on, perhaps this could have been prevented.

He reached for more straw, wincing at the pain in his hip. Those poor chiels. He should have gone to Gusland sooner, then he would have known what was going on. He was to blame. What could he do to make amends?

When he limped back to the house, the sky darkening and the bats fluttering out from their roosts in the linhay, it came to him. He had seen something that had reminded him of how the boy had talked of sailing ships and foreign shores. Back in the kitchen, he searched for the newspaper and read the advertisement again. He would get the harvest out of the way, and then he would look into it.

FREE EMIGRATION

TO THE AUSTRALIAN COLONIES,

In First Class Ships of large tonnage, chartered by and fitted out and dispatched under the immediate supervision of Her Majesty's Colonial, Land, and Emigration Commissioners.

FREE Passages, including provisions, medical attendance, &c., to Sydney, Port Philip, and Port Adelaide, are granted by the above authorities to agricultural labourers, shepherds, female domestics, and farm servants, and a few country mechanics, for whose services the most urgent demand exists in the above colonies, where wages are high, and provisions and clothing cheap, whereby steady and industrious persons may greatly improve their condition in life.

All Emigrants are absolutely free on arrival.

The fullest information and assistance may be obtained gratuitously at the Offices of Mr. J. B. WILCOCKS, agent for government emigration, 17, Cornwall-street, Plymouth; or from his agents, Mr. SAMUEL WORSFOLD, Castle Quay, Barnstaple; Mr. JOHN HAMLYN, Bideford; Mr. WM. TEPPER, South-street, Southmolton; Mr. HUXTABLE, Ilfracombe; or Mr. PULLIN, Witheridge.

Dated Office for Government Emigration,
17, Cornwall-street, Plymouth, June 7th, 1848.

North Devon Journal 27th July 1848

Mary slept little. At regular intervals, footsteps paused outside the door and the room lightened as a lantern was placed against the small barred window. Once, she heard faint snoring from the other bed; there was the scuttling of cockroaches. When she thought of Thomas lying awake in some other part of this huge building, she cried a few silent tears. When she did sleep, she was disturbed by terrifying dreams. But then she was woken by the sudden loud clanging of a bell, and she leapt up in fright to stand in her bare feet on the cold stone floor.

There was just sufficient light to see a woman climb slowly from the other bed. Like Mary, she wore only a shift and her straight brown hair hung to her waist.

She looked at Mary without interest.

'You came in late.'

She crouched to wash her hands and face in a bucket of water that stood at the foot of the bed. 'You must do the same; they'll be yer soon.'

Mary washed, and then followed the other woman's example by dressing herself. The woman was a good deal older than Mary, perhaps twenty-five or thirty, with a pursed, dissatisfied-looking mouth and sad, staring eyes. She observed Mary dispassionately while twisting up her hair and tying her coarse cotton cap, but she did not speak.

As she tied on her own cap, Mary felt she had to break the unnatural silence.

'What's your name?'

'Us don't have names in yer.' The woman was folding her blankets. 'Be quick and do your bed, they'll be in soon.'

'Us can't call each other by numbers! My name be Mary.'

The woman straightened up. Her eyes were devoid of light. 'Mine's Caroline, or it were.'

There would not have been time to say more even if Caroline had been willing, because the door was suddenly flung open and two scrubbing brushes were thrown in on the floor. Watching Caroline, Mary scrubbed out her side of the cell by dipping the brush in the washing water, and had barely finished when a woman somewhere outside bawled out two numbers, one of which Mary recognised as her own. She and Caroline then had to empty their slop buckets and refill their water containers. As she returned along the passageway to the cell, Mary caught sight of other women wearing identical clothes to her own scurrying along with bowed heads. The stench from all the buckets was almost overpowering.

A moment later a woman in prison uniform brought two bowls of gruel and two hunks of dry bread. They sat on their beds to eat the thin gruel which had a musty taste; the bread must have been at least three days old. Mary was too anxious to feel hungry, but she saw that Caroline ate with a quiet desperation. The thought that she too might soon feel hungry enough to look forward to such fare brought tears to her eyes.

They had barely finished when the bowls were removed. While they lined up in the passage with the other inmates, Mrs Gully moved down the row, prodding women who stood too close to each other; a distance of six feet was to be observed while they moved out into a yard.

'351, march!'

Mary, realising that Mrs Gully was shouting at her, quickly watched what the other women were doing. Walking was not good enough, they had to march with knees lifting and arms swinging, and so they went, round and round the yard. Mary learned to move at the correct speed, neither so fast that she caught up with the woman in front nor so slow that the gap between them widened. Once she had the rhythm, she was able to look around. At first glance, the women in their identical clothing all looked the same. She could not see anyone of her own age, but neither were there any very old women. All looked despondent despite their jaunty movements. Did she look like them? Would an onlooker, would Thomas, be able to pick her out from these identically-dressed women? They were prisoners, all of them; she was a prisoner. She was number 351. *I be Mary*, she chanted to herself in time with her marching; *Mary Mitchell, I be Mary Mitchell.* She wanted to shout it out for all to hear.

As she moved around the exercise yard, there was one point from which she could see the top of a tree outside the high wall, its branches waving gently in the breeze. It was the only natural, green thing she could see, making her long for the open fields, wooded hillsides and high hedgerows that she knew so well.

And Thomas was somewhere inside these walls, perhaps marching in another yard. Was he thinking of her? Was he afraid of the man who shared his cell?

Eventually they were ordered to stop marching. Continuing to keep six feet apart, they walked to a large hall lined with wooden benches. The benches had lines painted on them to indicate that they were to sit well away from each other. Mary was grateful for this when she cast surreptitious glances at the women alongside her; one had a hard, unpleasant expression and the other a constant twitch which contorted her face alarmingly.

It was not until a man at the front of the hall started to speak that she realised they were in a sort of church. She could understand little of what the man said because the words he used were long; he seemed to run them all together before taking a deep breath and commencing on another stream of sounds. When the women suddenly knelt, Mary had to hasten to follow their example, then after an unfamiliar prayer, they all stood for a hymn. As the singing commenced, the hard-faced woman leaned towards her, grinning.

'Do 'ee think our Reverend Worthy'd give us a look at what 'e's got under his gown?'

The woman with the twitch started to cackle, the sound drowned out by the voices around them.

''Tis a mighty one, I reckon.'

Mary, staring straight ahead, felt herself redden. She was used to coarse jokes out in the fields but never in chapel.

During the singing she became aware of male voices. She saw that the hall was larger than she had at first realised, being divided by a high wooden partition behind which the male prisoners must be standing. Thomas must be there, somewhere. She longed for his reassuring presence.

After another hymn and more incomprehensible words from Reverend Worthy, they were allowed to file out. Upon reaching an intersection, some of the women turned off to the left.

'Number 351, follow me.' It was Mrs Gully.

Mary hurried down the passage after her until they stopped by an open door.

'You are to undertake hard labour. This is to accustom your body and mind to work, so that in future you understand that, for someone of your station, work is the purpose of your life. It is not something to run away from.'

She stared at Mary, her small eyes almost disappearing in her plump face. Mary searched for the right response.

''Twasn't the work us runned away from, Ma'am. I be a good worker.'

'Are you now! And are you impudent as well? Insubordination is punished with solitary confinement, 351.'

The injustice silenced Mary.

'You ran away from your place of work. Here, you will learn never to do so again. Your brother will be working the treadwheel, but as that is considered too strenuous for females, you are to work in the laundry.'

The room they entered had a huge tank in the centre from which steam was rising. Lines of sinks ran along two walls and in front of each sink a woman in prison clothing stood waiting. An overpowering smell of unwashed humanity emanated from baskets piled high with clothing and sheets, and mingled with the biting smell of lye soap in the close, damp atmosphere.

'Everyone works here in silence. Number 68,' Mrs Gully pointed to a woman with a sad, gentle face, 'is permitted to tell you what to do, and you will work with her on the tasks that require two people. That is your sink.'

And with that, she walked off.

Mary glanced apprehensively around the room. All the women were looking at her. Their silent stares unnerved her. 'Stand yer by the sink. There'll be work to do soon enough.'

The gentle-faced woman spoke quietly, and Mary moved gratefully to stand alongside her on the wooden slats.

A large woman with muscular arms and the face of a pugilist stepped up on to a platform to peer into the vat of steaming water. Apparently approving of what she saw, she proceeded to hoist the nearest basket of washing into the simmering water and then to agitate it with a long wooden paddle. The steam curled up from the vat to hang just below the ceiling. After a few minutes large drops began to fall on to the floor and into the women's hair.

Mary's stomach was churning with anxiety. She had never done laundry work. Would she be punished for making mistakes?

She leaned towards the woman next to her and spoke in a low whisper. 'I don't know what to do.'

'Don't fret, I'll show you.'

There was the ghost of a smile. Mary felt gratitude flood through her; at least she did not have to be afraid of this woman.

When the clothes had been agitated in the boiling water for five minutes or so, the big woman used a huge pair of wooden tongs to hoist them out on to a drainer, from which the water streamed back into the tank. The other women then had to carry tin baths to the drainer and return with several garments. Mary tipped hers into her sink, then quickly stepped back as the hot steam rose up to scald her face.

'Wait now,' her new friend told her.

Hot water started to run along a channel behind the sinks. Copying her neighbour, Mary rolled up her sleeves and removed a bung to let the water stream into her sink, then rubbed the bar of soap over the fabric, took up the brush and started to scrub the garments.

She had three pairs of men's heavy trousers. The water was so hot that it was not long before her fingers were smarting. However hard she scrubbed, the dirt seemed to keep coming. The second pair of trousers she took up had a dark stain from which the most fearful smell emanated. Shocked, she took a step back, falling off the wooden slats that kept her feet above the wet floor. Her neighbour merely raised her eyebrows.

When the clothes were as clean as they could be, the water was let out of the sinks and rinsing water streamed in. The hardest part was wringing the water out of the clothes. The fabric was too thick for Mary's small hands to hold securely, and after a few attempts at twisting it, her hands ached so much she could barely move them. After two rinses her partner showed her how they could work together to give the garments a final wring, each holding one end and twisting until no more water came.

The windows along the length of the laundry were steamed up, but by standing on tiptoe Mary could see out of the upper part, which was open. She saw a narrow yard strung with washing lines, and two women hanging the clean clothes and bedding in the fresh air. It appeared to be a more enjoyable job than the washing.

'Will us get to do that?' she asked.

'Not until you've been here six months or more and behaved well,' came the reply.

When Mary returned to her sink after fetching more clothes, she could not find her bar of soap. Her partner, seeing what had happened, shook her head. 'I warned you to keep the soap in your pocket when you're not using it.'

It was true, she had.

'Where's it gone?' she whispered.

The woman lowered her voice further. 'The others'll take it so that they've some to use in their cells.'

'Silence!' shouted the supervisor.

Cautiously, Mary observed the women working alongside her. Both kept their heads down. Her partner helped her out of the difficulty by cutting a piece off her own bar of soap, but Mary was careful never to leave it unattended again.

There was a never-ending supply of washing. Before long, water dripped from Mary's hair, from the hem of her skirt and from her sleeves. The room had become so hot that sweat trickled down her face and back. The skin on her hands and wrists became red, ridged and so sore she almost cried with the pain, and every muscle in her body ached.

In the middle of the day, they were allowed an hour's break. She walked stiffly back to her dimly-lit cell to eat potatoes and a piece of gristly meat, then she lay in her wet clothes with her eyes closed until it was time to return to the laundry. She was far too weary to read her Bible, and she could not bear to think of Mrs Thorne.

Although the afternoon's work only lasted for four hours, it seemed endless. Now that Mary knew what to do, any communication from her partner was forbidden. The unnatural silence was unnerving. Working in the fields had been hard but she had been able to talk, laugh and even sing with her fellow workers if the maister was not there; she could breathe fresh, cool air, and when she straightened up to ease her back she could admire the distant views and hear the birdsong. Here there was no respite.

By the time she returned to her cell, her hands were acutely sensitive. When she was lying on her bed, she saw that the skin had been rubbed right off in places. Field work had calloused her hands, but had not protected them from the constant damp and abrasion.

She lay in a stupor, unable to contemplate the thought that the next day, and the day after that, would be the same.

Her cellmate rolled over to look at her. 'You've got hard labour then. Laundry?'

Mary nodded miserably.

'I was fortunate there, I reckon.'

Mary looked at her. 'Don't 'ee have to work?'

'Yes, but only knitting. Making stockings, they're for chiels in a charity school near here, so they say. Wish I could make some for my own three.'

'You have children?' Mary asked, surprised. 'Where be 'em?'

Caroline had withdrawn into herself again. Mary had to repeat the question before she would answer.

'Workhouse.' She was silent for a long time. 'Three months' prison for me and Workhouse for them, though they've done nothing wrong.'

'What did 'ee do?' She felt compelled to ask.

Caroline sat up. '*Vagrancy* they call it.' She spat out the word. 'We lost the cottage when my man was killed in an accident at work. We walked to my sister's but she had no room for us; she has four of her own. So I was begging when the constable picked us up.'

Caroline closed her eyes. Mary did not dare to ask her any more questions.

After a supper of bread and gruel, the cell door was suddenly unlocked and a man stepped inside. Both Mary and Caroline stood up in surprise. It was Reverend Worthy.

He told Mary that he had read her admission papers.

'I try to visit every prisoner, even if it is only once. This is a hard trial for one so young, but one that might stand you in good stead in later life.' He was a man of middle age with rather wildly curling hair. He had an authoritative air, but there was kindness in his expression. Mary, unsure whether a response was required, remained silent.

'Ah, you have a Bible; I am pleased to see it! Can you read?'

Mary nodded.

'But what is this?' He picked up her magazine. 'You are a Thorne-ite! Well-meaning people, but misguided. I hope that the influence of the services you will attend in prison will set you on the true path.'

He wandered over to the small barred window which was too high, even for someone of his height, to give a view of anything but a small square of grey sky.

'Have you found sufficient fortitude to withstand the day's work?'

Fortitude. It was a word she knew from chapel. God loved those who had fortitude, but she was not one of them.

'No, Sir!' The words burst out of her. 'I can't bear it!'

His expression softened. He sat on the bed next to her.

'Mary – I will call you by your name this one time – you have a hard task before you. While you are here, you must consider yourself a slave. Your every action must be as is commanded, and you must accept that. But remember that while your body is condemned to slavery, your mind, your thoughts and your heart are free; free to ask God for forgiveness, to pray to Him, to praise Him. The prison guards cannot command your thoughts. Remember that, Mary, and you will be able to rise above this trial and, before you know it, you will be free to start a new life.'

When he had gone, Mary lay back on the hard bed. She was still for a long time, staring at the ceiling. It was true; they could not control her thoughts. While she scrubbed the foul clothes with stinging hands and while the steam and the sweat dripped from her face, in her thoughts she could be somewhere else altogether, if she chose. She could be in Thornhillhead Chapel singing with her friends, their joyful voices reaching up to the rafters and beyond. She could be at Peppercombe with the waves rolling in towards the beach, the gulls calling and Thomas laughing at her side.

And if she listened very carefully she would hear the song of the skylark, because it was always there; you just had to remember to listen for it. She would turn to look beyond the cliffs where the flower-studded meadows lay in the sunshine, and the bird would start up from the earth, rising higher still and higher until it was just a dot against the azure sky, and its unending song would fill the air. Her heart would be rejoicing, but neither the women working around her nor the prison guards would know.

Chapter Twenty-Three

The prison door slammed shut behind her. Mary stood at the bottom of the steps, overwhelmed by the bright sunlight. So dazzling was it, she had almost stepped off the pavement on to the road before she saw the carts and carriages that passed so fast and close.

The buildings were high and the broad street full of noise and colour; carriages drawn by high-stepping horses, brightly-painted carts advertising their owners' trades; and all kinds of people passing to and fro on the pavement from ladies in wide, rustling skirts to poor children in ragged dresses. One or two, turning around to stare at Mary, perhaps guessed that she came from behind the high prison wall.

While she was changing out of the prison clothing and into her own laundered clothes, she had asked the warder what was to become of her when she left the prison. The woman did not know, but thought some arrangements had been made. What sort of arrangements? Mary asked. The woman could not say; Mrs Gully would know but she was busy with a new inmate. And what of Thomas, Mary had asked. Again the woman could not give her an answer. When, after half an hour, Mrs Gully had still not returned, Mary was let out.

Where *was* Thomas? Perhaps there was another exit from the prison. She ventured along the pavement until she could view the length of the prison wall but there was no other gate in sight.

She supposed that when Thomas came, they would walk out of the city to seek work. Would he know which way to go? Where would they sleep that night? She tried not to think of Caroline, who had been arrested for vagrancy because she had nowhere to sleep.

A passing woman, who had stared at Mary, turned back. She walked right up to her.

'Are you vitty, my lover? Are you waiting for someone?'

The woman's breath had a strong, unfamiliar smell. Mary tried to step back, but the wall was behind her.

'I'm waiting for my brother.'

'Folks wait a long time to come out of that place, my lover. Have you a bed to sleep in tonight?'

Mary was unnerved by the redness of the woman's lips and cheeks. 'Yes, my brother knows where to go.' She hoped God would forgive her the lie.

'Well, my lover, I'll be back this way later. If you're still waiting for your brother you could come along of me. I've a comfortable bed you can have for as long as you want.'

'Thank you,' said Mary stiffly.

The woman walked on, but stopped a short distance away to look Mary up and down again.

Mary stared down at the pavement, afraid now to meet the gaze of any passers-by. If only Thomas would come! She dared not consider the possibility that he would not be released today.

The time passed. She only looked up to watch the prison door, or the sun as it moved, very slowly, towards the west.

'Hey there!' The gruff voice was just one among many in the clamour of the street, so she took no notice.

'Mary Mitchell!'

There must be another Mary Mitchell, but she raised her head to look. A wagon with faded blue-and-red paint and drawn by two bay horses had drawn up adjacent to the pavement; the driver was looking in her direction but the sun was in her eyes, she could not see his face. It must be a mistake; she knew no one in Exeter.

'Mary Mitchell!'

Confused, she walked to the kerb.

'Come on, maid, I haven't got all day!' The man was middle-aged with a lined face and curly grey hair. She knew him.

'Mr Brook?'

'Yes, maid! Come up!'

Mr Humphrey Brook. He was the carrier from Thornhillhead, she knew him from chapel!

'Mr Brook, what're you doing yer?'

'Come for you, maid! And your brother. Where's he to?'

He held out his hand and pulled her up to sit alongside him.

'Us can't stay yer, us is blocking the way. I'll pull up over the road.'

She hardly knew whether to laugh or cry. Just a moment ago she had feared she would have to take her chance on the streets of Exeter, but now here she was sitting safely alongside the wonderfully familiar figure of Mr Brook.

When they had drawn up in a side road from which they could see the prison door, Mr Brook told his tale. Mrs Thorne had written him a letter which, being rather more wordy than his limited reading skills could cope with, had gone undeciphered until the following Sunday. Meanwhile, several people had asked him what was to be done about Thomas and Mary Mitchell. Then Mr Fulford wanted to know whether he was going to Exeter in the near future. So, when Mrs Thorne's letter was eventually read, and a collection of pennies made towards the fare as she had directed, it was arranged that he should collect Thomas and Mary.

Mary was amazed that all of those people should have been thinking of her and of Thomas.

''Twas lucky,' he said, 'that 'twasn't market day 'cos then I be in and out of Bideford, as busy as the best of 'em.'

'Did 'ee come all the way to Exeter just for me and Thomas?' Mary asked.

'There again I was fortunate,' he told her, 'Mr Reed wanted to go to the railway station, not liking the stage coach, see, and I had to pick up these fowls from the train for the Rector's wife, so I brought all the jobs together.'

Mary peered into the basket to see the strange hens that Mrs Colling had bought. The small golden birds, with long silky plumage resembling hair more than feathers, were crouched miserably in a corner of the basket.

'Mr Brook, be us gwain back to Gusland?' She was afraid that Thomas would refuse to go with them.

'No, maid!'

'But why not?'

At that moment, they looked up to see the prison door opening, and there was Thomas coming hesitantly down the steps.

She jumped down from the wagon, dodged between the horses and carts and leapt on to the pavement to throw her arms around her brother.

When she clung to him, all the loneliness and the fear she had experienced over the past month melted away.

'Look! Mr Brook's yer to take us home, over yer, look! Thomas, I thought you'd never come!'

Thomas was looking dazed. She took his hand and pulled him across the road, but when they reached the wagon he snatched his hand away.

'I bain't gwain back!' His mouth was set.

'But Thomas…'

'I bain't gwain back to Gusland!' He was shouting, and backing away from the wagon.

'But Mr Brook said…'

She looked desperately up at Mr Brook, who was observing them dispassionately. 'Mr Brook, tell him!'

'You'm gwain home, boy.'

Thomas did not reply, nor did his expression change.

'Thomas, listen to him!' Mary clung to her brother's arm, afraid that he might take flight. 'Tell us why, Mr Brook!'

'You'm free.' His placid expression suggested that he might be telling them the time of day rather than life-changing news. He pushed his hat aside to scratch his head. 'He signed the papers, Mr Phillips did.'

It took several more minutes of questioning before Thomas would agree to climb into the wagon, but Mary, too, found it difficult to take in the news.

'Us is gwain home? ' she asked. 'Home to Mam and Da? Be 'ee sure, Mr Brook?'

'That's where I'm to take 'ee,' he replied.

She sat pressed between Thomas and Mr Brook as they left the city behind. They did not speak for a while, and she guessed that Thomas was feeling as bemused as she was herself. They were not returning to Gusland. They need never see Mr Phillips again. Not ever. After all these years, they were going home.

Gradually, in response to her questioning, Thomas told her of his experiences in prison. He had been set to work on the treadwheel, which he said was the worst thing he had ever had to do. He described it as being similar to a huge mill wheel, made up of steps up which the men had to climb to make it turn.

'The steps were so high and the wheel so heavy to turn, 'twas harder than any work I've done before, Mary; you can't imagine…'

He told her that by the time he finished his hour and was allowed a five minute break, his legs would be shaking so much he would fall to the floor. As the days passed he became weaker; he was always hungry and developed stomach problems.

'I'm not so bad as I was, but feel how thin I be!'

Mary gasped when she felt his ribs protruding beneath his shirt.

Towards the end of the second week, he collapsed, falling from the wheel and narrowly missing having his foot crushed. After that he was put to work in the vegetable garden, but some of the men tormented him for not being able to withstand the treadwheel.

''Twas only because they wanted to do gardening too; they all hated the wheel.' He made light of it, but Mary noticed a yellow bruise on the side of his face.

Mr Brook stopped to rest the horses in Crediton, and again in the village of Beaford where he gave Thomas and Mary some ale and some bread. When the sky clouded over and rain started to fall, he pulled over the hood to keep them all dry. Lulled by the rhythmic clatter of the horses' hoofs, the creaking and swaying of the wagon and Mr Brook's soft, tuneless whistling, Mary let the events of the past few months run through her mind; it was over, all of it. She was going home.

'Thomas, what do 'ee think'll become of Joseph?'

But Thomas's head was resting on her shoulder, and she saw that he had fallen asleep.

The light was growing dim by the time Mr Brook pointed to the village at the top of the next hill. Mary stared at the silhouette of the church tower reaching up into the evening sky, the tower that, throughout the years of her exile, had marked the location of those closest to her heart. All that was over now; she would see her mother soon, in just a few minutes more.

As the horses slowed to a walk on the upward climb and the high hedgebanks hid the village from view, Mary moved forward impatiently on the seat, surely the horses were slowing still further? She would have jumped from the wagon to run up the road and into the village if Mr Brook had not been in her way.

'Us is nearly there, maid, look.'

And as they came around a bend there was a terrace of cottages. When she was much younger she used to run there to play with her friend, Ann.

Thomas nudged her. 'Look, there's the inn, do 'ee remember? I used to go to fetch Da home for his tea.'

As they passed, then, along the village street, people smiled and waved in recognition.

'Thomas, they know us! I thought people'd look down on us for being in prison.'

He squeezed her hand in sympathy, then cried out, 'Us is yer now, look!'

By the time they drew up by the village green next to the church, her tears were flowing. As Mr Brook helped them down, Mary's mother came running out of the cottage to greet them, her skirts held up almost to her knees and her hair in disarray. Mary fell into her warm embrace with Thomas alongside and, as she clung to her mother, she sobbed for all the times she had longed for this moment throughout the long and lonely years. And so they stood, until gradually she became aware that their father was patting their shoulders and telling them he was happy to see them back; and then Mr Brook was saying he really must be on his way before dark.

Only then did she wipe away her tears and take Mr Brook's hand.

'Thank 'ee, Mr Brook, for bringing us home.'

He scratched his head in embarrassment. Mary watched until the wagon turned the corner, and then she walked slowly, with her family around her, into the little two-roomed cottage that had been her home for the first nine years of her life.

Chapter Twenty-Four

In the days that followed, as Mary eased the burden on her mother by fetching water from the well or putting the washing out to dry, she was welcomed by the people she met. The usual greeting was 'You'm glad to be home after the hard time you've had, maid!'

Some people passed in articles of clothing for her or for Thomas, or some welcoming flowers from the hedgerow.

Each evening the family sat up late, gathering around the light of a single candle to catch up on the years they had missed. Mr Mitchell shook his head in disbelief at some of the tales, but Mrs Mitchell was more vociferous.

'Mr Phillips should be strung up!' she declared, jumping up from her chair and scattering the sewing materials that were on her lap. 'If I'd have known all that was going on, I'd have come down there and I... I...'

'You couldn't have done nothing, Mam,' Mary told her gently.

Five-year-old Jane, having recovered from her initial shyness, cuddled in on Mary's lap to listen to the tales, and slept in her sister's bed at night, while the two other girls shared a second bed. Thomas, who was looking more at ease than Mary had ever seen him, slept on a rolled out mattress downstairs.

It was during their first evening that they learned the details of the employment that had been arranged for them.

'Mrs Annie Fulford came to the door.' Mrs Mitchell leaned towards the candle to tell the story. 'Do 'ee know of her? Her's Mr Phillips' sister and married to Mr Bartholomew Fulford's cousin. Her'd called in once before and I wasn't inclined to welcome her at first, being as she is a Phillips, but a kinder woman you wouldn't meet. They farm down at North Hele, about a mile from here.'

Thomas stared down at the table, frowning.

'Anyway, her came in and sat just where you are now, Thomas, and said as the family wanted to make amends for the way the two of you have been served. She said she was very sorry for it. So her'd like you, Mary, to work in the house down at North Hele and help out with the hens and the pigs and suchlike four days a week. And her brother, that is Mr Richard Phillips as farms over at Brendon I think 'tis, he's offered to take you on, Thomas. Again, 'tisn't every day but, you see, they'm casting around for work 'cos they want to help. And you'll both be paid a proper wage.'

Mary did not know what to say. She wanted nothing to do with any member of the Phillips' family, and she could see from Thomas's expression that he felt the same.

'Bain't there work anywhere else?'

'No, there bain't!' put in her father. 'I'm fortunate if I can pick up four days' work a week even though 'tis known I'll work hard. There'll be some as wouldn't take you on after this business about running off, and prison. There just idn't the work to go around. You'm the lucky ones.'

Mary shifted uncomfortably in her seat. Her mother patted her arm reassuringly.

'Neither of 'em are asking that you give your word to stay a year, let alone twelve years like when you'm apprenticed. And you know us can't afford to feed 'ee if you'm not bringing in a wage.'

'I know, Mam.' Mary leaned into her mother's warmth. 'Us have got to do it, Thomas. Can't be worse than Gusland.'

On Sunday she and Thomas walked the three miles along quiet lanes to Thornhillhead. They had been told that the Phillips family had not attended chapel for some weeks and, in any case, Mary wanted very much to return to the chapel community. She felt sure that, even if the Phillips children were there, her friends would shield her from them. On the walk they caught up with Mr and Mrs Richards and their children who greeted them warmly.

'Us is glad to see 'ee back, midears,' said Mrs Richards, taking their hands in turn. They walked on to the chapel together, talking of the goings-on there had been in the weeks that Mary had been away. She was glad not to be asked about

Gusland, or the prison. She wanted to leave all that behind her now.

It was strange to approach the chapel from an unfamiliar direction, but as soon as she saw the little whitewashed building with its arched windows, she hurried forward, and could not hide her smiles when people gathered around her and Thomas to welcome them back. There were only a few who stood back and whispered. She did not care about them. She felt sure that in the eyes of God, and of Mrs Thorne, she had done nothing wrong.

The following Monday Mary set off for North Hele. Despite her nervousness, she had made up her mind that it was not up to her to be sorry for the things that had happened, and it was only right that Mrs Annie Fulford should want to make amends for her brother's actions.

She came to a comfortable-looking farmhouse set back from a yard where speckled hens pecked and crooned, and half a dozen white geese honked suspiciously at her as they waddled away to form a wary group near the gate. When she knocked hesitantly on the door, it flew open immediately.

'Come in, come in!' Mrs Fulford, a brisk, sandy-haired woman, hustled her into the kitchen. 'Have a dish of tea after your walk and I'll show 'ee around.'

Mary was introduced to Mrs Fulford's two daughters, both a little older than herself.

'You may wonder why I could use some extra help when I've these two at home,' said Mrs Fulford, 'but us has six boys to wash and cook for, see, they'm all out working on the farm. Us could manage indoors, but 'tis only right that someone in the family makes it up to you for what you've been put through.'

That was the only reference Mrs Fulford made to Gusland, and in Mary's time at North Hele, she never heard the farm or the Phillips family mentioned again.

When she returned after her first day, she was anxious to find out how Thomas had fared at Brendon. She watched for him from the window, but it was growing dark by the time he reached home after the three-mile walk. She saw at once from his expression that the day had gone well.

He had spent much of the day ditching. 'I didn't mind it,' he said, ''specially as I kept telling myself I was earning a wage.'

Mary had experienced the same feeling. It gave the work a purpose.

''Twas proper strange,' he said, 'when, at the end of the day, I left and walked home. Just think on all those years at Gusland when us wanted so much to do just that!'

A few days later he was sent to work in one of the lower fields adjoining Twitching Moors. He had only been there a short while when he noticed a familiar figure coming into the next field. Thomas watched for a while until he was sure no one else was around, then he called out.

'Joseph!'

Joseph, who was weeding turnips, looked up in amazement at hearing Thomas's voice. They both ran towards the hedge and Thomas scrambled up the bank so that they could see each other.

When Joseph learned how Thomas came to be working at Brendon, and had recovered from his surprise, he fell silent, kicking morosely at the bank.

'What happened after Mary and I went?' asked Thomas.

'The maister was in a foul temper, worst I've ever seen him.' He continued to kick the bank. 'But why didn't 'ee tell me you was going?' he suddenly burst out. 'I woke up and you'd gone! I could have come with 'ee, then I'd be other side of the hedge too!'

Thomas tried to explain that three people would have had even less chance of getting away.

'Don't forget, us was caught. Only reason us wasn't sent back was on account of Mr Fulford putting a good case about the whipping us had.'

He went on to suggest that Joseph send word to him if conditions at the farm deteriorated further, so that he could alert Mr Fulford. Hearing this, Joseph looked a little more cheerful.

'Leastways, looks like us won't have to plant so many teddies for next year. Maister's gwain back to having more grazing, keep more bullocks. 'Twill be less work. But still got all these turnips to weed.'

Thomas went back to his work, but he looked over every now and then at the small, solitary figure working alone in the immense field, and when he left, he gave him a shout and a wave.

'Maybe things'll get a bit better there,' he told Mary, 'or leastways no worse. I reckon the maister knows he could lose more apprentices else. And Lewis'll be finishing soon, it'll be easier for Joseph when he's gone.'

Although the work at North Hele was not too onerous and Mary was very glad to be earning a wage, she felt unsettled. She understood for the first time the difficulties of her parents' life: the unrelenting work, the constant anxiety about paying the rent and having enough to eat, especially since the potato harvest had again partially failed. They dreaded the coming winter; the hunger, the cold. She knew she did not want a life of extreme poverty. She did not want her own children to be sent out as parish apprentices.

She tried to communicate her feelings to Thomas one Sunday while they were walking to chapel.

'Will 'ee be happy to stay at Brendon? Marry one day, have a family like Mam and Da?'

Their boots rang in unison on the stony lane while she waited for his answer. When he eventually replied, it was with hesitation.

'I've been wondering 'bout that. You have too, bain't 'ee? You'm not settled.' There was understanding in his glance. 'I be glad, of course, that us got away from Gusland. And I should be glad to be working at Brendon, the maister's fair, and I be earning a wage. Little enough, but it helps at home.' He was silent for a few moments, then stopped suddenly in the lane and turned to face her.

'I do want a different life, Mary! Someplace else! I don't know where, but,' he ran his hand through his hair, 'I often think of that time when us was in Bideford looking at those ships. I really did reckon that us was going to Canada. I wish us could have gone!'

He walked on and she hurried to catch up with him.

'Think on it, Mary. Sail away, leave all this behind and start afresh.'

She too had had that dream at the back of her mind.

A few days later, they were all sitting around the table after supper when there was a knock at the door. It opened to reveal Bartholomew Fulford's smiling face. Mary took Jane on to her lap to make room for him at the table, and while her mother made him some tea, they talked about the weather, Thomas and Mary's work and the prospects for the winter ahead.

'Well now, I won't pretend I've come only to pass the time of day,' he said eventually. 'To tell the truth, it stuck in my mind, Thomas here talking of taking a passage to Canada. Now that takes money, as you know. But I saw this,' he took a folded newspaper from his pocket, 'and it crossed my mind that you might just be interested.'

He placed the paper on the table and pressed out the creases. 'See? Free emigration to the Australian Colonies. I've had a word with Mr Hamlyn in Bideford. He thinks as 'tis a possibility.'

Mary read out the advertisement for the rest of the family to hear. "*Steady and industrious persons may greatly improve their condition in life.*" Do 'ee hear that, Thomas? And it's free! But where is Australia? Is it near Canada?'

Mr Fulford explained that Australia was on the other side of the world, even further away than Canada. Mary looked from his face to the faces of her family; they were all listening intently. Could she and Thomas really go away together after all? She drew Jane closer and the little girl cuddled in against her.

'But, Australia, bain't that where the convicts get sent?' Her father was right; Joseph's father had been transported there.

'That's so,' replied Mr Fulford, 'but 'tis different, this scheme. See, it says "*All emigrants are absolutely free on arrival.*" The convicts, they have to work for nothing, terrible hard work too and poor living. But there's good wages for emigrants, so I'm told, three or four times what they would be here, and food cheaper too.'

Thomas had not said a word but was slightly flushed. When he spoke at last, his voice was husky with emotion.

'So us could go? Me and Mary, and at no cost?'

'Well now,' Mr Fulford leaned back in his chair, ''tisn't that simple. There's plenty to think on. I've a book yer,' he reached inside his jacket and pulled out a magazine, 'as lays it all out.'

Mary picked up the magazine called *The Emigrant's Friend*.

'It says,' he told them, 'that no one under the age of eighteen may go without their parents. So this is what you must think on; would 'ee all want to go, the whole family together?'

They sat up late that night. They talked for an hour or more after Mr Fulford had gone, and when the little ones had gone to bed, Mary's mother lit another candle and the discussion continued.

Mary read aloud from the magazine. It was startling to read about their current predicament in print; '*in England,*' it said, '*the poor agricultural labourer, at eight or ten shillings a week*' –

'What!' put in Mary's father, 'seven, more like!'

– '*has no expectations for his old age except the poor house.*'

The wages for a day labourer in Australia were one pound and four shillings a week, and items of food a little cheaper than those in England. They stared at each other in disbelief.

'What about rent?' said Mary's mother. 'Maybe that's costly.'

Mary searched quickly through the magazine, her fingers tingling with excitement.

'No, look, it says here six shillings for a town lodging. Might be less in the country. And a female house servant'll be paid £18 a year plus food and lodging.' She did some quick calculations. 'That's about seven shillings a week to spend on what you will!'

Thomas leaned over to study the booklet.

'You'm right! And look at the wages for a live-in farm servant! Da, us has got to go, it'd be a fresh start!'

Their parents were more cautious. They wondered about the journey, which could take up to three months.

'I don't know that I could stomach that,' said Mrs Mitchell. 'I've only seen the sea but once. And what sort of folks go out there? What neighbours would us have?'

Mr Mitchell wanted to know about the land, was it hard to work? Were tools supplied?

'I don't know that I've a mind to go sailing halfway around the world. Us knows no one that has been there! I reckon us should rest where us be.'

'But us wouldn't have the shame of turning to the parish for relief every winter.'

The discussions went on for the rest of the week. Mary's days were filled with thoughts of Australia, and at night she could hardly sleep for excitement. She and Thomas pored over the information in the booklet until they both knew it by heart, then they competed with each other in quoting passages in response to their parents' questions. Mrs Mitchell, once she was accustomed to the idea, was cautiously in favour, her husband less so. Mary managed to send messages to her siblings to tell them of the plan; Catherine and Edward were settled in their work and did not want to leave, but Elizabeth was keen to go.

When alone together, Thomas and Mary sought desperately for ways to persuade their parents. Finally, their determination won through.

'Well then,' their father said, 'I can't find fault with it. If Mr Fulford can arrange it for us, us'll go.'

Mary jumped up to hug her father. A new life was about to begin.

Soon after hearing that the Mitchell family were keen to emigrate, Bartholomew Fulford realised that his part in it was only just commencing. When he studied the application form in more detail, he realised that, due to their ages, Mr and Mrs Mitchell would not be eligible for a free passage. A contribution towards their fares, amounting to twenty-eight pounds, would have to be raised. He already knew that there were costs for which fund-raising would be necessary – there was the voyage from Bideford to Plymouth to reach the emigration vessel, there was all the clothing that each emigrant was required to take – but this extra amount of money meant that it was a considerable undertaking. Mr Norman, his fellow Guardian in the village, had already made it clear that he was not interested in wearing out shoe leather in order to raise money for the Mitchells.

Bartholomew decided to call on Reverend Colling first. Mr and Mrs Mitchell's attendances at church were irregular, but the Rector was, after all, responsible for everyone in his parish. Bartholomew knocked at the door.

Reverend Colling invited him in with a smile; married life must suit him. Before Bartholomew had time to explain the reason for his visit, he spotted a large pig from the drawing-room window.

'Heavens, Rector, what 'ave 'ee got there?'

Reverend Colling showed him what he called his model farm; it had been his wife's idea, he said, but they both liked the idea of husbandry. The pig was of a breed unknown to Bartholomew, there were five hens and a cockerel of most peculiar appearance, and a solitary sheep, all being kept in greater comfort than most villagers.

'We hope that by keeping them in ideal conditions, we might eventually breed superior animals and will then be able to suggest ways that you local farmers might improve your methods.'

Bartholomew scratched his head. It was one of the few occasions when he could not think of a suitable comment.

'To get to the matter in hand, Reverend…'

He benefitted from the Rector's expansive mood; he was given five pounds towards the emigration expenses which he considered a very good start indeed.

Next, he asked his congregation in chapel. The Mitchells were not Wesleyan Methodists but they were respected as hard workers, and the idea of emigration was approved of amongst non-conformist communities. He was able to collect a few shillings, which was more than the donors could really afford.

When he sent a message to the Bible Christian chapel at Thornhillhead, he was amazed at the response. Thomas and Mary were clearly valued there.

He broached the subject at the next Board of Guardians. As he had suspected, some, including Reverend Harding, were in favour of giving a small sum, no more than was necessary, because sending the family away would prevent them being a burden to the parish in future years. Others felt that they were a deserving case, and one or two saw it as their patriotic duty to help populate the colonies with a workforce capable of undertaking field labour and of consuming British goods. Sending a family of five girls to a colony populated mainly by men who wanted wives was seen as being particularly useful. It was hard to hear the Mitchell girls, of whom Bartholomew had grown quite fond, being referenced in such a way, but he gritted his teeth and accepted the offer of funding with thanks. Reverend Pine-Coffin added five guineas from his own pocket.

It was a hard winter. Generally Bartholomew took on some casual labour for occasional days in the winter months but he could not afford it after the previous summer's harvest. There was illness in the village, most of it caused by insufficient food. He knew the Mitchells were subsisting on a diet of turnips, cabbage and a small ration of bread; when he saw the older children walking the parish in search of an hour or two's extra work they looked distinctly undernourished, but he knew they were determined to add to their immigration fund, even if only by a few pennies.

The local landowners, Reverend Moore Stevens and Lord Rolle's trustees, lived at too great a distance for easy visiting, but when he could find the time Bartholomew wrote to them, stressing the worthiness of the Mitchells' cause. The fund gradually increased. By the time the first green shoots were pushing through in the oat field and the first swallows were wheeling and twittering above his barn, there was enough.

Chapter Twenty-Five

During the long months of waiting and hoping, three people were often in Mary's thoughts. When it became clear that enough money would be raised to enable the family to emigrate, she spoke of her feelings to Thomas.

'Us should go visiting. There's folks us must thank afore us goes away.'

'Who's that then?' Thomas, cleaning his boots by the fire, looked up at her.

'Mrs Thorne at Shebbear because her's been so good to us. And Mr and Mrs Prance.'

They set off for Peppercombe early the following Saturday.

The valley was as they remembered it; a magical place, different from anywhere else. Perhaps it was the smell of the sea that drifted up the valley to mingle with the birdsong, but it seemed a place set apart from the agricultural world they knew, despite the wagons that came to take lime back to the farms. Being a Saturday, there were no wagons that day to disturb the peace and they strode down the stony track without fear of meeting Mr Phillips. When they came near to the cliff they turned first to the right to revisit the ledge with its breath-taking view out over the sea. Mary clambered down to kneel there for a few minutes, relishing the sight of the waves rolling in towards the beach and the churr of pebbles as they pulled back. Turning to Thomas standing above her, she threw out her arm to encompass the wide bay.

'When us was here, us never thought us would have the chance to sail out there one day!'

He smiled down at her. 'I thought us would, even then.'

They retraced their steps to reach the cottage. While still quite distant, they saw Mrs Prance come out of the door to empty a bowl of water. When Mary called out and waved, she shielded her eyes from the sun, staring in bewilderment as they approached. She was wearing the same blue apron that Mary remembered and, for a moment, the light caught her silver-grey hair drawn into a knot on the crown of her head. As Mary hurried forward, her eyes filling with tears at the sight of the familiar figure, Mrs Prance suddenly dropped the wooden bowl with a clatter, and they ran into each other's arms. Neither of them could speak for a few moments, until Mrs Prance, patting her repeatedly on the back, cried, 'I've wondered and wondered when 'ee'd come back, chiel.'

Then she took Mary's hand and pulled her towards the front door, beckoning to Thomas to follow on.

The time passed quickly. They shared a simple meal and talked of the forthcoming journey. Mr and Mrs Prance had heard of Australia but knew of no one who had been there; most people thereabouts emigrated to Canada.

'Us has to get to Plymouth first off,' Thomas told them, 'so us'll be sailing from Bideford.' He got up to gaze out at the sea from the small cottage window. 'You'll be able to look out and see us when us goes past!'

Mary went to stand by his side. A ship was passing across the bay, so distant that its sails appeared no bigger than handkerchiefs. 'Will us see the cottage, do 'ee suppose? Us'll wave to 'ee anyway!' It was extraordinary to think that they would be out there, surrounded by water, and the land barely visible.

When the sun was sinking down towards the western horizon, Thomas and Mary reluctantly said their final farewells; as they climbed the steep lane Mary turned for a last wave to the elderly couple standing arm-in-arm by their cottage door, the sea stretching away into the distance behind them. The visit had completed that episode in her life; she had taken one more exhilarating step towards the future, and Australia.

It was to be a longer walk for Thomas and Mary to visit Mrs Thorne. They were told that it would take them at least three hours to reach Shebbear, longer if they stopped for a rest or dawdled along the way.

They made an early start. Their route took them first through the lanes to Tythecott and Thornhillhead, a way that was now familiar from their weekly walks to the chapel, and then along a wider road across Thorne Moor. There was a cool breeze but the high clouds pursued each other quickly across the sky, allowing sunshine to alternate with shadow on the road and on the patchwork of fields that stretched for many miles ahead. Mary had read that there were no fields like these in Australia, and that the weather was always hot. It was difficult to imagine it.

'Thomas, listen!'

A skylark was singing somewhere above them. They paused to shade their eyes from the sun, peering upwards until suddenly they saw it, a tiny bird fluttering to stay airborne as it sent forth a torrent of song.

'Do 'ee think there'll be skylarks in Australia?'

'I reckon so.' Thomas looked fondly at her. 'Maybe ostriches too – remember those birds as tall as horses that you read about in the magazine?'

'I don't know where they'm from, but us'll see kangaroos, Mr Fulford told us about they, didn't 'ee? They'm big too.'

They paused in Stibb Cross to look at the little chapel about which they had often heard, then continued on the long, lonely road to Shebbear. They passed few dwellings and met with only one solitary traveller. On this high, exposed land, the sky formed three-quarters of the view, and the hedgebanks, being lower than they were around the village, offered little shelter from the cold wind.

They were beginning to tire when they came across another chapel, this one standing alone at a crossroads.

'Look, 'tis Rowden,' Mary said, reading the inscription. 'Shall us rest yer? It can't be much further now to Shebbear and I reckon us is making good time.'

They passed through a gate into the graveyard and walked right around the chapel, looking in through the windows at its silent, whitewashed interior and empty benches, before sitting to rest on the front step. Mary leaned her head against the wall and closed her eyes. What a desolate landscape this would be without the simple sanctuaries the Bible Christians had built. It was hard to imagine Thornhillhead, Stibb Cross or this remote crossroads without chapels to provide places for neighbours to meet, to sing and to pray, often the only opportunity for social contact they had.

'Us must ask Mrs Thorne if there be any Bible Christians in Australia. I'd miss Chapel if us couldn't go.'

Mary already had a mental picture of Lake, where Mrs Thorne lived. There would be a large body of shimmering water beyond which would stand the house, and it would be no ordinary house. She associated Mrs Thorne with the evocative words they heard in chapel: *the promised land; celestial city; brightest glories; land of milk and honey.*

So it was a disappointment when she saw Lake Farm. It looked like any other large, whitewashed farmhouse thereabouts; there were hens strutting and pecking in the mud and pigs grunting in their sties, and even Lake Chapel and the buildings nearby did not look unusual. She asked a young man in dark clothing who was pacing up and down whether this was really where Mrs Mary Thorne lived.

'It is indeed; go on in.' He gestured at the open door of the farmhouse.

They found themselves in the doorway of a large and very busy kitchen. Mary looked around in confusion. There were at least ten people in the room talking and laughing, some reading at the table, others preparing food, and some young children playing on the floor with a kitten.

'Hello! Are you looking for Mother?' asked a girl. 'Mother! Visitors for you!'

The people around the fireplace moved aside and Mary saw a woman stirring a pot over the fire. She turned around; it was Mrs Thorne.

Her face softened. 'Dear children!' She hurried towards them and took their hands. 'Thomas, Mary, how good it is to see you here! How have you travelled? Has someone driven you here?'

'No, us has walked.' Mary, aware that everyone in the room was looking at her, felt herself redden. 'Us wanted to come and see 'ee before us goes away.'

'Did 'ee know that there's enough money now for us to emigrate?' asked Thomas, smiling at the faces gathered around. It was a question he never tired of asking.

Mrs Thorne had heard the good news, and explained their situation to the others. Mary could see now that most of those present must be her children, but there was also one servant girl, and two men sitting at the table who must be farm labourers.

'We will hear more about your journey when we are all seated at the table.'

It was many months since Mrs Thorne had seen them but, even here amongst her own family, she treated Mary and Thomas as if they were the most important people in the room, the directness of her gaze never faltering, the warmth of her voice never diminishing. Mary looked down in embarrassment as she felt her eyes fill with tears; she could not help it, she was so very glad to be here.

'Now come, sit here at the table and let me fetch you some milk to drink after your long walk. And of course you must stay to dinner, we will be eating before long.'

From the safety of a bench behind the long table, they sat to watch the proceedings. Three of Mrs Thorne's daughters helped her to prepare the dinner, two sons were laying the table and another held a young baby on his lap while he read a book.

The younger children playing on the floor seemed to Mary to use very long words.

'You are very fortunate,' said one, addressing the kitten, 'that you have not been banished to the yard for that behaviour.'

Mary caught Thomas's eye and they both had to hide their amusement.

'Please will you hold the baby while I call for the men and for my father?' The boy held the baby out to Mary. She sat the child on her lap and he looked solemnly into her face.

'His name is Paul,' said Mrs Thorne. 'He is a dear, is he not?' She ran her hand over the baby's soft head as she passed. She had a kind word or look for each of her children

313

as she went about her work, and even for the two labourers who sat at the end of the table.

Several men entered and took their places. Mary could see that one was another farm labourer but the others were smartly dressed young men, one of whom had directed her and Thomas to the farmhouse.

'These gentlemen,' said Mrs Thorne, as if reading her thoughts, 'are staying with us for the time being while they study at our Bible Christian college across the way.'

When Mr Thorne arrived they were twenty-one for dinner. He was the last one to enter, and it was then that the atmosphere changed a little. Mary saw that the children grew quiet and sat up a little straighter, the labourers shifted uncomfortably, and even Mrs Thorne's voice sounded a little strained. He was a clean-shaven, heavy-featured man. He neither greeted anyone in the room nor commented on Thomas and Mary's presence and, after saying grace, he remained silent throughout the meal. It was only after he returned to the printing works, accompanied by one of his sons, that everyone again seemed at ease.

In response to questioning, Mary shyly explained that on August 8th they would sail on the *Nelson* from Plymouth, and would expect to reach Melbourne in a little over three months. But first, of course, they had to reach Plymouth, which was slow and expensive by carrier's cart.

'It is a most dreadful journey!' put in one of the young men.

So Mr Fulford was arranging for them to travel from Bideford by sea. Mary answered Mrs Thorne's questions about employment, and the luggage that had to be taken, which was adding considerably to the costs.

'Us'll all have jobs to go to, except the little ones of course, most likely not together but nearby. Us each has to take six of this and six of that, two dresses! And two pairs of shoes each! But what I wanted to ask, Mrs Thorne, be there any Bible Christians in Australia? Be there any chapels?'

Everyone started talking at once, then. The students had received letters from Australia, and Mrs Thorne knew of many followers had travelled there from Cornwall. They had written with enthusiasm of their new lives, all remarked that food was plentiful, and some were hopeful of buying land.

'When I'm grown I shall go to Australia to become a preacher!' said the smallest girl. She was a tiny little thing with long brown hair and her mother's direct gaze.

Mrs Thorne smiled at her indulgently. 'So you shall, Serena. If you are determined to do something and pray to God for the strength to carry it out, you will achieve great things.'

'Mary, there are several followers for whom I have addresses!' She reached across the table and took Mary's hands. 'Might I ask you to do something for me? If you could put some pamphlets and two or three books in your trunk, items that we have printed here in Shebbear, perhaps one day you might be able to visit the addresses I can give you. I would be so very grateful.' She squeezed Mary's hands affectionately. 'If you cannot visit these people, never mind, you may keep the things for yourself, but it would be wonderful if they could be delivered, and it would be an opportunity for you to meet other Bible Christians. Our numbers are increasing in Australia and I am sure you will be able to find friends.'

It was an honour to be trusted with such an important mission. Mary felt overwhelmed with gratitude. She would not be leaving her chapel life behind after all, but would carry it with her; the love of friends, the knowledge of God, and wonderful memories of the chapels filled with music that drifted out across the fields for all to hear. And most of all, the influence of Mrs Thorne. It was a friendship that had transformed her life.

The day of their departure finally arrived. Mary's sister, Catherine, had come all the way from Barnstaple, and Edward from Frithelstock, to spend the last evening with the family, and were walking to Bideford to see them leave from the Quay.

Mary had been too excited to sleep. Although she was up before dawn to help her mother prepare the food for the journey and pack the last-minute items, they were only just ready when they heard the rumble of wheels. When they ran to the door, there were Mr Fulford and Mr Norman with their harvest wagons, each with two horses in harness. The men pulled up outside the cottage, and jumped down to help Thomas and Mr Mitchell carry out the trunks.

'Not like that!' shouted Mrs Mitchell. 'Mind what you'm doing, that's all our worldly goods you have in there!'

Mary stood at the cottage door holding Jane's hand, the small girl jumping up and down with excitement. When the trunks were loaded on to Mr Norman's wagon she took one last look at the room, bare now of all their possessions.

'Say goodbye to it, Jane. Our next home, 'twill be on the other side of the world!'

She felt no sadness at leaving it; that part of her life was over. But when she climbed into the wagon and settled the younger children on the straw behind Mr Fulford, she was astonished to see the village street lined with people.

Mary grabbed Thomas's arm. 'Look! Be 'em here for us?'

As if in reply, when Mr Fulford clicked his tongue and the horses set off, the onlookers started to cheer and clap.

'Safe journey!'

'We wish we could go to Australia!'

'Us'll miss 'ee! Good luck!'

'Oh my word!' declared Mary's mother, covering her face with her hands.

Even Mary's employer, Mrs Annie Fulford, was there, having walked all the way from North Hele especially to wave them goodbye, and Mary experienced a sudden wave of nostalgia for the village she was leaving, and for the people who had been so kind in helping the family on their way.

Suddenly, as they came around the corner, there was a loud clamour from the church tower high above them, then the ringers found their rhythm and the bells broke into a celebratory peal. The younger children, kneeling up on the straw, shrieked with delight, and Mr Fulford slapped his thigh and gave a hearty laugh, almost startling the horses. It was scarcely believable that the bells were being rung especially for the family, but when Mary saw Reverend and Mrs Colling waving politely from the grass verge, she knew that it must be true.

'Goodbye! Thank you!' she called out, her voice unsteady with emotion.

The music of the bells faded as they passed the last cottage and started to descend the long hill, but they had reached the valley road before their laughter and exclamations at the unexpected farewell party died down, and they started to look forward to the next stage of their journey.

Mr Fulford took the turnpike road along the valley; the steep ways were too much for the horses, one wagon being heavily laden with the trunks and the other carrying nine people.

'Remember the last time you rode into Bideford along of me?' he asked, turning around to Thomas and Mary. 'Us idn't doing that no more, sending chiels out, away from their homes to work for nought. It don't seem right now.'

At last, they came to Bideford. There was the old town rising steeply from the river where, beyond the ancient bridge with its many arches, the gulls mewed above the fishing boats, and the bigger ships were ranged side-by-side.

'See that one?' The wagon lurched as Thomas stood up, so he quickly knelt down again, pointing to the first boat moored alongside the Quay.

'That's a brigantine that's brought coal in from Wales!'

On several occasions he had walked to Bideford to wander along the Quay and talk to the men who worked the boats. A few weeks previously he had seen their ship, the *William*, which was now going to pick up cargo in Plymouth, and had agreed to take passengers on the outward journey.

When Mr Fulford stopped outside an inn, Thomas was the first to jump down, eager to find their ship.

'Hold on, now!' called Mr Fulford. 'Us has to find the *William* and draw up alongside.'

'I be gwain with him,' Mary said as she climbed down from the wagon. The dream she and Thomas had shared was now coming to fruition. 'Us'll find 'n together, Mr Fulford.'

They walked quickly along the Quay, dodging the coiled ropes, the nets, the stacked trunks and barrels, the handcarts and the swooping gulls, and as they walked, they read the names of each vessel in turn.

'The *Ellen Sophia*.'

'The *Torridge*.'

'The *Waterlily*.'

'There it is!'

'The *William*,' Thomas whispered reverentially.

He and Mary stood side-by-side, gazing at the handsome schooner as it creaked and swayed with the pull of the tide. Mary tipped back her head to see to the top of the tall masts and intricate rigging.

''Tis so big! Will the ship to Australia really be bigger still?'

'Much bigger.' Thomas's face was alight with pleasure. 'Come on, us'll show the wagons where to come!'

When the trunks had been lifted from the wagon, Mr Norman gave a brief wave and set off for home, but Mr Fulford promised he would stay until they were safely on their way. The family, who had been joined by Catherine and Edward, gathered in a close group on the Quay to watch the heavy trunks being loaded into the vessel, Mrs Mitchell holding tight to Maria and Jane for fear they would fall into the water.

At last, the crew shouted that it was time to board. Rather shyly, Mary approached Mr Fulford, having resolved that he must not be forgotten in the excitement of the moment.

She took a deep breath to steady her voice. 'Mr Fulford, I want to thank 'ee for all you've done for my family. If it weren't for you, I reckon me and Thomas, us'd still be at Gusland. And us'd never be gwain off to start a new life, the whole family together.'

'Oh, come now, chiel.' Mary saw that he was struggling with his emotions. 'Thing is, maid, you should never have been at that place. A young maid like you, and all you've been through, 'tisn't right. And 'twas me that took you there.'

He looked down at the ground, and it was a moment or two before he could speak again. 'I had to put things right, maid. I had to make amends.'

She took his hand. He was her friend; she would always remember him.

'None of it were your fault, Mr Fulford. And 'tis over now. Us is making a new start, all of us together.'

He patted her on the back, unable to say more.

Mary followed Thomas on to the *William,* holding a sailor's proffered arm as she jumped down on to the deck.

They had been told they must stay in the hold while the ship set sail, but Thomas had somehow persuaded the crew that he should remain on deck, promising that he would keep well out of the way.

But when they were all on board, he edged up to the captain who was standing at the helm.

'Please Maister, can my sister stay up yer with me, just the two of us?'

So, while the lashings were tightened and the moorings were released, while the ship creaked and swayed as it moved slowly out into the ebbing tide, there were Thomas and Mary, standing shoulder to shoulder at the bow. They felt the ship swing around and the breeze gather in the topsails, then orders were shouted along the length of the ship and the great sheets of canvas flapped noisily as they were unfurled and secured.

Mary lifted her hand high to wave to Mr Fulford, Catherine, Edward, and the cheering crowd that had gathered to see the *William* go out, and she watched until the waving figures and the little white town set on the hillside disappeared from sight. Then she turned her back on her previous life, on the suffering and the servitude, the mud, the poverty, and the beatings; she was leaving it all behind.

The *William* glided past tree-covered hills and lush meadows, and past the fishing village of Appledore. Bystanders waved, calling questions out across the water.

'Australia!' Thomas shouted as loud as he could, and they

laughed as the ship drew them away.

When the river began to widen, the green slopes that ran down to the river's edge gave way to undulating sand dunes. Mary drew her shawl around her as the wind strengthened and the ship swayed, but then they were through the rough waters of the Bar and the ship was rolling steadily and moving fast, leaving behind the thunder of waves on the long pebble-edged beach.

Mary felt the fresh salt air on her face as she looked out towards the open sea; towards her future. She knew that at last she had found freedom.

From the shipping list of the *Nelson* which sailed from Plymouth on 8th August 1849 with 253 emigrants, arriving in Melbourne 17th November 1849, a voyage of 102 days.

Thomas Mitchell	64	ag. lab.	6. Bideford	neither read nor write	Episcopalian
Charity Mitchell	50	housekeeper	6?	neither read nor write	Episcopalian
Elizabeth Mitchell	22	general servant	6. Littleham	read only	Episcopalian
Thomas Mitchell	17	ag. lab.	6. Littleham	read only	Thormite
Mary Mitchell	15	farm servant	6. Buckland Brewer	read only	Thormite
Ann Mitchell	13		6. Buckland Brewer		
Maria Mitchell	9		6. Buckland Brewer		
Jane Mitchell	7		6 Buckland Brewer		

THE POSTMAN POET
Liz Shakespeare

As a young boy, Edward Capern is desperate to read and write, but has to work an eighty hour week in Barnstaple's lace factory. As a man, he dreams of writing poetry and building a fairer society, but these aspirations cannot put food on the table. He fears he will never be able to marry the woman he loves, and it is Jane's skill as a milliner that eventually provides enough for them to set up a simple home together in Bideford.

Edward's fortunes change when he finds employment as a postman, allowing him to spend his days walking the Devon lanes he loves. He begins to write poems and songs that express his delight in the countryside and the people he meets, but neither he nor Jane can foresee the profound impact his poetry will have on their lives.

Liz Shakespeare's novel, telling the story of Bideford's Postman Poet from obscurity to national renown, captures the opportunities and inequalities of the Victorian age.

"Combining fiction, social history, and biography, *The Postman Poet* is an engaging and entertaining read that both brings a lump to one's throat and joy to the heart. Highly recommended." *Historical Novel Review.*

Also

The Poems of Edward Capern
Selected by Liz Shakespeare
Available from www.lizshakespeare.co.uk

The Songs of Edward Capern
Performed by Nick Wyke and Becki Driscoll
C.D. available from www.englishfiddle.com

ALL AROUND THE YEAR

Liz Shakespeare

These twelve poignant stories, deeply rooted in the Devon landscape, are each linked to a month of the year from January through to December. You will be transported from a sleepy village square to the wilds of Exmoor and from a summer beach to the narrow streets of a small Devon town, and introduced to a variety of memorable characters. In January, a young Croyde surfer tries to come to terms with her uncertain future. As signs of spring appear in the hedgerows, a farmer's wife starts a new venture. In August, a bereaved woman is deeply affected by an unexpected sight on Lynmouth beach. A Bideford man searches for a special Christmas present. All are at a moment of reckoning in their lives as they experience the subtle but significant events that make up everyday experience.

These stories of love and loss, of separation and reconciliation, will stay with you throughout the year.

"Sincere, emotional, touching; just three words that describe the stories in this book. Believable characters and the situations of everyday life which affect them are written in a moving and heart-warming way." *Devon Life*

"Liz Shakespeare's latest book is a collection of charming and compelling short stories rooted in the Devon landscape." *Exmoor Magazine*

"*All Around The Year* is a tribute to North Devon and to the people who live here." *Western Morning News.*

Available from www.lizshakespeare.co.uk

THE TURNING OF THE TIDE

Liz Shakespeare

Devon, 1871
Young and vulnerable Selina Burman from Clovelly and her
two young children are confined in the harsh environment of
Bideford Workhouse. She can only observe them from a
distance and despairs of a better future. Her prospects
improve when she meets Dr Ackland, a popular G.P.
committed to social change. He employs her as a servant in
his own household, despite the doubts of his wife and the
Bideford community, for whom any connection with the
Workhouse is a source of fear and shame. Selina's work gives
satisfaction, but her search for love and security does not
conform to the expectations of a middle class Victorian
family and threatens to damage both her own future and Dr
Ackland's career.

Set in Bideford and Clovelly, this novel draws on newspaper
articles, letters and census returns, and powerfully brings to
life the factual origins of the story.

'An immensely engaging story that captures the reader from
the first page.' *Historical Novel Review*
'A clever combination of fact and fiction, this book both
illuminates and entertains – an extremely gripping read.'
Family History Monthly
'Liz Shakespeare understands the period perfectly well,
describing the deprivation of the Union Workhouse as though
she had suffered it herself.' *Devon Family Historian*

Available from www.lizshakespeare.co.uk